# Gracelin O'Malley

# ANN MOORE

# Gracelin O'Malley

NAL Accent
Published by New American Library, a division of
Penguin Putnam Inc., 375 Hudson Street, New York, New York 10014, U.S.A.
Penguin Books Ltd, 27 Wrights Lane, London W8 5TZ, England
Penguin Books Australia Ltd, Ringwood, Victoria, Australia
Penguin Books Canada Ltd, 10 Alcorn Avenue, Toronto, Ontario, Canada M4V 3B2
Penguin Books (N.Z.) Ltd, 182–190 Wairau Road, Auckland 10, New Zealand

Penguin Books Ltd, Registered Offices: Harmondsworth, Middlesex, England

Published by New American Library, a division of Penguin Putnam Inc.

First Printing, August 2001

10  9  8  7  6  5  4

FICTION FOR THE WAY WE LIVE

REGISTERED TRADEMARK—MARCA REGISTRADA

LIBRARY OF CONGRESS CATALOGING-IN-PUBLICATION DATA:
Moore, Ann, 1959–
Gracelin O'Malley / Ann Moore.
p. cm.
ISBN 0-451-20299-6 (alk. paper)
1. Ireland—History—Famine, 1845–1852—Fiction.
2. Women—Ireland—Fiction. I. Title.
PS3563.05695 G73 2001
813'.6—dc21          00-052727

Printed in the United States of America
Set in New Caledonia
Designed by Julian Hamer

Printed in the United States of America

*For Rick,*
*who leads the way*

# ACKNOWLEDGMENTS

Thanks to the Bellingham Public Library and Wilson Library at Western Washington University for resource materials; to the many fine authors of histories and novels about the Irish famine, most notably Cecil Woodham-Smith and Liam O'Flaherty; to the members of U2 for the inspiration of their music and their politics; to poet William "Bud" Cairns, and metafictionalist Omar S. Castañeda—both gone now, but carried warmly in my heart; to Jean Naggar, literary agent and trusted advisor; to my beloved children, Nigel and Gracelin; to Teri and Peter Smith, Glen and Ezra, constant friends; and last, but most important—great thanks to my husband, Rick, for the thousands of hours he has spent listening, reading, researching, advising, and encouraging in more ways than anyone will ever know—I could never have written this book without his unwavering support.

And you shall hear of wars and rumors of wars: see that you are not troubled: For all these things must come to pass, but the end is not yet. For nation shall rise against nation, and kingdom against kingdom: and there shall be famines, and pestilences, and earthquakes . . . all in diverse places. But they that shall endure unto the end shall be saved.

—MATTHEW, 24:6–13

# One

CAMPFIRE flickered in the woods along the far bank of the River Lee. It was early spring and the tinkers had come. If they had waited but another day, they would not have witnessed the terrible thing that happened there, nor saved the life of young Sean from down the glen, a boy whose mother never let them pass without half a loaf and a good word.

Late winter and early spring are the same in the East; freezing rivers and a deadly frost that lies invisible on fallen logs and stone bridges. The tinkers know this—each year they cross the Lee with a watchful eye, a respectful pace. But a boy might not think of it, a boy puffed up with fresh evening air and the charge of driving a frisky animal for his pretty mother who sings beside him and laughs when he goes too fast. Such a boy would not be mindful of ice on the bridge.

They rose from a crouch, these tinkers, the sudden static of disaster pulling them up only moments before the fast-moving cart overturned, pinning the boy on the bridge, throwing his mother over the edge. They stood upriver, unable to help. Even if one among them had known how to swim, he could not have reached the woman—so furiously ran the river—and after an endless minute of struggle, she disappeared. It was to the boy they ran, pulling off the heavy cart, faces grim when they saw how badly hurt he was: leg with a bone punched through, arm and shoulder crushed flat. He was breathing, but unconscious now, and they were glad for the mercy of it. One man put the jennet out of its misery with a swift plunge of his blade; the others carefully carried the boy to a wagon and set out toward Macroom, for they knew now that this was the son of Patrick and Kathleen O'Malley.

Darkness and freezing rain descended upon them, but they drove on, urging the horse down slippery, muddy back roads, two men holding the boy firm in the back of the cart. When at last they reached his lane, lights shone through cabin windows and smoke rose from the chimney as those inside waited on mother and son.

With nary a word among them, the tinkers climbed down and lifted out the body of the broken boy, carrying it to the door. They kicked loudly with bare feet, then shouted to be heard above the din of the rainstorm. They were met by the face of the boy's father, stunned though it was and slow to see that the boy still lived. He peered at the cart, looking for his wife, and the tinkermen all shook their heads, offering up the boy instead. His eyes faltered but a second; then he took the body of his son, bearing him gently into the cabin and laying him down on a heather pallet. Ryan O'Malley, elder son, hastily threw more turf on the smoldering fire and fetched Granna's kit bag. Having seen the faces of the tinkermen and the shaking of their heads, Gran did not ask about her daughter. Instead, she went to work on the boy, soothing his moans as she cut away the heavy, wet clothes from his body, easing them over the terribly twisted arm and leg. Young Gracelin, her mother's pet and favorite of her brother Sean, crept as close as she could without getting in the way. Granna tossed aside a sodden jacket sleeve and Grace snatched it up against her, the damp soaking through her thin nightshift.

Word swept down the lane, and the door opened and closed, rain blowing in with each neighbor come to see what could be done, their presence pushing further into the corner the tinkers who had rescued Sean; they waited uneasily, these men, standing close together, eyes lowered, battered hats held tightly in their fists.

"Get your da's bottle from the shelf and give it to them," Granna said without looking up from the wound she stitched above Sean's eye. "When it's gone, wet the tea. There's bread."

"Aye, Gran." Grace stood slowly against the stiffness in her legs.

"I'll help." Ryan was there beside her, giving her a hand up. Together they went through the crowd, seeing to the drink, not looking anyone in the eye but the tinkers, who lived closer to the spirit world and knew the way of things.

"He'll live," one said quietly to Grace as she filled his cup. He nodded to the corner behind where Sean lay. "'Twas your mam awaiting him just there in the shadows, but gone away now, she has."

Grace stared into the corner long and hard until it dissolved and she could see beyond to the other place. She moved as if to go there herself, but the tinker's hand fell upon her head and kept her still. He turned her gently away from the vision and looked into her eyes, slowly shaking his head from side to side, aware that a child not long out of Heaven might still remember the way back. He blessed her in his strange tongue and Grace listened, not taking her eyes from his face. When they understood one another, he slipped out the door with his fellows and disappeared without another word.

The bone-setter finally arrived, cursing such a wicked night as this. He looked over Granna's work with approval, then went about his own, first pouring a glass of whiskey down the boy's throat. There was a scream, and another, as he pulled the leg, snapping the thigh bone back into place. The leg was shattered beneath the knee, but by the time he began to straighten it, the boy had again lost consciousness. The bone-setter was old and used to sounds of suffering, but the screams that arose from the wee girl disturbed his soul, and he was grateful for the women who gathered her up in their arms and rocked her until sleep drew its blanket over her head.

Later, later, in the gray hour before dawn, as she lay on her pallet next to Granna, Grace opened her eyes and listened to the stillness of the spent storm. It came upon her then that her brother lived, but her mother was dead—most surely dead—and a terrible pain cinched her chest, crushing all breath. Blood began to roar in her ears, but through it she heard her mother's voice, singing as if high on the hill that rose behind their cabin. The air in the room evaporated, locking her heart in an exploding chest; around her swirled the dark waters of the River Lee, greedy for the daughter of an angel. The singing grew louder, came nearer, and then her mother's voice rode over the top of the others, shouting, "Breathe, Gracelin! Breathe!"

Grace's eyes flew open and she gasped, unable to fill her lungs quickly enough. She struggled and flailed, and then Granna was awake, snatching her up and holding her so close that one heartbeat encouraged the other, one long breath showed the way for the next. Slowly, the panic subsided and each sip of air cooled the burn in her chest. The singing voices grew thin and high and faint, and finally slipped away, her mother's among them.

When at last Grace grew still and her eyes began to close again, Granna eased her down beneath the blanket. There she lay, though not asleep, but waiting patiently as if the wind itself might pick her up and bear her away. All that achored her was Granna's arm, wrapped tightly about her waist, and this is why, when she awoke, she found herself still in the world.

Kathleen O'Malley's wake was well attended, though the state of the body called for no viewing, so swollen from the river it was and hard to lay eyes upon. There were many in the neighborhood who had loved the young woman with her pretty singing, easy laugh, and bold eyes, and they came to comfort her old mother, her fine husband, Patrick, and their three children, the two sons and the wee daughter. Those who had known her best—Katty O'Dugan and Julia Ryan down the lane, Mary McDonagh from up the Black Hill—set to keening as soon as they saw the coffin. The wails rose from their lips and they rocked and swayed, clapping their hands and praising the dear girl who'd been taken from them. Every opening of the door brought in someone who raised the keen anew. It was many hours before the wailing eased, and everyone in the place found themselves with a full cup of Patrick's best Uisage batha—the water of life—and a fresh pipe. The room was warm and crowded, and men soon spilled out into the yard, where they started shaking their heads in the rhythm of sorrow, and storytelling in low, raspy voices. Women went in and out of the cabin with food, telling their own stories of children lost and mothers dead. They stayed the day, the night, and the next day until the coffin was buried high up on the hill and the O'Malleys closed their door to mourn their loss in private.

Grace could not look at Sean so white and motionless in his bed, could not comfort her father, who sat alone in the corner and wept and wept, could not erase the deep lines that had come into Granna's face, or ease the anger in Ryan's eyes. And she could not bear the hope that clung to her heart as she looked at her mother's chair and almost saw her sitting there, almost heard her laugh or the end of a song that still haunted the air. So she left the cabin—six years old and a half—and climbed the hill that rose up behind. There she wandered the field of daisies up and opened in sudden bloom, and when weariness came, she lay down among them and imagined Heaven, where she might close her eyes and rest her head forever against her mother's longed-for breast.

Sean was moved into the small room Patrick and Kathleen had shared, and there he lay in pain and fever for many days, moaning and calling out for his mother to hold on, he was coming, hold on. "Stay up, Mam!" he shouted again and again, until at last the delirium passed and he opened his eyes.

When he had swallowed some broth and could sit up for a short time, they gathered round his bed and waited for him to speak. Haltingly, he told them how the stone bridge across the swollen Lee had been slick with frosty rain, how the mule had lost foot and thrown the cart, pinning half of Sean's body beneath it on the edge of the bridge. He'd seen her in the churning current, fighting to stay afloat, her heavy skirts and boots weighing her down. She'd called to him, struggled against the frigid water as long as she could, and then she'd called out once more before slipping beneath the waves. He remembered nothing else, he said, tears running down transparent cheeks, until he'd awakened this day to Gran's gentle voice, telling him his mother was dead.

Patrick grew smaller and smaller as he listened to his son's words. He patted the boy's hand, then sighed and left the room, and the man Grace had always loved simply disappeared beneath the waves. He sang no more songs, told no tales of their ancestors, carried not even the smallest smile in his pocket. She was only near to him when she crawled into his lap and felt his warmth, breathed his smell of tobacco and earth. With her head upon his heart, she was certain that even its beat was weaker and more sorrowful than when her mother lived. She put his hand on the top of her head, hoping he'd stroke her hair as he'd always done, but it fell away into his lap, so lost had he become, and he'd say to her after a while, "Shush now, child, and be off with you."

She did not know this old man—her father had always been full of plan and action, like the great Chieftans of the West who sailed from Connaught. The greatest of them, Granuaile, daughter of Owen, had become the famed Pirate Queen, feared by the English and revered by her people, and Patrick had named Grace for her because, he said, at the moment of her birth, it was clear that the light of the sea shone in her eyes. Her father was directly descended from the O'Malleys in the North, who'd held a large estate, but lost it all with the defeat of James II at Boyne and the subsequent Penal Laws. These had destroyed the great old Catholic Irish families, her father said, forcing them to divide their lands until nothing was left, depriving the Catholic Irish of education and a voice in politics, refusing them government jobs and the right to maintain their religion. His forefathers had been Oak Boys and Ribbon Men, meeting in the foggy bogs to plot revenge, but they'd never regained all they'd lost, and the bitterness of that was in Patrick's voice each time he told these stories to his children.

What Grace could not know was that Patrick felt his nobility, and had suffered shame for his ragged, defeated parents, who drifted aimlessly from county to county, living in mean lodgings and scraping by on nothing. Their sudden deaths from typhus had left seven orphans, three of whom died soon after, the rest to be scattered by the local priest. There was no family to take Patrick in, and he spent three years in the workhouse at Dublin before running away at age ten. He lived in summer ditches, wintered in abandoned bothans, stole food from pigstyes, and wore rags tied to his feet. After one terrible winter of near starvation, he went back to the Brothers, who agreed to take him in as an indentured servant. He farmed during the day, sheared their sheep and spun their wool, cleaned their house, made their candles, and often stayed up at night to pray for their dead. He suffered beatings for his laziness and ingratitude if he fell asleep or asked for more food, and he was forced to pay heavy penance for wicked thoughts or lack of goodwill. The fasting, fatigue, and endless work had eaten away at mind and body, until his only strength was a small flame of rage, which he fanned in secret. Determined to be his own master, even if it meant sleeping with pigs and sharing their slop, he ran away again. Childhood had left him and he was a young man then, although his body was small and thin, yellow with hunger, and the scars across his back made others suspicious. He never entered a church again, and he kept his views about God to himself.

But Kathleen harbored a deep love of God and a need to worship Him with others of like mind. She was Protestant—great-granddaughter of a Scotsman on her dead father's side—and though she was nearly alone in a sea of Catholic countrymen, she saw no reason to let religion divide them. Patrick had allowed her to attend the Church at the Lake, with the understanding that it was not for him and she was not to ask. Granna did not like to travel so far from home in a day, Ryan was too much like his da to allow religious emotion into the order of his life, and Gracelin was yet too young. But Sean had always been happy for the chance to get out on long rides through the countryside, where he spoke to his mother of his dreams, the magnificence of Ireland, and the wonder of God. They would begin early on a Sunday, before the sun was up, harnessing the donkey to the rough wooden cart and setting out with a dinner pail of warm porridge and Saturday's bread. They followed the winding path of the Lee through Inchigeelagh, past the rippling waters of Lough Allua, crossing the river at Ballingeary, and heading toward the Shehy Mountains until they reached the small stone chapel that sat on the shores of Gougenebarra Lake, the source of the Lee. It was a tiring journey and they would not return home before nightfall except in the long days of summer, so they never went more than thrice in any season, and that was plenty even then, according to Patrick.

In the months after Kathleen's death, Patrick sat on a stool outside the cabin each evening, smoking his clay pipe and thinking about his wife. She'd given up her whole way of life for him, and what had he given her besides children and the occasional day at church? When they'd married, he'd hardly a penny to his name, just dreams and plans. She'd given up the family bakery in Cork, which she'd run with Granna, and used part of the money to lease land in Macroom, buy seed, a plow horse, tools—a start. He'd promised to make it all up to her once the farm prospered, and he never thought about the life she was leading as the wife of a struggling farmer instead of the successful business owner she easily could've been. He carried the guilt of it now like a stone in his heart, along with a grief that never eased. Now that he alone shouldered the burden of their children's future, he saw how heavy it was, and he was afraid for all he'd leaned on her. He'd depended on her too much—for advice and encouragement, for comfort, for love. With dull eyes and a heavy spirit, he knew he had reverted to the bitter man he'd been until the lucky day he'd met Kathleen Dougherty, and he grieved not only for the loss of her, but for the loss of himself, as well.

On the nights when Patrick sat outside on the hill with the sheep, brooding and smoking his pipe, Granna tried to lift the heaviness of the house by telling the children stories of their mother.

"She was a true Irish beauty." This was how she always began, in Irish, her eyes moist with memory. "Skin the color of cream, a high bloom in the cheek, hair darkest red and curling with pleasure . . . and her eyes, arrah, her eyes—blue gray like a thundering sea. You, Grace," she'd add, smiling fondly at the little girl near her feet, "you have your mother's eyes." Here, she'd always sigh. Then, "And wasn't she always singing, even as a wee girleen? And coming out with such funny things about the neighbor folk? So bold she was, and full of life! Your da loved her the very minute he set eyes on her."

"Tell us," Sean always demanded first.

"Shrove Tuesday, 'twas, with all the lads about their games, and all the girls looking to be caught by them as they wanted." She laughed, then put her hand over her mouth and glanced toward the door. "Your da had just hired on at the mill and he came to our shop for onion bread and a cup of the mead that made your mother famous." She pulled herself up and deepened her voice, wagging her head in imitation of Patrick's youthful cockiness. " 'I've eaten all over Ireland, Miss,' he says to her. 'And your bread is finer than any I've tasted.'

" ''Tis my mam does the baking,' she says to him, hands on her hips, but a blush to be seen miles away—she was shy, our one, but you'd never know it for all her fire.

"He steps as close to her as he dares and says, looking bold into her eyes, 'Herself will have to live with us when we're married, then'.

"He made her laugh and that was it. Your mother always knew what she wanted." Gran sighed, but not without pride. "They were married after Easter and then went looking for a small bit of land to lease in County Cork, which is where your da wanted to settle. I thought I might open a baker's shop along the square in Macroom, but they wanted me here, so I come, not having no one else to stay for. Faith, they loved each other true as the sun, they did. Your mam didn't think twice about giving up city life to be a farm wife. Strong and independent, she was, with a great passion for scooping up life and patting it in around her."

The children listened, their hunger for stories of their mother matched by Granna's need to speak of the daughter she'd loved so well.

She and Kathleen had smuggled in religious tradition where they could, and, perhaps because they were Protestant, Patrick had turned a blind eye to most of it, sometimes even staying in the kitchen to hear stories of Christ's miracles while they made sweet pancakes for Shrovetide, a last treat before Lent. Most of their neighbors made due with one meal a day during the forty days before Easter, but Patrick wouldn't hear of such nonsense and insisted on two good meals a day for his family. When he'd gone up to the fields, Kathleen would wipe her floury hands on her apron and speak seriously to the children about the Lord's suffering before His death, and the importance of keeping it in mind by giving up a little something themselves. Granna seemed to think that Kathleen's death covered the giving up for the rest of their lives, and she no longer asked for personal sacrifice at Lent.

Once a year of grieving had passed, Granna began to speak more freely of Kathleen and openly continued the traditions that she knew had been important to her daughter. Sean and Grace were her only audience now, as Ryan was old enough to work with his father. Patrick still could not bear the singing, so this, too, they did when he was out, Granna teaching them the words to "John O'Dwyer of the Glens," the melody to Thomas Moore's "Tho' the Last Glimpse of Erin," and their mother's favorite, the ancient "Derry Aire."

There was no talk of attending services. Sean did not even ask, although he missed the church and the hymns, the sound of the lake lapping at the shore.

"Your da is angry with God," Granna explained to them. "He cannot make sense of his life without your mam, and he cannot forgive Him for taking her away. But is he not the good father he's always been, and are we not to be a comfort to him now? 'Tis what your mam would want of you. Leave it to the Lord to soften his heart."

But as time passed, the lines in Patrick's face only grew deeper, and his once auburn hair was shot with white. He was closest to Ryan, who now worked each day with him and was learning to run the farm, but he remained distant from his younger son and daughter.

Grace emerged from childhood even more beautiful than her mother had been, though she couldn't have known it. She'd long forgotten Kathleen's face, and this troubled her heart, although at times the night would bring her comfort and she'd awaken to the sound of gentle humming. There, a figure would stand in the corner of the little room, braiding the long hair that trailed to her waist, her face turned just enough to hide its features. A wonderful peacefulness would sweep through Grace, but when she reached out her hand or tried to awaken Granna, the figure would turn away and disappear.

"God's not forgotten your loss," Granna would whisper to the weeping girl, stroking her hair. "I carry her face in my heart, but you've no memory of that."

And in the morning, when Grace asked again why she and no one else saw such a thing, Granna said to her, "Sure, and hasn't the Lord always blessed you with visions of angels and the like, signs of the otherworld since you were in your mother's lap? Wouldn't you warn us away from corners for fear we'd tread on the toe of an angel?" She laughed, then looked up from the onions she peeled. "Don't question it, child. I wish upon my soul I had the gift to look upon her just once more."

Sean spoke up from his hob near the fire, where he spent most of his days. "I dream of saving her, you know, of pulling her from the river. Every spring when the water rises, don't I have the same dream?"

Granna peered at him. "I know you do," she said. "I hear you thrashing around some nights when I go out back."

"Why was she taken from us?" The anguish was still clear in his voice, even though they had talked this out many times before.

Granna shook her head. "It was her time and that's all." She paused. "I'll tell you a story: Long ago, the Irish were blessed with knowing when their time would come, and all were content with living their lives fully until then. But there came a man who saw he was to die after harvest, so he built only a makeshift fence for the sheep, and barely patched his roof. The neighbors began to talk on this so loudly that an angel came to see the man. 'Why have you not secured your sheep, or made good repair on your cabin?' he asked. 'I see no reason if I'm to die after harvest,' said the man. 'Let the next one do the work.' The angel saw that this was no good and spoke to God, who then took back the knowledge of death from the people so that they might not give up on life before their time."

Grace listened to the old story and took the words into her heart, but Sean just shook his head.

"Some give up on life and hope for death, anyway," he said. "Like Da."

"Aye, 'tis wrong," Granna allowed. "But he doesn't really want to die, your da. He wants to know how to go on living, for he sees no plan to his life a'tall."

"Nor do I," Sean said bitterly, staring down at his twisted arm and leg.

Granna slapped down her paring knife. "You know better than to question the way of the Lord, Sean O'Malley. You think God has punished you by leaving you a cripple, but that's looking at what you don't have instead of what you do. Were your limbs strong and your body big, you'd be out in the fields with your da and brother, or working at the linen mill, or down in Cork City on the docks. All of it hard work, day in and day out—with no time left for the books you love!"

Sean raised his eyes and she saw the pain in them.

"I know it's not been easy, agra. Fourteen years old and no running with the other boys, except Morgan McDonagh, bless his heart. No dances, not much life outside this house, and sick most of the winter. But your mind is strong, boy." Her eyes burned into his face. "You've got your mother's quick way of thinking and your father's strong will. Reading and writing is your ticket into the world and you'd never have learned so much or studied so hard if you were working with your body."

Grace moved close to her brother and put her arms around his neck. "Isn't it you taught me to read and write, then?" she asked softly. "Where would I have learned it if not from you? I'm sorry you're cripple, Sean . . . but I thank Jaysus for letting us keep you, a'tall."

Sean squeezed her strong arms and smiled weakly. "Ah, never mind me. I'm still an eejit for all my books. What's that the old ones say?" He thought for a moment. " 'The lake is not encumbered by the swan; nor the steed by the bridle; nor the sheep by the wool; nor the man by the soul that is in him.' I think I'd best take hold of that."

Granna and Grace smiled, not following a word of what he said, but relieved that the depression that often fell on him would slip away easily this time.

"Are we not due a visit from Morgan?" Granna asked. "That talk of the lake makes me want salmon. The two of you've not been fishing for over a fortnight."

"Missus O'Dugan says his mam had the baby, another girl," Grace said. "And his da's gone off to sea again."

"Leaving the boy to look after them all, the scalawag." Granna clucked her tongue. "'Tis a hard life, he has. A day of fishing would do the both of you some good."

But Morgan did not come, and they resumed their work, sewing steadily until their eyes were dry and tired. Sean had earned a reputation as a steady hand with the needle, taking in piecework from the mill and some custom orders from the gentry. Granna had taught him as a way of keeping his fingers nimble and his mind occupied, and now he'd gotten enough of a trade to bring in a bit of change. Grace had taken it up to keep her brother company, and had quickly showed a gift for design. She embroidered handkerchiefs, collars, aprons, and lapels, and made beautiful samplers. Those who could afford it often called upon her to sew up wardrobes for newborns, and in this she was assisted by Sean, who could make up dozens of nappies in no time. Although his posture was awkward, he was quite adept at cutting out and stitching up the nightgowns, hats, blankets, little jackets, and robes, which Grace then detailed with embroidery and ribbon. An order like that could bring in a fair amount of money, but it was not steady work and could not be depended upon. Granna and Kathleen had kept up their baking skills and had sold breads and rolls at the market in Macroom; but even with Grace's help, this was now too difficult for Granna, who had to contend with Patrick's refusal to send them off in the wagon any distance at all, let alone all the way to Macroom.

Theirs was a rural neighborhood like any other; most of the families around them struggled to make it through each year and there was never money for extras. The cabins were sparsely furnished, the clothing simple. Further out into the countryside and up into the mountains, housing was rarely more than a windowless mud hut, one or two stools or big rocks for sitting, a pot for boiling potatoes over the fire, straw in the corner where the whole family bedded down at night with the animals. Potatoes and water were the mainstay, supplemented by whatever the land might yield: nuts, berries, small game, fish, herbs, and bitter greens. Those who dwelled in the mountains wore their clothes to rags and were lucky to have a blanket to share among them.

Life was better for folks like the O'Malleys, who lived closer to the main roads that led to town. Theirs were small, stone cabins with thrush roofs across which were thrown lines of stone-weighted rope to keep the straw from blowing away. There were windows and half-doors, cobbled paths and swept yards, boulder-fenced pastures, wider lanes for travel. Inside, there were a few sticks of furniture, a cup and plate for each person, stuffed mats and blankets, an extra change of clothing. Most of the men planted their holdings in potatoes, but also hired out as labor to some of the bigger estates or went away part of the year to work the mills or go to sea. No one had a rich, comfortable life, but because of Kathleen's head for saving, the O'Malleys had more than most. The pigs stayed out in a shed of their own and didn't muck up the big room of the cabin; there were a few pictures on the walls, luster jugs, a set of plates and crockery. They had utensils and their mother had insisted they use them, not just scoop food into their mouths with their fingers, as was the custom. They had good pans and sharp knives, mended by the tinkers who came down the lane now and then, and even a tatted rug on the stone floor. In addition to the hobs and stooleens, there was furniture that Kathleen and Granna had brought from the bakery: a table with benches, a sideboard, two chairs, and a rocker. Painted benches were built in around the walls, and dried wreaths and flowers livened the room. They slept on proper pallets—large pieces of flannel sewn together and stuffed with straw—and had quilts to warm them at night. Her mother had drawn the suspicion of the neighbors by whitewashing the cabin twice a year and by leaving the sweeping broom sitting in a pail of disinfectant, but many of the fevers that swept through their county did not touch the O'Malleys, and Gran said they had their forward-thinking mother to thank for that. Granna was as mystified as the others about Kathleen's modern ideas and the confidence she showed in executing them. She insisted the girl had been switched by tinkers with the baby of a queen, but her eyes twinkled with joy, and pride was there in her voice. Grace knew the money her mother had saved was long gone and that they now struggled to pay their rent in labor days to the landowner, but in this they were no different from anyone else. All the folk grumbled about landlords, just as they all squinted at the sky and scooped handfuls of dirt to sniff, made forecasts about the coming potato crop, and claimed accuracy no matter what. It was their life.

And so the seasons passed, one after another, marked with the holidays and small feasts they all celebrated, although Patrick kept to himself and worked all days as if they were the same. His only conversation was with Ryan about the condition of the farm and how to come by the rent that had doubled in the past year. Rack rent was a constant worry, and Quarterday, when the agents came to collect, loomed ever large. Ryan had now assumed his father's dour disposition; Sean and Grace considered him an old man since he could no longer be counted upon for a song to mark the day or a game of checkers on a winter's night. It was as if two families inhabited the house: one resigned to the struggle of their life, the other just as determined to find joy in the day.

Christmas was not bountiful, but Grace was a stranger to the word, and she delighted in the ribbon Sean had for her hair, the rag doll Granna made with leftover bits of material, the absentminded kiss and hard peppermint from her father, bootlaces from Ryan. She had small trinkets for them, as well: fish hooks, a pair of woolen socks, an embroidered bookmark, a wax-sealed jar of summer preserves. This was the only day her father would relax some, although he still went to work when they began to sing.

On St. Stephan's Day, Granna insisted that Grace blacken her face with the other village children and trim the holly bushes with scraps of ribbon. St. Brigid's Day came in February, which Granna celebrated on the sly, not being Catholic, but having great feeling for Brigid. "A true Irishwoman," she'd say. "Much more suitable for us than Patrick—the old snake charmer."

Candlemas, the Feast of Lights, was followed by Shrove Tuesday and then Lent. Hungry children from the lane would appear at the O'Malleys' half-door, knowing Granna or Grace would give them a bit of tea brack or gingerbread. On Ash Wednesday, the Catholics wore smudged ash on their foreheads; Grace stayed indoors because her difference from them was all too apparent on this day, and she wanted to avoid pitying looks from her neighbors, as well as scowls from the priests. Good Friday was a somber day, rare in that Granna would not work more than was necessary, then spent the evening sitting in the dark, telling them quietly the story of Christ's terrible death on the cross. Easter Sunday, the day of His resurrection, brought with it a celebration of renewed life, with a feast of roast lamb for any who had it. The first of May was Beltaine, Grace's favorite, when bonfires lit up the hillsides all over Ireland, and the cows were driven between them to get rid of murrain. St. John's Eve, at midsummer, also meant bonfires, but in the middle of town. Grace, Sean, and even Ryan would jump on the haywagon that came down their lane and ride it into Macroom to watch the dancing, Ryan sometimes joining the other young men who leapt through the flames in a show of daring and strength. Lug's Day, the first of August, was the welcomed day of digging new potatoes, and big plates of colcannon sat on every table.

Autumn passed quickly with harvesting and winter preparations; the children celebrated Samhain with apple bobbing, blindman's buff, and rounds of Black Raven, a board game Sean played with Morgan in front of the fire. Although she still baked the bram brack, Granna no longer put into it the rings, coins, or other tokens that were traditional. The year she died, Kathleen had found no token in her cake at all, an unheard-of occurrence; there'd been no fortune to foretell her coming year, and this had haunted Granna ever after.

By the looks of the carts and rigs that passed down their lane, Ireland was getting more crowded every day, according to Gran.

"Can't hardly walk down my own boreen without some jennet near squeezing me out," she often complained. But she enjoyed the population moving by her windows, and had a special place in her heart for the tinkers who stopped to peer in and bless the cabin.

It was 1840. Grace was eleven, and the world had grown smaller, or so it seemed with all the coming and going down the lane. The past twenty years had doubled the population in Ireland, but the people still lived on potatoes, filling themselves with ten pounds a day or more; one acre could yield as much as six tons, so even the cottiers—who held no land—hired themselves out and leased conacres to grow enough to support their families. Land was life; to lose it was a death sentence. The O'Malleys rented a relatively large holding of ten acres planted mainly in potatoes, but also in grains, and pastureland for sheep grazing. They kept a kitchen garden, and raised chickens and pigs. With a long-term lease, there had been incentive to homestead. Now the lease had run out and Patrick could not afford the stamp to renew, so he paid quarterly like everyone else around them. He had followed his wife's advice and resisted dependence on potatoes alone; she'd kept a small botha filled with preserves, sacks of meal, and salted meat. Patrick had teased her about stockpiling and said they'd gain a reputation for miserliness, but Kathleen had put her hands on her hips and insisted they could say what they liked, hadn't the potato failed before and most surely would again? Come terrible times, she would not see her family starve.

Their land and all that around them was part of Squire Donnelly's estate and it was to his agent they paid their rent come Quarterday. The squire, son of an English Lord and twice widowed, kept to himself at Donnelly House, sometimes traveling to the North where he had business. Talk was, his youthful escapades in London and lack of obedience to his father had earned him banishment to the family estate in County Cork, but it seemed he'd come to savor independence and had made Donnelly House his home. His rents were fair enough, though he'd raised them twice to support the new mill in Galway, and it was supposed he sent a fair portion back to the family home in England. His agents were curt, but not rude, and no family was turned out but of their own accord. He'd got a name for himself as dry and humorless, but it was not followed by a mean spit in the dirt, as were the names of so many other squires.

A man like Patrick could not dream of buying land even if it were to be had, so he paid his rent on time and hoped to hold on to the farm for his sons and their families. He'd counted on farming with both Ryan and Sean when they came of age, perhaps even gaining the hands of a son-in-law when Grace married. He would have divided the land among the children as they settled into family life, keeping a small plot for himself and Kathleen. Now he only hoped to hold on until Ryan married and assumed the responsibility, but he had no hope of a future for Sean. He could barely stand to look the boy in the face, and it pained him to see his young son bent awkwardly over a needle. The money Sean and Grace brought in was a help; it clothed them and bought additional food, but it was not enough to save. The money Kathleen had hoarded pennies at a time was long gone now due to

Patrick's indecision and poor judgment. He had not her head for figuring costs, and his impatience was terrible. Two divided acres had
been leased out to cottiers, but the daily work of keeping up the rest
was taking its toll. He was not the kind of man to content himself with
scratching out a lazy bed of potatoes and leaving it at that. He'd seen
fields abandoned because the soil simply had nothing else to give after repeated plantings of the same crop, so he rotated, which gave the
local men no end of knee-slapping amusement. Dawn to nightfall saw
him out plowing, tending sheep and pigs, planting, hoeing, mending
the haggard, in all kinds of weather, mostly rain. Other men found relief of a kind in the shebeens that dotted the network of lanes con-
necting the farms, but Patrick was not a drinking man, taking a small
glass only at weddings and wakes, or when he fell ill. Ryan worked
steadily beside him until nightfall, then set off to the O'Douds' to
court the comely, outspoken Aghna. The sour look had left his face,
replaced by one of moony lovesickness. Patrick kicked at him and said
his work was worthless, so distracted had he become. They could all
see his need to marry.

Granna got the porridge together in the mornings and made the
daily soda bread. Grace, now fifteen, saw to supper, laundry, the
kitchen garden and food preserving, sweeping out the house, and to
farm chores like egg gathering and milking. Sean was able to help
some in the kitchen garden and had become an expert fisherman,
pulling his body into the cart and lying across the seat to drive the
mule to the river or, when the salmon weren't running, to the lake.
He'd roll out of the cart, then drag his leg behind him to the edge,
where he'd fish for salmon or trout. They had enough to eat, but
Patrick's setbacks had cost them. He'd invested in cattle, hoping to
export salted beef, but his timing was bad and prices fell once England turned to America's cheaper market; he'd slaughtered the heads
he couldn't afford to feed, and took a loss on the local market. Then,
he'd tried wheat and barley, but the Irish considered those grains animal fodder, so he'd lost his investment there, too. Now they kept only
the milk cow, some sheep, a few chickens, and two pigs. One pig would
be sold, the other butchered.

There were doctor fees and medicines for Gran, who'd suffered a
stroke, and for Sean, who was also sick with a deep, racking cough in
his chest through that damp, blustery autumn and most of the cold

winter that followed. Granna was still weak and sat down often during the day, despite the bowls of beef tea Grace kept simmering over the fire. Sean also recovered slowly, the sound of his breathing like bare winter trees groaning in the wind; he was terribly thin and pale, and his spirits lagged. Even the sight of Morgan, blowing in wet and muddy on a cold day, singing good cheer, could not rouse him. Grace would walk into the silent kitchen after an afternoon of cutting turf on the bog, full of fresh air and a high heart, and there they'd be, sitting still as statues, minds elsewhere, and she'd shake with fear that they'd both give up their will and leave her. She chattered tirelessly to them about the promise of spring, bringing in every new blossom she found, leaving the doors and curtains open so that the warm light might shine on them, cooking all day to tempt their appetites. She traded a day of washing muddy work clothes for a bucket of clams from Cork City, and made Granna a rich chowder. She emptied the storehouse, and combed the woods and streams for ingredients to make chicken and ham pie, mutton pie, Sean's baked salmon with sorrel sauce, Finnan Haddie and hot buttered toast, roast rabbit, fried mushrooms, boiled bacon and cabbage, potato cakes, colcannon and dulse, soda bread, brown bread, boxty, and pratie oaten. She gave them endless cups of tea, which had become dear and depleted her bargaining chest, and she made them scolleen on damp days or in the evenings when the hot milk, butter, honey, and whiskey warmed them through and picked up their spirits. She felt as if it were her sheer will that kept them going, and when spring ended and summer began, she found her reward in their ability to walk slowly out of doors, in bodies that had finally begun to fill out, in faces that bloomed with the promise of renewed vigor, and in eyes that shone with love whenever she walked into the room.

"You brought them through the winter alive, girl," Patrick said to her one evening as she sat milking in the barn. " 'Twas your own hard work done it."

Grace kept at her milking and said nothing, unused to her father's praise.

"Not that it's of much use, themselves being what they are." He wiped a hand tiredly over his face. "Faith and they'll be lucky to see another year. Your granna's gone old now, and our Sean . . ." He sighed.

Grace looked up, aghast. "How can you say that, Da?" Her cheeks burned with anger. "Granna is old, true to you, but Katty O'Dugan's grandmother still rocks in her chair and isn't she a one to remember Brian Boru himself?"

Patrick snorted.

"And Sean will get better, he's stronger every day!" She raced on. "It's that shoulder hunched in makes the chest take cold so easy. . . . Could we not take him to Dublin, to the hospital there?"

Patrick shook his head. "There's no more money for travel or doctors, wee girl, so don't pin your hopes on that."

Grace bit her lip. "Blood and ounse, Da! You can't just give up as if he's already dead and buried!"

Patrick frowned. "There'll be no cursing in my house nor my barn, and you'd best not forget that, or feel the sting of my belt."

Grace lowered her head, contrite. "Sorry, Da."

Patrick allowed her a small smile. "Your mother let fly a good curse now and then, and don't you sound just like her?"

He took away the full bucket and handed her an empty one to put under the cow's udder. "It's not that I'm giving up on our Sean, agra, I'm just not fooling myself about it, either, is all. If he gets well, praise God, and hope He sends answers for the other worries."

"What other worries, Da?"

"Well, for one thing, who's going to care for him when Granna and I are dead and gone?"

"Who do you think?" Grace looked at him in surprise.

"Maybe you'll have a husband who'll take in your crippled brother," Patrick said pointedly. "And maybe you won't."

Grace's eyes widened in anger. "And do you think I'd be such an eejit as to marry a man who wouldn't have my own brother in the house?"

"Might have no choice in the matter," he said evenly. "As it stands, will I not be pressed to make the best marriage I can? Contrary to your own way of thinking, a girl's brother is not considered part of the usual dowry."

Grace ducked her head and yanked on the cow's teats.

Patrick picked up a hay straw and fiddled with it. "He'll stay on here at the farm, is what I'm thinking. He'll live with Ryan and Aghna, and—God willing—he won't be too big a burden."

"'Twill be the other way round, like as not," Grace muttered into the cow's warm flank. "And anyway," she spoke up. "He'll not be needing their help, or anyone's—he's going to get stronger, he is, and be healthy, as well, and have a fine life and a wife of his own, and many, many children!"

"Hah!" Patrick got up from his stool. "Sure of that now, are you, girl?"

She held his gaze fiercely, and he softened.

"Ah, well, that's fine for you. Hope is for the young."

He left her to finish the milking and cool her anger, but for many days after that, Grace thought of their conversation and took extra pains to see that Sean got rest and food, that he exercised his weak limbs. He did get stronger, if only through a desire to find a purpose for his life. Granna had given him Kathleen's Bible and he pored through it when his father was not in the house, searching the scripture for guidance. He began to believe that God would set before him a meaningful life when the time was right, but that he must be ready for it, and he studied the verses as if deciphering a secret code.

"'I love those who love me; and those who diligently seek me will find me'." His voice was a whisper, barely heard above the hiss of the fire in front of which he and Grace sat. "'Riches and honor are with me, enduring wealth and righteousness. My fruit is better than gold, even pure gold. And my yield than choicest silver. I walk in the way of righteousness, in the midst of the paths of justice, to endow those who love me with wealth, that I may fill their treasuries.'" He marked the spot with his finger. "Did you hear that, Grace? 'My fruit is better than gold.' That's the Lord talking to me. Do you hear?"

Grace nodded, her fingers doing the fine work automatically as she looked up at him. "I hear you, Sean." She had to laugh at the earnestness of his face, the zeal that lit up his eyes. "You're thinking of riches again."

"Ah, no, sister, 'tis more to it than that." He closed the book on his finger and leaned over the pile of cloth in his lap to make himself more clearly heard. "He says He'll fill our treasuries, and all He wants in return is our love."

"Have you not said often enough that things like love and honor, faith and charity, cannot be bought?" Her fingers smoothed the threads of a woman's embroidered cuff. She tied a tiny, nearly invisible knot and snipped off the end. "Here I thought my brother a noble man, only to learn that his greatest desire is to be a rich landowner. Did you not read out just this morning that it is to be the meek themselves who inherit the land?"

Sean frowned and started to rise, then winced with the pain of pushing up on his foot. He reached down to massage the knotted flesh. "You've got it all wrong, Grace. You're not thinking deeper than the words themselves. He says that those who love Him *despite* reward will be the ones to gain. And as for owning my own bit of land, dear sister, you know that's not in my future, short of some blessed miracle."

"Miracles happen all the time," Granna commented from her place by the window. She seemed content these days to merely watch their faces and listen to their conversation; sometimes it was as if she wasn't in the room at all.

"Aye," Sean nodded. "True enough. Look at us sitting here, well again." He turned back to Grace. "But I'll not keep fighting to live in order to spend my days doing piecework by the fire just to earn my keep. The Lord will give me work worthy of His name. I have faith in that."

"Faith is nothing more than stubborn wishing. How do you know the Lord doesn't want you to stay right here and do humble work?"

Sean's face fell. "Sure, and that could be true, Grace. That could be true, indeed."

He shook his head so sadly that Grace reached out and patted his leg.

"I'm not saying it is. Haven't we always said God's got grand plans for our one, Gran?" She looked over her shoulder and smiled at her grandmother, whose head rested against the back of her chair, mouth slightly open in a twilight sleep.

"Could be you'll face a long life of struggle," she whispered to her brother.

"I don't mind struggle," he said thoughtfully. "I'm not afraid of that. Struggle can be good if it strengthens our faith in God. It's the struggle without meaning that buries a man before he ever dies."

"Like Da."

"Aye." He nodded. "Da's given up on a meaning for his life. He just works until he's tired enough to sleep. Then he gets up and works again."

"But he believes in God, true enough!"

"He believes in God, but he's lost his faith. There's no finding it on your own when you've suffered a blow like Da. If he had a church life, there'd be a chance of finding it again."

"Are you saying I've got no faith because I've never been to church?" Grace set down her needle and frowned at him. "And yours is strong because you've been a handful of times?" She shook her head. "That's faith in the church you're talking about, not faith in God."

"You're partly right and partly wrong. When Christians use the church for their own end, it becomes no more than a councilhouse. But when they use the church for the good of God, it is a mighty place with power to lift us all. We're meant to seek out such a place as that. God says we must be part of a Christian community—'tis the body of Christ, after all."

"And are we not a community here ourselves?" she asked.

"Aye, we are. But who leads us? Who is our shepherd? Not Da. He won't have anything to do with religion, nor will he let us seek it out on our own. He's respectful of God and he's shown us that road, true enough, but it's a long, long road and he's given us no manner of map for the journey."

Voices came from outside, loud over the sound of the rain. Sean pushed open the basket that held his threads and needles, and slipped the Bible down into the very bottom, picking up the linen collar and resuming his work as the door opened.

"It's pouring buckets out there," Patrick said as Grace got up to take his dripping oilskin.

"Ryan's not coming in?" she asked as she hung the slick on a peg.

Patrick shook his head. "Make up a pail of food for him, will you, Grace? I'll take it when I go back out."

"Where is he, then? I thought I heard him." Sean set down his basket and moved over on the hob, making room for Patrick to sit and warm himself.

Patrick stood instead, his back to the low flame. "The ewes are lambing and there's a vixen in the wood makes us edgy. He won't leave them. If comes a break in the rain, we'll bring them to the shed."

"No Aghna tonight, then?" Sean smiled. "And won't they enjoy a night of peace over there, not that our Ryan is the talker of the match."

Patrick frowned. "O'Doud's fond of the boy and it's clear enough Aghna's set her cap for him. He speaks of marrying come summer, and wonders about bringing her to live . . ." His voice trailed off and he looked down at his boot tops.

"Aghna's always been a one for getting ahead. She's a proud girl," Granna said. "I don't suppose she'll be wanting to start off her married life in a small cabin with an old woman and a young girl in the way of her housekeeping."

Patrick, his body warmed, settled on a stool nearer to Gran and lit his pipe, sucking vigorously on the end of it and cursing the damp tobacco. "He says she has dreams of getting off the farm, going west to her mother's people in Galway, though not to the fishing life. It's the towns and all, fills her head." He paused to draw on his pipe. "Our Ryan, he's no townsman, but what can he offer so terrible smitten he is?"

"He'll not go away from us, will he, Da?" Grace asked, worried.

"I've said I'll add on here once we get a little coin in our purse. The bait of a lovely room all their own, plus independence here, might turn her eyes closer to home. With most of us moving on, they could have the place to themselves soon enough."

Sean looked at Grace, then his father. "What do you mean 'moving on,' Da?"

"Well, won't I soon be out of the way, an old woman like myself?" Granna put in, smiling comfort at Grace, who rose to protest. "Faith, and it won't be too many more years, agra, before you're married into a home of your own, as well, with no more need of this one."

"Aye, you'll both go and leave me here to sit by the fire, sewing till my hands go blue, bouncing all the babies on my one good knee like a good uncle." Sean smiled around at them, but it was as twisted as his arm and there was no mistaking the bitterness in his voice.

Patrick puffed on his pipe and narrowed his eyes at the boy. "You'll be lucky to have it, you will. Fed and cared for by your brother and his wife. Where in the world else would you go, crippled as you are?"

Grace's head was down over her work, but she could see Sean's hands clench together in his lap, although he, too, kept his head down. She put aside the stitching and said quickly, "Supper's been warming in the pot and there's plenty of bread and fresh butter to go along."

"Some of that good stew, I hope. And your buttermilk scones like clouds. That's all a man needs at the end of any day." Patrick pulled too hard on his pipe and began to hack, finally spitting black juice into the fire and wiping the sweat off his forehead.

The other three watched him. Something was wrong. They gathered quietly around the table and began eating when Grace filled their bowls, Granna and Sean watching Patrick make small talk as he'd never done before. Even Grace seemed aware that there was something her father wanted to say, but could not.

At the end of the meal, Grace brought out a bowl of stewed plums.

"You're going to be a fine wife, Gracelin," Patrick said, then suddenly put down his spoon and wiped his eyes.

"What is it, then, Da?" Grace asked gently. "Has something gone wrong?"

"Are we to be evicted?" Granna covered Grace's hand with her own.

Patrick remained silent, staring down at the table.

"Tell us, for God's sake," Sean demanded.

"There'll be no taking in vain of the Lord's name in this house." Patrick looked up angrily.

"There's none of the Lord's name in this house as it is," Sean answered defiantly.

Patrick rose up off his stool. "Listen here, boy. Have I not told you more times than I care to count? The word 'Irishman' existed long before anyone ever thought of adding 'Catholic' or 'Protestant' to it. Although they'd like you to think it, they've not cornered the market on belief, you know." He slammed his fists down on the table. "I'm Irish, by God. *That's* my religion. You'd make it yours, as well, if you had any sense!"

Sean lowered his eyes, chastised.

Patrick sat down again, the high color leaving his face as he calmed himself. He picked up his spoon, then put it down again. Finally, he cleared his throat, not looking at Grace.

"It's good news, it is, and now it's ruined by fight." He glowered at Sean. "Might as well just say it straight out." His gaze moved around the table, stopping on Grace. "I've found you a husband, and a better match no father could make for his own."

Grace's eyebrows rose to her hairline. She looked immediately at

Sean, whose mouth had fallen open in amazement, eyes fixed on his father's face.

"A husband for me, Da?" Grace said, then turned to Granna. "But I hadn't yet thought of marrying," she added quietly.

Granna's face was as shocked as Grace's, but she quickly regained her composure, nodding as though the wisdom of the decision were suddenly clear to her. "Aye, you seem so young to us who love you, but fifteen is not a child anymore." She paused, then said gently, "Your mother was but fifteen when she married your da."

Grace shook her head as if to clear it. She looked at her father. "Who is it I'm to be marrying?"

Patrick was still again for a moment. "Squire Donnelly," he said at last.

Dead silence fell upon the table as they all stared at Patrick.

"He's thirty if he's a day!" Sean burst out. "Closer to your age than hers! And he's married twice before. The man has no reputation for keeping a wife!" He looked pointedly at his father. "You know what I mean, Da. Grace can't be marrying the likes of that one!"

Patrick slammed down his pipe. "Have I not fixed it for him to marry *her*, and not yourself? Have you not caused enough trouble here tonight?" He stopped and took a deep breath. "The man lost his first wife in childbirth, and the second to fever—can he not lose a wife without blame coming upon him? Have I not lost a wife myself?" He paused again, then seeing no acceptance in their faces, lost his temper. "It's not as if he's making her his tallywoman, for God's sake—he's asked for her hand in marriage! Squire Donnelly is the largest landholder in the county, and the son of a lord! Use your head, boy—think what this will mean!"

"Is that it, then?" Sean's good hand gripped the edge of the table. "You've sold her out to him for a break on our rent?"

Patrick knocked back the stool and was up in an instant. He leaned across the table and grabbed the front of Sean's shirt, yanking him up, face to face. "Don't you ever talk to me like that again, boy, do you hear? Who in the name of God do you think you are?" He shoved Sean back down onto the bench. "I've not sold her out. I'd not do that to my own daughter. We've made a bit of a deal, 'tis true." He looked to Granna for support. "But it's all to the good for Grace. She's got no dowry except what she's sewed for herself, and who else is she to marry but some poor pegeen who can't understand a word of English and can't give her anything but lots of children and maybe a few young years." His eyes pleaded with them to understand. "She'll never get a chance like this again in her life. It's a wonder he picked her at all, him being a squire with plenty of choice from the other big houses. But it's Grace he wants, he's made that clear. And it'll help us all if she marries him. We'll keep the farm, no matter the year; Ryan and Aghna can come to the house and he's offered to build on new rooms, as well as a new plow horse. He'll give Grace everything she deserves—a big house, lots of help, a doctor for the babies . . . a decent life!"

"But she doesn't love him," Sean said quietly.

"And what would you know of that but what you've read in books?" Patrick demanded. "Isn't there more to marriage than love or would none of them last? Love grows out of respect, and sure enough, it'll come once they're wed."

Grace heard herself ask, as if from far away, "Why is it me he's chosen? Does he even know the look of me?"

"He saw you at the bonfire on St. John's Eve. Brigid Sullivan told him who you were, and when he came back from the North, he asked after you." Patrick smiled at her with pride. "Some of the other squires' wives and daughters been showing off your needlework and telling what a gift you got. He says it's the best he's ever seen, and he travels, you know, to England and Scotland."

"Are you telling us he wants to marry her because of her embroidery?" Sean narrowed his eyes at his father.

Patrick shook his head. "Of course not, you eejit," he said. "But her having a talent like that lifts her up above other folk, not to mention she can read and write a bit, and her English is as good as her Irish. She's not just some country girl living in a rough with pigs and sheep to keep her warm at night." He waved his hand around at the walls of their cabin. "Hasn't your mother made a reputation for living a better life, and isn't Grace her mother's daughter? He's been told what a fine cook she is and that her mead is as good as Kathleen's. He knows she's young and strong, and the man's desperate for an heir." Patrick looked at Grace as if they were the only two in the room. "I've been to see him. He's made a generous offer to the family in consideration for your hand. You'll never want for anything, agra. He's given me his word as a man of honor."

"A man of honor," Sean spat. "He's a landowner. And a bloody Englishman, for all that. They hand their word to the Irish like a piece of meat—fresh today, but rotted before week's end."

"His word'll pay for a doctor to look at your leg there, boy, so don't be so quick to condemn the man. Who are you a'tall to sit in judgment?" Patrick rose from the table and reached for his slick. Grace got up immediately and helped him into it, then brought him the pail with Ryan's dinner. He took it, laying his hand over hers.

"You don't have to marry him, Grace," he said, suddenly weary. "I did what I thought was best for you. He'll be wanting an answer come morning."

Grace looked at her father's dear face and didn't hesitate. "I'll marry him, Da. You can tell him that." She kissed him quickly on the cheek, then rubbed the stubble affectionately with her open hand. "It'll be all right. And haven't you done fine by us all, then?"

He pulled himself up straight and smiled into her pretty face. "You're a smart girl, like your sainted mother. It'll be you raises the name of O'Malley to its rightful place."

Grace watched him disappear into the driving rain, then returned to the table. Sean had pushed away his uneaten plums and sat staring at the wall. Granna picked up his bowl and carried it slowly to the sideboard.

"Have you nothing to say to me, then, the two of you?" Grace asked when the silence had grown thick around them all.

Sean looked up at her and shook his head, sandy hair falling into his eyes. "There's nothing to say, now you've made up your mind."

Granna turned, leaning on the edge of the table. "Do you not want to think more upon this, Grace? Isn't he a squire, after all, and an Englishman, as your brother says? They're different from us. Will your life not be changed forever?"

Grace looked from one face to the other and back again. Her eyes filled with tears. "My life will change no matter who it is I marry, and am I not to trust the good judgment of my father in this? How can I know what is best for myself when I still act like a child?" She bit her lip, blinking hard. "At St. John's Eve, Morgan McDonagh stood close by, and when he tried to hold my hand, I near jumped into the flames myself! I couldn't get home fast enough, could I? Dreaming is a fine thing, but one day you must wake up. Sure and I thought married life lay far down the lane, but here it is—knocking at my very door!" She wiped her eyes, then stared at her damp fingers. "Look—dirty and ragged. Not gentle hands, these." She sighed and hid them under her apron. Then her face changed, the misty eyes grew determined, and her chin rose firmly. "But can I not learn to *be* the wife of a gentleman, as I would've learned to be the wife of a farmer or a shopkeeper, a teacher or a baker?" she asked. "Am I not blessed to have for my husband a man of good fortune? A man to provide us with peace of mind, so that we all might know comfort. Through him, I'll be able to do for the both of you—warm clothes and meal in the winter, medicine and doctors . . ." Her voice trailed off at the sight of their forlorn faces.

Granna stepped forward and put her arms around the girl. "There now, child. Of course you will—we've no doubt of that. And as for learning to be the wife of the Squire, why, you've got the makings of a lady in your heart already, sure enough, and wouldn't your own dear mother be proud?" She held Grace out to look at her. "You're a fine girl, and you're doing right by your father and mother. We just want your happiness in the bargain, don't we, Sean?" Granna stared him down until he gave up his glowering look. "He'll make a fine husband. Hasn't he had plenty of practice, then?" Granna's eyes twinkled and even Sean laughed, despite himself. "Your mother, too, seemed young at fifteen, but she had a strong character, just like yourself, and a noble heart like yours, as well."

Grace looked up into her grandmother's face. "She and Dad had love."

Granna nodded. "Faith, they did." She squeezed Grace's shoulders and said firmly, "But more's the marriage that begins like yours. Love will come, as your da said—the Squire would have to be blind and dumb not to fall for such a one as you, and we know he's not that."

Sean pushed himself up from the table. "I'm tired," he said abruptly. "My leg hurts tonight." He managed a weak smile before bumping out the back door to the lean-to that was his room.

"Gran?" Grace watched the door bang shut.

"It'll be all right, child," Granna whispered. "He's had you to himself all these years, and he's not been thinking of giving you up so soon."

"I won't be far," Grace said. "Donnelly House is but a half-day's ride."

"It's a world away, child, and you might as well get used to that." Granna sighed and untied her apron. "I'm going to bed now, too. Kiss me when you come in?"

"And now, as well." Grace brushed her lips against the papery cheek that smelled of potato flowers and onions, and her heart surged.

After Granna had gone, Grace finished cleaning the dishes and putting away the food. She filled a pot with cold water, added oats, and covered it, ready to fire in the morning. Then she set aside oats for the laying chickens. When this was done, she paused and looked around the cabin with its whitewashed walls and stick furniture. In the dying light of the fire, it felt snug and safe, and she was filled with a terrible ache at the thought of leaving it. There was a smudge on the chimney from the smoke; nearby lay a pile of turf ready to throw on; her stool and work basket stood next to that. A sampler hung on the wall and curtains she'd fashioned from bawneen brightened the windows. There was the rug Granna had made from old, torn rags, and the shelves Sean had nailed a little lower than the rest so that she might easily get at the pots and pans without a stool. Picture postcards from her mother's youth were nailed up on the walls, landscapes, mostly: the Mourne Mountains sweeping down to the sea—Heartache Hills, her father called them, claiming to have hiked them as a boy; there was one of goats grazing the cliffs near Kilkee; and another of the Golden Vale's rich grasslands, which her mother had loved best and which hung in the kitchen; and near the front door of the cabin, a larger picture of the fiery, sun-going-down sky above Bantry Bay, sitting in the shadow of Hungry Hill. All testimony to her parents' love of the achingly beautiful Irish land, a love they had passed on to her. She would miss the cabin and her quiet life in it, but it came to her then that she might finally see the rest of Ireland for herself. She might even travel to other countries. The thought steadied her, and she turned to speak to Sean, but saw only shadows in the corner where he usually sat.

She crossed the room and stepped out of the kitchen into the cold, evening air, walking quickly through the mud to the outhouse. It had stopped raining, and on the way back, she lingered, looking up at the sky streaked with dark clouds, just a hint of the starlight that would be so bright later on. Lamplight shone through the oilskin window of Sean's room and she tapped quietly on the door.

"Who is it?" Sean barked.

Grace had to smile. "And who was it you were expecting, then, Mister O'Malley, sir?"

She heard him limp across the floor to open the door. "I'm worn out, Grace," he said, and looked it.

"Sean." She touched his cheek, serious again. "Are you angry with me, then?"

He bent his head, trapping her hand between his face and his shoulder for just a moment.

"Musha, Gracie." He brushed the hair out of her eyes. "How could I ever be angry with you? Don't I love you more than anyone on earth? Many's the night I've wished the Lord would take me home, but for you, Grace. You and Granna. Gran giving me Mam's Bible has helped, but it's you that's shared most of these long days with me . . . even teaching me to stitch!"

"For which you've cursed me ever since," she teased.

He laughed, too. "But I've always been grateful for your company."

"And I for yours. You're a fine brother, teaching me to read and write, and figure my numbers, and telling me about Mam."

They were quiet, listening to the night settle around them, the cow lowing in her stall, the rustle of chickens in the coop.

"Life will change now," Sean said softly. "You'll be a married woman. No more gossiping over the needle with your old crippled brother." He smiled, but Grace could see the sadness in his eyes. "I'm happy for you, really I am. Jealous, too, I'm thinking. You're off and away to a new life . . . and I'm going to miss you, is all."

Grace hugged him tightly to her. "You won't have time to miss me, eejit. I'll be seeing you more often than not."

Sean suddenly squeezed the breath out of her, his face in her hair.

She pulled away from him. "Won't I?"

He didn't answer.

"Why won't I be seeing you, Sean O'Malley? What's going on in that ever-whirling head of yours?"

He wouldn't meet her eyes. "I'll stay long enough to see you settled in your marriage, and to make sure Squire Donnelly lives up to his promises." Now he did look at her. "But you can't ask me to stay here forever. I fetch so little coin, it barely pays for the doctor and laudanum."

"But we'll have money for that now!" Grace whispered urgently. "We'll be able to take you up to Dublin, to the hospital there. A modern doctor will straighten your arm and leg, and you'll walk properly again!"

Sean tipped his head, and with the lamplight behind, he looked like an angel.

"You're not to think of going out on your own, Sean, do you hear me?" Grace shook his good arm. "What about Gran? It'd break her heart to lose the two of us all at once!"

"Granna knows I must make a life for myself."

"But where will you go?" Grace said frantically. "What will you do?"

Sean shrugged, but there was strength in his face. "The Lord has plans for me, but He's not going to hand me a piece of paper with instructions. I've got to go out into the world and be ready. Ryan and Aghna will be having a family, and just looking at me makes Aghna shudder. She thinks I'm cursed. I can't live with that every day. It'd be miserable for all of us."

"Then you'll come to live with me at Donnelly House," Grace said firmly.

Sean smiled, but shook his head. "I could no more live with your squire than he with me, Gracie, and you know that's the truth of it."

He saw the desperation in her face and weakened. "Fifteen," he said gently. "I forget what a slip you are. How is it possible you're to be someone's wife?"

Grace sighed. "I don't know. It's not real. I can't do it if you're not here."

"All right, then, wee sister. I won't go anywhere until you tell me it's time. But then I'll have your blessing as I take up my pack for Scotland . . . or maybe even America."

Grace pulled him close to her again and held him for a moment before saying reluctantly, "That's a promise, then. You won't leave until I say."

Sean eased out of her embrace. "I promise." He scowled at the look on her face. "I made the promise! I won't break it," he insisted. "I'm not going to disappear before morning, if that's what's worrying you. I'll see your married off to old man Donnelly first." He puffed up his chest and looked down his nose. "The wealthy landowner, don't you know. I'll be calling you Missus Donnelly, your ladyship, now."

They both laughed; then Grace kissed him on the cheek and whispered good night. She slipped back in the kitchen door, taking off her muddy boots and shaking out her skirt. Her father would be in any time, so she left hot water in the kettle and a piece of bread and cheese on the table, then went to the back of the cabin, where she shared a wide pallet with Granna. She took a candle with her, pausing in the doorway, the mellow light falling across the sleeping figure in the bed. At the foot of the mattress sat a wooden chest filled with her mother's handwork and some of her own—things to take when the time came to marry. Setting the candle on the sill, she bent over the chest now and lifted out a set of clean folded sheets with the edges turned and hemmed; pillowcases with wildflowers twisting up the open edge; a tablecloth Kathleen had given her to embroider and which she'd edged with dancing men and women, singers and musicians. There were doilies and sachets, samplers and napkins, lace collars, underslips with roses and hearts, and a long white nightgown, a gift from Granna two years ago, that Grace had stitched with birds and flowers cascading down the front to a beautiful field of goldenrod and daisies. This last she lifted out and held up to herself. She'd not thought of wearing it for years yet, and a blush rose to her cheeks at the thought of her wedding night. A country girl, she knew the ways of getting life, but being the youngest in the family, she'd never seen her mother pregnant or bearing children, and suddenly she was afraid of what she didn't know. She undressed quickly and pulled on the nightgown. It was meant to be worn on the night her new life began and, she decided, that was tonight. The fabric was heavy and cool against her skin, the front ties silky in her fingers. She smoothed down the folds of fabric, then unbraided her hair and brushed it as the vision in the corner had done on so many nights.

"So I'm to be married, then," she said quietly to herself. "Gracelin Donnelly. Missus Donnelly. Missus Bram Donnelly." She paused. "Landowner." This last sent her into a fit of laughter and she pushed her fingers against her mouth to stifle the sounds before they woke Gran. The laughter turned quickly to sober tears and the smile faded from her face. She blew out her candle and got into bed, lying on her back so that she might see through the tiny window the glow of starlight strewn across the sky. As she felt her body give way at last to the drowsiness before sleep, she prayed silently the prayer her brother had taught her: Our Father, Who art in Heaven, Hallowed be Thy name. Thy Kingdom come, Thy will be done . . .

"Thy will be done," she repeated slowly, words whispered aloud, the comfort of them settling in around her and leading her safely into sleep.

# Two

SEAN was waiting on the wooden bench outside the cabin when Morgan McDonagh came up the lane in his father's rough cart. The jennet, old and nearly blind, was stubborn and moved at a pace slower than a happy man's stride, but Sean could never have walked the distance to the river without pain, so Morgan brought the cart.

"'Tis a fine evening for it, O'Malley!" he called, tossing aside the reins and hopping down with an easy swing. He was a strongly built young man with thick, nut-brown hair like all his family, and hazel eyes set in a smooth, tan face, a smattering of freckles running away over one high cheekbone.

Sean stood carefully, always happy to see him, then handed over the pole and tackle kit to put inside the cart, alongside the empty basket for their catch. He clapped Morgan on the shoulder. "Evening's always best for spring salmon," he said happily. "We'll have a fine catch to bring back. Thanks for coming out, Morgan. I know they need you at home."

Morgan nodded soberly. "Faith, it never ends. That's the truth of it. Not with eviction hanging over everyone's heads now that rents have gone up again." He tossed in the small stool Sean took for sitting on the riverbank when he tired. "Nearly forty pounds a year, man, can you believe it?" He shook his head. "And all those extra bits tacked on—a pound if we whitewash the place or stone the walk, a levy for bringing baskets of turf across the lake, fines for not giving duty days if we're sick when they call us, or if some relation misses his rent. Even a fine for getting married without his lordship's leave! Blood and ounse, a man can hardly turn around without it costing him!"

"O'Flaherty's a bastard," Sean said, stepping into the foothold Morgan made with his hands. He pulled himself into the cart with his good arm. "I hear he's thrown out everyone over in Castle Rock, knocked down the cabins, and posted soldiers to make sure they don't sneak back and rebuild."

"You heard right." Morgan climbed into the cart and settled himself. "Most of those families held on a hundred years or more. They made their rents with nothing left over, but now they've been raised and levied till there's nothing left. He's going to graze sheep and cattle on that land. Money there, he says. No money in keeping people alive what worked your land all their days." Morgan spat, then slapped the reins along the jennet's backside to get her moving.

"A few passed through the lane here." Sean moved over to the edge of the driver's bench, giving Morgan more room. "Looking for relations to take them in. There's so many on their own, you know, and what's to become of them?"

Morgan shrugged. "Well you might ask. O'Flaherty's agent—spawn of the devil, that Ceallachan—says they'll pay for immigration, but they only go because it's that or die in the road. Paying the five-pound passage is cheaper for O'Flaherty than standing their rent another year, but I hear he sends them to Canada to die in the fever sheds . . . if they survive the crossing in those stinking holds. That done, they're still living under English rule."

"Grace says she saw whole families living in the bog, when she was cutting turf with Ryan."

Morgan nodded. "Aye, some live in the bog, some in ditches. Respectable folk all their lives, living now like tinkers, only worse 'cause they don't know how to beg their food without losing their pride."

"Would it not be the better choice to risk passage than to starve in some muddy bog with only brack water to drink and roots to eat?" Sean rubbed his withered arm with his good hand. "It's come upon me often enough, though Lord knows I've got good shelter and my belly's full." He looked down wistfully at his twisted leg. "A man can make something of himself over there. Every man an equal to every other man in America, they say."

"Do you not think they've got rich and poor, just like here?" Morgan asked. "Because you're daft, if you don't."

Sean frowned. "A man can work himself hard every day of his life in Ireland and never get ahead. He can't even leave the bit of land he works all his life to his children. But in America, if he works hard every day, he can own his land and his family has something to show for his toil!"

"'The Land of Opportunity,'" Morgan said wryly. "Sure, and some do all right, they go west and get a patch of their own, or stay east and send a bit of money home to the old folks. But most you never hear from again. The girls that come home, they're silent as the grave." He snapped the rein. "My cousin Colleen was in service at a grand house in Boston, sent money home regular, but after a year, she come back. Brought her mother a sewing machine and ten pounds, then went straight into the convent. America's a wicked place, if you ask me." He looked up into the blue sky filled with billowing white clouds and sailing blackbirds, took a deep breath, and said passionately, "It may be a hard life here, but you couldn't pay me enough gold to leave Ireland."

Sean smiled. "True enough. You're an Irishman the likes of Finn McCool and Brian Boru. You should've been a king."

Morgan glowered. "I'm the son of one, same as you—descendants of the seven hundred kings that once roamed this island. 'Tis no blood stronger or more noble than Irish blood, and it still beats in the hearts of men like William Smith O'Brien and John Mitchel." He shook his head in disgust. "We've let the bloody English bully us and make peasants of our fathers, but it's time we stood up for our rightful claim. It's time the Irish ruled Ireland again."

Sean's smile faded. "That sounds like sedition, my friend," he said softly.

Morgan met his gaze. "Call it what you like. I call it truth."

They rode along in silence, each one deep in thought. Sean's father, mistrusting the Catholics, was not an active Repealer, though Sean knew he wished for it fervently. Morgan, however, was steeped in the politics of his father, who attended all the rallies when he was home from seafaring. But Smith O'Brien and Mitchel were names associated with the new Young Ireland party, radicals in the eyes of the

Repealers, for they refused to take the oath against bearing arms. He wondered how deeply Morgan was involved.

Unhindered by cloud, the late afternoon sun beat down and warmed their shoulders. A cuckoo called in the wood. Morgan sighed and shifted in his seat.

"You'll not be paying a marrying tax for Gracelin, I don't suppose," he said all of sudden, glancing at Sean, then back at the road. "And, of course, you'll not be worrying about living in the bog any time soon."

Sean reached over, snatched the reins, and stopped the cart, then twisted in his seat to face Morgan. His voice was calm, but his eyes blazed.

"My sister is no man's tallywoman, Morgan McDonagh. So, if that's what you're implying, I'll have to kill you now."

Morgan's eyes widened in surprise, and he put up his hands in defense, despite his obvious physical advantage. "I'd never call her that, and you know it, you daft boy. We all love your Grace! Some more than others, to be sure," he added under his breath, and then his hands fell into his lap. "Ah, brother, I'm a gabby eejit, is all. These days have my thick head whirling."

The anger died and Sean's shoulders drooped. "That makes two of us, then." He sighed. "To say the truth, I'm jumpy about Grace marrying him. It seems so queer. Our Grace marrying a squire and going off to live in a big house with servants and all. I can't see it."

"You're not alone." Morgan picked up the reins and set the cart in motion again. "Tongues are wagging up and down the valley, they are, all wanting to know how it come about."

Sean rolled his eyes in disgust. "It's all over him wanting an heir. And to get himself a boy, he's convinced he needs a strapping country lass instead of a genteel lady, seeing as how he's tried that in the past, don't you know. He saw Grace in Macroom at St. John's, and Brigid Sullivan, who keeps his house, told him all about her. He's been up North to Ulster, but now he's back, determined to have her. He put it to Da that he'd marry Grace, not just keep her. And her with no dowry—but of course, it makes no difference to him." He stopped and took a breath, then looked Morgan square in the eye. "And, the truth of it is, Morgan, he says he's going to make life easier for ourselves. Ryan can marry Aghna O'Doud and come into the house, because Donnelly's going to build rooms onto the place. Now Ryan will stay on the land instead of going west to Galway as Da feared. There's to be a new plow horse, as well, and a Dublin doctor for me. And, of course, we won't be put out if times get hard, though we can't do a thing for our neighbors. I feel ashamed of it all, somehow," he added. "As if we're selling her off to make our lives easier."

Morgan drove the cart with one hand, laying the other on Sean's stiff leg. "You can't blame your da," he said firmly. "He's better off than some, but poor men are always poor in Ireland, you said so yourself. If he's struck a bargain that stands well by yourselves, then he's done his duty to you, and you can be sure it brings him some relief."

"Him being saddled with an old woman and a cripple son, you mean," Sean interjected bitterly.

"Eejit." Morgan whapped him. "That's not what I'm saying at all, as you well know. Sure and your body is crippled. But not your mind, and are you not thankful for that? You're no burden to your da. Look at the coin you earn."

"Pays not the doctor seen once a year." Sean looked away into the woods where sunlight dappled new grass between the trees. "It's why I'm thinking of America, of striking out on my own. But, faith! What could I do?" He pounded his lame leg with his fist. "What am I good for, then?"

"Usually, you're good for a bit of easy talk." Morgan grinned. "But not today, I'm thinking."

Sean hung on to his frown stubbornly.

"You're good for keeping knowledge and figuring things out," Morgan volunteered. "You've been blessed with a sharp mind, sharper than any man I know, and that's God's truth."

"Cursed, is what you mean. Cursed with a sharp mind . . . and a body too useless to house it." Sean rubbed his forehead, his face tense.

"Doesn't God tell us to count the blessings and shoulder the burdens?" Morgan peered through the trees for a glimpse of the river up ahead. "Does He not give both for our better good?"

"And what burdens do *you* carry, then, Mister McDonagh?" Sean asked, testily. "You with your bit of land, strong body and good looks, and a voice that makes all the girls want to lose their better judgment? What burden has God given *you* to shoulder?"

Morgan stared straight ahead. "I've got them, sure enough."

"You care for your mam and the girls—I know that," Sean acknowledged. "But that's duty, not disappointment."

"Of late, my friend, I've made good acquaintance with disappointment." He paused. "I've come to love a girl who can never be my wife."

"She must be blind and deaf both!" Sean replied. "Tell me her name quick, so that I might call upon her this very day!"

Morgan laughed despite himself. "Nay," he said, shaking his head. "She'd not have you, though love you truly she does."

"What?" Sean punched Morgan's arm. "Out with it, man!"

Morgan looked at him briefly, his white teeth worrying his lower lip. "You must promise never to speak of it."

"I swear on the soul of my father, the king," Sean said, raising his hand.

"Then I'll tell you that she's more beautiful than the fairies and more gentle than any new mother. She is as brave as the pirate whose name she carries, and her mind is as quick as that of her brothers."

Sean stared, then blinked twice before he found his voice. "Morgan!" he shouted. "Morgan, man! You're in love with our Grace!"

Morgan smiled sheepishly. "'Twas at that cursed bonfire last summer, St. John's Eve. Did every man fall in love with her that night, I wonder?" He shook his head. "She was standing next to me and I could smell the wood smoke in her hair. She looked up all of a sudden like and smiled that sweet, gentle smile she has, and I . . . it just come over me then that I loved her."

"Why did you do nothing about it?"

Morgan looked at Sean, one man's regret an even match for the other man's amazement. "I took her hand," he said, then laughed, remembering. "And she near withered away of shyness. She couldn't get away quick enough. But I knew, as I watched her run up the hill in the moonlight, that the time would come soon enough for me to speak." He stopped and swallowed hard. "I told myself I'd wait till spring to come courting. I thought I'd get a jump on the line of boys I knew'd be waiting for her hand." His laugh this time was short and tired. "It never occurred to me that Squire Donnelly would squash the line and claim her as his own. So, you see, Sean O'Malley, you're not the only man to carry a stone in his heart."

Sean said nothing until they got to the river, an offshoot of the

Shannon that came tumbling over smooth, round rocks, sparkling in the light—a clear, cold river teeming with salmon in the spring. They got out their poles and tramped to the river's edge to follow the thin path through the grasses that led to the salmon stand. When they came to the shoal where the fish tried to get up to the redds, they set down their baskets and Sean's small stooleen, then rigged up for the first cast.

"She's not married yet," Sean said, when their lines had settled.

"Aye, but she's promised."

"Many a promise has been broken for less."

"No." Morgan shook his head firmly. "If he were a country man like myself, you can be sure I'd press my case." He pulled gently on his line. "But he's not a country man. Nor even a city man. He's a squire. Son of an English lord, for pity's sake. What can I possibly give her next to that?"

Sean grabbed Morgan's arm, stopping him before he stepped into the water.

"Love," he said simply.

Morgan didn't smile. "You're a dreamer, Sean. Sure and I love her more than any other girl I've ever known. Love is a double comfort in a man's life . . . but not in a woman's. Don't I see it all around me? Have I not watched my mam suffer for her love of a wandering husband? I'll not burden Grace with the fact of my love when she's a chance for more."

"She has no feelings for him."

"And who's to say she has them for me!" Morgan jerked his pole angrily, then sighed in disgust at the loose line lying tangled in the water. "Devil take you, Sean O'Malley, what are you doing to me here?"

"You're the better man, by far," Sean insisted. "Grace will see it, if she's given the choice."

"And what choice would that be, then?" Morgan spat. "Life in a hovel with me and all the babies, scraping by to pay the rent and put oats in the pot . . . or life in a manor house with servants and warm clothes, and plenty of meat for her sons and daughters, and a chance to turn her mind to other things than should we buy a cow this year or can we do without shoes till winter?"

"He's no kind of husband for her!" Sean kicked the fish basket out of his way and sat down heavily on the bank.

"It's not for you to say." Morgan ran a hand, wet with river spray, through his hair. "Even if she did love me, it couldn't last. Don't you see? Not now. Think it out, man—if she agreed to marry me, she'd regret it as we got older and life was so hard on her children compared to what she could have given them. And if she didn't choose me, she might be left wondering—in the comfort of her home—about the love she passed over." He stepped closer to where Sean sat. "You think you'll be giving her a choice . . . but the truth of it is, you'll only give her doubt. It's best she never know my feelings. It's best she marry Donnelly and come to love him. And she will, if we don't get in the way. Do you understand me now, brother?"

Sean was still, then slowly he nodded. "You're a better man than myself, McDonagh. I'd grab my chance and run. Will you forgive my badgering?"

Morgan smiled. "Always do."

"I had high hopes there for a minute. Don't we already love you like one of the family?" He smiled, too. "Even if you are thick with the priests."

Morgan raised an eyebrow. "Not so thick now, boyo. I knew your da would never let a Catholic marry his daughter, so I've been thinking and reading on my own this past winter. Don't think your badgering falls on deaf ears."

Sean stared. "Go on with you! You'd never leave the church?"

Morgan shook his head. "No—Da would cut my throat if I did— but a man must do his own thinking if he's not to be a fool, and some of these priests act like thinking's a sin. Are they not men, after all, and no different from us in the eyes of God?" He stopped to think. "What's that verse in First Corinthians you wrote out for me?"

"'Know ye not, that they which run in a race run all, but one receiveth the prize?'"

Morgan nodded. "'So run, that ye may obtain it.'" He paused. "And the end bit, 'I therefore so run, not as uncertainty; so fight I, not as one that beateth the air: But I keep under my body, and bring it into subjection: lest that by any means, when I have preached to others, I myself should be a castaway.'"

"You've taken it to heart," Sean said softly.

"Aye." Morgan looked around at the wild landscape. "And I understand what it says: Those that preach the word of God should strive to be among the best of men, and yet they should be humble and serve the people of their church, as Christ served God." He paused and looked at Sean. "I must run in this race. Not just as part of the church, but as a servant to my people. God's servant."

"How did you come by a Bible?"

Morgan laughed. "Your gran had one belonged to her mam, and she insisted I take it, though she swore me to secrecy and begged me hide it away somewhere my da wouldn't find it."

"I wondered where that had gone!" Sean laughed, too. "Faith and she's a sly old thing."

"Aye," Morgan agreed. "But I love her dear. Mam doesn't know what I'm at, just sees the candle lit at night, and she boasted to Father Brown that her Morgan is quite a reader thanks to that bit of schooling with the Brothers. He's taken it upon himself to keep me well-provided now with pamphlets on modern farming and personal cleanliness." He laughed. "Wouldn't he be clutching at his heart, now, and fearing for my salvation if he knew I was puzzling through the Good Book on my own!" The smile faded. "Sure and it's a hard thing, though, making sense of it all."

Sean nodded. "Aye, you have to live in it before it starts to become clear."

They fell silent then, watching the black water, the shadowy shapes of the salmon swimming beneath the surface, now and then a glint of their silver sides. Sean felt a tug on his line and played it, bringing it in slowly but with an expert hand. Morgan waded out and caught it on the gaff, then took the hook out of its mouth and tossed it to the bank, where Sean hit it once with a club. When it was still, he ran a stick through the mouth and gill, and secured it in a shallow pool to keep it fresh. He went back to his place and cast his line again, looking over to where Morgan stood under the chestnut trees, white blooms drifting down lazily from the tall cathedral of branches.

Morgan looked up and caught his eye. "I'm not speaking against the church, mind you now. I've known more good priests than bad, and Father Brown is one of the finest men alive, priest or no."

"He's a good man, I'll give you that," Sean conceded. "He's made a life among the people, doesn't hold himself apart." He paused. "It's the mixing up of religion with politics gets me so angry. What right have they to tell the people who to back?"

Morgan played his line, then waited. "I don't know that you can separate one part of who you are from the other part." He waited. "If we're to be Christians in this world, we cannot hide ourselves away from the business of it. We cannot pretend that our neighbor's plight is not our own."

"True enough," Sean agreed. "Why then do they bully the people, telling them to pay rent when their children are starving or face the wrath of God for not rendering unto Caesar? Is it right, do you think, to tell them that oppression and famine are the will of God and they must accept it silently, with heads hung humbly down?"

"No." Morgan frowned. "A man must pay what he owes in good faith—that's rendering unto Caesar—but there's little good faith to be had in Ireland anymore. These swaggering agentmen go about collecting higher and higher rents for landlords who don't even come down to the country! How can a man living in Dublin, let alone England, understand the suffering of people he never sees? God does not want His people sacrificed for sheep and cattle, or for another man's rich life. No, He does not." The hazel eyes flashed. "He wants us to rise up and insist on a Christian country where all can count on a plate of food at the end of the day and a man's family is not turned out on the road in the dead of winter, his house and belongings smashed for all to see . . . a place where life is not so desperate." He stopped and lowered his voice. "Men like Father Brown use their persuasion to rally support for O'Connell and the Repeal Movement, and that's a good thing. But we cannot, in good faith, continue to be part of the great silent mass."

"I can hardly believe what I'm hearing, Morgan, man." Sean squinted at his face. "Are you true serious?"

"Ireland is coming upon harder times, still." Morgan bent over and cleaned his fingers in the clear water. "I feel it. She can't be pushed much further. There's been too much famine in the past, too much fever, too much work . . . too little hope." He stood and wiped his fingers on his trousers. "Whatever comes, I had thought to have Grace beside me as my wife and you as my brother. My heart fights against it, but I'm trying to accept the Lord's will in sending me down another path."

Sean looked at Morgan. "Can it be His will, truly Morgan, do you think? About Grace, I mean?" He paused, then said with great discomfort, "Have you not heard the talk? Da says it's lies put out by jeal-

ous men. But, faith, I . . . I don't know." He shook his head. "It troubles my heart to hear it. I lie awake hours at night in worry."

"What talk is that?"

Sean's face turned red with embarrassment. "Have you heard
nothing, then? About the way he . . . they say he visits houses in the
city, in the North, and that he . . . he mistreats the girls there." His
eyes filled with anguish. "And what about the truth of two wives dying?
The second in such a way that no one speaks of her but in a whisper.
Who is this man that will take away our Grace, and how will I be able
to help her, should she need it?"

Morgan's face had grown still with anger and he stood straight,
shoulders back, strong hands clenched at his sides, his voice deadly
calm when he spoke. "I'd not heard that about the women in the
North. Though it's a dull man doesn't wonder about the fate of that
poor English girl he married second time around." He thought a
minute. "Talk or no, we'll keep an eye on him. And if he's a minute
less the man he should be with our Grace . . . well, then, won't we put
himself straight, you and I together? You have my word on that." He
put out his hand. "God as my witness."

Sean took Morgan's hand in both of his, and they stood bound together, one boy strong and broad as the Shillelagh oak, the other bent
and twisted as a blackthorn hedge, drawing courage from one another
as around them the trees swayed in the wind and the river hurried
out to the sea.

# Three

GRACE'S wedding was like nothing she'd ever imagined—there was no singing of the old songs, no room full of family and neighbors drinking poteen and offering toasts in Irish, no tinkers with their ballads, and no dancing. No animals stood at the windows, staring in at the commotion, no small children ran through the crowded room, excitement blooming in their cheeks, flower garlands atop their heads. It was, instead, a solemn day: the tall, stately minister at the front of the chapel; her family all in a pew behind her, sitting straight-backed in stiff collars and vests; the rest scattered throughout other rows, all unfamiliar faces—Bram's gentry crowd, along with fellow businessmen and English officers, and of course, the wives. Grace wore her mother's long ivory dress unpacked from the trunk and smelling of lavender, aired in the sun and made over to suit Grace's longer neck and waist. There was a garland of spring roses and ivy, and Irish lace to cover her face. Bram's wedding gift to her had been a short strand of beautiful pearls that had been delivered in a velvet case by young Nolan Sullivan, his stable boy. Grace had opened the case gingerly and lifted it out for her family to admire, wondering inside about the man who would choose such a costly gift. They had yet to meet; it had been his wish to negotiate their future together completely through her father, so that when she first saw him, it would be at the altar.

The morning was overcast, and the hills glowed with green intensity against a low gray sky. Delicate berry blossoms scattered pink and

white petals across the lane; hedge roses added their deep color to
the day. It was the kind of light that heightened Grace's awareness of
beauty's ache, that filled her heart and tore at it in the same moment,
and all of this made even more poignant by the sense she had that she
looked upon it for the last time, that today she would be forever
changed. And then, when she'd thought she could not bear a minute
more, and must certainly tear off the dress and run away to the fields
on the hill, the sun broke through with its promise of calm, and the
carriage was at her door.

She followed Granna out into the light, holding her skirts carefully above the dirt and grass, waiting while Granna was handed in by
Nolan, whose father, Jack, drove the team; Grace was aided by her
own father, who then walked back to the tub cart and climbed in
with Ryan and Sean, ready to follow the carriage to Macroom. All of
the neighbors had come out of their cabins to see her off, and she
waved to Julia Ryan, who stood clutching Katty O'Dugan's arm and
weeping, the children shouting and jumping up and down while the
husbands doffed their caps, Tad O'Dugan shuffling his feet and looking embarrassed by all the display; out came Old Campbell Hawes,
wobbling in the doorway, his nose red from drink and emotion as he
shouted a blessing, his wife telling him to shush now and don't embarrass the girl; the Sheehans and the Dalys stood together—Fionna
and Shane close at the shoulders, though not touching; there were
the Kellys, Irial with his fiddle, son Kealan on the pipe—all lined the
lane to see her off, tossing flowers and beseeching God to bless this
happy day. The young men fell into a group behind the carriage,
singing "The Paisteen Fionn," and Grace was sure she could hear
Morgan McDonagh's strong, familiar tenor among the voices that
followed to the end of the lane, behind the steady clip-clop of the
horses' hooves. They stopped walking as the carriage turned onto
the avenue, and she closed her eyes, straining to hear the last of the
beautiful song:

> "O! You are my dear, my dear, my dear.
> Oh, you are my dear and my fair love!
> You are my own dear, and my fondest hope here,
> and oh, that my cottage you'd share, love!"

She blinked back the tears she'd been fighting all morning, then turned stiffly in her dress to look out behind, but the singers had faded back into the lane.

"Homesick already, are you?" Granna chafed Grace's cold hand between her two warm ones. "There's naught to fear, you know," she said softly, mindful of Jack Sullivan, who was known to gossip. "Are you not to be married this day to a fine man, and wouldn't your mam be ever so proud?"

"I'm not afraid, Gran," Grace answered softly in Irish. "Sean says God's angels will fill the church and Mam will be among them." She smoothed the beautiful skirt across her lap, steadying her hands.

"Faith and the boy is full of fancy," Granna said fondly. "But as you'd be the one to see her, mind you show me where she sits so I might have a quiet word and catch the scent of her again." She paused, then laughed self-consciously. "And would your one not be having a change of mind if he heard us speaking of such things? And in Irish, as well! We'd best keep your gifts to ourselves and speak only the Queen's English, or he'll be wondering what he got himself into!"

Grace joined the laughter. "Won't he be wondering that anyway after a few days of living with me, now?"

Granna's eyes sparkled with love. "Sure, and you're the finest girl in the county, Gracelin. In all of Ireland, true enough!" Her smile faltered and she glanced down at her hands, fussing with the unaccustomed gloves, a blush coming up in her cheeks. "I've not yet spoken to you as a mother should, Grace, for I could not find a time with no one about."

Grace frowned, puzzled.

Granna shook herself and said firmly, "I'm talking about your wedding night, agra. Are you in a way of knowing about it?"

It was Grace's turn to blush. "Sure and I've heard the wedding shouts all my life," she stammered. "And the cows and sheep . . ." Her voice trailed off.

Granna slipped an arm around her shoulders. "Put that out of your head. 'Tis not like the animals a'tall, but a thing of beauty, the coming together of man and wife." She glanced at Grace's downturned face and plunged on. "When the time comes, he'll leave you alone. Put on your nightdress and get into bed to wait for him. Don't mind your shyness. He'll understand."

Grace's face was intensely red and she dared not look at her grandmother.

"What comes next is natural and God's way for man and woman. Trust him to do what's right and let it be done. Find pleasure in his love for you and know that your love for him will grow out of this. And won't it give you children, which are such a blessing to a man and his wife?"

Grace looked up quickly, her eyes wide in alarm. She threw her arms around the old woman's shoulders, clinging to her. "Can you not come with me?" she begged.

"And what exactly is it you'd have me do, then? Stand at the foot of the bed and whisper encouragement?"

They stared at one another, picturing it, then burst out laughing.

"Ah, now," Granna murmured when both had sobered again. "I should've spoken up long ago, and the shame's on me for it." She straightened Grace up, and smoothed her hair and gown. "Don't vex yourself now, child. A bride must shine like the sun on her wedding day if she's to warm her husband's heart."

Grace nodded, but her smile was tense and fleeting. She took up Granna's warm, familiar hand and held it all the way to the chapel.

Clouds now blew in tatters across the sky, alternately masking, then revealing sharp glints of sunlight that streaked the hills and valleys. Grace's composure had returned and she felt fairly steady as she stepped out of the trap into the brisk spring breeze. She gently shook free her fluttering skirts, smoothed the fitted bodice, took a deep breath, then entered the church on her father's arm. But the sight of her future husband waiting at the altar turned her knees again to jelly and sent her vision swimming. It was an endless walk down the aisle, even with Patrick's reassuring face and firm grip on her arm.

"You look every inch a queen, and wouldn't old Grainne, the pirate, be pleased with the sight of yourself?" he whispered, his breath moist with the warm, woody smell of whiskey. He winked at the surprised look on her face. "Can't have your old da fainting from nerves on your very own wedding day, now, can you, darling girl?"

Her heart swelled with love for him, and impulsively she kissed his cheek, catching the glint of tears in his eyes as they reached the altar and he put her hand into that of the man who stood waiting.

And there they stood, side by side, listening to the words of the minister as he spoke about Christian marriage and the duties of husband and wife. She stole a quick glance through the lace of her veil, expecting to see formidable sideburns and a sober countenance. Instead, she was surprised by his youthfulness—a face that was tanned and fit, lines only at the corners of his eyes and mouth, no sideburns, but a full mustache of sandy hair, lighter than that on his head. He turned slightly and she saw that his eyes were as pale blue as the high summer sky, and was startled when suddenly he winked at her. She bit her lip and blushed, turning quickly back to face the minister, who was asking them to state their vows. Shyly, she repeated the words after him about loving and cherishing her new husband, and obeying him in all things, answering soberly that she would do so until death parted them. When it was the Squire's turn, she heard the amusement in his voice, and felt the firm squeeze upon her arm when he announced loudly, "I do!"

They turned to one another as directed, and he slipped onto her finger a wide gold band with an inset diamond, then lifted her veil and looked into her eyes before bestowing upon her a kiss so gentle, it was as if a feather brushed against her lips.

Listening to the minister finish his blessing, she was acutely aware of her new husband's solid presence beside her, the smell of him and the feel of his good cloth coat against her arm. The clarity that had come over her with her mother's death now swept through her again: Life would never be the same. Then, it had come with an overwhelming sadness; now, it came with excitement and a sense of destiny. God had chosen this man for her helpmeet. Her children would be educated in a proper school and never want for food or clothing, and her new position meant that she could now help her family and her neighbors. She stood tall, then—shoulders back, chin up—and all who looked upon her as she left the church on the arm of her new husband were taken with the light that seemed to radiate from her face, the confidence that shone in her eyes.

Too quickly, the ceremony was over and the wedding breakfast eaten. With Gran's help, Grace changed out of her beautiful dress and into traveling clothes for the journey to Dublin. It would take two days, as Bram had business on the way. She bid farewell to her family, then set off in a trap for Cork Harbor, where a light boat awaited them. She had never been on a boat in all her life, though she'd spent many pleasurable hours watching sails hoisted in the harbor.

The day was bright and the water brisk, but not too choppy, and she was pleased to find her sea legs. Bram spent a good deal of the voyage talking to the captain about grain transportation, so Grace was left to enjoy the sights. It was queer looking back on Ireland from the water, but she felt a swell of pride at the beauty of her island, the strong dark hills and lush pasturelands. Spring had just given over to summer, so all the trees were dressed in tender new leaves, their light color fresh among the darker shades of green that covered the hills. Even the sea had more green than blue, capped as it was with white tips.

They followed the shore, Bram occasionally calling out landmarks: Youghal Bay, Dungarvan Harbor at County Waterford, and finally Wexford Bay, where they docked. The captain wanted to take them all the way to Dublin Bay, but Bram informed him that he had business in County Wicklow and Kildaire.

From Wexford Bay, they traveled by coach to Blessington where Bram had hired a room for the night. Grace, tired and sleepy from the emotional morning and long day at sea, barely tasted the egg and butter, dish of trout, and wheaten bread set down before her. She held a cup of steaming hot coffee in her hands, blowing at it between drowsy sips. Bram bade her eat up and retire, as he was to meet Captain Hastings from Kildaire at the public house down the road. This was her wedding night, but he took her aside and explained that their honeymoon would begin properly in Dublin, that tonight she would have her own room here at the inn so that she might rest comfortably. She was surprised, but accepted that he knew best.

The housekeeper, a Mrs. Garrity with tight orange curls escaping from a white muslin cap, showed her to a small, neat chamber on the second floor.

"Right to bed with you and enjoy the peace, for sure and it's the last you'll see in a good while," the woman admonished, adding a wink for good measure.

Grace smiled weakly and, when the door was closed, changed into her nightdress, settling down for what she thought would be a long, wakeful night. Instead, she fell instantly and deeply asleep.

She was awakened at dawn by Bram's polite knock on the door. When she answered, he put his head in to say that breakfast was waiting below. She dressed quickly, tidied her hair, and joined him, though she had little stomach for more than bread and tea. Her lack of appetite was fine with Bram, who was greatly animated and rubbed his hands in anticipation of the journey ahead, confiding in her quietly, though with great pride, that Captain Hastings had paid a handsome price for a partnership in the Kildaire linen mill.

"You're bringing me good luck already," he said, his face glowing with satisfaction.

He took her outside into the cool morning air, where she learned that he'd booked two seats on the Bianconi long-car that went to Dublin City, another new adventure for Grace, who was beginning to feel well-traveled. Their luggage, along with that of the other travelers, was stowed in the middle of the open carriage, leaving room all along the outside for the passengers to sit facing out, their feet resting on a board barely higher than the ground. A canvas awning covered everyone from the light rain that fell occasionally along the way. There were six others along, and a coachman in a glazed hat and long coat, reins held tightly in one gloved hand, whips in the other to drive the four great horses at a brisk pace. They made only two stops to let off and pick up, and Grace was charmed by the bustle of the inn yard, where waiters hurried out with trays of drinks to refresh the passengers.

The silent bogs and quiet woods gave way to more populated, noisy villages, and finally to Dublin itself. Grace sat, stunned, as they drove into the great city, more magnificent than anything she'd ever seen. There were soldiers everywhere, guards in smart uniforms, students in tasseled caps, immaculately dressed ladies and gentlemen, sailors, merchants, barristers in their wigs, and, above all, beggars. Although Grace had lived door to door with poverty, she had never felt poor herself, and had not given it great thought until she witnessed the beggars of Dublin: ratty children screaming like seagulls, women in rags with a babe in each arm, old men without legs or eyes, sick, crippled, exhausted, following anyone who might have a penny, hands out, promising eternal fortune, God's blessings, a dance, a song, or a curse if no penny came forth. Bram told her to ignore them and passed by as if they were invisible, occasionally nudging one out of the way with his cane. But Grace could not look past them, and they flocked toward her at every opportunity. She clung to Bram's arm and wished for a purseful of coins to hand out, especially to the thin, dark-haired little girl in bare feet who followed them all the way to their hotel.

Doormen shooed away the beggars, including the little girl, and swept Grace and Bram inside to another world that was hushed, plush, and fragrant with flowers arranged in huge urns by the staircase that curved grandly up and away from the lobby. Bram went to the desk and registered them, then took her arm and escorted her to the third floor, followed by a bellhop with their luggage.

It was a magnificent room, and Grace felt her knees go weak as she looked around at the heavy curtains on wooden rings, ornate wash-stand, dressing table and pier glass, enormous wardrobe, and two comfortable velvet chairs near a writing table by the window. Her eye fell at last on the large double bed and she quickly looked down, pretend-ing to admire the thick Chinese carpet with its intricate pattern of birds and flowers.

When the bellhop had deposited their trunks, received his tip, and gone out, Bram pulled Grace into his arms and kissed her quite unlike the way he'd kissed her in church. She was caught off guard by the force of it, the roughness of his mustache and his urgency, but she did not resist and her nervousness gave way to the beginnings of pleasure. They smiled at one another, then kissed again, more politely this time.

"You've weathered the trip well," he said, unpinning her hat with a practiced hand and smoothing her hair. "You've a good constitution." He stood back and admired her, then straightened his own coat. "I'll leave you to get settled and changed out of your traveling clothes."

"And where are you going, then?" Grace was suddenly anxious at the thought of being left alone in this great city.

He smiled at her apprehension. "Downstairs. Gentlemen's club. I'll look at the papers for an hour, then return." He paused, feeling in his pocket for his watch. "We'll be hungry. I'll have dinner sent up."

Grace swallowed hard and nodded, hoping that was the response he wanted. It seemed to make him happy and he left the room whistling.

He was gone no more than a minute when there was a rap on the door and a maid arrived, saying her name was Alice and she'd come to help the missus unpack. Not knowing what else to do, Grace let her in and pointed to the small valise and Bram's trunk.

While Alice went expertly about her work, Grace sat gingerly on the edge of the nearest velvet chair and shyly admitted that this was her first trip to Dublin. Alice smiled reassuringly and began to tell her about the wonderful sights of the city, then paused to ask about the state of country living down South. Grace's shyness evaporated as she spoke of her little village and the simple life she'd left behind, the evidence of which she knew Alice could see as she began to unpack Grace's own small valise, shaking out the embroidered nightdress and laying it on the bed, hanging up the one good dress Grace owned besides what she wore, and putting away the simple underthings in the dresser drawer.

"Have you another trunk coming, ma'am?" Alice asked as she set out Grace's brush and comb on the dressing table.

Grace made herself sit very straight. "I don't," she said. "As there'd be nothing to put in it."

The maid nodded and said, "Very good, ma'am," as if this were a perfectly acceptable answer, then closed the valise and stored it in the wardrobe.

"Begging your pardon, ma'am," she said, her back to Grace. "But would you be wanting to know where to acquire some things while you're in the city?"

"I don't know," Grace admitted shyly.

Alice snapped open the locks on Bram's trunk. Seeing the quality of his clothes, her eyebrows went up and she smiled.

"You'll be wanting to go up Sackville Street way," she announced. "Lovely shops there—dressmakers, milliners, and the like. It will take time to make up a full wardrobe, so go right away in the morning. When the things are ready, they'll be sent on to your home."

"Ah, no." Grace clasped her hands together in her lap and glanced out the window. "Sure and I won't be needing much if I'm only meant to be living in the country, then?"

Alice kept busy, going to the window and opening the curtain so Grace could have a better view. "True enough, you country ladies get by with fewer dresses than town ladies, but you'll need at least three good frocks for entertaining, as you know." She didn't look at Grace, but tied back the curtain with a gold sash. "And you'll be wanting two or three warm dresses for morning work, a wool shawl and riding jacket, a good winter coat—sealskin or oiled wool is what they wear round here—shoes, of course, a pair of boots, an everyday hat and one for each of the fine dresses, gloves, petticoats, slips, corsets . . ." She ticked them off on her fingers, then glanced at Grace's figure. "Not that you need any shaping, but it's how the fine lady dresses."

"All that?" Grace asked weakly.

"Aye." Alice nodded. "That's the least of it."

Grace sighed, thinking of the cost.

"It's all right, ma'am," she said, reading Grace's mind. "He can afford to dress you proper . . . and you should expect him to. You mustn't let him get by on the cheap. Not that I'm saying he would," she added quickly. "A lady don't concern herself over cost, as does, say, a *farmer's* daughter." She ran a duster over the writing table, then, seeing Grace's face, added kindly, "Sure and you're not the first to marry up, you know. I've seen plenty come in from the country, scared as wee church mice in the beginning. Give it a few days. Some new clothes, a few fine meals, a bit of refinement, and you'll feel the part. He'll respect you more for demanding the best, that's how they are, these gentlemen. You must take a step up and not leave your feet hanging down in country mud."

Grace's eyes widened. "Shows as much as that, then?"

Alice shook her head. "Not a bit. I wasn't sure at first, though the dress give you away some. You carry yourself well, head up and all, and you're a beauty, as any can see."

Grace let out a long breath, relieved.

"And I've seen your husband as he come down the hall," she added. "You could've done worse. Some marry those old, gout-ridden bachelors with mountainy manners. But he's a fine, handsome man, yours."

Grace rose and put out her hand. "I'm Gracelin O'Malley." She shook her head. "Grace Donnelly."

The maid didn't take her hand, but curtsied instead. "Missus Donnelly. It's a pleasure to serve you, ma'am. If you'll be needing anything else while you're here, please just ring the desk and ask for me."

She left then, and Grace went to the washstand to clean her hands and face. She began to take off her dress, but realized she could not sit in her nightgown for dinner. She brushed her hair and tidied her appearance as much as she could, then sat down to wait.

The knock at the door startled her, although she'd been listening for it. In came the waiter, pushing a tray on wheels. A collision of different smells—all delicious—filled the room, and Grace's stomach began to rumble, much to her embarrassment. The waiter paid no attention, but spread a cloth on the writing table, pulled up the velvet chairs, set out the china and covered dishes, then bowed as he went out, nearly bumping into Bram, who was entering. Bram smoothly put a few coins into the waiter's hand, then dismissed him.

"You're still in your traveling clothes!" he exclaimed once the door had closed.

"I . . . I'd nothing else to put on," Grace stammered. "And I wouldn't shame you by sitting here in my shift like a girl who knows nothing a'tall." She looked at him frankly, despite the heat in her face.

"That would have been fine, covered with your dressing gown," he said.

"I've not one of those. Just my other best dress."

"Hmmm." Bram stroked his chin. "I hadn't thought. But of course you'll need a proper wardrobe. We'll go tomorrow and get you all fitted out. There must be dozens of women's shops around here."

"In Sackville Street!" Grace said confidently.

He laughed. "Well, I see you've got all the information you need. Isn't that just like a woman?" But he seemed pleased and held out her chair.

The dinner was as delicious as its promise and he filled her wineglass with champagne several times before she begged him to stop or she'd drop to the floor. She'd had champagne for the first time at her wedding breakfast, and was unused to the light-headedness that came upon her so quickly. However, it did ease her nervousness and she was relaxed and mirthful by the time the meal ended, at which point he discreetly suggested she attend to her toilette while he had a nightcap in the gentlemen's bar. When the dishes had been collected and Bram had excused himself, Grace hastily removed her clothes—fumbling with the buttons—then hung them crookedly in the wardrobe. She washed her face and brushed out her hair, slipped on the beautiful nightdress that still smelled of her mother's trunk, and crawled into the enormous bed to wait for him. Again, she fell instantly asleep and awakened an hour later to find him sliding into bed next to her. He wore silk pajamas that felt so wonderful, she could not resist running her hands across the fabric. Pleased with what he thought to be her initiative, he pulled her to him and kissed her deeply. She tasted the brandy he'd drunk and the cigar he'd smoked, shreds of tobacco catching on her tongue, floating in her mouth, all of it so strange.

Her wedding night was as Granna had said it would be. Bram's deep voice in the darkness and his sure hands finding such obvious delight in Grace's young body made up for her discomfort and nervousness. It ended surprisingly soon, and afterward, he fell into a heavy slumber, one arm holding her close to his chest. She lay wide awake, going over in her mind all that had happened to her in the last two days, not the least of which was lying in a real bed for the first time in her life, surrounded by such luxury as she'd never known. She eased herself out of this awkward position and got comfortable on her own pillow; there she lay, arms tucked beneath her head, listening to the strange sounds of the city—the distant whistle of the train, the clatter of carriage wheels on cobblestone, the shouts and calls, songs and curses, that went on and on without pause through the night.

In the morning, her shyness returned and she dressed in the room with the bathtub. All through the breakfast of kippers, fruit, bacon, and scones, she stole glances at him, trying to connect this briskly proper person—more father or teacher than husband—with the passionate man who'd been in her bed the night before. He made no mention of their first night together, other than to suggest they go about the business of organizing a wardrobe this morning, so that she might rest in the afternoon. He seemed to think she should be exhausted, and so she pushed up a few yawns for his sake, but in truth, she felt more alive than ever before, invigorated and charged with excitement.

Dublin was fascinating; rounding each corner brought further astonishment. Bram took her to the dress shops immediately following breakfast, and had her fitted out as promised. He was more than generous, urging her to buy all she would need, as this would be their last time in Dublin for a year or maybe more. She would have to make due with the shops in Cork City, he said, as if this would be a hardship on her. He had her measured for an evening gown cut so low across the front that Grace could barely look at herself in it, although the feel of the plush velvet against her skin was stirring. On the advice of the formidable woman who ran the shop, he bought for her a pair of French gloves, a scarf of Limerick lace, two plumed hats, and a striking blue bonnet to wear right away. He left the room when the assistant brought out shifts, petticoats, whalebone corsets, silk stockings, garter belts, and panteloons. Grace stared at herself in the mirror, a young woman draped in lengths of fabric, wondering if she was the same girl who'd awakened just three days ago on a straw mattress shared with her old gran, the girl who jumped up, splashed water on her face, brushed her hair, and pulled on the same cotton shift she'd worn nearly every day with darned stockings and old boots. This new wardrobe brought about such great change; she breathed differently and held herself more stiffly now, no longer darting and dashing from place to place, but moving more slowly, regally, as if she were balancing eggs on her shoulders. She was beginning to feel like a manor wife.

That evening, after her rest and long bath—another first, and what a wonderful thing compared to washtubs and summer ponds!—Bram took her to dine at the Black Swan which was lit as much by the jewels ornamenting the other ladies as it was by candlelight. Three waiters attended them throughout each of the nine courses and Grace was dizzy from all the different dishes and wines, when at last Bram ordered the brandy that signaled the end of the meal. When he had finished, she asked to walk instead of ride to the theater where they were to see the famous comedienne actress Peg Woffington. He readily agreed, and the fresh evening air did much to clear her head and ease her stomach; she did not see how men and women in society could eat and drink such great amounts and still keep their wits about them, but she vowed to learn the trick. Once seated in the theater, she could barely contain her excitement and Bram had to tell her quietly— a stiff smile on his face—that she was gawking like a peasant. This shamed her into stillness and she was glad when the houselights fell. Miss Woffington took the stage to great applause which she acknowledged with a grand flourish before beginning her excellent mimicry. Grace again forgot herself and burst out laughing, reminded only by Bram's firm grip on her arm that this was unseemly. Sobered, she glanced around and saw that the other ladies tittered discreetly into handkerchiefs. When laughter came upon her again, she followed suit and was rewarded with an approving nod from her husband.

After the performance, they walked slowly in the cool midnight air, crossing the River Liffey on slender Halfpenny Bridge, stopping midway to look at the lights reflected in the water.

"Happy?" Bram asked, taking her hand.

Grace nodded, then smiled up into his face. "Aye, 'tis like a tinker's dream, so full of wonder and shine. Sure and isn't it a fine thing for Ireland to have a grand city such as this?"

Bram frowned slightly. "One day, perhaps, I'll take you to see a truly grand city—London, perhaps, or Paris."

"I should like that true enough." She sighed in anticipation.

"But first we shall smooth your edges a bit," he said as if amused. "Rid your speech of those charming colloquialisms."

Grace bit her lip. "Sure and I don't understand what it is you're saying?"

Bram smiled briefly, then mimicked her speech. "'Sure and I don't understand . . . Faith, 'tis but a tinker's dream . . .'" He raised his eyebrows. "See what I mean?"

Grace straightened herself ever so slightly. "I'm too country in my talk, is what you're saying. I give you away for marrying low."

"Now, now," he soothed. "Not too country. Just too Irish." He took her arm. "Pay closer attention to my speech and try to copy it, so that people might understand and take you seriously. Is that too much to ask?"

"Nay," Grace said, then corrected herself. "No, it's not too much to ask, and certainly I can learn to speak correctly." She clipped off the ends of her words in perfect mimicry.

Bram laughed delightedly, then bestowed a smile full of fondness upon her. "Well done! You're quick. I'll give you that. No one could tell, simply by looking at you, that you're fresh up from the barnyard."

Grace turned away, pretending to look over the edge of the rail into the water.

"And the men!" He laughed again, then reached into an inner jacket pocket for his cigar case, opening it and selecting one. "They can't take their eyes off you, did you know that? You're the Irish version of a beauty, my dear. All high color and flyaway curls."

He felt for his lighter and held the flame to the end of the cigar, puffing until an ember glowed at its end and thick, strong smoke curled into his hair. He bent over her then, holding the cigar away from her hat, and kissed her lightly on the corner of her mouth.

Grace did not understand the emotions rising within her, but suddenly she was angry, and before she could control herself, she'd wrapped both arms around him tightly and kissed him with all the passion she could muster in order to erase the acidity of his words. When she'd done a thorough job, and her anger was spent, she let go and stood back, hands on her hips, hat askew, triumph lighting her face.

It took him a full minute to regain his composure, after which he glanced up and down the bridgewalk. It was empty but for them; still, he turned a stern face upon his wife.

"What in God's name do you think you're doing?"

Grace's look of triumph faltered and her hands fell away from her hips, but her tone was determined. "I just wanted to remind you that I'm here while you're talking about me, Mister Donnelly. And that hard words spoken well still hurt when tossed about."

"Ahhhh. You're a sensitive girl—is that it?" He took several short puffs of the cigar, eyeing her as she stood against the rail, her back up, head held high. "Well, before you start correcting *me,* my dear, you'd do best to work on yourself." He looked at the half-finished cigar, then tossed it into the water, where it spit and went out. Quick as lightning, he yanked her into his arms and kissed her forcefully until she began to struggle, unable to catch her breath. His teeth ground against his own lips and hers, and she tasted blood. She shoved at him with both hands but could not break his embrace until, at last, he was finished. One arm still firmly around her, he tipped his head to one side and spat in the water, then touched the back of his hand to the cut on the corner of his lip, eyeing the blood that came away. "Is this what you're looking for, then, my little maid? A little roughness? A tumble like those with the stable boys in your father's barn?"

"No!" Grace said in astonishment, her mouth still throbbing in pain.

"Because I'm happy to oblige, my dear," he continued, pulling her tightly against his chest. "Don't misunderstand me—I'm quite fond of boldness and high spirit. I like a woman who can take what she wants. Who can give me what I want." He pressed his mouth against her ear, so that the words hissed. "But not in public. Ever. Is that clear?"

"Yes," she whispered against his chest, fighting back tears.

"And one other thing. A minor point. It's *Squire* Donnelly. Not 'Mister.'"

"Squire," she repeated softly.

He relented then, but still held her head firmly against the silky cloth of his jacket. "I fully intend to give you a good life, my dear," he said softly. "But you must respect me in all things. At all times. You will do everything the way I tell you to do it, because you are living in my life now."

She nodded, but said nothing, walking along in silence back to the hotel. He seemed not to notice, chatting away about the magnificent dinner and the evening's performance. Later, in bed, he was even more gentle with her than the night before.

In the morning, it was as if no battle of wills had ever occurred, and Grace was sobered. She had not realized her anger could rise so quickly, or that it would be met by an iron fist. Was she willful and disrespectful, or merely young and naive? And had her husband been right in his correction of her? Certainly, she felt older this morning than she had the day before, and a lesson in restraint had been learned. But his words still troubled her; were they not meant to share this life together . . . or had she—as he'd said—only entered into his, hers to be left behind? Her new maturity whispered that he would always be separate from her on some level, something that she had never considered in a marriage. Perhaps it was best. Maybe a wife should not know all that went on in her husband's head. And, by the same token, perhaps she should learn to keep a private room within herself, as well. These thoughts left her confused and wary, but as the day passed, his charm and seeming devotion won back her heart and convinced her that she had overreacted, that her youth had led to foolish fancy and that she had no more knowledge of the ways of men and women than a hen.

The honeymoon resumed smoothly, and over the course of a week, they visited Christchurch Cathedral and Dublin Castle, strolled with other couples in Phoenix Park, taking refreshment in the teahouse at its center, and attended the first classical music concert Grace had ever heard. The symphony from England performed concertos by a man called Haydn, and the soaring strings moved Grace to yearn for some untenable thing; she had not realized she wept until Bram nudged his handkerchief into her fingers.

There was only one place in Dublin that had soured her spirit, and that was the old church of St. Michen's, where, preserved almost perfectly by the limestone that surrounded them, a number of ancient skeletons and mummies were set out for general viewing. The muscle and tissue had deteriorated, of course, and papery skin fell tightly over sharp facial bones; fingernails and hair had grown long and dry. Grace had stood and stared, both mesmerized and disturbed, until Bram said in no low voice, "There they are, Grace, the warrior kings of Ireland, your noble ancestors. Still hoping for a drop to warm their bones before Judgment Day." He had laughed helplessly over this poor joke, wiping at his eyes, before halfheartedly apologizing. Grace had had a moment of revelation then, had looked for a brief moment through the part in the curtain, and knew it came to this: His English pride would always ride roughshod over her love for her own countrymen; he would always attempt to trample down what he thought was the lesser life, never mind that his wife came out of it and that his children would carry the song of it in their hearts. This would always come between them, unless she cast herself in another mold. She had looked again upon the poor beggars lying out in the cold stone room, and her pity turned to compassion. The nobility of her ancestors lay in their spirit, not in their shells, and her husband could not be blamed for his blindness—he was English, after all, and everyone knew that the English had no gift for seeing within.

She had begun to grow weary of Dublin after that; her head was loaded down with sight and sound, her heart raw with new emotion. It was too much for a girl who'd only had the market town of Cork City once a year, and she hoped they would soon travel home to begin their real life together. She'd watched and kept mental note on how to give orders and speak to servants, what was needed for a squire's housekeeping. Bram had given her money for her purse on one of the days he had to spend at the solicitor's, and with it she bought presents for her family: an Indian cashmere shawl for Granna, a woolen fisherman's sweater for Sean, a shirt and vest for Ryan in which to be married, silver candlesticks for their wedding gift, and a pocket watch for her father. Back at the hotel, she wondered at her amazing fortune to be mistress of accounts that could provide such bounty simply by asking for it.

It was on this same afternoon that Grace put the last piece of her new self into place. Alice had come to hang up two dresses, just delivered, and was showing Grace the proper way to wear her new things.

"What a lovely pattern." She held up a cotton dress with flowers scattered across the skirt. "And isn't the blue just perfect with your eyes and that fine hair?" She smiled at Grace, then tipped her head and studied the young woman from head to toe.

"And why are you peering at me in such a way?" Grace asked, touching her face instinctively.

"Would you mind a piece of advice, Missus Donnelly?"

Grace bit her lip. "Sure and I'd trust you in anything, Alice. What is it I'm doing wrong, then?"

"Nothing, ma'am . . . It's your hair, you see, ma'am."

Grace's hands flew to the thick dark hair pulled back and twisted so that it hung in a thick rope over her shoulder.

"Braids is fine for a young girl," Alice continued. "But married ladies don't wear them, as a rule."

"What a country clod I am." Grace yanked on the braid. "Of course they don't. I've seen nary a braid on any of the fine women about. Thank goodness the Squire's not caught that one yet." She grimaced. "How *should* it look?"

Alice came around behind her and coiled the braid up into a bun. "It should come up high, like this, only softer," she said. "You've got a fine neck, so you can wear it better than most." She took a few pins from her pocket and secured the bun, then stepped back to look. "That's not bad, but you need someone does it proper to show you."

"Can you not do it, Alice?" Grace asked anxiously. It was a beautiful hairstyle and made her look far more sophisticated, but she was afraid of being intimidated by a true ladies' maid.

"There's a woman comes to do hair for other ladies in the hotel," Alice said, reading her thoughts. "A nice woman, not a bit snobby. You'd like her, ma'am. I could ask her to see you this afternoon before the Squire comes back, and then you could wear it dressed when you dine out tonight."

Grace agreed and the hairdresser came up shortly with pins, combs, and brushes. She was an older, grandmotherly woman and her eyes lit up with delight when she saw Grace's beautiful thick hair. She patiently showed Grace how to brush it up from the neck, twist it, and secure it high with the ends tucked in, then had Grace do it herself to make sure she understood. A few wisps escaped at Grace's temples and at the nape of her neck, but this only added to the attractiveness of the style. Grace thanked the woman profusely and put a few coins in her hand, earning a grateful smile.

She had agreed to meet Bram in the lobby of the hotel and was gratified by his stunned expression when she glided down the staircase. He remained speechless during the short walk to the restaurant and throughout the appetizer course. Food revived him, and he proceeded to tell her an amusing story about a man he'd met at the races, but still, he shook his head often and broke off from what he was saying to tell her how very beautiful she looked tonight. This was the final transformation she'd needed, and now, feeling taller and more refined, she was ready to face her new home.

*Four*

THE honeymoon ended, and a weary Grace gladly boarded ship the next morning. The wind was high, making it a fast trip to Clonakilty Bay, where they spent a night in Roscaberry before taking a carriage back up to Macroom.

Coming up the avenue to the big house, Grace realized with a shock that she was now truly mistress of the manor and in charge of the servants who stood waiting on the porch. Bram was a working squire and had a keen interest in his farms and mills, but he still lived in grand style.

It was an entirely different life from the one they'd lived in Dublin, but at least she was on familiar ground and had a better understanding of her husband. She knew that he loved his position as landowner and rode out daily to look over his holdings, checking tenant land and his own close in, sometimes working alongside the field hands. His solid body and good looks earned him admiring glances wherever he went, and Grace did not miss these, seeing him afresh in the eyes of others. She found she had pride in her husband, and determined to follow his wishes about her dress and manner; indeed, about all the ways their life was to be run. He was older, he was wiser, he'd known married life. She'd put herself completely in his hands and trust his advice.

"Welcome to your new home," he'd said, helping her out of the carriage. "This is my housekeeper, Brigid Sullivan"—he indicated the woman who stood next to the door—"and her husband, Jack, my butler and driver." A tall, thin man with hooked nose and reddened cheeks bowed stiffly. "Their son Nolan, the stable boy."

"Welcome home, ma'am," they all murmured, then stepped down off the porch to gather the trunks and boxes from the carriage.

Bram took her through the front door and into a great hall. "This is not a house full of servants," he said. "I don't believe in supporting that kind of expense just for show."

Grace nodded, looking around at polished woodwork and brocade curtains draped at the windows, family portraits and ornately framed hunting scenes. It was a cavernous house, a man's house, handsome and strong.

"Brigid and her husband live in the gamekeeper's cabin down in the glen behind the barns. I like my privacy and those two have more children than I can count, though I believe they've stopped at Nolan. The others are completely unruly; I won't have them about the place at all except as seasonal hands."

Grace nodded again, unable to think of what to say. She knew the Sullivans. She'd gone to school with some of them and never thought them rude or wild, although the older boys had a bit of a reputation. There had been two daughters after Nolan, both dead at young ages, she vaguely remembered, but she said nothing to Bram of her familiarity with the family.

They came into a great room where a big log fire burned and a tray of sherry and biscuits sat on a side table.

"This is the kind of nonsense I despise." He walked over to the fire and kicked it apart with the toe of his boot. "It's wasteful to burn good logs or even turf on a summer day. Brigid likes a fire and she'll burn one in every room if you let her." He looked over his shoulder at Grace and said pointedly, "You'll have to have a firm hand in running the house."

"Yes, Bram." Her voice was soft.

He nodded. "Now"—he rubbed his hands together—"meals are simple around here, no need for a cook. Brigid sees to that and the house. She's got a girl in to help on laundry day and when she does the heavy work. Sullivan acts as butler when we've got formal guests, but there aren't enough of those to keep him in tails every day. He cleans and stores the game, keeps up the wine cellar, and pokes about in the garden, although we've got to do something about that. Their oldest boy's usually out of a job." He stroked his chin. "Or Nolan can take it on . . . days are longer now. Ah, it's good to be home."

"What would you have me do, then?" Grace asked, mentally checking off all the tasks that would be done for her.

Bram crossed the room and put his arms around her. "You, my fair bride"—he nuzzled her hair—"will concentrate on giving me an heir."

Grace smiled. "That takes care of my evenings," she said, and was pleased to see his eyebrows go up at her boldness. "But how will I fill my days?"

He cocked his head. "You'll run the household, of course: plan the menus, do a little cooking if you wish—God knows we could use a change—oversee the kitchen garden and the pantry, the laundry, general housekeeping. I suppose you'll go calling, and receive, as well . . ." He frowned. "Though, not too frequently, I hope. These old ladies in the neighborhood like gossiping to new brides; I would discourage intimacy. Do be *polite*," he warned. "Social connections are important, and we've got your humble beginnings to contend with."

Grace was dizzy from all the instruction. "I'll not embarrass you," she murmured.

Bram poured her a small sherry, then showed her the rest of the house. Compared to the great houses of Dublin, it was small, but to Grace, it was enormous, the big rooms square and high-ceilinged, long windows set into paneled walls. The main floor was laid in stone, layered with thick carpets in the drawing room, runners down the wide hallways, a large, faded Turkish rug in the center of the dining room on which sat a grand polished oak table surrounded by twelve chairs and over which hung a brilliant chandelier, and yet another carpet—this one simple and threadbare in places—in the entry where they'd begun. Grace found herself wondering how many days each month were occupied with the taking up and beating of these rugs.

There was an entirely separate room at the back of the house for preparing and cooking the food. No rugs covered the flagstones, though she noticed a colorful rag braid in front of the chair by the cookstove. That was where Brigid must sometimes sit of an evening, Grace thought, seeing now the work bag of mending tucked into the corner. Beside the great black cookstove, there was an open fireplace with a kettle hook, and this was a relief to Grace, who had never cooked on anything else! A thick wooden safe sat in one corner, away from the stove and fireplace, and there was a basin built into a table set underneath a water pump. Pots and pans hung from a rack over her head, and a series of shelves housed the crockery and utensils. In the middle of the room sat a huge wooden worktable with four stools pushed under. Grace was stunned at the size of the kitchen, which was nearly as big as her entire cabin, and at the array of cooking tools. She had always loved preparing meals and she would have pushed up her sleeves right there and then, had Bram not steered her back out into the entry and up the stairs.

There were three fireplaces on the first floor—in the kitchen, the dining room, and the great room—and four more upstairs. The upstairs flooring was pine with a single long carpet running the length of the hallway. There were six rooms total: three bedrooms, a study, a nursery with a small grate and stovepipe, and next to that, atop a short flight of steps, a door that Bram did not open, referring to the room as "unused." A longer flight of stairs at the end of the hall led to the attic. A peek into the bedrooms showed her that they were complete with ample bedding, wardrobes, mirrors, dressing tables, and washstands. It was all so grand and Grace was thankful that she'd been to Dublin first, so that the shock of this did not render her stupid. The study was at the head of the stairs, across from which was clearly Bram's bedroom, so Grace was surprised when he led her back down the hall to the room across from the nursery.

"This will be yours." He opened the door to the largest room, which was clean and shining, ready to welcome her.

She turned to him in amazement. "Are we not to be sharing the same room, then?" she asked.

"Whatever for?" he teased. "Ladies and gentlemen need separate quarters for dressing and retiring."

"But . . ." She bit her lip, unsure how to ask the next question.

He waited, enjoying her discomfort, then led her into the room and closed the door. "I'll come to you at night," he said quietly. "After you've performed whatever magic you ladies do before retiring. I may spend the night." He glanced at the bed. "Or I may return to my own room in order that we might both reap the benefits of an undisturbed night's sleep."

"Oh." Grace felt very small.

"Your dresses have been delivered." He nodded to the open

wardrobe and the garments that hung inside. "And your trunk is ready to unpack." A slight frown took the light out of his eyes. "You won't require a maid, will you?"

"A maid?" Grace thought of the prim and proper ladies' maids she'd seen following their mistresses in and out of shops around Dublin.

His frown deepened. "To help with all this," he said. "Your wardrobe and personal tasks. We've had them here before, though I've never cared for it myself. Little busybodies. Always in the way of . . . things."

Grace was no more fond of the idea of a maid in her life than was her husband. "I can dress myself, you know," she said quickly. "Haven't I been doing that all my life?"

His frown disappeared. "Quite right! There's the spirit!" he said approvingly. "No need to have a maid around. Brigid can lend a hand when you need it."

Grace moved quickly into his arms, kissing his neck. "I'm so happy, Bram. I just want to make you happy, as well."

He dropped his mouth to her hair, hands running down her back and up her sides. "You have," he whispered, kissing her gently, then with greater urgency, arms tightening around her until, finally, he lifted her off the ground. They kissed like that until Brigid came down the hall, clearing her throat and knocking politely at the door.

"Yes, Brigid," he said hoarsely, lowering Grace back to her feet. "What is it?"

"It's Missus O'Flaherty come to pay her respects to the new bride," she said evenly. "Shall I say she's not fit to be seen?"

Grace's eyes widened, but Bram shushed her.

"Tell her Missus Donnelly will be down in a minute, Brigid."

They looked at each other as the sound of Brigid's shoes slapped on the stairs. They heard her voice drift up from the entry.

"Well?" Bram stepped away from her. "What are you waiting for?"

Grace bit her lip. "Shall I go as I am or do I change?"

Annoyance flitted across his face. "Have you never received callers?"

"Aye," she said. "Nearly every day! I set them down near the fire for a cup of tea and slice of bread, and we talk a bit about the neighbors and such."

He tried to maintain his frown, but amusement won out. "Well, it's not so different really," he said. "Brigid will see her into the draw-ing room and 'set her by the fire.' You'll come in, make her acquain-tance, and offer her tea and cakes from the tray Brigid will bring."

"All right, then." Grace raised her chin with determination. "I can do that."

"Neaten your hair and wear that shawl around your shoulders, that should do. Say your wardrobe has just arrived and you've not yet unpacked. Pour out the tea, and make polite conversation. Not about the neighbors, however, as you've not yet met anyone of any standing. And certainly you know not to discuss our private life." He went to the door.

"And where will you be?" she asked, alarmed.

He smiled. "You're on your own, Missus Donnelly. This is your debut. I'll be out riding my lands like a good squire. Best of luck!" He gave her a mock salute, then hurried downstairs, pausing only to greet Missus O'Flaherty and ask after her husband before taking leave of the house.

Grace stood before the mirror, smoothing her hair and pinching color into her cheeks, although they already glowed with good health. She settled the lace scarf over her shoulders, then slowly descended the stairs.

"Missus O'Flaherty," she said warmly, coming into the great room. "I do hope Brigid has made you comfortable after your long ride. Tea shall arrive momentarily." She had to turn away and pretend to adjust an arrangement of flowers to hide her amusement at the oh-so-proper sound of her own voice.

Missus O'Flaherty perched on the edge of the divan, the long peacock plume in her hat swishing over her head. "Oh, yes. I'm quite comfortable, thank you. I didn't want to impose, Missus Donnelly, but wished to greet you right away and welcome you to the neighbor-hood." She made no attempt at discretion, but took stock of Grace quite frankly while she talked, eyeing the expensive shawl, new dress, and sophisticated hairstyle. "You look well after the rigors of travel."

"You're very kind." Grace seated herself on the divan opposite her guest. "My husband and I are so pleased to be home."

"Such a beautiful city, Dublin." Missus O'Flaherty spoke long-ingly. "We keep a house there for the season, but Mister O'Flaherty prefers the pleasures of country living."

"Cairn Manor is said to be a beautiful estate," Grace complimented.

Missus O'Flaherty smiled weakly. "Indeed it is, but one does miss the uplifting society of sophisticated people. There is so little amusement here for our son when he is home from university, and, of course, no suitable callers for the girls. Not anymore," she added pointedly.

Grace did not know what Missus O'Flaherty meant by this, and fought the urge to bite her lip.

"My daughters could not recall having made your acquaintance, but that cannot be so, as surely you have met one another? Eleanor, my younger daughter, is quite stately in her manner and an accomplished pianist. She is always asked to play at gatherings. Brenda is two years older and has the most lovely skin and elegant head, if I do say so myself. She and your husband were quite good friends at one time. They had many interests in common, and shared a love of fine horses, attending many shows together. Chaperoned, of course."

Grace shook her head. "I'm afraid I've not had the pleasure of meeting Miss Eleanor nor Miss Brenda."

Missus O'Flaherty appeared puzzled, her fingers fluttered about her chest. "No? But do your people not come from this part of the country?"

Grace weighed her answer. "Yes, but I lived a quiet life."

"Kept under wraps, were you?" The old bird tittered. "Where exactly were you raised, Missus Donnelly?"

"I come from the next valley through the back wood and before the Black Hill. Near the river."

"And your father?"

Grace hesitated only a moment. "Still lives there, of course."

Missus O'Flaherty forced a little laugh. "Of course. You're very charming." She paused, eyeing Grace's brooch, the fine bones of her cheeks. "I mean, *who* is your father?"

"Patrick O'Malley."

There was a rattle of silver and Brigid entered with a large tea tray.

"Thank you, Brigid," Grace said, relieved, and stood to clear a small table near the fire.

"Patrick O'Malley." Missus O'Flaherty had ignored Brigid and was working on an appearance of confusion. "Patrick O'Malley. The name is not familiar to me. Though O'Malley is common enough in these counties. What is your father's occupation, did you say?"

"He is a farming man." Grace settled the delicate china cups and saucers, and checked the pot under its cozy.

"Oh, my. Ah, yes." Missus O'Flaherty seemed to have become clear to herself. "I do remember someone saying that Bram had found himself a farm girl. But, I must confess, I thought they meant someone to do the milking!" She tittered again behind her hand, endlessly amused. "Oh, my, you must forgive my innocence, dear girl. . . . I'm quite unused to this progressive notion of one marrying whomever one wishes." She collected herself and leaned forward with big eyes. "Well. You must tell me all about how you and Bram came to this . . . arrangement. You must be a very clever girl indeed to have captured him so completely away from us!"

Grace poured out the tea, though her hands shook and her face was flushed. "How do you take yours, Missus O'Flaherty? Milk and sugar?" She raised her head and caught the look of naked disdain on the older woman's face. "Or do you, perhaps, prefer a wee drop of Uisage batha for your health?" she added, the words out before she could stop them. "They say it's the only thing to sweeten soured milk."

Missus O'Flaherty's mouth clamped shut and her eyes narrowed. She rose to her full height, tossing her head so that the feather trembled violently.

"I cannot stay," she clipped, pulling on her gloves with a series of short tugs. "You seem to have misunderstood my intentions, dear girl. I merely wished to help you get started on the right foot—so very important if one is going to acquire friends of any standing . . ." She shrugged. "And, of course, if one has any aspirations for one's children."

Grace's heart rose up into her mouth and froze there. She had made a promise to her husband and broken it in the same day.

"Missus O'Flaherty," she stammered, her speech losing the unaccustomed formality in her race to undo the damage. "Please forgive the stupidity of a young country girl. I confess my wits are all scattered after the wedding, the excitement of Dublin town, and now this grand home that I've taken hold of only today. I'm shamed to be caught unprepared, so new I am to all this, and knowing only what we offer guests at home. And yourself such a fine and respected lady of the community. Can you not find it in your heart to forgive me this one time, God willing, as I have no mother to teach me such things and could only benefit from coming under the wing of one such as yourself?"

Missus O'Flaherty relaxed slightly, reinstated as she was upon her pedestal. "Well, my dear, I would not be a Christian if I could not forgive the slights borne upon me. A woman of my standing invites envy, and I am used to the frantic desires of others to rise above or pull me down." She smiled sympathetically. "I do feel for you. There is so much one must learn when one is not born to one's position." She reached out and patted Grace's hand. "I could teach you many things and you are wise to look to me for advice. But not today. Another time for tea, perhaps, and you and Mister Donnelly must come to dinner at Cairn House when you've settled in here."

"You're very kind," Grace said meekly. "Thank you so very much."

Missus O'Flaherty leaned in conspiratorily. "I've known your husband since he first came over from London and I'm sure I can help you with him. He is an aristocrat, you know, and they can be very demanding."

Grace glanced at Brigid, who was turfing up the fire and pretending not to hear a thing. "I'd be grateful," she said, putting out her hand, then letting it drop to her side when it was not taken. "Thank you for calling, Missus O'Flaherty, and a safe journey home."

She watched until the trap was brought and the woman had ridden nearly out of sight down the avenue in front of the house.

"Of all the nerve," Brigid muttered, coming up behind her. "There's trouble for you there, Missus, so watch out for it."

"She's right about one thing, though, Brigid." Grace shut the door. "I've a lot to learn if I'm going to get on here."

"Aye." Brigid carried the tray to the kitchen, setting it down on the wide plank table. Grace sat down in front of it and nibbled from the plate of cakes, then poured a cup of tea for herself and one for Brigid.

"If you don't mind my saying so, Missus, you shouldn't be sitting in the kitchen having tea with your housekeeper." She paused and listened for a moment. "Leastways, not when the Squire's due home anytime."

"Oh." Grace stood quickly. Then she sat again, her cheeks burning red. "But is this not my house, as well? Am I not allowed to keep company with those around me?"

"No," Brigid said shortly. "This is Squire Donnelly's house and no woman he brought home to it was ever allowed to forget that. I'll not be saying more on the subject, you being a new bride and all, but take it to heart—he may have wanted a country girl to bear his children, but he wants a lady to run his home. And it is *his* home."

Grace nodded slowly, no offense taken.

"Not that the old hen didn't deserve it," Brigid chuckled. "But it's bound to get back to the Master, and he's not going to be pleased. Everyone knows Missus O'Flaherty has a nose for the whiskey, and everyone knows not to say a word."

Grace's mouth fell open.

"Watch what you say to these people, Missus. It's all cat and mouse, if you ask me. Best run along upstairs now, and hang up your pretty new dresses."

Grace rose mechanically and went to her room, sitting by the window and watching as afternoon turned to night and still Bram did not return. She was undressed and in bed when she heard the sound of his horse come up the gravel drive. Moments later, he appeared in the doorway of their room.

"Offering the neighbor ladies whiskey in the afternoon is no way to begin your life here," he said firmly.

"I'm sorry, Bram." She pulled the sheets up around her. "It was childish. I'll not give in to it again."

Suddenly, he laughed and collapsed into the chair by the window. "I'd've paid good money to see her face, the old warhorse. I'll bet the carriage wasn't halfway down the drive before she'd pulled on that flask she keeps buried in her handbag." He pulled off his boots, coming in stocking feet to sit on the edge of the bed. "Watch your step, though, little wife," he added, picking up her hand. "I'll not be made a laughingstock."

Grace gasped. "Never! Oh, Bram! Can you not forgive me?"

"This time only," he said, his eyes taking in her loosened, glistening hair and flushed cheeks. He leaned over and kissed her. "I'll let you make it up to me."

She smiled at him without blushing, another first in her short married life.

* * *

She awoke in the pale to the clear, strong call of the larks, urging the others to join them for morning song. Next to her, Bram breathed heavily, still deeply asleep, his body warmly pressed against her own. She was glad he had stayed, glad he'd not left their bed for his own. She touched the hair on his arm gently to make sure this wasn't a dream, that she was here in this grand house with this grand man, and that she was surely carrying the child for whom he longed. She closed her eyes and pictured the life stretched out before her, the bumps in the road nothing at all compared to the length of it, and for this she gave fervent thanks to God.

# Five

GRACE'S presence lingered on in her old home, her voice whispered in the corner and laughed in the yard, her scent clung to the bedding, her shawl hung waiting on the peg by the door—everyone missed her terribly, though none would admit it to the others.

Ryan announced that he and Aghna would marry come summer's end, and it was to celebrate this good news that Grace visited at last. She'd come alone, explaining that she couldn't stay long, as she was needed at the manor house. Granna was surprised at how quickly Grace's appearance had changed. And it was more than just the lovely dress and hairstyle; this was an older girl than the one who'd left them six weeks ago—it was in her voice and the way she carried herself. It had taken half an hour of Sean's teasing to loosen her up and bring out the old spark in her eye; she'd rewarded him with an account of the grand library at Trinity College and her opinion that not one of the students there was half as bright as her own brother. The words spilled out then and their Grace emerged in the eagerness of her tales of travel and the sights of Dublin, the restaurants, theater, concerts, shops, museums, and all the different people. She brought out her presents for them, which they received shyly. Granna only held the shawl gingerly, feeling its luxury between rough fingers, until Grace shook it out and draped it around her shoulders. The warmth was immediate and she settled back into it with a sigh. Sean tried on his sweater, wrestling his crooked arm through the sleeve, and pronounced it a perfect fit. Ryan kissed her cheek gruffly, but smiled with pleasure at the wedding vest and shirt, and Patrick was visibly moved when she put in his hand the silver pocket watch.

"You mustn't spend the Squire's money on presents for us," he said by way of thanks.

"The coins he puts in my purse are my own," Grace answered firmly. "And so they are yours, as well."

They had begged her to stay the day long, to share a meal at least, but she'd not had the liberty. Granna reassured her, saying they'd see her again soon, but in her heart, she suspected the Squire had already set about weaning his beautiful young wife from her tenant family.

That had been many weeks ago, in June. St. John's Eve had come and gone with no one feeling much like riding down to the bonfires, and Lug's Day was a week past, the cold room now filled with potatoes and no one but Ryan with much appetite. His wedding was two weeks away, and although she tried to keep her mind on the festivities and Ryan's happiness, Granna could barely contain the fierce longing she felt to see Grace's shining face in the room again.

Ryan had become nearly impossible to live with, determined as he was that everything should be perfect for his new bride. The stones were quarried and masons had been hired to build on the new room that he and Aghna would share, a luxury by neighborhood standards.

"'Tis a wedding gift from Grace and the Squire," Granna told each neighbor who put a head through the window to marvel at the addition and wonder at the cost. "Such a good girl, our Grace."

"Only one of the lot," Patrick would mumble. He'd stopped speaking to everyone now that Ryan had announced his intention to convert.

"Bad enough you marry a Catholic girl who'll fill the house with priests and nuns," he'd yelled. "But you let her browbeat you into joining that herd of cattle!"

"Mind what you say!" Ryan had yelled back, a shock to them all. "I'm doing what's right by her and God, and that's all there is to it!"

"I'm still head of this household," Patrick warned the boy.

But Ryan had found confidence in his new position as husband-to-be. "Have I not earned my right to half this house?" he spoke boldly. "Working with you as I have, day and night, never asking for naught? And I'm not asking now. Aghna and I will worship God as Catholics, and we'll not be treated as whipped pups because of it. Do you hear me, Da?"

Patrick had kicked over a chair in disgust, grabbed his hat, and gone out into the rainy night. He'd stayed gone two days, but when he returned, it was with the masons and the quarry stone, and without a word to anyone, he'd begun building the extra room.

Sean and Granna poured their spare time into stitching a cover for the newlyweds' bed, keeping at it as the silence hung on around them.

"Being Catholic's not the end of the world," Granna whispered after Patrick had gone out.

"It is to Da," Sean said. "You know how he hates the priests and bishops, even the nuns! He says it's unnatural and an affront to the life God puts in a body. He says Ryan will never find happiness in that church."

Granna clucked her tongue. "Sure and he will." She pulled at the thread in her needle. "He's not a deep thinker, our Ryan, and he'll not question the authority of the church, just as he's not questioned your da's authority all these many years."

"Could it be that, then, what's making Da so angry?" Sean asked. "The church taking his place in Ryan's eyes?"

Gran nodded. "'Twould be your da's way of thinking, sure enough, but I don't see it myself. Themselves are cut from the same cloth as ever there was, and Ryan could never depart from your da, despite the shouting and hard words." She shrugged. "And besides, a little religion will be good for the boy. He needs something other than your father's word as law. A wife and church life will round him out, bring him into his own manhood."

"Hard to picture our Ryan in church, saying his rosary, isn't it, Gran?"

They both laughed at the image of tall, gawky Ryan scrunched down on his knees on the hard stone floor.

"He'll go for a while, to prove out your da; then he'll let Aghna take over that side of their marriage." She was quiet for a while, bent over her work, then said casually, "And so, everyone is getting married around you, Sean." She waited for him to look up so she could see his eyes. "How is that for yourself?"

He set down his cloth and picked up the cup of tea that sat at his feet, blowing away the steam, then sipping at it gingerly. "I'm happy for the both of them," he said, evenly. "And I'm looking forward to being an old uncle."

Granna kept her keen eyes on his face. "Do you not think about marrying yourself one day?"

Sean set the cup down again, shaking his head. "No, Gran. I do not." He met her eyes. "The Lord has blessed me in many ways, so I'm not looking to Him for a wife, as well."

Granna started to speak, but he stopped her.

"Who would have me, Gran?" he asked directly. "Even if some poor girl took a fall for my wonderful self—and what girl wouldn't want a man who could keep her in dresses," he said with a smile, "her family would never allow it. Look at me. I'm small and thin and twisted. I don't look as though I'd survive my wedding night, let alone find work and support a family!"

"I pray every night that the Lord will send someone to love you, my boy," Granna whispered.

Sean reached over and took her hand. "Hasn't He though, Gran? Haven't I been given you and our own Grace?"

"Aye, you have, though 'tis not exactly the love I'm speaking of, as yourself knows good and well," she minded. "Ah, no . . . I miss the girl, I do. So good she was at keeping up your spirits."

"My spirits are fine, Gran. Don't worry about me. Though I'd not mind seeing her face about the place a bit more myself."

"I thought she might have come again by now, but it's to be later rather than sooner, by the looks of things."

"It's just all that fine cooking you're missing," Sean teased. "She spoiled us, she did, waited on us hand and foot."

Granna laughed. "Remember that hot, buttery whiskey she'd bring us in the night, and her good brown bread with a little coffee, when we had it?"

Sean grinned. "I miss that sauce she'd put on salmon, and her colcannon."

"Oh, and her wild berry jam—we've none of that this summer," Granna said sorrowfully. "Nor none of her singing while she makes it."

Sean rose stiffly and filled her teacup. "Well, old woman, you'll just have to make due with bitter tea, boiled bacon and cabbage, and my own sour self for company."

"Ah no, agra. The tea's never bitter, I've lived on boiled cabbage more than once in my lifetime, and as for yourself . . ." Granna roused herself. "I'd not trade you for any other man."

"She's promised to come to the wedding. Maybe we can get her to cook something for us then!"

Granna laughed again. "I wouldn't be counting on that," she said. "The Squire will not want to see her scraping in the kitchen of her old cabin home."

Sean frowned. "I hope he's good by her."

Granna nodded. "I, too, boy. She looked well enough, though a mite tired. It's clear he's generous in the way of her dress. We'll see if his kindness lasts the honeymoon. For her sake, I hope they soon have a child."

The days flew by and the new room was finished. Into it, Patrick moved the large bed he'd shared with Kathleen, and Granna covered it with the new embroidered spread. Aghna was not used to more than a shared straw tick in the back of a cabin, a cloth hung from the ceiling for a wall, so Granna knew she'd be pleased and her desire for a bettered life well met. Sean had stuffed two pillowcases with moss and herbs, and the room smelled as bright and fresh as it looked. Ryan was pleased, going back to look at it every time he came in the house.

The night before the wedding, he made an announcement at the dinner table.

"Aghna comes tomorrow," he said, as if they might have all forgotten. "And, Granna . . ." His face was worried. "She'll be wanting to take on the householding."

"Fine by me, boy," Gran said and smiled down the table at Sean. "We'll be looking forward to a good meal around here again."

"How's her colcannon?" Sean winked.

"Ever bit as good as Gracie's," Ryan insisted. Then he paused. "You don't think Grace'll show her up at her own wedding, do you now? She won't be coming in that fancy dress with her hair all done up, will she?" His face creased with alarm.

Sean waved his spoon in the air and scowled. "What are you saying, you thickheaded eejit? Our Grace would never put on airs!"

"She's a squire's wife now," Patrick said, eating steadily, eyes on his plate. "She's got no choice but to dress like one."

They waited for him to say more, but he just finished his meal, pushed away his plate, and said he'd be going to bed now, with tomorrow's long day before them.

When Granna got up to clear, the door off the lane burst open and in tumbled a group of neighborhood boys: Morgan McDonagh, Declan and Paddy Neeson, Tad O'Dugan, Aghna's brother Rory, and Quinn Sheehan laughed and pushed each other, shouting at Ryan to get his coat and come for his due, it being his last night as a free man.

"Don't keep him too late, boys," Granna laughed. "He'll need his strength for the morrow!"

They roared and answered in kind, as Ryan pulled on his coat and grabbed his hat.

"Sure and you're coming, as well, Sean?" Morgan waited in the doorway.

Sean waved him off from where he still sat at the table. "No, you go on," he said. "I'll just slow you down."

Morgan came back into the room. "We're just going over to Agahmore, to O'Devlin's public house. You'll not be slowing us down unless you plan on preaching to us while we drink!"

Sean looked at Granna.

"Go on with you, now." She shooed him with her apron. "Have a bit of fun, why don't you?"

"It's settled then—you're coming," Morgan announced. "Declan's got the wagon." He strode across the room and lifted Sean from the bench. "Now, will you be a man and walk . . . or will I carry you like a bride over the threshhold?" He puckered his lips and kissed the air, tossing a wink at Gran.

Sean laughed. "I'll walk, thank you very much." He pulled on the sweater from Grace and kissed Granna, the men outside shouting for them to hurry up.

As they went to the wagon, Morgan said in a low voice, "Sure and I'm glad you're along tonight, being as you're the only man can keep me from adding to the wealth of the Guinness family." He paused. "And is she coming then to the wedding and all?"

Sean nodded.

"Ah, well." Morgan gave him a hand up into the wagon. "All the more reason to get it out of my way tonight, softhearted fool that I've become."

The other men piled into the back of the cart, Ryan in the seat of honor next to Declan, who slapped the reins. As they rocked down the narrow lane, big Quinn Sheehan started them off with "Thank

You, Ma'am, Says Dan," his hearty baritone sailing out into the red-rimmed twilight.

> "'What brought you into my room,
> to my room, to my room,
> What brought you into my room,'
> said the mistress unto Dan.
> 'I came here to court your daughter, ma'am,
> I thought it no great harm, ma'am!'
> 'Oh, Dan, my dear, you're welcome here!'
> 'Thank you, ma'am,' says Dan."

As he sang, Sean gazed off at the Derrynasaggart Mountains, blue shadows against a flaming sky. He left off singing the third verse, leaned over, and whispered in Morgan's ear, "There's no reason to come at all, man, and put yourself through it, you know."

Morgan wasn't singing. "The truth of it is," he said in a low voice, "I'd not be able to keep away." He turned aside and rubbed his hand hard against the rough, splintered wood of the wagon. "Nor would I," he added softly, "not for all the gold in the world."

*Six*

WEDNESDAY was as fine a day as they come—clear blue skies and a warm wind stirring the trees—but Squire Donnelly wouldn't hear of attending the Catholic wedding of a country tenant, wife's brother or no, and so Grace would not see Ryan and Aghna married by the priest who'd come all the way out from Cork City. A week of long sighs and sorrowful eyes, no singing, and pitiful meals led Bram to reconsider, and he had finally agreed at last to a short afternoon visit to the wedding party.

They arrived at midday, long after the bride and groom had made their joyful entrance. The small cabin was crowded with people from all over the county, but they fell away and made a path for Grace, warm smiles cooling ever so slightly when Bram came in behind. She made her way through the room, stopping to greet all the old neighbors: the O'Dugans, Old Campbell Hawes and his wife, Mister Neeson and the boys, the Dalys, and Bully Ryan, who was pulling on Julia's arm to get him another cup. It is a rare Irish room that falls silent, but the talk in this one had hushed all the same. The eyes of the women quickly took in Grace's simple blue silk and the slippers on her feet, the pearls around her throat, and the beautiful hair now swept up and held with two mother-of-pearl combs. They did not miss the thick gold band on her ring finger or the powder dusted across her bosom. She had dressed as plainly as she dared without displeasing Bram, but she could not so easily downplay the way she carried herself now or the manner of her speech, which had changed under her husband's constant correction. The older women smiled proudly to see her—a girl of the lane—and the younger girls watched her with admiration and envy, smiling shyly as she passed. The men couldn't snatch the hats from their heads quickly enough to nod respectfully when she greeted them; Bram they sized up with steely eyes, though they called him "sir" and "Squire" to his face. He was stopped by someone behind Grace, but she worked her way through the room until she saw Granna near the worktable and Sean on his stooleen.

"Gran!" She rushed into the old woman's arms and breathed in her scent of herbs and flour.

Granna folded her in tightly, cooing against her cool cheek, before holding her out to have a good look. "Ah, I can't get over how grown you look, child, with your hair up and your missus dress." She looked back over her shoulder at Sean. "Not at all like our Gracie come flying in from the bog with mud on her face and squished up between her toes, eh, Sean?"

They all laughed.

"Or with jam up to her elbows on a black batch morning." Sean put out his hand. "Come say hello to your dying brother."

"Sean!" She came immediately, peering into his face.

He pulled her down onto his lap. "Just dying to have another look at yourself there, girl," he said, and laughed again.

She punched him, then kissed his cheek.

"And here's Morgan! I didn't see you standing in the corner." She stood up and smoothed her dress. "How's your mam? And the girls?"

He smiled. "Herself is well, Grace, thanks for asking. Home with the newest McDonagh, another sister for us all. Barbara's looking after them, but the midlins have come along." He tipped his head toward a group of three girls, softer versions of himself, standing in the corner, surrounded by admirers. "Wouldn't miss a chance to dance and show off their pretty selves, those three."

"They look wonderful." Her voice was wistful as she watched the chattering, laughing girls with their long braids and flowered skirts.

"And you, as well." He stepped out of the corner and handed her a bough of wild roses wrapped in moss. "Didn't I trouble myself to pick these for your gran, and herself without a jug to put them in? Ask Grace, she says to me, and thank God you're here before they wilt away."

Grace turned, flustered. "Up top there, near the rafter, that's where I kept it."

"Here, now." Morgan stood on tiptoe, reached into the cobwebs, and brought down a luster jug. He handed it to Grace, who arranged the roses and set them on the window ledge.

"Faith, and aren't they sweet? And yourself as well, for bringing them along to an old woman." Granna smiled at him, then turned to Grace. "Morgan and Sean have been making the long days pass, surprising me with the odd treasure from their lollygagging in the woods."

"Still wasting your days on the riverbanks, are you?" Grace teased.

Sean nodded, his eyes twinkling. "Aye. Morgan comes by regular to fill his basket with fish and his head with dangerous thinking. We have long conversations about God, the state of Ireland . . . and love." He put his hand over his heart and fluttered his eyelashes.

Morgan shot him a warning look, then turned to Grace. "Himself is still full of worthless prattle, in case you're looking for improvement. But you, now. Your face shines with the good life you're leading."

"You'd not believe all the new things I've seen and learned! My head spins when night comes and I'm hours falling to sleep!" she said wondrously.

Morgan smiled at her enthusiasm, then lowered his eyes to the ring on her finger. "Ah, well, that's fine then, and I'm happy for you."

Granna slipped an arm around Grace's waist. "Arrah, and I hate to send you away from us, but your Squire's been cornered by Father Keating and he's looking none the happier for it."

"I'd better go," Grace said anxiously. "It was hard enough to get him here in the first place." She kissed Granna's cheek and hurried across the room.

"Ah!" Bram said too warmly when she joined them. "Father, this is my wife. Gracelin dear, meet Father Keating, a true Irish priest and a veritible font of information on the lives of minor saints."

Grace recognized the tone in her husband's voice and said immediately, "Bram, I'm afraid Da is too eager to show you the new rooms on the house. He's waiting in the yard."

Bram feigned disappointment. "I'm sure you'll excuse me, Father, as I leave you in much prettier company." He ran a finger along Grace's jaw to her chin, lifting it slightly, then sauntered out to the yard, extending his hand to Patrick.

Grace turned her attention back to the priest, slipping two gold sovereigns into his hand. "Thank you for coming all this way, Father."

He looked down at the coins gratefully; the usual method of payment would have been by collection, a poor bet by the looks of this crowd.

"It's a fine start for my brother and his new wife," she added. "To be blessed by the church."

Father Keating nodded soberly. "Are you a believer in the True Faith, then, Missus Donnelly?"

"My husband is a Protestant, Father," she said.

"Well, one can be a True Believer and a Protestant," he allowed, the coins warm in his hand. "But one must work harder at it, you know, for the Lord has less to work with."

Grace nodded, listening with half an ear as he went on to praise her well-made marriage and the gentry class for setting such a fine example of higher living. His only regret, he whispered conspiratorily, was that there were not enough Catholics in the bunch. Still, he said, if God bestowed such a fine life on Protestants, who, as we all know, are dancing on the edge of the Pit (begging your pardon but there's the hard truth of it), just think what might come to hardworking Catholics! Grace was glad when a bottle appeared; she took it and filled the priest's glass, urging another drop on him before he started out on the long journey home. He drank to her health, swallowing heartily, then, with reddened cheeks, he loudly blessed the bride and groom, and departed.

After his donkey was out of sight, the talk grew louder and more free. Grace made her way around the room, filling glasses with poteen, then with punch. Bram had finished several glasses along with Patrick's tour and was holding court out in the yard, when tinkers appeared at the half-door off the lane, blessing the house and all in it. They were invited to share the wedding feast and paid their way with a long, moving ballad, offered up by the oldest woman in the tribe. She invoked the beloved name of Carolan the Blind and brought out her ancient harp, which she stroked nimbly until the room quieted and all eyes were turned upon her.

The sound of her high, quivering voice and the solemnity of the song drew Bram in from the yard.

"What in God's name is the old hag singing about?" he breathed heavily in Grace's ear.

She frowned at him, then tipped her head and listened to the Irish. "It's about a young man who falls in love with a girl of better class. He watches her all day at the fair, and that night she comes to him in a dream and says it will not be long until they marry, but first he must make his fortune."

"A bit like us." Bram's words were slightly slurred. "Except for the girl being of better class." He took a sip, swirling the burnished liquid in his glass. "I never said before, but I watched you that night at St. John's Eve, you know, standing near some ruddy brute of a farm boy. You were the spitting image of the girl who'd appeared in a dream I'd had. Quite vivid, actually."

Grace looked at him, astonished.

He nodded. "Quite true." He pulled her back into the corner and lowered his voice even more. "I'll tell you." He smiled indulgently. "In this dream, I fell into a deep well and couldn't get out. Rain was filling the damn thing up and I knew I was lost. I heard a voice singing, and a baby appeared in the light at the top. I startled it by yelling for help, and it fell down the shaft right into my arms—a fat, naked, howling boy. I looked up and, in the light, saw a mass of red curls framing an anxious face—your face." He touched her cheek. "I called out for you to save me, but you were frightened and shook your head. Only when I held up the boy and begged you to save us both did you shake loose your hair and allow me to climb up on it. When I reached the top, I put the baby in your arms. You looked at it for a long time, then kissed it tenderly and gave it back to me, saying this was *my* son now."

Grace's mouth hung open in astonishment. "One afternoon at an Irish party, and haven't you become as grand a storyteller as the best of them!"

Bram shook his head. "It's no story," he said gravely. "The next night, there you were at the bonfire, every bit the girl in my dream. Younger, perhaps, but who could mistake all that hair?"

Grace was thoughtful. "If what you say is true, then it's more than a dream you've had." She bit her lip, her eyes growing wide. "It's a sign."

Bram rolled his eyes, retreating back into his world of modern sensibilities. "You Irish and your signs. One of the many things that keeps you from joining the modern world." He tossed off his drink.

"This is not about Pookahs and Banshees. It was simply a dream, a vivid dream at best, but that's most certainly all. I must've seen you before in the village, and your face remained in my subconscious."

"Yet you married me without a word between us," Grace challenged. "That's not me looking for answers in signs, now, is it?"

Bram's face grew still. "I want a son," he said simply.

Grace's heart went out for the yearning in his eyes, something she had never seen. She hesitated only a moment before leaning against him and whispering in his ear, "Bram. It was a sign from God most surely. I'm meant to have a baby come spring."

His stare was blank. Then his face lit up and he let out a whoop that she attempted to smother.

"We must announce it," he whispered loudly.

Grace shook her head. "This is Ryan and Aghna's wedding day. It would be bad luck to steal happiness from them."

"I must tell someone," he begged. "Your father! Let me tell your father, then. In private! Outside!"

Reluctantly, Grace agreed, wary of intruding on her brother's joy. But she watched with pleasure as Bram took her father's arm and led him out to the yard.

The old woman finished her song and Irial Kelley began to tune his fiddle in the corner. The floor was cleared and four couples began to dance, arms to their sides, feet flying in complicated steps as much a part of them as the music itself. Others pressed against the wall, leaned in on windowsills, or crowded the doorways. Ryan and his fair-haired bride skipped around the room with eyes only for one another, and Grace was happy for the light that shone in their faces. She did not notice Morgan's approach and was startled when he put a hand on her arm.

"A quick step while your husband's not looking, then, Missus Donnelly?"

"Morgan," she scolded. "Bram's not at all like that!"

"So the answer is 'yes', is it?" His eyes twinkled, knowing she was caught.

Grace glanced out the window to see Bram again holding court with the young farmers, puffed up with his secret, and drinking more than he should.

She bit her lip, but could not help smiling as Morgan moved her

out onto the floor with the other couples. They took their places in
the line, waited for the fiddler and piper to call the song, then smiled
at one another and began to fly.

Granna and Sean watched the musicians and dancers from their
chairs in the corner, more than content with their place on the edge
of the party.

"Morgan's got Grace to dance," Sean said, pointing them out.

"Aye." Granna sipped daintily from the finger of whiskey Sean
had poured her. "'Tis a shame he's so full up of love for her."

Sean sprayed his drink on the floor in front of him, and turned to
her, eyes wide in alarm.

Granna shushed him. "Ah now, don't worry yourself. There's no
one to see but ourselves who love them both." She paused. "Why did
he not speak of it?"

Sean wiped his chin, then moved his stool closer to her chair.
"Donnelly got there first, but didn't I beg him to say something even
then? He made me swear never to tell a soul. He said there was no
choice to be made, and that putting it before her would only bring
her heartache."

"God knows I'd have rather called himself son than that other
great beast of a man." She gazed into her glass. "But there's nothing
can be done for it now. Grace is married to him and happy enough.
'Tis our own poor Morgan will have to find happiness where it lies."

Sean looked to where they stood, waiting for the next song,
flushed from the dance, Morgan just now brushing a bit of loose hair
away from Grace's face.

"He will," he said, lifting a glass to them. "He is."

The couples spun through two more sets; then Aghna's father
stood to sing "Barbara Allen," a favorite of the crowd. Other singers,
Morgan among them, granted requests, and there were many trips to
the poteen barrel to refill glasses for hearty toasts to the bride and
groom, may they have long life and many children, a bit of land and
love in their hearts. Gone was the currant bread and whiskey punch;
the men drank straight whiskey now, getting teary over songs of lost
love and hard battles, and of Ireland, the most beautiful woman in the
world. Barefoot children, eyes shining with merriment, shirts un-
tucked, flower wreaths askew on their heads, ran shouting through

the legs of grown-ups, who kissed instead of cuffed them on this happy day. And in the long, warm, bright summer evening, the women sat around them all, keeping track, and talking their talk of weddings remembered and wakes recalled, babies born alive and dead, children raised to good or bad, and men who never changed.

# Seven

THE McDonaghs gathered before the hearth on their knees, rosary beads in hand, to say their morning prayers. Nally McDonagh, the father, led them rapidly through it, eager as he was to get on with his day. With his wild hair just going gray, pulled back and tied like Morgan's, and a gold ring hanging from each earlobe, he looked like the pirate he longed to be. The mother—a tired, faded beauty at thirty-five—knelt in their midst, one hand rocking the cradle of the newest babe; smaller children leaning against older. All the feet that showed were bare and black on the bottoms from the dirt floor and summer roads, all the earnest faces sun-browned and freckled.

"Amen," Nally said emphatically as each one made the sign of the cross. He kissed the beads and hung them on a peg by the hearth before sitting down at the board for breakfast. A knife and a tin cup marked each seat and in the middle sat a heavy black cooking pot filled with steaming boiled potatoes, a crock of fresh butter, and a bowl of salt. They stuck their knives into the pot, pulled out a potato, dipped it into the butter and salt, and ate it from the knife, washing it down with cups of buttermilk. When there were no oats for porridge, this was breakfast, and dinner, too, more often than not.

Mary McDonagh put the baby to her breast and watched to make sure everyone got their share. She'd given birth to eleven children, eight of whom still lived. Although she loved her seven daughters with a full heart, she was most attached to Morgan, her firstborn and only surviving son. He sat across from her, feeding the two-year-old on his lap hot potato from his hand.

"Musha, eat up now," she said softly to him. "'Tis a long walk your-selves will have to the fair."

Morgan looked up and smiled at her. "And don't I wish you were coming along, Mam? You who loves the market days."

"We'll bring yourself back a bit of something, Mam," Aislinn said, wiping her hand on her skirt. She would be the oldest daughter going, as Barbara was staying home with her mother and the wee Erin.

"Just be sure you get what's on the list," Mary said sternly. "Mind you don't get flighty as you're wont to do."

"Not me, Mam!" Aislinn said earnestly. "I'll get Katie to go round with me and gather it all." She looked across the table at her younger sister, who nodded vigorously, cheeks stuffed with potato.

Nally stood, wiping his mouth with the back of his hand. "You'll all stay with me till we get a price for the yearling cow and the pig. Then we'll square up with the Squire's agent and see what's left for the cupboard."

"You're selling a pig?" Morgan frowned at his father.

"Aye." Nally's eyes darkened. "We'll barely pay the rent after sell-ing the calf, so the pig's got to go."

"That leaves but one to eat, none to bear." Morgan looked around at all the faces at the table.

"'Tis not my fault all the piglets took sick and died," Nally said an-grily. "Now I've naught to sell but the old one, be lucky to get a decent price for him as it stands. We'll just have to trust our good fortune and find the sow a mate come next spring. Let yourselves be finished now and get on." He donned his market hat, dark brown with a slouchy brim, then stepped out the low door into the yard, whistling for the dogs.

Mary looked after him wistfully. "Arrah, himself is a fine-looking man in his linen shirt and vest. 'Tis what he wore to marry me away." Her face took on that far-off look that came over her so much of late. Morgan knew she was missing her home in the Black Valley, poor and scruffy though it was, and her mother and da long dead. She had been a true mountain girl, her cabin three walls of the mountain itself, no windows, and a low, narrow door, her father and brothers driving the sheep up the steep, narrow paths to the small patches of grass, her mother weaving the frieze for the tailor to sew into workshirts when he came round once a year. Nally, making the tramp to Galway to see about getting a ship, broke his arm in a terrible fall and was found by her. She helped him back to the cabin and sent a boy for the bone-setter. He gave over his heart for the shine in her eyes and the way she listened to his talk about adventure. They married and he brought her back to the family farm, but he never conquered his desire for the sea, and every few years he left the growing family to set sail and bring home riches. Rarely did the riches amount to more than he could've made had he stayed on the farm, but now and then he enjoyed a small bounty, and he told fantastic tales around the winter fire.

"He'll be leaving us again soon," Mary said, her eyes still on the yard and disappearing figure of her husband.

"But he's not been back a year!" Morgan was dismayed. There was so much to be done and he needed his father's help.

"Aye," Mary said. "But I can see it. Himself is restless and can't look me square to talk about winter coming."

Morgan stood and set the two-year-old gently down on the floor. He shook his head. "I'll speak to him, Mam. 'Tis no time for him to go."

Mary sighed. "Never is, but go he does, so sure he is that treasure and riches are only to be found at sea."

The girls had neatened their hair and tied their cloaks around, and now called for Morgan to hurry.

He stooped to kiss the toddler, then the baby and Mary. "I'll speak to him, don't worry yourself. Rest today. Let Barbara do for you." He smiled at his sister, a serious young woman, tall and strong-boned like himself.

"Off with you now," Barbara said. "I'll watch after our mother and the babes. You know I will."

Morgan kissed her and hurried into the yard, where the party had already begun moving down the road. The girls carried their stockings and shoes in their hands to keep them clean until they reached the town, and their faces were flushed with excitement. Up ahead, his father drove the yearling calf and the sow with a long stick. The wind had picked up and Morgan held his hat on with one hand as he caught up to his father.

"No rain to slow us down," Nally said by way of greeting.

"True for you," Morgan said, keeping the sow in line with his stick. "I'm thinking we can buy some seed at the market if we get a fair price for the pig."

"What kind of seed?" Nally spat tobacco juice to the side of the road.

"We could grow a small vegetable garden in the spring."

"Vegetables!" He shook his head firmly. "'Tis a break with custom and I'll not be a party to it. The neighbors would laugh to see me waste good pratie ground on the planting of vegetables."

Morgan gripped his stick and tried to keep the anger out of his voice. "We've got the room for it. I could clear that rocky patch on the south end of the cabin, put in a few seeds—turnips, carrots, onions . . ."

"Onions grow wild in the wood, and berries and nuts. God provides us with what we need." Nally spat again.

Morgan tapped his stick against the hide of the slowing calf. "That doesn't make sense, Da," he said. "Why grow potatoes then? Why keep chickens, pigs, and cows? We could grow the oats we feed the animals and save the cost!"

"So it's oats you want to grow now! Grain and vegetables! You want me to run a squire's farm—is that it?" His voice was loud and angry on the quiet road. The others had fallen silent behind him and were listening fearfully. "Well, let me tell you something, boyo. To run a squire's farm costs a squire's coin. The minute we put our spades to the earth, they'll raise the rent. When the grain and greens start to grow, they'll raise it again. When it begins to look as if we might have enough to eat and are prospering, they'll take half of it for themselves and add a tax, as well. And on top of that, our neighbors will suffer envy and steal what they think should be rightfully shared." He shook his head. "Makes no sense to do things different when the custom of the land is against it."

"But, Da," Morgan protested. "Hear me out, at least."

Nally struck the ground hard with his stick and stopped. "No! No, boy. You're wanting to be like those O'Malleys of yours. Didn't your mother, as well, bringing home the strange way of that Kathleen, and did it not serve her poorly? 'No pigs in the house,' she says to me, and what happens but they all die of the cold, away from the hearth ash. 'I'm moving the hen coop to the yard,' she says and catches a terrible fever, losing the babe she carried, all from going out in the rain to get eggs from high and mighty chickens must have their own place!"

Morgan felt the slow burn of rising anger. "Your thinking is all wrong. We've had less sickness since the animals are out of the cabin. The pigs died of swine fever from that rogue you caught in the wood and put in with the others, and as for the hen coop—it was away off in the bushes where you made her put it because she stood up to you for once in her life. Have you not noticed that it's now built onto the side of the cabin, and all's been well with it?"

Nally squinted into Morgan's face. "I hear plenty of blame in your words, boy, but it wasn't me raised the rent when your lovely work come under the notice of the landlord, now was it?" He started walking again. "Those O'Malleys are Protestants—no good can come of their way of thinking, for they're not guided by God. Patrick's got a good place, 'tis true, but he pays a high price for it and works like a slave. And he's as cursed as Job, he is—herself dead and the boy a sickly cripple, his only daughter in the hands of Satan's agent."

Reminded of Grace, Morgan felt his breath leave him; defeat settled on his shoulders and he sensed the full weight of it—but only for a moment, and then he shrugged it off.

"We can't go on as we have, Da." He glanced at his father's stern profile. "Either you stay on the land and help us live"—he paused and took a breath—"or it will be myself runs off to sea."

Nally stopped again, the girls behind coming up short. "Go on ahead," he shouted angrily to them. "Go on now."

When they were out of earshot, he turned to his son and said with menace, "I've never run away from anything in my life, boy, and I should beat you down right now for such talk as that." He raised the herding stick.

Morgan did not flinch. "You leave us when the money gets thin, when it's too big a burden." He paused. "Are you not already planning to leave again before winter comes?"

Nally stared a moment, then lowered the stick. He looked away down the road toward town; beyond the mountains was the sea. "I'm thinking on it," he said quietly. "There's little money to be got out of the land this year. I can bring more back from working the ships."

"And when will that be?" Morgan was no longer angry. He saw the stoop of his father's shoulders and, in the sunlight, the deep lines on his handsome face. "One year? Two? Maybe three, this time?"

Nally shrugged. "As long as it takes, wherever the work is. Whatever I can do to keep the family going."

Morgan waited until Nally looked at him, and then said quietly, "There's no guarantee we'll be left alive here in another year, Da. Rents go up, we starve every summer until the potatoes come in, fever hits."

"The girls'll be marrying away soon," Nally said defensively.

"One goes, one more is born." Morgan's voice was hard with the fact of it.

Nally pushed back his hat and put his hands on his hips. "Is that it, boyo? You're wanting to be married yourself, making your own children like a man?"

Morgan shook his head in disgust. "I care naught for finding a wife. But let you be honest, Da—I run your farm and I'm raising your family. If you want me to keep on, then there's a price to be paid."

"Hah!" Nally spat. "Pay you to look after your own mother and sisters? What kind of a Christian are you?"

Morgan ignored the slight. "You'll pay me in seed and you'll let me plant what I want on the farm, or I'll not stay another day."

"I'm calling your bluff, for I know you'd not desert your own mother."

"I'll serve her better by leaving the family and forcing you to stay," Morgan said firmly. "So, let you give your answer by the time we reach the town or I leave you there and hike the road to Dublin."

His father stared at him, then growled deep in his throat and started off at full stride, Morgan keeping his distance behind until they caught up to the girls.

They walked on through the clear autumn morning, a sharpness in the air the only hint of winter to come. As the path broadened from trail to lane to road, they were joined by more people driving their animals to the market fair, baskets of goods carried on their heads or tied to their backs, smaller children riding on donkey carts, legs swinging behind. They called hallos and speculated about the prices they hoped their animals would fetch; there was optimism on this morning, even though most of the money would go to make up rent. Women in their wedding clothes—the only good dresses they owned—walked carefully around piles of manure and muck running down the middle of the road. Men in their Sunday shirts and vests, top hats or fedoras, stiff brogans on their feet, clay pipes in their pockets, held out the hope for picking a winner at the horse races that afternoon and enjoying a pint or two from the keg that was sure to be there. The children hoped for an extra penny to spend on sweets or a toy from the woodcarver. By the time they walked into the village, the noise was deafening; already a fiddler was playing alongside the hucksters' tents and a few men, merry with drink, were trying a jig. Morgan hurried to speak to his sisters, whose faces were highly flushed with excitement and the awareness of glances from all the young men.

"Mind you watch yourselves in this crowd," Morgan said to Aislinn, who nodded without giving him so much as a look. "Do you hear me, girl?" He put a hand on her shoulder.

"Aye," she said impatiently. "Of course I hear you with your big voice. Don't be looking to spoil our fun so early in the day, Morgan, you old man. Aren't we big girls now?"

"You may be a big girl at fifteen, Aislinn," he reminded. "And Katie at fourteen. But Maureen is just eleven and Ellen only eight. Keep them tight with you, or leave them with me."

"I'll stay with you, Morgan." Ellen slipped her small hand into his and looked up at him with adoring eyes. She had been the victim of her sisters' sport more than once, and worshiped her older brother.

"Not me." Maureen slid over nearer to Katie. She was a stout girl for her age, but with a delicate face, and fine, thick hair.

Morgan sized them up, narrowing his eyes at Aislinn. "All right then. But keep ahold of her, I say." He looked to where his father was leading the livestock to the sellers' ring, then down the street to the big office on the end where people were already lined up. "Meet us down near the agent's at midday and we'll square up then."

The three girls turned and hurried into the crowd, skirts swinging over hastily pulled on stockings and shoes, their heads close together in conspiracy.

"Come on then, you," Morgan said affectionately to Ellen, squeezing her hand. "Let's go find our da."

They walked into the ring where buyers were making offers on livestock. Nally was thick in with a butcher from Cork City, sharing a nip from the flask the man offered. When Morgan handled the sale in the past, he almost always got a better price than Nally, but he was not about to step in today.

"Let you go over to the marionettes across the road," he said softly to Ellen, pointing out the performance that had drawn a small crowd of laughing children.

She looked at him anxiously, shy of letting him go. "Will you come for me?"

He nodded and kissed the top of her head before sending her off. He watched her cross the road and stand near the back of the group, her little shoulders stiff under her blouse and cloak. Soon, however, she relaxed and he was glad to see her laughing along with the rest. He turned his attention to his father, who had gotten down to serious business with the butcher and was now counting coins. They spat and shook hands, completing the deal, and the butcher took away the calf on his lead. Nally looked up and hailed Morgan, then pushed his way through the group.

"We got a fair price for that one," he said, showing Morgan the little pouch of coins. Morgan counted quickly, hiding his disappointment; he could've gotten half again as much.

Nally eyed him, then scowled. "Aye, you think you're the only one with a head on you." He was feeling the effect of the whiskey and his face was close up to that of his son. "Well, let you go and sell the pig, then, you who knows so much about everything."

"I'll hear your answer first." Morgan took off his hat to show respect.

"Answer?" Nally looked puzzled, then his face cleared. "Aye, then, my answer." He paused and pulled back his shoulders, as if realizing for the first time that his son now stood taller. "Myself heads this family, Morgan, and let you not forget that. Yourself has grown into a man without my marking it, but that cannot be helped." He paused, warming to his speech. "It's not been easy for me to leave your mother and her children, but I've done it because there's been no other way. My own father now, God bless his miserable soul"—he wiped a tear from his eye—"was a one-a-day man: one meal a day, one beating a day, one word a day and never kind, one look a day, to size you up. I've not done that to you children, no, I've not." He shook his head vehemently. "I've kept food on the table and love in my heart and a kind word in my mouth for herself and the babies. I've been a better man than my father was, which is a son's duty. So don't pass judgment upon me till you've fathered your own and made a man's way in the world."

Morgan was unmoved. "Let you give me seed money and I'll do just that."

Nally's eyes hardened and the misty look left his face. "This is my answer, then, boy: Since I cannot bear to break your mother's heart by robbing herself of her only living son, I'll give you the money for seed and let you plant as you will."

"And yourself?"

"I will go out and make a living for my family, best as I know how."

"Done." Morgan put out his hand.

Nally shook it once, hard, then let it drop. "Go sell that pig, boy, and meet me at the track. The butcher tipped me off to a sure first."

"The money." Morgan held out his hand again.

"Take it out of what you get for the pig." Nally pocketed the pouch. "Don't waste the morning bargaining for pennies. Get what you can and meet me afore midday." He strode away down the street to the field where the horse races were beginning.

The marionette show had ended and Ellen was waiting for Morgan, hands under her apron, eyes anxiously searching the growing throng. The sun was climbing the sky and the day in full bloom. She smiled in relief when he called her name.

"Where's Da?" she asked, taking Morgan's big hand in both of hers.

"Watching the horses run." They could hear the shouts from the field. "I've got to sell the pig and buy some seed. Then we'll eat. Have you not seen hide nor hair of your wicked sisters, then?"

She grinned up at him and shook her head, then pointed a tiny finger. "There they are! Going into the dry goods."

He turned and was glad to see they still had Maureen with them. When they disappeared into the store, he and Ellen walked on to the pigstye. They passed the first fistfight of the day; two men, stripped to the waist, sweat pouring off their bodies, traded punches while others cheered them on and the odd coin traded hands. The larger, dark-haired man was taking the worst of it from his lighter, quicker opponent; blood flowed freely from his nose, and a cut above his eye blinded him. His lip was split open and his jaw red and swollen, but still he stood, swaying about with a weak swing.

"Fall down!" Morgan yelled as he passed, and the crowd booed good-naturedly.

Further up the street, another group—mostly women and old

men—circled a priest who was preaching the virtue of avoiding drink and bad women, and offering God's blessings to all who behaved in a civilized manner on this day. Young men were strangely absent from this lecture, but Morgan saw the cause across the road behind a huckster's tent. Looking furtively around, a tall, red-bearded fellow addressed the men in quiet though passionate speech, pounding his fist into his hand, and pointing a finger at the priest across the street, then at the Protestant minister handing out clothes from his doorstep, and at the guards lounging on the steps of the jail, now paying more attention to this particular crowd of young men. Morgan wished he could step closer and hear what the man was saying. He was sure it was recruitment for the new Young Irelanders said to have broken bitterly from the Old over the taking up of arms. He'd heard nothing from them but fighting words and was not eager to join another group of hotheads. Still, he was intrigued and considered stopping to hear this speaker, but the nearness of the soldiers and their narrowed eyes cautioned him away. There would be another time and a better place.

He quickened his step and led Ellen down an alley to an open barn. Here he bartered and bargained and came away, at last, with a price near to what he'd hoped to get. The market was poor again this year and people were holding their money close. He went on to the storehouse and looked through the available seed, choosing turnip, onion sets, carrot, corn, oat, and rye. The keeper wrapped them in brown paper packets, which Morgan pushed deep into his pocket with a pat, thinking of the future.

"Will we find Da now, or the girls?" Ellen asked, squinting at the sun full up in the sky. "I'm hungry."

"Keep a lookout for your sisters near the agent," he told her, then spied them coming out of the Catholic ladies bazaar.

"Aislinn!" he hailed, noting the look of annoyance on her face when she saw it was only him waving them over.

"We'll get Da at the track and have a bite from the basket Mam sent," he ordered. "Then let you gather the supplies and we'll rest before walking home."

"Won't we dance, then?" Aislinn began to pout and Kate looked over her shoulder at a group of teenage boys winking and whistling in their direction.

Morgan eyed the group, as well. He was happy for his sisters to keep young company, but these were bold boys from the town and he didn't like the brazen way Aislinn flirted with them. He didn't think she knew what she was letting herself in for.

"We'll stay for a bit of dancing," he said. "But mind you keep hold of yourself in this fast crowd."

Aislinn gave him one of her dazzling smiles and he marveled again at how rapidly she could change from viper to vixen. She was a queer one and needed a firm hand, but his mother was too tired from the babies, and Barbara could do nothing with her. Nally, of course, wasn't around, and when he was, he encouraged her nature as he saw in it his own desire for the bold life.

They walked as a family down the street, stopping now and then to greet a neighbor and give out news of their mother. They could hear the excited cheers of the racing field and the thunder of pounding horse hooves. Nally stood near the rail, nearly mad with urging his horse, a strong-looking chestnut bay with powerful legs and a long stride, well ahead of the pack. And then it was down, coming too sharply into the curve, losing its footing in a streak of slippery mud. The rider was thrown and lay on the track before coming to his senses and scrambling out of the way of the oncoming horses. The bay stayed down, her foreleg clearly broken.

"Get up, get up and *run,* you bloody bitch!" Nally screamed, pounding the rail, spit flying from his mouth with the curses. "God-damn you to hell, you miserable nag, and your damn fool rider, as well!" His shoulders began to shake and tears coursed down his blotched face.

Morgan told the girls to wait and walked up quietly behind him. "Your horse went down."

Nally stiffened at the sound of his voice. "'Twas a freakish thing. Never seen anything like it a'tall in all my life."

"Bet on her, did you?"

Nally turned slowly, his face tight with anger. A shot rang out as the horse was put down, and he winced then, the color draining from his face, leaving behind a pale, shaken old man.

"Aye," he said, his eyes glazed.

"All of it?" Morgan could barely breathe.

"Most." Nally wiped a hand over his face. "The butcher said it was the sure bet—wasn't it his own brother riding the damn beast, and himself betting on her, as well? I knew it to be true!" His eyes sparkled briefly, then faded again in disappointment. "But God would have it otherwise. 'Tis a sign that I should go right away to the docks. This very day. My luck is not on the land."

"How are we to pay Ceallachan?"

Nally hesitated. "What did the pig fetch?"

Morgan shook his head. "We'll still be short a pound, and nothing left for the cupboard."

Nally looked over his shoulder at the dead horse and the weeping owner. His face was grim. "We'll speak to him . . . tell him we've had bad luck, sickness in the family. He knows I'm good for it. Haven't we always paid?"

Morgan held his tongue yet again, swinging Ellen up onto his shoulders as they walked back down the crowded street to the house on the end where hung a brass plate reading GERALD O'FLAHERTY, ESQUIRE: BREASAL CEALLACHAN, AGENT. There was a short line of people waiting to settle their debts; the mood was somber as no one wanted to part with the hard-earned money in their hands, let alone beg for mercy if they were short. The line moved up a step and into the room where Ceallachan sat at a desk, a ledger opened upon it. Behind him stood a broad man in a too-tight jacket, the handle of a gun peeking out above his waistband. Seated in a chair on the other side of Ceallachan was another man, clearly a gentleman by the look of him: clean-shaven with a nary a nick nor scratch across his smooth cheeks, well-cut suit of clothes, polished leather riding boots, heavy wool jacket over his shoulders, and the silver chain of a watch fob stretched across his vest. His hands were clean and unmarked, and he had the good health of one who'd never missed a meal. He was a hand-some man, except for yellow hair that curled tightly about his head and collar, and a sparse mustache smoothed often with a finger that bore a heavy gold signet ring. Morgan caught his father's eye and raised his eyebrows in question.

"Young Gerald O'Flaherty," Nally whispered. "Cut like his father, but for all that pretty hair and the thing above his lip."

"What's he doing here, then?" Morgan kept his voice low.

"Finished at school." Nally paused to cast a frown at Aislinn, who'd crowded close to listen. "Studied drink and cards, word is. Waiting for a commission from the queen's army. Got to stay out of trouble till then, I suppose."

As the line moved forward, Aislinn stood at its edge, pinching her cheeks and smoothing her hair. They were now near the desk.

"Four pound six, Mrs. Galligan." Ceallachan ran his finger down the ledger.

The old woman counted out her few coins with a trembling hand.

"You're short two and six," he barked. "Put it on the table now, missus. Don't take all day."

The old woman bowed her head. "God bless you, sir, but I've not got it. I'm widowed this year, you see—buried my Mike in the winter and himself being all I've got to home."

"What about the boys?" Ceallachan's eyes were hard.

"Dead, sir, but for the eldest gone to America and the next sent to Van Diemmien's Land."

"Transported? On what charge?" O'Flaherty asked, his voice more gentle than that of the agent.

"Attempted murder, sir." The old woman turned her pleading eyes on the young man. "He went mad when the guards came for his da, and he near killed the one, God save his soul. The judge give him six years. Put him on the boat to Australia right then."

"What's she saying?" O'Flaherty directed the question to Ceallachan.

"The Galligans are a rabble lot, sir. Always fighting their neighbors, always in some kind of trouble, they are." Ceallachan scowled at the woman. "Her husband sold his cow to Hynes, the shopkeeper, then stole another cow when Hynes butchered the first. Her son flew into a rage and beat the guard who came to arrest his father, smashing the man on the side of the head with a rock and leaving him stupid, and blind in one eye."

"Begging your pardon, sir," the old woman interrupted. "Mister Hynes was holding the cow on good faith for her butter and cream till our bill was met. When the month passed and my husband, God rest his soul, went to get her, he found her butchered and the meat sold. We cannot live without the cow, sir—we'd paid our debt. Mister Hynes said to take another, an old one, and he did, my Mike, but then the guards come, and Mike terrible sick in his chest and they took the cow and hit poor Mike with their clubs. Martin, God save him, struck out with his fists at the guard." She spoke rapidly now. "I pray for the guard and his family. God knows I do . . . and for our Martin, who suffers in prison on the other side of the world . . . and for my Mike, who's gone out of it and left me alone." She began to weep into her hands.

The agent snorted in disgust. "They can tell a story to break your heart and the next minute laugh at you for the pennies hidden up their sleeves." He frowned at the widow. "You've got chickens and a pig on that ground of yours. Anything else?"

"No, sir," she said quietly, wiping her eyes with her sleeve.

"Leave the money, bring in the animals."

"But how will I live?" she begged. "How will I pay next Quarterday?"

The agent shrugged. "That's not our concern."

Missus Galligan turned, stunned, then fell down in the corner, pulled her apron over her head, and started to keen, rocking from side to side.

Ceallachan spat in contempt. "Get her out of here," he said to the group huddled by the door.

Nally motioned to the girls, who went to the widow and helped her up. They spoke gently to her, getting her to the door, but before they left, Aislinn glared boldly at O'Flaherty, who watched the scene with horrified amusement.

Morgan and Nally shared a glance. If there was no pity to be had for a suffering widow, what chance had they? Two other families paid what they owed and then it was their turn.

"Ah, McDonagh." Ceallachan tapped his pen on the ledger.

Nally put his money on the table. "I'm short, Ceallachan," he said directly, his eyes not wavering from the agent's face. "But you know I'm good for it."

Ceallachan shook his head slowly. "I expected better than that from you, McDonagh," he said. "You've never missed a day."

"Aye," Nally narrowed his eyes. "And I've often paid ahead when I've come back from sea."

"When do you go?"

Nally nodded. "Today, and I'll be sending money home before next quarter."

"And if you don't?"

"My boy, Morgan, will see you get your due. We'll have the piglets by then and another calf on the way."

"Bet the horses today, did you, then, Nally?" The agent smirked.

Nally was still. His eyes flicked to the face of the young Squire, then back to Ceallachan. "I was unlucky, true for you, but 'tis not the cause of our trouble."

"So you were gambling with money that rightfully belonged to the Squire." Ceallachan looked over his shoulder. "That's stealing, wouldn't you say, sir?"

O'Flaherty was looking at Nally, but his gaze suddenly shifted to the open door as Aislinn and her sisters came back in and joined their father. Aislinn had taken the shawl from her head, and her hair, thick and loose, glistened in the light. She had pushed back her cloak and untied the top string of her blouse so that her fine collarbones and the hollow at the base of her throat showed clearly. Her shoulders were back and her figure was perfectly molded inside her clothes. She met the young gentleman's gaze with one of her own, direct and unafraid. Her eyes sparked as she moved closer to her father.

O'Flaherty didn't take his eyes off her face as he spoke. "My father does not approve of credit, as you know," he said. "And far be it from me to encourage debt in a family that has avoided it all these years." He paused, looking her slowly up and down before shifting his gaze to Nally. "We have need of a servant for my grandmother, who is ill and bedridden." He paused again, as if considering. "Your daughter may prove sufficient, and certainly it would be a step up for her to come into service at Cairn Manor."

Nally said nothing, but Morgan felt him stiffen.

"She can easily work off your debt in two months' time. After that, the money she earns is her own." O'Flaherty glanced again at Aislinn, who was now demurely looking down at the tips of her shoes.

Nally struggled to work it out, then looked up, incredulous, as he realized how much money Aislinn stood to make.

"She'll work especially hard and pay off your debt," O'Flaherty quickly amended. "After that, if her work is satisfactory, she'll be paid a fair wage to be determined at that time." He paused. "Well?"

Nally looked at Morgan, who was shaking his head, then at Aislinn, who turned her yearning eyes full upon him. It took him only a moment to decide.

"'Tis against my way of thinking for a young girl to leave her Christian home and enter service, no disrespect to you, sir." He ignored the stricken look on his daughter's face. "But my way of thinking does not always follow that of our Lord's, and if it be His will to set this path, then I will walk it. Provided, of course, that her brother may call upon her, and that after paying our debt, she may come home to her mother if needed."

O'Flaherty raised his eyebrows at the impertinence of conditions on his generous offer, but after another glance at Aislinn's bosom, he accepted.

"Very well," he said, shrugging his shoulders and forcing a yawn. "See that she arrives first thing in the morning." He glanced briefly at Morgan, sizing him up, and then again at Aislinn, tipping his head in the slightest of bows, and earning a shy smile in return.

The McDonaghs left the room, followed by a wave of silent disapproval from the others. Tongues would wag tonight, but Aislinn cared not at all; her face glowed, her eyes danced, and she could barely contain the smile that threatened to turn into laughter.

They made their way through the crowd to the edge of the field, where they sat down under a birch tree to eat the bread and cold potatoes Mary had packed in Kate's wicker basket.

"Mind you watch your step in that house, girl," Nally growled around a mouthful of potato.

"Aye," she said meekly, then flung her arms around his neck. "Oh, thank you, Da. Thank you for letting me go to such a fine house!"

He pushed her off, but smiled despite himself. "Ah, well, it worked itself out, didn't it now, and I'm thankful for that. But don't I know the sons of gentlemen, and how quickly their manners are forgot?" He frowned again. "He'll be looking for amusement before he goes off to the army. You'd best keep your head on your shoulders and your feet on the floor, or you'll be coming home with more than pay in your pocket."

Aislinn blushed, stricken, and lowered her eyes. They finished their meal quietly, no one sure of their father's mood. Ellen fell asleep, her head in Morgan's lap, and then Nally hauled himself up, belched, and announced that the girls may have a turn at dancing while he went in search of a pint from another seafaring gentleman. Morgan watched them all go off in opposite directions, glad for a moment alone to sort out the day. He leaned back against the trunk of the tree, pulling Ellen along with him, resettling her head on his leg and smoothing the silky hair off her forehead while she slept.

"A quick step while your father's not looking, then, Mister Mc-Donagh?" teased a light, familiar voice.

His heart began to pound even before he opened his eyes into Grace's smiling face. She moved out of the sun and came closer, pointing to the sleeping child in his lap.

"Can that be your Ellen? Arrah, what a tall thing she's become!" Her voice was soft so as not to awaken the girl.

"Aye, and heavy, as well." Morgan patted the ground. "Will you sit awhile, or are you . . . expected somewhere?"

Grace glanced over her shoulder. "Bram's off buying his pigs, and then I suppose he'll drink on it with the men." She knelt beside him. "Did your sisters come, and your folks?"

"Where would the girls be but dancing, and Da trading sea stories for ale? Mam's tired with feeding wee Erin, and Fiona's a right terror, she is, so Barbara—our blessed commander—stayed home to care for the lot." He realized he was rattling on and took a deep breath. "I've not seen an O'Malley all day."

Grace smiled. "Only Ryan and Aghna came, to get a price for the pigs and two calves Da wants to sell. He wouldn't come himself—you know how stubborn he is about giving up a day of work. I saw them holding hands near the dance square, still starry-eyed for one another." She laughed. "Can you believe our Ryan actually smiles these days!"

"A good wife will do that for a man," Morgan said, then added quickly, "I'd hoped to see Sean and have a word."

"Aghna says he's down with a bad cough again, and Gran has made him stay in bed near the fire with the mustard cure."

"It's the damp now that settles in where that shoulder crowds his chest." He frowned. "I was hoping he'd not be so sick again this winter. I'll go round to see him in a day or so," he added, by way of comfort. "He'll be happy to hear all the news of you."

"I miss him so." Grace picked at the grass. "I don't see him near enough."

"You're a squire's wife, now," Morgan teased gently. "So many duties to fill your day—hair, dress, order the servants about . . ."

Grace laughed, despite herself. "It's not quite like that," she admonished. "Though I could wish for more useful work." She blushed suddenly, then looked up at him. "I do have news. I'm to have a baby in the spring."

Morgan was caught completely off guard, but recovered quickly. "Well, and isn't that grand news," he congratulated. "Won't you have plenty to keep you busy now! I couldn't be happier for you. And the Squire, as well."

Grace looked down in shyness, her hand brushing her belly, and Morgan suddenly had a clear picture of her with a baby in her arms. It was so lovely that the tightness flowed from his heart and he was able to smile in earnest.

"And won't you be a fine mother?" he said.

The tenderness in his voice raised her eyes to his and they sat a moment looking at one another. Grace had forgotten the way the freckles ran down and away under his eye like the mark of tears long dried; it brought upon her a queer sadness, a pain in her heart, and finally she had to look away, pretending to watch the dancing in the square.

"Do you not have a sweetheart among the fine ones out there?" she asked, to change the mood.

"Ah, many!" He laughed, glancing toward the quick-stepping girls. "But my favorite—and the most beautiful—is right beside me, as well you know."

The color drained from Grace's face and her eyes went wide, but she did not turn her head to look at him.

"Asleep here on my lap," he added, instantly aware of his gaff. He glanced down at Ellen, who had begun to stir.

Grace laughed and shook her head to clear it of the impossible thought that had suddenly flown in. Her cheeks flushed again and she reached down to smooth Ellen's skirt.

"She's devoted to you, 'tis true. But what of the others, all those happy maids who are surely waiting for you to call?"

"Are you trying to marry me off, then, when I've already a family to support?" Morgan chided.

"'Tis your father's family you support, not your own."

Morgan shrugged, then sighed. "He's off again today, you know.

Drinking enough to convince himself he's doing a manly duty by us all, going away to sea." He narrowed his eyes. "And he's put Aislinn to service at Cairn Manor."

Grace drew back, surprised. "Truly? That doesn't sound like your mam. I always thought she'd see the girls in a convent before she'd allow them to go into service. Especially for that bear O'Flaherty. He eats them alive, they say."

"Mam doesn't know yet." Morgan looked out to where Aislinn was dancing freely, long hair swinging out behind her. "Da worked it out with young Gerald today as a way of paying the debt we owe."

"Are you behind, then?" Her eyes darkened with concern.

"Da bet the ponies. 'A sure thing'—until it fell and broke its leg." He grimaced. "I'd already bought seed with the pig money, so we were short. O'Flaherty suggested the work, and it was all said and done before I could . . ." He shook his head. "We'd already had a right terrible row over him going off again, so there was nothing left for it."

Grace felt for her purse. "I've not much in here, but I want you to have it. All of it. For the family."

"You shame me, Missus Donnelly. I can pay my own way in the world, as you well know." His voice was more sharp than he'd intended.

"Sure and I meant nothing by it," Grace said abruptly, and to her great alarm felt her eyes fill with tears. She wiped at them fiercely. "Only that you are like my own brother and I want to help."

Morgan shook his head, disgusted with himself at having upset her. "Ah now, you mustn't mind me, Grace. 'Tis the day that's put me off my mood." He was full of contrition, but unable to show it. "Thank you for the kind offer, you've a good heart. But we'll get by as we always have, God willing."

Grace nodded, and they sat in awkward silence, each one mortified by the exchange.

"I've been gone too long," Grace said, standing and hurriedly tying on a beautiful blue bonnet that covered over her lovely hair and hid her face. "It was good to see you, Morgan. Give my love to your mam and Barbara."

"Grace," he called after her, but she did not turn back before fading into the crowd. "Damn my words," he muttered to himself, and cursed the day for not giving up more of its luck.

By late afternoon, Nally had still not come back. The girls were tired and stood grumbling, while Morgan searched the top of the crowd for his father's hat. His eye was caught by the figure of a man in sailor's pants weaving a crooked path down the road, ragged and dirty upon closer inspection, and terribly drunk. The sailor's eyes lit up when he spied Morgan and the four girls standing by the tree in the field, where Nally had said they would be.

"It's from yer father, fine man that he is," the man slurred, handing Morgan a small brown paper packet. He sniffed and wiped at his eyes with the back of a trembling hand. "Gone to sea to save the life of your poor sainted mother, and her blessed babies, though it's tearing his heart in two. Be brave," he spoke gravely. "For he'll come back to you soon enough, God willing, with gold and riches to ease your way of living." He saluted them, then turned on his heel and stumbled away.

Morgan fingered the paper, then slipped it into his pocket.

"Come away now," he said softly to his sisters.

They left the bustle of the town behind, walking long through the twilight, the call of crickets and frogs rising to greet them from the bog, the dirt turning cold and damp beneath their feet. Now and then they shared a word, but otherwise walked quietly, each one with their heart in another place: Morgan stood in the garden he would grow, surrounded by rows of carefully nurtured vegetables; Aislinn worked hard in Cairn Manor, pretty in her new uniform and sleek from delicious leftovers, now and then flirting with the bold young squire; Kate was there, as well, sure that Aislinn would find a place for her and the two of them would escape the hard life and rags of the country; Maureen stood in a beautiful dress with flowers on her head next to Gavin McVey, the white-haired miller's boy with sweating hands who was often her partner at dances; and Ellen hummed a lullaby and thought of the lovely babies at home waiting for her to play with them.

Cows lowed in the neighbor's field and mice rustled in the grass along the fence as the weary walkers turned at last into their lane. They were cheered by the light that spilled out the cabin windows, and the smoke that rose from the chimney, the promise of a warm fire and buttermilk before bed. Mary came to the door, drying her hands on her apron, peering out into the darkness. Morgan hallooed and waved his arm, and she came rushing out to greet them. She saw at once that Nally was not there, but said not a word, shepherding her children inside and listening to their tales. Aislinn had been ready to do battle, sure she would be dismissed without Nally's support, but Mary's quiet acceptance of the plan left her first elated, then confused, then teary as she realized this was her last night at home. Mary took her daughter's hands and murmured gently about honoring the family and doing God's will, and Aislinn listened as she never had before. Finally exhausted, she climbed into the loft, followed by each sister in turn. Barbara had long since gone to bed, tucked up with Fiona, and the others settled in around them.

"He's gone away then, has he?" Mary asked, quietly accepting the paper packet Morgan handed her when they were alone.

"Aye." He stooped to kiss her cheek, closing his eyes to better take in the soft milky smell of her.

"You're a good son," she whispered, her hand against his cheek.

He kept his eyes closed against the tears that threatened to come and felt her arms go tightly around him.

"'Twill be all right, agra," she soothed. "You've a Father in the Lord and He'll look out for us as He's always done."

He nodded, kissed her again, then went to his corner of the cabin. He lay down in his clothes, turned his face to the wall, and fell immediately into a dark and dreamless sleep.

Mary sat on her stool, staring at the embers in the hearth until the cabin had grown quiet but for the sounds of sleeping, and then she bowed her head and prayed with an open and weeping heart. An hour passed, and then another, and finally there was nothing left to beg of God, only that for which to thank Him—the lives of her children, a roof over their heads, food for tomorrow. She stood stiffly to cover the embers with ash, then went to the back of the cabin and lay down alone on the straw, drawing the thin blanket up to her chin and setting carefully under her pillow Nally's gold earrings—all that was left of him now.

# Eight

ALTHOUGH the evening air carried within itself the kiss of a fine mist that would lie upon the ground before morning, Grace felt no chill. It was in anxious anticipation of the evening ahead that she briskly rubbed her arms, bare in the low, sleeveless evening gown Bram had gotten for her in Dublin. This would be her last chance to wear it before the baby was born; already it had gone snug about the waist. She would have to sit tall and eat very little to remain comfortable during the long evening at O'Flaherty's.

"Gracelin!" Bram shouted up the stairwell. "Come on now! I shan't keep the horses standing any longer!"

Grace winced at the irritation in his voice, but did not jump up. She took a long, deep breath, then covered the powder bowl and rose carefully, pausing briefly before the looking glass to check her appearance. Rich midnight blue velvet fit against her like a second skin, taut across her growing bosom and hips; a small flounce at each shoulder only rendered more smooth and white the skin of her shoulders and arms. She had never spent a summer out of the sun, never given it a thought, but Bram had insisted on hats and long-sleeved gauze work shirts when she was out of doors and the result was this creamy, lightly freckled skin. The low-cut bodice that had made her blush on her honeymoon now caused her no embarrassment; she had learned her husband's appetites and knew he would take pleasure in the other gentlemen's enjoyment of her figure.

"Grace!"

She grabbed the cashmere shawl, picked up her heavy skirts, and went carefully down the stairs. "Here now, you can stop your stomp-ing and barking," she teased. She let down her skirts once she stood in the entry and looked up into his face. "Shall we go, then?" There was no answer. "Bram?"

He closed his mouth and shook his head as if to clear his vision, then came closer, running an open hand down the side of her neck, across her collarbone and down to her bosom. "Perhaps we should skip the damn dinner and stay in tonight," he said hoarsely, kissing her neck.

She pushed him away gently. "Shame on you, Squire Donnelly, after putting the fear of God in me to mind my manners around the O'Flahertys and their high guests, after making me spend all my evenings these past weeks practicing 'proper pronounciation and the polite conversation of the parlor,' after insisting I spend all afternoon squeezing myself into this dress and—"

"All right, all right," he laughed despite himself. "You've made your point. We're off." He turned and clapped his hands. "Brigid!"

The housekeeper appeared in the doorway with a greatcoat for Grace and a carriage blanket for the ride home, which she handed to the Squire. "Missus Donnelly shouldn't take chill in her condition, sir," she said respectfully, adding, "'Tis a beautiful gown on her, and the two of you so handsome together."

Bram screwed up his face, but Grace could see he was pleased.

"Say a prayer for me tonight," she whispered to Brigid as the older woman settled the coat around her shoulders.

"Won't be needing any dressed like that," Brigid whispered back reassuringly.

They left the warmth of the house, walking down the steps to the waiting carriage; Jack would drive them over the hill to Cairn Manor. It was to be her first foray into country high society and she would meet some of the other families who made up the Twelve Tribes of Galway. They comprised Bram's social circle, and several of the men had provided financial backing in his mill enterprises, for which they were realizing a generous return.

Bram was more nervous than she'd ever seen him, questioning and quizzing her throughout the short trip.

"After dinner, you'll go with the other ladies while I retire with the gentlemen for cigars and brandy."

"Where is it the ladies go?" Grace asked.

Bram waved his hand vaguely. "Up somewhere. To fix their hair and neaten their dresses." He leaned in close. "They'll no doubt make reference to your good marriage; how will you reply?"

Grace bit her lip.

"Stop that," Bram flicked her mouth with his gloved hand. "It's childish. Now, what will you answer when they ask, 'And how do you find Donnelly House?'"

"Well, I'll tell them it's easy to find, being so grand and all, and the only one off the avenue by the lake!"

"Be serious!" Bram glared at her.

Grace drew back slightly and cocked her head at him. "Do you really think I'm as thick as all that, Squire Donnelly?"

His anger faded as quickly as it had come up, but his voice was still firm. "This is important, Grace. These people are my friends and my business associates. They will be judging you . . . and by my choice in you, they will be judging me, as well."

"I understand." She turned away and looked out her window into the dark countryside, saying a silent prayer to calm her nerves.

"Bram," she said suddenly. "Will they be holding me up against"— she glanced at him and away quickly—"your first wives?"

He frowned, but said nothing. Then, "Why?"

"They were ladies, were they not? How can I measure up to that?"

"You can't," he said simply. "That's why it's doubly important you rise above your humble upbringing. They'll behave more generously to you if you're shy and demure, and if you keep up a bit of mystery. So no rattling off about ways to prepare potatoes and cabbage, or where's the best bog in which to cut turf."

Grace turned away, stung. "I'm no fool, Bram, and if you don't know that by now . . . well, then it's your mind they'll be questioning, not mine."

"Just do as I say, Grace." He squeezed her hand tightly until she faced him. "You've a high spirit, and that's fine at home . . . in private." His eyes flicked across her body, then back to her face. "But not in public. Not with these people." He moved so close, she could feel his breath on her face. "We'll be raising our children with their children, educating and socializing them together, sending them off to university together, marrying them to each other. You must not bring shame to our children, Grace."

She nodded, her cheeks hot with the unfairness of his words, her throat dry and choked with tears.

And then they were there. The horses stopped and stamped their feet, while Jack opened the carriage door and let them out. The chill evening air cleared her head and braced her with its familiar autumn smell of wood smoke, dying leaves, and fading marigold.

Cairn Manor was a true manor house, enormous by country standards, with a formal garden and hedges, and light blazing from every window. Occasional bursts of laughter shot out into the dark; Grace shivered and put her hand over her stomach.

Bram took her arm and whispered, "You look beautiful."

The door opened and a butler in full dress took their cloaks, passing them to a maid before leading the couple into a crowded drawing room.

"Squire and Missus Bram Donnelly," he announced stiffly.

Conversation died within seconds and all eyes turned upon them. Grace lowered hers to the floor to compose herself, then looked up and smiled, singling out their hostess.

"Good evening!" Missus O'Flaherty hurried toward them, bringing them into the room.

Talk began again, quietly and politely in its separate circles, although Grace caught the end of covert glances whenever she looked around.

"Same old crowd." Missus O'Flaherty was dismissing Bram with an aggressive smile and coquettish batting of the eyes, at the same time she took possesion of Grace. "You know everyone here, I believe, Squire."

Bram took his cue, kissed Grace on the cheek, and moved toward the circle of men near the fireplace, who hailed him boisterously and clapped him on the back.

Missus O'Flaherty led Grace from one group of ladies to the next, nodding and smiling and reeling off long names with bits of ancestry. Grace murmured and lowered her eyes, trying desperately to commit all of it to memory. There were several lords and ladies, many squires, a few land agents whose names she recognized; she knew the solicitor, and Doctor and Missus Branagh, but none of the young married ladies, or the debutantes. This latter group in particular eyed Grace with a mix of spite and curiosity, making little effort to hide their scorn for the country girl who'd snatched away such a prize as Bram Donnelly, a man so far above her station. Thinking of her fine mother and father, her dear grandmother and brother, Grace stood as tall as she could and met every gaze, kind or not, with the graciousness that had been born into her.

With the arrival of new guests, Missus O'Flaherty left Grace in a group of older matrons much caught up in the subject of fine teas. With one ear to the conversation lest a question be put to her, Grace let her eyes wander over the room, which was far more grand than that at Donnelly House. Ornately framed portraits of ancestors and their dogs and horses covered the walls, porcelain figurines and carved ivory from Mister O'Flaherty's adventures in Africa sat on sidetables, shelves, and mounted glassed cabinets. The wood in the room glowed with polish; the window glass gleamed; fire and chandelier light caught and danced in the crystal from which they all drank; diamonds and emeralds and rubies sparkled around the necks and wrists and fingers of the women; the gold and silver of the men's rings, watch chains, cigar clips, and cuff links added to the luster of the room. Grace put her hand to her neck and realized she'd not worn the diamond teardrop Bram had given her, although smaller diamonds hung from her ears. She sipped the sherry someone put into her hand, and was just beginning to relax when dinner was announced.

Bram came immediately to her side, smiling to let her know he was pleased, and offered her his arm into the dining room.

It was all Grace could do to keep from gasping. The room was enormous—a long table ran down its middle with padded chairs all around. Behind the chairs, up against the wall, were twenty servants, the girls dressed in black muslin and starched white caps and aprons, the boys in jackets and white shirtfronts. Grace saw Aislinn McDonagh and began to speak, but caught herself and settled for an exchange of nervous smiles. Brenda O'Flaherty suddenly appeared and coquettishly claimed Bram's arm, her brother Gerald claiming Grace's with equal charm. They were escorted to opposite places at the table: Grace's toward the head, Bram's across and down at the other end. She looked down the long table at Bram in alarm, but he silenced her with his eyes and entered into conversation with Brenda, who was seated on his right.

The table was magnificently set with bowls of hothouse flowers, crystal, china, and silver. Watching the others, Grace placed her linen serviette in her lap, then sat quietly while her dinner partners were seated. Mister O'Flaherty sat at the head of the table with his wife at the other end. On his right was Lady Helen Ashton, visiting from Cheltnam; Gerald O'Flaherty; Grace; Lord David Evans from London; Miss Julia Martin, whom Grace knew to be at college in England; and seven others, including an Austrian count on honeymoon with his new wife, and a lone duchess, on down the row to Missus O'Flaherty, who had seated Bram on her right followed by her daughter Brenda. Doctor Branagh, several debutantes, and the solicitor made up the far side of the table; Eleanor O'Flaherty sat directly across from Grace, her stern, unhappy gaze making an uncomfortable place to rest the eyes. Grace looked down the table to Bram and was rewarded with an encouraging smile.

Gerald gave his attention to Lady Ashton and Eleanor, and Lord Evans was engaged in a political discussion of some heat with Miss Martin, although both seemed to be enjoying it. Grace did not mind her own absence of conversation, was in fact relieved, and concentrated on the lovely surroundings and excellent supper, which was course after course of the most beautifully dressed food Grace had seen since Dublin: oyster bisque with floating butter, a molded salmon salad, slices of roast venison, duck in plum sauce, pears and apples with cheese; and for dessert, cherry preserves, cool refreshing ices, and chocolate gateau, all of it washed down with French wines.

Grace was unable to eat more than a bite or two of each dish for fear her dress would burst, and she was very aware of the waste of food being sent back to the kitchen. She felt apologetic each time a serving girl removed her plate. Aislinn stood across from her, behind Eleanor, and Grace soon realized the girl was in a kind of silent communication with Gerald. Eleanor quickly caught on to the flirtation and tried to shame her brother with a look of obvious distaste, but this only made him more bold, signaling for Aislinn and causing her to bend over so that he might whisper in her ear, presumably about the underdone venison on his plate. Aislinn's eyes widened and a blush spread across her face, her hands trembling as she picked up his untouched plate and carried it back to the kitchen, returning moments later with another cut, prepared more to his liking. Eleanor then signaled to the girl and made similar comments about her own plate; thus, Aislinn was kept moving throughout the entire dinner until her face was pale and drawn, and her eyes harried. Grace's heart went out to her and she wondered if the girl would survive this house. She resolved to speak to Morgan about it, and in the next moment remembered the pained look on his face when she'd offered him money. That gaff had nearly cost her their friendship, and she mustn't let it happen again.

"They're just having a bit of fun with her." Lord Evans spoke in a low voice, dabbing the corners of his mouth with his serviette. He smiled when she turned. "One should not become distressed over the plight of servants. Especially when one is surrounded by good food, excellent wine, and a fascinating dinner partner who is feeling neglected."

"Forgive me," Grace said softly. "I did not mean to neglect you. I thought you were discussing the Repealers with Miss Martin."

Lord Evans sighed. "You are not also interested in Irish politics, I hope."

"I care about my country," Grace said, and then remembered Bram's warning. "But my opinions are closely held."

"What a relief!" He leaned back in his chair and smiled. "Now tell me, why are you troubling yourself over that child?"

"She is the sister of my oldest friend."

"Ah!" Lord Evans's eyebrows rose in amusement at her sincerity. "I take it your friend's family has fallen on . . . difficult times?"

"No," she said, puzzled. "They live as they always have."

"I beg your pardon." He took a delicate sip from the wineglass in his hand. "I do not understand. Your oldest friend is of a . . . how shall I say it . . . less elevated class? And your family encourages this friendship?"

Grace pulled herself erect, then glanced down the table at Bram, who was engaged with Brenda in lively conversation. Safe for the moment, she dropped her guard. "We consider it a blessing to have such good friends as themselves, sir. The McDonaghs are a fine family— honest and hardworking. I know of none better."

"Among the tenant class."

"Among any class." Grace's eyes flashed but she worked to keep her brogue down.

Lord Evans hid a smile in another sip from his glass. "You are a champion of the poor, then, are you, madam?"

Grace did not know what to say to this; she was aware of Gerald's silence on her left and feared he might be listening.

"Poverty and wealth are conditions of the soul, Lord Evans," she said firmly. "An impoverished spirit can befall any man, and indeed, I see more poverty here in this room than I have in any country lane."

Lord Evans tipped his head, studying her with new regard. "Well said, madam." He raised his glass. "May I propose a truce?"

Unsure, Grace reached for her glass. "You've not seen many battles, Lord Evans, if you think we were at war."

He laughed, and moved his chair closer to hers. "To whom do you belong? I must know." He looked around at the table guests. "Wait!" He held up his hand. "Don't tell me. Let me guess."

Grace smiled at this, then nodded.

"I can rule out O'Flaherty and his son—oh, no . . ." His face fell, and he lowered his voice conspiratorily. "You're not with Master Gerald, are you?"

Grace looked at him as though he were mad.

"No, no, of course not," he laughed again, and continued surveying the table. "Not the count—too Austrian," he added.

"And newly married."

"You're clearly not a woman of the world," he teased, then pursed his lips and frowned. "Not the solicitor . . . much too old; nor the doctor, of course . . . I know his wife, lovely woman. Certainly not that chap next to her, and definitely not that one with the mustache . . . hmmm, who is left? Lord Stevens?" He arched his eyebrows at the possibility, examining her.

Grace shook her head, unsure of whom they were speaking.

Lord Evans squinted down to the end of the table, stopping abruptly when he came to Bram.

"You're Missus Donnelly. I'd heard he'd married again." He turned back to Grace, but his smile was stiff now, forced. "You've married hardworking Squire Donnelly, then. Lord Donnelly's son."

"You know my husband?"

"Slightly." He finished off his wine in one gulp. "My father and Lord Donnelly are members of the same gentlemen's club. I must say, I'm a bit taken aback. I'd just assumed he'd married old Brenda."

Grace looked again to where Bram sat, now talking quietly and closely with his dinner partner.

She folded her napkin in her lap. "I know little of my husband's life before we married."

Lord Evans signaled for more wine, directing that Grace's glass be filled first.

"Just as well." He winked in an effort to restore the mood. "He wasn't worth knowing then. Bit of a rogue, you know. It's marriage makes the man, they say—and clearly he's made himself a fine one."

Grace remained serious. "Did he break a promise to Miss O'Flaherty?"

Lord Evans's laugh was short. "Probably." He lowered his voice and spoke close to Grace's ear. "Don't worry about the O'Flaherty girls, Missus Donnelly. What they get, they give back threefold. They like a little intrigue in their rather dreary lives, and are not averse to drama." He paused to moisten his lips. "Trust me."

Grace pulled back, eyes wide. She glanced at Eleanor, who was watching them suspiciously.

"I'm sure I'd rather not be knowing anything else about that, Lord Evans," she said quickly, then winced at the sound of her own country accent.

"Yes." He nodded and she realized his thoughts were swimming in wine. "Quite right. And men can change, rare though it is. I myself bear witness to that."

She swallowed, and glanced around the table for help. All the other guests were engaged in conversation, except Eleanor, who now openly glared at her.

"How old are you, my dear?" Lord Evans appraised her with a knowing eye, taking in the luxurious hair, the smooth skin of her neck and shoulders, and her powdered bosom, where he lingered far longer than was polite.

"Surely that's not a question for another man's wife?" She drew herself up.

Lord Evans nodded. "Right you are. Quite right," he acknowledged, then continued anyway, frowning slightly. "He likes them young, always has. That last one was twenty, but Abigail wasn't much older than you are now. Eighteen, when she left England. And you're not a day over sixteen."

"Seventeen," Grace insisted, then added quietly, "On my next birthday."

Lord Evans nodded. "Lovely age," he said dreamily. "So much ahead, so many possibilites. You look a bit like her, you know."

"Who?" Grace's curiosity got the best of her.

"Abigail. His first wife, a beauty like you . . . my cousin thrice removed or something like that." He waved his long fingers, then let the hand fall to his knee. "We're all related in England, you know, one way or another. Her father was against it—they eloped and came out here. She died in . . . childbirth. He married again rather quickly. But, of course, you know all that."

Grace shook her head.

Lord Evans frowned and peered at her more closely. "You really are an innocent, aren't you? Who are your people?"

Grace again looked round the table, and seeing that everyone was otherwise engaged, said softly, "My father is a tenant farmer on Squire Donnelly's estate."

Lord Evans's eyes grew wide in amazement. "Dear God, you're fresh off the farm! An honest-to-God country girl!"

Conversation suddenly faltered around them and Grace was acutely aware of eavesdropping on either side.

Lord Evans lowered his voice. "Terribly sorry," he said firmly. "Please don't be embarrassed. My fault entirely. I quite understand."

"Understand what?" Grace kept her eyes on her plate.

"Why I'd never seen you before. Why you seemed so genuine, so unspoiled. Why you look at your husband with such open love."

"Is that so surprising? Does he not deserve my love?"

"No."

The hardness in Lord Evans's voice startled her, and she looked up.

He shook his head, then smiled wanly. "I mean to say, dear lady, that I'm sure no man is deserving of a love as pure as yours. You mustn't mind the ramblings of an old drunkard, you know." He slipped his hand into her lap and covered her fingers with a squeeze. "It's only jealousy."

"You're no drunkard." Grace gently removed her fingers from his grasp and took up her wineglass, although she made no move to drink from it. "And you're certainly not old. And I feel no embarrassment coming from a family as fine as my own. So," she said firmly, "let us talk of other things."

He bowed his head to her in a gesture she found at once elegant and dear.

"You are most gracious," he said, then put on his best conversational face. "Quite a wind picking up outside tonight, Missus Donnelly, wouldn't you say?"

She laughed quietly, then paused to listen to the whistle as the wind sped past the corners of the house. Her smile faded as she thought of her family at home in their snug cabin. "Winter's on it's way, sure enough, Lord Evans."

"Then I shall be leaving soon for a warmer climate," he commented.

"Leaving?" Mister O'Flaherty boomed from the head of the table, silencing the guests at that end. "You're not leaving yet, Lord Evans, are you? Not without treating us all to a song."

Grace's eyes widened in surprise. "You're a singer, are you?"

Eleanor laughed sharply from across the table. "He's considered quite a bit more than just a singer. Lord Evans is an accomplished musician and vocalist whose work is known throughout Europe."

Grace lowered her eyes, abashed.

"I am a violinist and composer," he said quietly to Grace. "But my love is the Spanish guitar, which I have spent some years studying. And, in the course of things, I have learned to sing a bit, as well."

"That's very fine. My own mother had the gift of music," she added wistfully. "The most beautiful voice in all the valley."

"I'm sure it was."

Their eyes met and Grace was startled by the emotion she saw there. She did not look away.

"You must play for us tonight, Lord Evans," Eleanor interrupted loudly.

Lord Evans had not looked away, either. "Shall I, do you think?" he asked Grace, as if it were just the two of them in the room.

Grace nodded slowly. "It would be an honor to hear you, sir."

Mister O'Flaherty thumped the table. "Very good! Very good!" he boomed. "If your bellies are full, then push away. Ladies." He looked at his daughter. "Miss Eleanor will show you where to freshen up—not that any of you need it!" He laughed hard at the joke, the others joining in politely. "And, gentlemen, we'll adjourn to the library for cigars and cognac, then on to the drawing room for a bit of music from our own Lord Evans, what do you say, sir?"

"You honor me, Mister O'Flaherty." He paused, then looked across the table. "And it would be my pleasure, providing Miss Eleanor will accompany me on the piano."

Eleanor blushed and fluttered, picking at her skirts and murmuring, "Oh yes, an honor, oh my, I'd be delighted, thrilled actually."

Mister O'Flaherty beamed at them and Grace saw the glow of his matchmaking, although it was behind her own chair that Lord Evans now stood, ready to escort her out of the room.

"Thank you," she said, rising smoothly. "I enjoyed our talk."

Lord Evans smiled. "You didn't, but you're too kind to say so." He paused, as the others began to gather by the door. "I'll be looking for your face in the crowd, Missus Donnelly." He took her hand and kissed it. "Until later."

Grace watched as he left the room with the other men, including Bram, who shot her a quizzical look as he left.

"Let me show you where to go."

The sweet Irish voice belonged to Missus Branagh, the doctor's wife. She slipped her arm through Grace's and led her out of the dining room. As they passed through the entry, she said quietly into Grace's ear, "Lord Evans is quite a charmer, isn't he?"

"That he is," Grace agreed, then her smile faded and she stopped dead in her tracks. "Did I do something wrong, Missus Branagh? Is that why you're speaking to me now?"

"Don't look so alarmed, child." The older woman patted her arm. "You're doing fine." She glanced toward the stairs, where the last of the women were climbing to the second-floor powder room. "The O'Flahertys are looking to match Lord Evans with Miss Eleanor, but I'm afraid you thwarted their intentions by sitting next to him at dinner."

Grace's hand flew to her throat. "'Twas Gerald showed me to my seat!"

Missus Branagh frowned. "There's little brotherly love the boy has for his sisters, and I said to the doctor, he's not changed one bit for all his years away at university."

"What am I to do now?" She thought of Eleanor's sharp eyes.

"Nothing, my dear." Missus Branagh smiled. "What's done is done. But you must try to avoid further conversation with Lord Evans this evening, or it won't look well."

Grace nodded. "I would not want to damage his reputation," she said gravely. "Thank you for telling me."

Missus Branagh took up her arm again and led her to the stairs. "It's not *his* reputation I'm looking after here, Missus Donnelly." She paused, then whispered in confidence, "I married up, as well, you know. I was but a country girl, like yourself, when Doctor Branagh set his cap for me. It took me many years—and many tears, I might add—to learn how to handle this bunch. I don't want you to have it so rough as I did, so you can count on me for friendship."

Grace squeezed her arm gratefully.

At the top of the sweeping staircase was a large room, now crowded with ladies adjusting their hair, smoothing their dresses, powdering their faces, and applying lip rouge.

"Bad enough he marries low and brings her along to flaunt in front of poor Brenda." It was Eleanor's voice. "But then she spends the entire evening flirting shamelessly with my Lord Evans!"

"Actually, she made very interesting conversation," Miss Martin put in coolly. "Which, in your case, would be an oxymoron."

Grace stood frozen in the doorway until Missus Branagh said in a loud voice, "Here we are, Missus Donnelly. Freshen up a bit. Then we'll all go back downstairs and hear some of that delightful music." She led Grace into the room and positioned her in front of one of the full-length mirrors.

Grace could see the redness in her cheeks, but she willed the color out, and out it went. She pretended to adjust her hair and fix the wilted shoulders of her gown, conscious of the diminished conversation around her. Miss Martin caught her eye in the mirror and sent the slightest wink of comradeship before taking herself out of the room and back down the stairs.

When Missus Branagh had done with herself, she collected Grace and the two of them began the long descent, but not before Brenda's voice chased out into the hall after them.

"The lane girls have found each other," she pronounced snidely, and a few of the remaining ladies tittered.

Missus Branagh pulled up the slumping Grace as they went down the staircase. "Stand tall, girl!" she insisted. "It's just sour grapes. He chose you over her."

"And for the life of me, I'll never understand why." Grace shook her head.

The doctor's wife smiled then, and smoothed back the hair on Grace's forehead. "He needs you," she said gently. "He knows you can change his life for the better."

Those words comforted Grace as she entered the music room and joined the other guests. She could not see how she had wrought any change in Bram compared to the enormous change he'd brought to her life. Still, she could see that the women who truly seemed to hold her marriage against her were few and that she could find friendship with interesting women if she sought it. She returned an acknowledging nod to Miss Martin, the woman who went to college and studied law, who was rumored to write articles for the newspaper, not about flower clubs and ladies' leagues, but about O'Connell and Irish politics. Sean would like to know a woman like this, Grace knew, and was gratified when Miss Martin chose the seat next to her before the music began.

"I am not in the countryside long, Missus Donnelly," she said in a lovely throaty voice. "But might I be so bold as to invite myself to tea one afternoon next week? I think you and I might share common ideas about our countrymen." Her eyes were quick and dark brown, full of mischief.

"You'd be more than welcome, Miss Martin," Grace said warmly. "Which day did you have in mind?"

Miss Martin bit her lip, thinking, and Grace smiled—it didn't look at all childish.

"Would Tuesday next suit you?" She looked at Grace directly.

"Tuesday." Grace nodded, then turned to Bram sitting on her other side. "Bram, I've invited Miss Martin to come to tea on Tuesday. Is that fine?"

Bram gave her a look of intense irritation. "Of course," he said, but his eyes threw daggers, which Grace chose to overlook.

"Fine then." Miss Martin nodded briskly, patted her arm, then turned her attention to the front of the room, where Eleanor had seated herself at the grand piano with Lord Evans leaning over her shoulder, plotting their course of music. Grace could see that Eleanor was barely paying attention to his instructions, leaning as she was, ever so slightly against him.

Bram stifled a yawn next to her, and when she reached for his hand, he moved it purposefully away. He was angry now, she knew, tired of the evening and of her making an invitation without his prior approval. Well, she'd convince him of the success of the evening and make it up to him when they got home.

The music was beautiful; Lord Evans had a rich, melodic voice that flowed into the room and eddied around them like swirling pools. It was opera, strange to Grace and in a strange tongue, but there seemed no place he could not go and no place he could not take them. Half an hour passed and he was not the least bit hoarse; indeed he was warmed up and in fine voice. Eleanor's playing was very good and only once did her fingers stumble, making a quick recovery for which he sang even more strongly.

"Now," he said, taking up a beautiful guitar from its case. "If you'll permit me, I would like to sing for you one of Ireland's most beautiful ballads. I dedicate it to Missus Donnelly, whose mother, I'm told, had the finest voice in the valley."

His eyes found Grace and he sang the entire ballad to her. It was "A Rose That Blooms" and Grace's eyes filled with tears to hear the very song her mother had sung so often when she lay abed, a little girl. She clapped more fervently than the others when he was finished, and he seemed gratified by the emotion on her face. Bram, however, was not, and when the musicale had ended, his grip on her arm was like steel.

"We'll say our good-nights now, dearest." His voice was pleasant enough, but she knew that he'd had enough.

Hastily thanking their host and hostess for a lovely evening, and saying a quick farewell to some of the other guests, Bram steered her out into the entry where their coats were waiting.

"Donnelly!" Lord Evans hurried out into the cold night after them.

"Evans." Bram stopped and faced him. "Still in good voice, I see. How's your father?"

Lord Evans shrugged. "I rarely get back to London. And yours?"

It was Bram's turn to shrug.

"You've made Ireland your home, then." Evans blew some warmth into his hands. "And I've met your lovely new . . . wife."

"So I see."

"Aren't you going to invite me to dinner some night?" He smiled at Grace, but his tone was a challange to Bram.

"Certainly," Bram countered. "How long will you be in Ireland? Grace can arrange an evening with Miss Eleanor . . . and her mother, of course."

Evans grimaced. "I was thinking of something a bit more . . . relaxed, shall we say. Just the three of us and some of that good Irish ale you keep in the barn. You do still keep a keg handy, don't you?"

Bram glanced at Grace, who was nothing less than baffled by the entire conversation. "If it's drink you're after, then ride over any evening and I'll fill your cup until dawn. But if it's anything more, then you'd best tie your horse up under Eleanor's window."

"My good man!" Lord Evans lifted his hands in defense. "You're raising ghosts long since put to rest."

"Are they?" Bram eyed him a moment longer, then turned to help Grace into the carriage.

Lord Evans sought Grace's face in the darkness. Moonlight showed up the pools of her eyes and made pale the cool skin of her cheeks.

"Take care, Missus Donnelly," he cautioned.

She dared not return his farewell, but nodded her head slightly.

"Be off!" Bram shouted.

Jack snapped the reins and urged the horses toward home. They had only ridden a few miles and Grace thought Bram had fallen asleep, so silent was he against the opposite side of the carriage. She scooted closer, thinking to put her hand warmer under his head for a pillow, when he snatched her up and thrust her away from him, her back hitting hard the wall of the carriage.

"Bram!" Her voice rose over the sound of the horses' hooves. "What are you doing?"

"You disgust me," he snarled. "Country whore."

She heard the metal slip of the cap from his flask and the swish of whiskey poured down his throat. She held her breath in shock, unable to reconcile the depth of his anger with her actions of the evening, but then, she'd not realized he'd brought his own drink in addition to what he'd had at O'Flaherty's. He had a temper when he drank whiskey; she'd learned that much, but always before she'd managed to stay out of his way and he'd spent his anger somewhere else, falling into a dead sleep for half a day when he got home. He did not appear anywhere near sleep now, and there was no way out of the closed carriage, which was moving at a brisk clip through the lonely wood.

"Disobeyed me at every turn," he muttered, swigging from the flask. "Every turn, damn you!"

"No, Bram," she urged, hoping to persuade him away from his fury. "I did just as you asked."

"Flirting with that damn Evans the entire evening! He called you a farm girl in front of everyone and you let him! You let him!" His speech began to slur now as the whiskey took hold. "I saw him fawning over you, looking into your eyes, and you just smiled away like an idiot. Don't you know what he was up to?"

"Bram," she interrupted.

"Shut up!" He yelled. The horses slowed. "Faster, Jack, stir them up!" he called, and when their hooves began to beat a steady pace along the dirt road, he turned to her again. "It's Abigail all over again, but he won't win this time, either. I'll see to that." He finished off the flask and threw it into the corner of the carriage.

He was so still, Grace dared not move. Then suddenly he smashed his fist against the side of the carriage and his rage was refueled.

"Never knew a day of hard work in his life. You wouldn't know what to do with a man like that, would you? Could you satisfy a man like Evans?"

"No," she whispered, drawing the blanket more tightly around her.

"You made a fool of yourself playing right into his hands, and then you gossip with the doctor's wife—that village hag—instead of finding a suitable friend among the ladies. Don't think I don't know everything you did tonight, Gracelin . . . O'Malley." He spit out her last name as if it were something rotten in his mouth. "You willfully disobeyed me. And over what? Tea with Miss Julia Martin, that highbrow bitch? She's not interested in a village dimwit like you. She just wants to amuse herself! And you fell right in with the joke! You made yourself out to be the evening's fool. They're all laughing over you right now, every one of them, having a good laugh over my simpleton wife."

Grace closed her eyes, humiliation washing through her. She'd spent an entirely different evening from the one he pictured for her, but she saw the truth in his accusations: She had allowed Lord Evans to enter into a bold flirtation with her—had in fact enjoyed his attention—disrespecting her position as wife of Squire Donnelly. Missus Branagh had seen it, had felt compelled to speak to her about it. Everyone knew. And she'd been so full of herself to think that an educated woman of breeding would actually seek out her company. These people cared nothing for her; she had been foolish to think she could count friends among them. Oh, how could she have been so blind? Her eyes filled with tears and she leaned forward to beg his forgiveness.

Instead, he hit her. Hard—hand open, carrying the full weight of his anger. Her head snapped back, hitting the brass lock of the carriage door. She raised her hands in front of her face, but in the dark, his fists seemed to come out of nowhere.

"Stop, Bram, please!" she begged as the blows fell on her face and arms, slammed down on her thighs. "I'm sorry! You're right—I'm a fool!"

He paused for a moment, so that she thought it was over and lowered her hands. The moon came in behind him, and although she could not clearly see his eyes, she believed he was smiling. She relaxed.

"Come here." His voice was hoarse from shouting and the drink, but it was the coldness of it that sent a chill through her body. "Now."

When she didn't move, he slapped her again, grabbed her hair, and pulled her across the seat to him, holding her tightly with one arm. She could barely breathe, didn't dare speak. He ran the fingers of his other hand down the middle of her face, giving a small push to her nose, rubbing her lip against her teeth, pinching the end of her chin, then down her neck, pushing off the wrap, his open hand stroking her chest, down her bosom, squeezing her thigh so hard that she cried out.

"Not so full of yourself now, are you?" he whispered into her ear, biting the lobe. He gripped the front of her dress and yanked, ripping it away from her shoulders and chest, leaving her exposed to the cold air. She could not cover herself, her hands still pinned at her sides, so she closed her eyes. He laughed and buried his face in her bosom, pushing her backward onto the bench. She struggled, but this only seemed to excite him more, and when he couldn't undo her dress, he pushed it up instead, his hands rough and prodding.

"No, Bram, you mustn't," she begged. "You'll hurt the baby."

He laughed again and pinched her inner thigh until she bit her lip to keep from crying out. It was rough and painful, her tears brought no reprieve, and she thought that it would never end, until suddenly he was whispering in her ear that he loved her, he would always love her, she was his world. Abigail, he called her, and began to weep. Abby, oh, Abby. He fell into a kind of stupor and she was able to pull herself out from under him. She huddled in the corner, clutching the torn velvet across her chest, staring out at the moonlight as owls swooped down on tiny fieldmice.

And then they were home. Home, she thought, but it was not her home. Her mind was pulling in its own direction and her thoughts unraveled.

Bram had awakened with the halt of the horses. He shook his head to clear it, then became aware of the moaning and rocking in the corner of the carriage. He sobered immediately and covered her now freezing body with his own coat, whispering that he was sorry, he was so sorry; it would never happen again, he was too easily provoked, he was sorry, it would never happen again. Never. Ever. He would make it up to her. She fell into a kind of daze, his words following her even into her dreams, where they made her groan and shiver. She awoke again in his arms as he carried her up the stairs and put her to bed, gently removing the torn dress, sucking in his breath at the sight of bruises and welts, rubbing her body with flannel and building up the fire until a little color came back into her face; easing her into her nightgown. She looked up at him through her dreams and imagined Morgan had come into the room to kill him. He didn't know how terrible Bram could be and she tried to speak, to warn him away.

"No more," Bram echoed what he thought he heard her say. "Hush now, my darling. Sleep now. You'll feel better tomorrow."

After he'd turned down the lamp and left the room, she lifted her head to see if Morgan still stood behind the looking glass. He was there, and Sean, too, sewing on a stool in the corner near to where Gran bent over the kettle and Da was lighting his pipe, speaking low to Ryan. They were all there, even her lovely mother, who sat down on the edge of her bed and held her hand, leaning over to place a cool cheek against Grace's feverish one. Grace could feel the softness, could smell her mother's scent of rosemary and lavender, could hear the sweet, gentle melody of "A Rose That Blooms." She was with them all again; she had never gone away. It had all been a dream.

# Nine

"How much longer?" Bram waved his spoonful of dripping egg yolk at Grace's swollen belly.

"Another month, I'm thinking." She smoothed her apron, then winced as another kick pushed against her ribs. "Near Eastertime."

"Let's hope so." Bram shoveled down the rest of his breakfast, wiped his mouth, then pushed back the chair and reached for his hat. "It's going to be a busy spring and I won't be around much of the time." He paused, frowning. "I don't like you here on your own."

"You're often away, and I do just fine, don't I?" Grace picked up his plate. "Besides, I've got Brigid."

"Not much, you haven't," he said sharply. "You give her too much freedom, Grace. She comes and goes as she pleases. I want her here all day, every day until this baby is born."

Grace nodded, hoping that Bram hadn't noticed Brigid's absence again this morning.

"I'll be gone again all day," he announced. "That damn agent of mine hasn't collected half the rents, and it's well past Quarterday. Foley can't pay at all. Just as well," he muttered.

"You'll not turn him out, will you, Bram?" Grace held up his jacket, waiting. "He's farmed that piece his whole life. Would still be at it, as well, but for all the sickness they've had."

Bram shrugged his shoulders. "That's not my concern." He slipped his arms into the jacket, then turned to look at Grace, his expression softening at the disappointment on her face. "Well, of course

I feel for the man, and I've given him every chance to make good. But I can't carry him forever; I've got money to pay on my end as well."

"Aye, true enough." Grace handed over his saddlebag. "There's some bread and cheese, a bit of cake, two apples. Don't just work all day, now. Stop and eat what I've given you."

"I always do." Bram slung the bag over his shoulder. "Give us a kiss, won't you, Missus Donnelly?" He bent down to meet her mouth. Their lips touched, pressed harder. He put his hand on her stomach and grinned. "Felt that one. It'll be a strong, healthy boy, for sure. I've got money on it all over town."

"So I'm hearing. They say the birth of a girl will break us!"

Bram laughed. "Never happen. Besides, *your* mother had sons and *my* mother had sons. We'll have sons, as well."

They walked out to the front gate, Grace drawing a shawl over her shoulders against the February mist that hovered over the hills. Nolan was just leading out Bram's prized stallion, the great black.

"Wait." Grace touched Bram's sleeve, then turned and flew into the house.

Bram watched her go, annoyed. "Grace," he called. "I want to leave!"

Nolan brought the horse around to the gate and handed the reins to Bram.

"He's feeling it today, Squire," the boy said, running a hand down the horse's nose. "Must be the bite of spring on the breeze."

Warrior reared, snorting and shaking his enormous head. Bram kept a firm hand on the reins, pulling him slowly back down.

"Easy now, boy. Steady." He turned to Nolan when the horse was settled. "I'm heading to Tib Foley's place. And I've got other stops on the way back, so I'll be gone most of the day. No lying about, now," he ordered. "Or I'll see you whipped. Muck out the stables and mend the fence in the sheep pen. Mind you, mend it properly this time or it'll cost you your job. I don't intend to lose any more sheep to the foxes this year."

Nolan looked down at the toes of his worn boots. "Aye, sir. Sorry, sir."

"Bring in fresh hay and oats for the horses, and stretch the mare. Missus Donnelly can't ride her right now." He put his foot in the stirrup and swung up, then added, "Keep an eye on Missus Donnelly. If anything should happen, get your mother up here quick. Then run for the midwife." He paused. "But only if it's absolutely necessary, hear me?"

Nolan nodded, twisting his cap in his hands. "Aye, sir. As you say."

"Good." Bram glanced at the clouds that had gathered above the clearing mist. "Where is she?" he muttered. "Grace!"

She flew out of the house, leaving the door open. Bram winced at her awkward gait. She handed him a grease-spotted, brown paper package.

"For Mister Foley," she said, catching her breath. "Some mutton and a bit of cake. And a jar of that strawberry jam he's partial to."

Bram stuffed it into his saddlebag, swearing under his breath about old men and pregnant women. Then he pulled up the reins and dug in his heels, calling, "Hah!" to the eager horse.

Grace stood in the gateway, waving him off, although he never turned back to see it.

"Well, he's gone for the day, he is." She turned to Nolan, who stood beside her. "And didn't he leave you with a long list of chores, then?" She smiled sympathetically when he nodded. "You do earn your keep, sure and that's the truth of it. Come in now, and have a bit of food before you start. It's warming in the oven."

Nolan shook his head, then pulled on his cap. "No, thanks, Missus. I better be getting on with it."

Grace watched him as he walked across the yard to the stable, knowing full well he had nothing more in his belly than a hunk of dry bread and maybe a bit of thin gruel; Brigid ate well at the house, but could take nothing home for the children. Nolan was small for ten, but able-bodied; of all the young Sullivans, he was the most serious. The others seemed to come and go with the seasonal work, especially the older boys, but Nolan was there every day and had earned himself a steady job and wage. She knew his brothers only by sight, but she'd been at primary school with Moira, who was a year younger. Even then, Moira had been a veritable font of information concerning the ways of men and women, and she held her place as leader of her peers by dispensing this information bit by detailed bit. Grace had been privy to a few of her stories, and even now, when Moira came to do the milking or churn butter, she painted such explicit scenes that Grace wondered where she got the fuel for her fire. She could only attribute it to Moira being part of an extended family where everyone, including parents and married brothers and sister, slept in the same room. But Grace now had so little contact with anyone outside Donnelly House that Moira had become entertaining company, and Grace enjoyed her frank manner, even the good-natured jealousy over Grace's fortune in "snagging the master."

Moira was curious and pried boldly into Grace's intimate life with the Squire, but Grace just laughed it off, giving away nothing. She carried the knowledge of her beating that terrible night of O'Flaherty's party like a stone in her heart, the weight of it a steady reminder that her marriage was not an open and free place to roam. Moira spoke of the beatings her father sometimes gave her mother, of the way her brothers handled their wives, and so Grace came to the cautious belief that this was the way between most men and women, although she could not remember any such roughness in her own family. They never spoke of it, she and Bram. He'd come to her early the next morning and told her she'd had a terrific fall getting out of the carriage and that she should stay in bed for the next day or two for the safety of the baby. He'd be going away, he said, not meeting her eyes, to the North, to Ulster, on business. It would take most of a week. She had not replied, just watched his face, her body aching and stiff, her heart bruised. He had tossed a small sack of silver on the bed and told her to have Jack take her to Macroom on market day, where she was to buy some things for the nursery. Except on their honeymoon, he'd never offered her money like this, and she recognized the gesture as an apology. Two days later, she'd gone into town and spent most of the money, squirreling away the remainder in the bottom of her wardrobe.

By the time he returned, she had already sewn curtains for the windows, rearranged the great room, and started in on the baby's layette. They never spoke of that night—not the dinner party nor the ride home—but their marriage had been altered and their positions in it shifted. Grace stepped up and claimed her place as mistress of Donnelly House, feeling intuitively that some price had been paid, and Bram stepped out of his position as sole owner. They began a new marriage of uneasy partnership, but soon the uneasiness became a part of them and they no longer recognized it.

The winter had passed slowly with little company to break up the dark days. She had gone once at Christmas to see her family, and once Sean had ridden to the edge of the wood to whistle for her. She had never asked him not to come to the house, but he seemed to know he would not be welcome there. Lord Evans had not pursued an invitation to dinner, for which Grace was thankful, and Miss Martin had returned to Dublin, where it was rumored she stayed late in the pubs, smoking and drinking with other university graduates and arguing the politics of the day like any man. They say she called openly for repeal in her writings, and Grace scanned the newspapers Bram brought home for articles; she did not find them, but followed avidly instead the growing arguments between O'Connell's passive Old Irelanders and the new, aggressive Young. Now that she was obviously pregnant, and forced to avoid public appearance, she sorely missed the company of her brother around the fire and what would surely be passionate opinion and compelling theory.

But she was not unhappy. The dramatic sight of Donnelly House rising from the avenue—the heavy stone walls and massive chimney on one end, with smaller chimneys scattered across the tiled roofline— always gave her pause. Small, leaded glass windows opened to the morning air, catching and reflecting back the sunlight. Ivy grew up thick in the front around the main entrance, and on the sides up to the bedroom windows. Grace had quickly come to love the house, once she'd made her mark on it and felt less like a visitor. She never took for granted its beauty or convenience—especially the indoor privy and the washroom with its big iron tub brought over from England by Bram's second wife. Grace had never had a lying-down bath in her life and enjoyed the luxury of this one, although carrying the kettles of boiling water was too much of a chore for her now and she hated to ask Brigid to do it more than once a fortnight. She kept the house clean and neat, working alongside Brigid rather than hiring extra help, which she knew pleased Bram for the money saved, and she'd put her mastery to work making curtains and draperies, covers for the chairs, and pillow slips.

Bram did not approve of her moving about so much now that she'd grown big, so evenings were spent doing handwork by the fire while Bram looked at the papers or went over his books. They talked generally about the day, or if he was animated, he might discourse on the progress of business deals and his plans for the future. But never did he talk about the past, and Grace knew instinctively that any inquiry would be unwelcome. Nor was he interested in the life she'd led before entering his, and did not encourage reminiscence. Their world was confined to the present day—the two of them and their small household, their business holdings, and the approaching birth of their son.

Realizing this, Grace sighed and wandered into the library. There was much she could be doing around the house and garden; the women she knew worked hard up until the moment the baby came, but she was under strict orders from Bram to rest. She ran a dust cloth over the spines of the beautiful books, having already looked through most of them. There were names on the flyleaves: *Abigail Dunstone* in a fine, firm hand graced novels and art histories; *Mercy Steadham* was the spidery slant in poetry books and ladies' journals. Grace had found herself standing before these books more and more often as her time drew near, running a finger over the names, wondering about the other wives. She was sure that the silver and china had come from England with them, and some of the furnishings, as well, but she did not know exactly. The only other trace she'd found of their lives in this house was a velvet-covered case in the bottom of Bram's steamer trunk. The lid was fine needlepoint, two entwined hearts bearing the initials *A.D.* and *B.D.* It was surely Abigail's, the name Bram sometimes called out . . . in his sleep. Grace lifted one of the leather-bound novels from the shelf and held it up to the window light to see again the strong hand.

"She was a beauty, like yourself." Brigid had come quietly into the room and was shaking out the heavy drapes. "The toast of England, they called her, and with a different suitor every day of the month. She was engaged to marry a fine young lord, but when she and the Squire set eyes on one another, that put an end to it all. 'Twas she brought most of these books, but scarce else."

"How long were they married?" Grace ran her fingers over the handwriting.

Brigid glanced around the quiet room, then out the window, listening.

"He's gone out for the day," Grace said.

Brigid frowned, hesitant, then moved closer. "Four years, they were married, if that."

"How did she die?"

"Hard birth." Brigid kept her eyes off Grace's belly.

"Tell me about her?" Grace put the book back on the shelf and sat down.

Brigid glanced again out the window. "'Tis a longish tale," she said anxiously.

"He's ridden out to Tib Foley's," Grace assured. "It'll be hours. Please, Brigid. I'd like to know."

Brigid nodded and wet her lips, pausing for a moment to remember. "Well, they were both young and headstrong people, used to getting what they wanted. Lord Donnelly had arranged a different sort of marriage for the Squire, and Miss Abigail was engaged to a wealthy lord. But when she and the Squire set eyes on themselves, they could have no other, and so they run off. Miss Abigail's father turned his back on her for the shame of it, and Lord Donnelly was furious. Wasn't the Squire his favorite son and all sorts of grand plans made for him? But it was a scandal, so Lord Donnelly sent them here." Brigid moved away from the window and sat down on the edge of the divan. "I'll say this for Miss Abigail—she was a true lady, gracious as any queen, and she loved the folk here, always riding out to see the way of it herself, coming right into the cabins to sit at the table and share a meal, taking on our problems as her own, and working to make things right. She'd come as close to death as a person can with the terrible birth of her first, turned around and tangled up he was, dying and trying to take her with him. But she loved life and fought her way back. They buried him in the cemetery on this land. She should never have tried another baby, but being herself, she did." Brigid shook her head and sighed. "The young lord she'd left behind came to Ireland, here to the house, but Miss Abigail's time was at hand again and I think she knew she was going to die this time, as she sat upstairs and would see no one. He stood in the courtyard, in the pouring rain, calling her name, but we run him off before he could upset her." She stopped. "'Twas ten years ago, and myself a mother six times. Seemed terrible unfair. Himself went near mad with grief, and when Miss Abigail's brother came from England to claim the body, they had to wrestle the poor Squire out of the house. He wanted them buried here with the other, you see, mother and dead sons, but her family wouldn't hear of it and Lord Donnelly sided with them." She frowned. "Odd it is, that neither wife was buried here."

"Neither one?" Grace asked softly, hesitant to interrupt.

"Miss Mercy's family come to claim her body, too, after she died. There was a fight, sure enough, left both men bloody. Her father and the Squire, that is. Mister Steadham accused the Squire of . . ." Brigid caught herself and closed her mouth firmly.

"Of what?" Grace leaned forward.

Brigid stood up, anxious again. "Well, isn't it all over now? Himself finally settled down with a good wife, a child on the way. Wouldn't he be angry at me talking up his past misery?"

"Please, Brigid," Grace implored. "I must know all of this if I'm ever to understand him and make him happy."

"Ah, Missus, you don't want the trouble of it! 'Tis nothing but a pack of lies. The English, what do they know of us, anyway?" She crossed the room and stood before the fire, warming her hands.

"The Squire is English."

Brigid slumped. "Aye," she said quietly. "I forget sometimes he's not one of us." She squeezed her hands together. "No sense in trying to understand him, then, is there? Just try to get along."

"You must tell me," Grace said firmly. "I swear no one will ever know."

Brigid smiled weakly. "Wouldn't matter if they did. There's many thinks they know the story already . . . but no one really does."

"How long were Miss Mercy and the Squire married?" Grace asked, sitting on a low stool near the fire.

Brigid counted on her fingers. "Not two years."

"And how did she die?"

"Brain fever," Brigid said grimly. "She was weak, had a cough even when he brought her home from England. I don't know as I ever saw her in good health. She was the daughter of his father's cousin, one of those English beauties with pale skin and fine bones. And money of her own, of course. Not strong and full of life like the first one. Lovely hair and a good figure on her though, and a love for children. Many times that first year, she come down to help after my Mary was born and I so weak all the time. Looked after the little ones and cooked a bit, till the master said she must save her strength. They were hoping for a child themselves, you see."

"She never carried?"

"No." Brigid shook her head. "Just wouldn't take. She'd miss her monthly and get all excited, but in seven or eight weeks she'd take to her bed with the heavy bleeding of it. Brain fever come for her in her second winter here; she was sick for months and died in the spring."

Grace looked into the low flame of the fire, her heart heavy.

"When they come for her, of course, they saw how wasted she'd become locked away in that room. Her father stood right where you're sitting now, pointed his gun, and accused the Squire of murdering her."

"Murder!" Grace was stunned.

"Aye." Brigid twisted the corner of her apron in her fingers. "'Twas a terrible thing. Terrible."

"But why murder?"

"She'd gone mad, you see." Brigid became agitated. "Ranting and raving. Himself had to lock her in for her own good! At first he'd go to her at night, to talk and be a bit a company. But it got worse each time until she'd start screaming the minute he opened the door, throwing and smashing things, calling him names not fit to repeat. He had to do it to keep her safe. We took out most of the furniture and anything that might break; anything she could hurt herself with, he said. And then, of course, when she tried to throw herself out the window . . ." Brigid paused, her shoulders sagged. "We had to tie her to the bed. He took her meals in himself and fed her when she was calm, and he'd wash and care for her, as well. She was too violent, he said, to risk anyone else going in to her and he wouldn't hear of putting her away. And then, finally, she died, may God have mercy on her soul." Brigid crossed herself fervently.

"My God." Grace could hardly believe what she was hearing.

"My God, indeed, Missus," Brigid echoed.

Grace took a deep breath, then let it out slowly. "How terrible. For all of you. How very terrible."

"Aye." Brigid frowned. "And I've put it all in your head now. Can be no good for the baby. This house needs no more misfortune. God knows it's true."

"It's all right, Brigid." Grace took her hand. "It's better for me to know this from you, rather than finding it out from others who don't care about him. Thank you for telling me."

"Please, Missus, don't bring it up to him. Just leave it buried."

Grace had never seen Brigid beg and it made her uncomfortable. "Would I do a thing like that?" she reassured. "It'll be our secret."

Brigid sighed in relief, then jumped when the big clock in the entry struck the hour.

"Sure and that can't be the time!" She untied her apron. "Me and Jack have to take the wagon to fetch our Decla's husband into Macroom. He's catching the boat out of Cork City for London tonight, then he's off to America to make their fortune." She laughed a little. "Just looking for a bit of adventure, is what me and Jack are thinking, but Decla stands by him." She paused before going through the door. "Is this all right, Missus?" Her voice was anxious as she took in Grace's belly. "No one's on the place, then, but Nolan."

"I'll be fine." Grace shooed her away. "I've another month to go at least, by my counting, although 'tis true, I'm big as a barn."

Brigid didn't smile. "Be sure to call Nolan for any lifting or carrying."

"I will." Grace stood slowly and stretched. "Don't worry about me now. I'll just sit here by the fire and sew."

"Good." Brigid set Grace's work basket at her side. "I'll be back come evening."

Grace heard Jack hallo for his wife and Brigid's answering, "Hush you," then the crunch of wagon wheels against rock as they set off down the drive. She went to the window and stood, aware of the great quiet that settled on the place now that it was practically empty. Her mind was full of Bram's earlier life and all the suffering, and she thought she better understood now the helpless rage that came out of his drink. And yet she was troubled by the hints of violence that forced her to recall the episode of months ago. Who was this man—really— to whom she now belonged? He was her husband, certainly, but not her friend. Friendship involved loyalty and trust. Was he loyal to her? Could she trust him?

A nervous anxiety took hold of her and she felt sick to her stomach. It had been a long morning; she needed to eat. She would have a slice of bread and butter, a cup of tea. The food comforted her, and she looked around the spacious kitchen. It had been a long time since she'd prepared a really grand meal, and it would occupy a mind that now felt so unsettled. There was a cut of beef to roast, and potatoes from the storehouse. She'd make a gravy from the drippings, and suet pudding, and she'd boil winter greens from the nearly bare garden.

She drank the last swallow of sweet tea, brushed the crumbs from her blouse, then got out the heavy pan and fired the oven. While the oven heated, she went out the door and carefully through the mud to the little patch of green sheltered around the side of the house. Crossing to the storehouse, she gathered the best-looking potatoes, herbs, a squash, and some dried apples, filling her basket so that she had to carry it with both hands out in front of her.

When she returned, the kitchen felt close and oppressive after the fresh, breezy spring air. The anxiety that had spurred her to action now gave way to sudden depression, and a deep fatigue spread through her limbs. She would have stopped, but it was well past noon and there was no time for a nap or supper would be left undone. She nibbled at an apple, then scrubbed the praties and put them in a pot to simmer, leaving the cut greens to soak in salted water. She rubbed the meat with salt and herbs, and set it in the pan. The kitchen was now warm and fragrant, but she could not put down her uneasiness and growing sense of foreboding. Mechanically, she went to the oven and took out the browned apple cake, setting it on the counter to cool, then lifted the meat pan to the oven. As she slid it in, a terrific pain tore through her belly, dropping her to her knees, hands pressed against her abdomen until it passed and she could breathe again without pain. Five minutes went by, then ten, then another spasm gripped her, stronger than the last, and she closed her eyes, moaning, sweat beading on her forehead. Water puddled beneath her, soaking her skirts.

"Oh, dear God," she whispered, crawling slowly to a chair near the window. She rested for a moment, then pulled herself up. "Nolan," she called, but her voice was too weak.

She watched him cross the yard with the water buckets, then disappear. A moment later he returned, water spilling over the edge of the buckets.

"Nolan!" she cried again, but he didn't hear, and she put her head down on her arms, holding herself very still. Then came another pierce of the knife deep within and she clamped her teeth as pain ricocheted through her body, blacking out all thoughts except survival. When it subsided and she could breathe again, she raised her head and spied a wooden bowl lying on the table. Steadying herself, she pulled it toward her and gripped it in both hands. She waited, afraid that another pain would come and she'd miss her chance. Finally, he came into view and she heaved it through the window, shattering the glass. He turned, startled, dropped the buckets, and ran toward the house.

"The baby," she gasped when he burst into the kitchen. "It's coming."

He turned white. "I'll fetch Mam."

Grace shook her head, another contraction beginning its rise. "No," she panted. "Gone."

"I'll get someone! Don't worry!" His voice rose with panic.

Grace opened her mouth to speak, but screamed instead, frightening him out of the house. She heard him yell for Moira, and then she fainted.

Stinging slaps to her face brought her back to consciousness. She opened her eyes and saw Brigid's face, dark with worry.

"Thank God you've come back to us," she said. "Stay awake now. It's time."

Grace's head swirled with confusion and the darkness of the unbearable pain. It was as if her body had caught fire and she could not escape it.

"Raise your knees, now, Missus," Brigid shouted, pushing them up herself when Grace did not respond. "Come on now, girl, you must do this!" Quickly, she tied a clean apron over her skirt and moved a stack of cloths closer to the bed. "God forgive me," she muttered. "'Tis my own fault for raising ghosts, then leaving her all alone with them. Up now!" she commanded. "You can't birth it lying flat!"

Grace did as she was told and was rewarded with such a searing burn that she wanted to crawl right out of her skin.

"I can't stand it," she gasped. "Am I dying, Brigid?"

"Only for a little while," Brigid said grimly. "You've got to take the pain and go with it. Listen to your body, now. When it tells you to push, that's what you're going to do."

Grace lay back, breathing deeply. Steam rose from the basin of boiling water in the corner of the room and someone had closed the curtains against the coming night.

"I was in the kitchen, cooking . . ." she rambled. "How did I get here?"

"Hush now," Brigid clucked. "Don't waste your strength talking. Jack's gone for Doctor Branagh. 'Twas myself and Nolan carried you, though sure the poor boy could've lifted you up with one hand, so shook he was. Never been so glad to see his old mother in all his life. Carries his heart on his sleeve for you, that one does."

The pain, now familiar, began its steady climb. Grace reached for Brigid's hand and tried not to panic.

"First one's always hardest," Brigid soothed. "Feels as if you're giving birth to twenty grown men instead of one wee babe, but it'll soon be over. Trust me, now. Haven't I done this thirteen times and lived to birth yours, as well?"

She gripped Grace's hand in answer to the grip she recieved, and moaned when Grace moaned, calling through the haze of pain, "Push, now, girl! Push!"

Pushing felt better than not, so Grace gave into it, stopping when her body seemed to signal a stop, pushing again when her body demanded it. There was an enormous pressure, then almost instant relief from the pain and she heard Brigid's voice saying, "You've done it, Missus! It's a boy! You've got a son!"

Grace laughed and cried as she looked down through her legs at the red, screaming baby covered with what appeared to be a white paste. Then another pain pulled and twisted deep inside.

"There's more," she panted.

"Just the afterbirth," Brigid said confidently, cutting the umbilical cord. And then she gasped. "Jesus, Mary, and Saint Joseph himself! 'Tis another one, true enough! Just look at that head!"

Grace had only to push a little bit when she felt the baby slide out, and then there was that blessed relief.

"A girl!" Brigid was astonished. "A wee little thing!"

"A girl," Grace repeated weakly, listening to the cries of her babies.

"You've not got any more in there, now, have you?" Brigid peered tentatively between her legs.

"No more," Grace wheezed, then let her head drop back against the mattress, resting while Brigid cut the second umbilical cord, then set to work cleaning up the two babies.

She finished the boy first, wrapped him tightly in fresh linen, and laid him on Grace's breast.

"Get him to suckle a bit," she said, brushing a fingertip over the baby's lips. "He's smaller than the girl, but he's got a good-size head on him."

Grace supported the hot little head with its damp crop of silky hair, resting the baby's mouth against her nipple. Her breasts did not yet feel full, and so she was not surprised when he refused it. His lips quivered, but soon his eyes closed and he fell asleep.

"And what will you be calling them?" Brigid lifted the limp baby and placed him in his cradle, returning with his sister. This baby latched on immediately and began to suck with such vigor that Grace winced.

She looked into the tiny face where wide, dark eyes stared back. "She's Mary after my gran, and Kathleen for my own mother. Mary Kathleen," she whispered to the infant, who widened her eyes even more and sucked harder.

"And the boy?" Brigid glanced toward the still bundle in the cradle near the low fire.

"He shall be called Michael after the Squire's grandfather. And perhaps Brian for a second name."

Brigid nodded. "Aye. For the great king." She bundled up the linens and set them near the door. "'Tis a fine name that: 'Michael Brian Donnelly.' A strong name." She went near the cradle and looked down into the baby's face.

Grace felt her eyes closing. "Can you take Mary Kathleen, Brigid? She's done and I'm slipping away as I speak."

Grace fell immediately into a deep, exhausted sleep, even while Brigid was changing the rags for fresh and washing her legs. The room was quiet but for the breathing of three tired souls and the tick of the clock, and the snap of the fire now and then as the flame began to burn low. Brigid found herself drawn again and again to the cradle where the two babies slept. The girl looked well enough, but the look of the boy troubled her. Something was not right there, but she couldn't see it, although she'd counted fingers and toes three times now. She'd never had early babies herself, let alone twins. She shook her head as Grace moaned in her sleep.

"Sure and they're a month early by the looks of them, but the boy's head . . ." she mumbled to herself, worrying her lower lip with her teeth. "That's what it is, all right. The head appears swollen."

She sat down in the rocking chair and pulled out her rosary, fingering the beads as she moved her lips in prayer, starting again when she'd finished, keeping a watchful eye on her charges.

Bram was late coming in, and drunk. Having been met by young Nolan with the news of the birth, he'd begun celebrating immediately with a round of drinks at O'Devlin's. His singing woke Grace and she listened as Brigid flew down the stairs and told him to hush now, mother and babies were sleeping. He had a son, she began to tell him, and a . . .

"A son!" Bram's voice boomed through the house. "I knew it would be! I'll see for myself!"

He brought with him the smell of fresh, cold night air and strong whiskey. His wet hair dripped on Grace as he bent to kiss her.

"Out in the rain without your hat, were you, Squire Donnelly?" She smiled up at him, drowsy with warmth and contentment.

"We've got a son." His eyes filled with drunken, dreamy tears.

"Over there." She tipped her head toward the cradle in the corner. "A wee daughter, as well."

His eyes went wide with amazement. "A daughter? A boy and a girl?" He hurried to the cradle, peering in as if he'd never seen two babies in all his life. "Which is which?" he whispered.

"The boy has a bit of light hair, the girl's is thicker and darker."

He lifted the boy out and held him awkwardly before placing him in Grace's outstretched arms.

"He's a fine-looking lad, young Michael."

"I thought Michael Brian, if it's to your liking," she said shyly.

He nodded. "A fine name." He looked into the little boy's face, lifting the tiny chin with one finger.

"And the girl is Mary Kathleen after Granna and my mother."

Bram kept his eyes on the boy. "Fine," he said softly. "She's your daughter. Call her anything you like."

Mary Kathleen woke then and began to cry for her milk. Grace bade Bram put the boy back in the cradle and bring the girl to her.

Bram brought her the red-faced girl and watched as Grace unbuttoned the top of her nightgown to nurse the child. His gaze was so intent as the baby began to suck that Grace became flustered and her nipple popped out of Mary Kathleen's mouth. The baby screamed with frustration, her tiny fists flailing until Grace got her resettled.

"Demanding, that one," Bram said, but Grace heard approval in his tone.

He stayed until she was done, took a last look at his son, then left to bed down in his own room.

In the morning, Brigid brought her breakfast in on a tray, but Bram came up shortly after with his coffee. He was as polite and tender with her as in the early days of their marriage, and Grace rested peacefully for the first time in months. But two mornings later, she knew that little Michael was not well. Mary Kathleen had awakened regularly every two or three hours to nurse until she was full and milk dribbled out the side of her mouth. Michael had yet to give more than a few tentative sucks before whimpering and falling into a fitful sleep. She was anxious for him all that day and kept him tucked into the bed with her, putting him to her breast as often as she could and cooing to him to wake up now and eat.

"He's not well," she said right away to Bram when he came in with her dinner tray. "He cannot suck."

Bram shrugged, tired from the long days and sleepless nights, damp and muddy from the constant drizzle that had fallen since the babies were born.

"They sleep a lot in the beginning, women tell me. He'll wake up hungry any day now."

"But his color's odd—he's gone yellow in the face and hands. And he whimpers in his sleep." She set her jaw and looked up at Bram. "I think we should call Doctor Branagh."

Bram frowned and rubbed a hand over his face. He needed a shave.

"We're not going to call in the doctor for every little thing. Especially that hayseed Branagh. I don't want everyone knowing our business." He looked at her with irritation. "Besides, I thought you farm girls knew all about babies."

Grace stared at him, then picked up Michael and held him in her arms. She said nothing.

Bram relented. "Well, anyway, he's gone to Cork City. I passed him on the road yesterday afternoon, and he asked about the babies."

"What did you say?"

"That they were fine."

Grace's eyes filled with tears.

Bram shifted in the chair. "Well, they *were* fine then, weren't they? You're overwrought, is all. Tired from being up all night with that greedy one over there." He glanced toward the cradle where Mary Kathleen slept. "What does Brigid say?"

"That Mary Kathleen might be taking most of the milk. She says keep him in the light and the yellow will go away, and then he'll wake up enough to suck."

"Do that, then." Bram stood and walked to the window.

"I have! But it's been so dark!"

As she spoke, clouds gathered and rain began to spatter against the glass. Bram stared at his reflection.

"Send the girl out to nurse," he said and Grace's heart lurched. "There's a woman, out toward Agahmore, nurses newborns. Husband's dead, so it pays her rent. Have Brigid take the baby to her tomorrow."

"Send her out?" Grace could not hold the tears and they spilled over her cheeks. "Oh, Bram. I couldn't send her away from me. How could I do that?"

Bram turned and gave her a hard look. "Send her out or lose our son." He softened his voice, trying to convince her. "It won't be for long, Grace. You said so yourself. A few days in the light and he'll start in. Give him a week or so to put on some weight and get the best of your milk, then you can bring the girl back and care for them both."

"Can we not bring the woman here?" Grace pleaded.

Bram shook his head. "She's got children of her own and a home to tend. And other babies in her care. I'll pay her well. The girl will get plenty of milk, and she'll be well looked after."

Grace bit her lip and looked down at her quiet, yellow son. "All right, then," she whispered. "If you think it's best."

"Good girl." Bram came and patted her on the head. "I do think it's best. And if young Michael hasn't improved in a few days, we'll have someone out to look at him."

"Doctor Branagh," Grace said firmly, eyes down.

Bram sighed with annoyance. "Or the midwife, or someone who knows something about babies, and can keep their mouth shut."

Grace slept not at all that night. Michael sucked fitfully, but never opened his eyes. Mary Kathleen looked so healthy next to him, with her pink cheeks, dark hair, and bright, shining eyes. She cooed and nursed with as much vigor as always and Grace cried each time at the thought of letting her go. Morning came and she nursed the baby one last time, holding her so tightly that Mary Kathleen yelped and scowled. Brigid stood silently nearby, then scooped up the baby, bundled her, and took her out into the cold morning air. Grace got out of bed, made her way to the window, and watched until the carriage was out of sight. When Brigid returned an hour later, she reported that the baby had taken enthusiastically to her nurse and was doing fine.

Grace dressed herself, then sat by the window, rocking Michael and praying fervently for sunlight to break through the dark clouds. She sang to him, whispered love to him, begged him to open his eyes and suck, and he would, but never for very long and never so much that his mouth overflowed with her milk. Bram came in the evening and said to give it a few more days, he was getting all the milk now and would soon be fine. In the end, however, it wasn't Doctor Branagh they called, but the casket maker.

Grace's son died deep in the night of his eighth day, head swollen atop a thin body, his skin the color of marigolds. He lay next to his mother in the bed, her arm loosely around him, her ear near his mouth to mark his breathing. It had been steady, though light, and she had fallen into a weary sleep wherein she dreamed the dream that had saved her life so long ago on the night of her mother's death. Again, Kathleen's voice came singing down the hill with the choir of angels, again hers rode over the top of the others calling out, "Breathe, breathe!" and Grace awoke with a start, pulled the still bundle into her arms and cried out the same words, but it was too late, she had not been strong enough to anchor him in the world as Granna had anchored her. Unbelieving, she loosed the blanket around his tiny shoulders and chest, felt for the weak beat of his heart, touched the golden skin of his face, and willed him to open his eyes. When he did not, she sat up in the bed and cradled him in her arms, crooning softly to him every lullaby she knew. Her breasts ached from all the milk he could not drink, and she held him tightly, brushing her nose along his downy head, breathing in the sweet scent of him, rocking, rocking until the first light of morning crept quietly into the room and her vigil was ended.

         ✧   ✧   ✧

When Bram came striding into the room after his breakfast, Grace was still holding the dead child, singing softly, her voice now hoarse. She looked up and saw him as if from far away, watched as his rested, confident face paled with shock. She frowned when he reached for the baby, and shook her head. He sat down in a chair across from her and they regarded one another; she with great detachment, he with stunned bewilderment. And then he got up and left.

He had always been, if nothing else, a decisive man, and in this he buried his grief. Brigid was ordered to Grace's room, where she soothed the disturbed mother, and eased the child out of her arms. The casket maker was called, and the wood chosen.

"He'll have the best!" Bram insisted, then shut himself away with a bottle of whiskey. "He's a Donnelly, by God!"

The whiskey broke down his fortress, and he ranted and raged at God and his wife. The storm passed as quickly as it had come, and though new lines of bitterness marked his face, he seemed resigned to this latest blow of misfortune. He remained distant from everyone, especially his heartbroken wife.

Grace could not lie in a bed that was empty of both husband and baby, and so she arose and dressed, resuming her duties mechanically. She knew that grief had made her numb, but she had no idea how to save herself. Perhaps the other child, the girl. But she was afraid of losing her, as well, and so left her where she was. Unable to cry, barely able to think from one moment to the next, she carried her son's new-born gown through the house, becoming frantic when the smell of him began to fade. She folded the gowns he'd worn, the nappies, booties, and cap, wrapped each piece in tissue, and laid them in the bottom of her keepsake chest. The other clothes she sent to Mary Kathleen's nurse. With nothing to hold now, nothing to fill her empty hands, she turned again to her needle and began to embroider a casket cloth. Her hands did what she wanted, but there was no light in her design. She could not remember joy. In despair, she contemplated her own death.

# Ten

THEY all came to the wake—Ryan and Aghna, Granna, Patrick, and Sean, who suffered the cold, jolting ride in the wagon. It was he who finally calmed the waves of grief that smashed against her heart, quoting his beloved book: "And all wept and bewailed her, but He said, 'Weep not, she is not dead, but sleepeth.'"

He took her hand and led her out into the sharp night, away from the hushed voices in the sitting room. There was no loud keening as there had been for their mother—Bram's proper English sensibilities would not allow for such an emotional scene—and now Grace understood what a relief it would have been to make that sound, to throw her apron over her face and let go of all the tight, burning pain that banded her heart. Instead, she had to restrain herself and act as though she had accepted this blow. She sat quietly in mourning, graciously offering tea or coffee or whiskey to her husband's guests and nodding at their stories of other sorrows. Sometimes she thought she might burst out laughing as she looked at the ladies whispering over their teacups; other times she was shocked at the rage that welled inside her.

"We're all of us sick at heart for you, Grace," Sean said when they were outside away from other ears, his voice full of anguish.

"And what do you know of it?" she asked bitterly, hating the sound of her own voice, but unable to alter it. "You've never had to hold the dead body of your innocent child in your arms."

"No," he said. "Nor will I know the joy of one that lives."

"Then you're blessed, to be sure." She wrapped her arms around herself and stared at the hard, black ground.

Sean stayed quietly beside her, the hushed voices of those inside the only noise around them.

"You don't mean that." He put his hands on her shoulders and turned her to face him. They were the same height, brother and sister, and they looked eye to eye. "He must've been grand, Gracie, and I'm sorry I never knew him."

His words penetrated the fog of her pain, and suddenly she felt it so sharply, she thought she could not bear it. She clutched her heart, and he caught her as she began to fall, holding her tightly in his arms.

"Weep, now, and never mind them inside," he whispered. "What are they to you that you must hide your grief in front of them?"

She began to wail then, blinded and choking as tears ran thick and heavy down her face, soaking her brother's shoulder, shaking his body along with her own. The voices inside the house had fallen silent as her shrieks swept through the hills and echoed in the night.

"Would you like me to call out your husband?" he asked gently when her sobbing ebbed and she was still.

She shook her head against his chest.

"Is he no comfort to you, then? Because the boy is lost? His heir?" He stroked her hair, felt the heat of her emotion in its dampness.

She wiped her eyes on his jacket, then lifted her head. "He dares not say anything about it," she said. "Because it may be he who weakened the baby."

Sean frowned. "And how would he do such a thing?"

She studied his face, her beloved brother who should already know in his heart what had happened to her and not make her say the words.

"Was he cruel to you, Grace?"

"Aye," she confessed, and the weight of it fell from her shoulders. "Early on, before Christmastime. It was only the once," she added quickly. "And he was drunk, I'm ashamed to say."

"It's not you should feel ashamed," he said, his face hard. "What kind of man is it, beats a woman carrying his child?"

She had no answer.

"Why did you not tell us?"

"What could you have done?" she asked plainly. "And after a while, it seemed as if it might have been just a bad dream. We never spoke of it."

"You should never have married him." Sean glanced over his shoulder at the shadows of those inside. "He doesn't love you."

"And how do you know that?" she demanded.

"Because I've seen the face of a man who does, and the light in his eyes when he speaks your name makes the eyes of your one in there seem cold and lifeless as an empty hearth."

They stared at one another.

"What are you saying?" Grace whispered.

"Morgan loves you," he said simply. "He's the man you should've married."

Grace slammed her fists into his chest, knocking him back against the porch post, her face red with fury. "Damn you, Sean O'Malley," she cried. "Damn you for saying that!"

He caught her fists before she could strike him again. "Don't you love him, Grace. Because God knows I think you do!"

She shook her head, weeping.

"Leave Donnelly," he insisted. "You should never have married him in the first place. Leave him and marry Morgan."

She yanked her wrists out of his grip, and in the light that spilled from the window, he saw how terribly tired she was, how defeated and heavy with the weight of her life, and he realized he'd done nothing but pile on another stone. But he could not take back the words.

She pulled her shawl tightly around her shoulders and turned away from him. "It makes no difference who I love and who I don't," she said, her voice weary and far away. "I stood up before God and married Bram Donnelly. For better or for worse, I promised. Before God. I cannot break my promise to God, Sean. He's already taken my son."

"God doesn't cause the misery in our lives," Sean said softly. " We do that ourselves. God is our path through it." He pulled a ragged book from his pocket and put it into her hands. "Mam's Bible. Take it now and use it to find your way, for who better than God can understand the pain of losing a son?"

Her eyes filled with tears.

"And there's something else. Not about Morgan." He hesitated. "Though I want you to know that Donnelly will pay if he ever lays a hand on you again. I may be no match for a man like that, but nothing will stop Morgan from coming, mark my words."

"I know," Grace said, remembering the night Bram had beaten her and the later vision of Morgan behind the looking glass. "He was there." Her eyes cleared and she turned them fiercely on her brother. "And that will be the last time we ever speak of him this way."

"Grace . . ." he pleaded.

"No." She held up her hand, then added softly, "I couldn't bear it, Sean."

"All right," he said. "But what I had to say is about Mary Kathleen." He took her hand. "Your husband has made you believe that a son is everything and a daughter beside the point."

She started to protest.

"He has," Sean insisted. "Or why would you keep her at another woman's breast when your own are aching for her?"

She stood for a long moment, thinking. "Aye," she said at last. "I must have been out of my mind to send her away."

"You were," he said gently. "And isn't it time now to bring her home?"

Brigid went for Mary Kathleen at dawn, over Bram's protests. It was too much for Grace to cope with so soon after Michael's death, he insisted; let the baby stay out to nurse for another month or two, until summer, at least. But Grace held firm. She'd have no milk soon and then the baby would have to stay with the nurse; she'd not know her own mother by that time. The child was a Donnelly, boy or not, and she was coming home. They argued through the night until Bram at last gave up, outwardly disgusted with her insistence, but inwardly unnerved by her refusal to bow to his wishes. He maintained the upper hand by forbidding her to go in the cart over the winter frozen ruts in the road, and she was now savvy enough to concede this point. However, she stood in the doorway the entire morning until Brigid placed the warm bundle of her baby daughter back in her arms.

With Mary Kathleen in a cradle by her feet, Grace took up her needle and finished the burial cloth that would drape her son's small coffin. She announced that the burial would take place in three days and she insisted they place the tiny body out in the storehouse where it was coldest. No one argued; they could see she had changed. Bram came and went silently, not daring to interrupt the reverie in which she worked. All who glimpsed the casket cloth said it was the most beautiful piece of work to visit the earth. Pale morning stars in gold thread, angels with magnificent wings wrapped tenderly around the children they carried, a hundred mothers' faces turned toward the sky, garlands of roses and lilies and love-lies-bleeding, intricate banners with God's promise of life everlasting. And above all, Lord Jesus at the gate, arms waiting to receive the children, His heart in His hand. It was an extraordinary vision, and all who looked upon it came away with wonder.

When the child had been buried and the magnificent cloth folded and put in the chest, there were those who said she would never again do such work, sure and weren't her hands nearly crippled from holding the needle and cloth for too many hours too many days in a row? And hadn't her heart been emptied of all its vision in this one burst of grief? Wasn't it a miracle she'd done the work at all? What, they asked themselves, would happen now to this girl, still so young, whose eyes were filled with such immense sadness, but whose face had become so calm, nearly radiant, in her mourning? There was nothing they could do now but wait and watch, the strangeness of it carried deep within their hearts.

# Eleven

MORGAN worked the heavy handcart down to the bottom of the garden and tipped out the stones he'd dug from the earth, sweat stinging his eyes and soaking through his shirt. The wall was waist-high and nearly done; his shoulders throbbed and his back ached, but he was glad for physical work that left him too exhausted at night to toss and turn. He puzzled the chunks of rock together, stacking them tightly into a sturdy wall that would protect their crop from animals. The gray-green stone framed nicely the chopped and furrowed rows of his garden, where he could now recognize pointy stalks of corn and fragile tomato shoots, the bushy leaves of potato plants near slender onions, feathery carrot tops, delicately tangled peas, the climbing trellis of beans. He was enormously relieved that anything had come up at all, so hard was the soil after a bitter winter, so touchy the weather that threatened a late frost. But Father Brown had encouraged him to follow his instincts, had reassured him that he was on the right track with this kind of compatible, planned farming and soil preparation. The amiable priest had listened to his ideas for hours one night over a short pint and a long fire, and had then suggested that Morgan meet with other young men who also wanted to advance their farming. Morgan had done more reading than all of them put together, he said, and proved himself true when Morgan was voted the leader of two separate groups from neighboring parishes. He met with one group each week to discuss the latest information on soil treatment, seed selection, crop rotation, and irrigation. Throughout the long winter, he distinguished himself by presenting his own theories and was soon considered something of an expert—even though he had yet to plant his own first crop. This was a private joke between him and Father Brown, who told him to remember the Book of Hebrews, which said that faith meant believing in what one hoped for. Morgan repeated this to himself each morning upon rising.

Vision blurred by sweat, he stripped off his shirt and poured a bucket of well water over his head, letting out a fierce yell at the shock of its chill. Heart pounding, he wiped himself off with his shirt, then perched on the completed wall to survey the work. He lifted his face to the sun, and Grace danced into his mind's eye, but he pushed her gently away, his heart still too raw to dwell on that loss. Now and then, the reality of his terrible mistake in not speaking for her hand washed over him and he nearly drowned in the pain. He confided in no one— would not even talk about it with Sean—and slowly, slowly, the drowning days were becoming fewer.

He had not allowed farming to become his life's passion, only something on which to focus while passion burned itself out. He hoped that if he worked hard enough and profited enough to satisfy the landlords, he might somehow be allowed to purchase his own piece of ground. He tried his best to ignore the hard fact of a government that would never allow him such advancement, but his heart knew the truth and this fanned the fire of his discontent, a fire readily fueled by the political pamphlets someone had slipped into his weekly bundle of agricultural literature.

"Did you have a look through Martin and Mitchel, then?" Father Brown had asked him casually.

Morgan had been surprised. There were a fair number of Irish who believed the future lay with British rule, and gladly reported subversive conversations to the other side. He did not discuss his views openly with anyone but Sean; Father Brown was either taking a risk, or baiting a trap.

"The articles on fertilizers?" Morgan had pretended ignorance.

But the priest had already gauged the situation, and pressed on. "Change is in the wind, my boy," he said resolutely. "There's many of us take note of you—how you head your household, the reading you do, and the way you lead others, your standing among your peers. And don't they all look up to you? Give it some thought, is all I ask. We could use a young man of your ability."

Morgan had long flirted with daydreams of revolutionary change, but it now occupied more and more of his thinking. He was not yet ready to commit to the untested ideas of the Young Irelanders, but it was a relief to feel something other than remorse, and there was excitement in change. It opened up possibilities of a life of which he had only dreamed.

On the other hand, it was not just his own neck he stuck out, but the necks of every member of his family. His involvement would implicate them all, and tenants had been turned out for less. They'd had no word from Nally since the market fair, but Aislinn's work had paid last quarter's rent and her wages were helping with the first quarter of the new year. Morgan had traded on his strong back at every opportunity to bring in money or a piece of meat, but the family still struggled. Mary had not been well through winter and they'd had to buy a milk goat for the baby, who in turn became sickly and pitiful. Barbara had been ready to enter the convent and become a noviate, but delayed her plans in order to run the house until Mary was strong again. This was hard on them both, as Mary's deepest desire was for one of her daughters to join the Holy Sisters, and it was Barbara who most strongly heard this call.

They all felt Aislinn's absence in the house, not just her helpful hands, but her liveliness and the excitement she brought into their lives. Mary worried about her at O'Flaherty's; Aislinn had accustomed herself to life at Cairn Manor with an ease they found unsettling. She sent word home now and then, and paid into their rent account directly, for which her mother was very grateful, but rumor had it she'd become the infatuation of young Gerald O'Flaherty, and no good could come of that. Both Kate and Maureen worshipped her, especially since seeing her in proper clothes and receiving from her pretty little presents at Christmastime. Their talk was almost always of when they, too, would work in the manor house and wear fine things. Ellen, now nine, had assumed responsibility for her three-year-old sister: getting Fiona up, feeding and dressing her, and keeping her near while doing the chores. She kept a distance from the two older girls, although she was close to Barbara and to her mother, and she still adored her big brother. Morgan watched her now, crossing the dirt yard to the chicken shed, little Fee trailing along behind, prattling on in the language only Ellen and Mary seemed to fully understand. He waved and motioned them over.

"Have you finished it, then, Morgan?" Ellen asked when she reached his side. She shaded her eyes with one hand and peered down the neat rows. "And isn't it a beautiful thing to have?" she said enthusiastically.

He laughed. "Won't be much longer and you'll be eating carrots and peas, then onions, corn, parsnips, squash . . ."

"Quish?" Fionna dug her hands into the dirt and squeezed.

"She wants to know what's squash," Ellen interpreted.

Morgan shook his head. "I'm not sure myself, wee Fee," he said. "It's a gourd, and it's hardy and you can eat it, according to the pamphlets Father Brown left."

"Will we not have potatoes?" Ellen asked anxiously.

"Aye. We'll always have those to fill our bellies."

"Then why plant all the other things?" She pushed a lank piece of brown hair away from her freckled face.

Morgan regarded her. She knew tales of famine, and sure she was hungry often enough. But she'd never felt the really great hunger itself.

"Well, now, Miss Never-Change," he teased. "You plan on eating potatoes and only potatoes for the rest of your life, do you?"

She giggled and took his hand. "I don't know," she said shyly.

He squeezed her hand. "Change is a good thing," he said. "It keeps life interesting." He looked down at Fiona, who was eyeing the dirt in her fists. "There now, you, don't eat that! Here's a child not afraid to try new things!" He swept Fiona up into his arms and settled her on his shoulder, his free hand in Ellen's once again. They stood for a moment looking across the ready garden, down the hill to the road that wound through the trees.

"Who's that coming up our lane, then?" Ellen asked.

Morgan squinted as the cart drew closer, its driver leaning at an awkward angle over the reins.

"Why, and isn't it Sean O'Malley making the trip!" he said in amazement. He thought again of Grace, and his heart stopped. She'd lost her boy child three months ago, and what if the daughter had passed now, as well? He swung Fiona down to the ground and put her hand into Ellen's. "Run, now, and tell Barbara that Sean's coming in the wagon. Put the water on and see if there's anything to eat in the house. I'll go across the field to meet him."

He hallooed and waved; Sean waved back and slowed the horse when he saw Morgan running over the field, leaping fences and jumping gulleys. He was there in a matter of minutes.

"What's happened, then?" he asked, taking in Sean's pale face and wide, excited eyes.

"I . . . I had to come right away," Sean stammered. "I had to tell you, you've got to come, it's . . ."

"Slow down." Morgan climbed into the cart and took the reins, supporting Sean's back with his arm. "Is it Grace?"

Sean shook his head. "No, no, nothing like that." He was trying to catch his breath; two small spots of color burned in his cheeks as if he had a fever.

"Your da? Granna?"

"No." Sean frowned with irritation. "Wait." He took two deep breaths and relaxed his body. "Nobody's hurt, you great oaf. I've just come from a meeting, is all." His eyes burned bright and he looked around before lowering his voice. "A secret meeting. And it's continuing on tonight. They're waiting for someone to give a talk. A man come to organize us."

Morgan's eyes opened in surprise and then he said angrily, "Are you telling me, Sean O'Malley, that you've ridden all the way here because you've been to a meeting of the Young Irelanders?"

Sean nodded enthusiastically. "Aye, and wasn't it grand! They have plans, these boys, plans to change Ireland for the good . . . forever!"

Morgan shook his head. "I know all about it." He snapped the reins and the horse began to make its way up the path to the house. "They're low boys with high ideas. It all sounds good, the speeches and the wild cheering, but I've not heard anything leads me to think they're men of action. They have no solid plan at all."

Sean grabbed his arm. "That's where you're wrong," he said excitedly. "They've formed small bands, maybe a hundred, spread all through Ireland! This man who's coming, he's got military training and money for guns and shot. He goes about from group to group, organizing them. It's a real movement now, secret though it is."

"Secret because they're breaking the law," Morgan said quietly. "And getting their families evicted in the process."

"It's English law, not Irish, and it'll be the death of us, so why not go down fighting?"

"You think we'll go down, then?"

Sean looked up at the McDonagh house with its patched roof and ragged fences, boiling kettle of laundry in the yard, Ellen and Fee standing at the stone fence in mended shifts. "It's not the winning or the losing matters anymore, really, is it? Only the fact that we stand up and fight for what's ours. This is Irish land." He looked at Morgan, dead serious. "Wasn't so long ago you spoke of sedition yourself."

"Hah!" Morgan snorted. "Wasn't so long ago, you spoke to me of a man's Christian duty."

Sean smiled. "I'm first to admit when I'm wrong."

"Sure and that's a terrible lie." Morgan drove through the gate and stopped the cart. "We'll not talk of this in front of Mam and the girls," he warned. "Tell them the foxes are after your sheep, and I'm to come trap them out."

Sean's eyes widened. "So, you'll come, then? To the meeting?"

"I'll come," Morgan said. "But only to look after your daft self."

They met in the cave up the hill behind Irial Kelley's farm. It was twilight and the entrance was hidden behind tree boughs against boards blocking the opening to the cave. It was a struggle for Sean to get up the hill and sweat poured down his face; he'd vehemently refused Morgan's offer to piggyback, insisting he'd walk in on his own two feet like a fighting man.

The cave was crowded and hot, despite the cool stone walls. Someone had brought in a small keg of beer, and a whiskey bottle was making the rounds, but no one was drunk yet. Indeed, Morgan thought, the mood was serious and sober. Torches and lanterns provided wavering light, many men seemed to prefer the shadows, and each new arrival was greeted with wary glances for fear of spies and reproval. Morgan and Sean were acknowledged with nods from the groups of farmers Morgan knew, the other young men in their parish, and from many of the older men, as well. Morgan looked for a bench and found one in the back; Sean sank gratefully into it, his face strained.

Morgan leaned against the wall and listened to the talk around him. These were mostly Catholic tenant farmers like himself, the older ones remembering a hard-won Catholic emancipation in 1829 and the more recent work of Daniel O'Connell, a brilliant solicitor who'd given up the bar to devote his life to Ireland, a man whose enemies deemed his flamboyance vulgar and called him "Swaggering Dan." His followers were pledged to obtain repeal of the Union only by legal and constitutional means, but the more radical, like the men gathered here, had abandoned those orders in what they felt were desperate times. Some of these men had been to O'Connell's monster meetings where hundreds of thousands flocked to hear him demand repeal. Had it been only a year and a half since he'd called for the greatest meeting of them all? They were to gather on the fields of Clontarf, near Dublin, where eight centuries ago Brian Boru had driven the Norsemen into the sea. Government waited until more than fifty thousand people had arrived before ordering the guns of Pigeon House trained on Clontarf; warships entered Dublin Bay, and troops occupied the only approaches to and from the meeting place. O'Connell then addressed the crowd, calling out that "human blood is no cement for the temple of liberty" and begging them to go home rather than face mass execution. The crowd, shocked, had quietly dispersed. There had been no meeting and no disturbance had taken place, yet O'Connell was arrested on a charge of trying to alter the constitution by force. He was convicted by a packed jury and sent to prison. The verdict was later reversed and O'Connell released, but his health had been broken and he'd lost his nerve. Ireland had lapsed into this helpless hostility, fed by the British, who maintained a military occupation. Morgan's father had attended the Great Meeting at Clontarf and had spoken with bitterness about O'Connell's imprisonment and subsequent change of heart. Tonight, Morgan heard again those same sentiments echoed all around, and the old anger began to burn.

"I'll find us a drink," he said quietly to Sean, then made his way across the room to the keg, where Kelley himself pulled two clay mugs for Morgan, blowing off the foam before handing them over.

"Who's this speaker coming tonight then, Irial?"

"Don't know his name for sure, though some call him 'Evans.' He's known by his yellow hair. Most of the boys call him 'Captain.'" Kelley sucked the head off his ale. "He's late tonight. Coming all the way from Kanturk, he is."

"An Irishman?" Morgan took a swallow of the cold ale. It whet his thirst and he drank again more deeply.

"Hell, he's a bloody Englishman, if you can believe that." Kelley's eyes roamed over the room as he talked. "An expatriate, they say. From Spain or some such place. He's got money—or friends who've got money—and he's firmly behind us, that's God's truth. Came last summer and started moving from county to county, taking toll of our numbers, and making great maps."

"Trusted, is he, then?" Morgan asked.

"By the best men there are," Irial told him. "Glad to see yourself here among us," he added pointedly.

Morgan thanked him for the drink and went back to Sean, who took his mug gratefully. They drank their ale and wished for food, but didn't complain.

Another hour passed and then there was a commotion near the entrance of the cave. Fresh air swept in followed by a group of men, one of whom wore a heavy cloak and felt fedora pulled down low over his face. This man moved to the front of the crowd and took off his hat, exposing a shock of yellow hair. The talk died at once.

"Gentlemen." He addressed them in a sure, confident voice. "I know you've been waiting a long time." He paused and looked from face to face. "Nearly six hundred years, to be exact."

Instantly, the men rose and cheered in one roar. Evans held up his hands for silence.

"The wait is nearly over, now that you have agreed to take up arms against your oppressor. You tried to win their respect with marches and protests, legislation and speeches, but all you won was continued poverty and starvation. Your families have been divided by loyalties to the Old and to the Young, and the British laugh up their sleeves at you. Do not waste time fighting among yourselves, work instead to unite your brothers. Show them the way to victory—you are the men to do it."

Another cheer swelled, leaving in its wake an excited murmur that quivered throughout the crowd.

"Presently, there are troops posted in every major seaport, billetted in forts or outposted in boarding houses. They ride out regularly for exercise and to keep us aware of their presence here. As if we needed the reminder," he added with a small smile.

The men chuckled appreciatively and pressed closer.

"This is war, Young Irelanders." His smile vanished. "And you are now enlisted soldiers. It will take great courage to pull the trigger, but pull it you must." He paused. "Your target is the British uniform. Do not miss."

Morgan glanced at Sean, whose face glowed with the intensity of his emotion.

"Captain Evans."

Heads turned.

"Who's that?" The Englishman peered into the shadows at the back of the cave. "Step forward."

The men jostled one another and made way for Morgan to move up, some of them reaching out and patting his shoulder with encouragement.

"McDonagh's my name," he said firmly. "And I want to know why you think we Irishmen need a Brit to lead us. Are you not just another superior-thinking European come to rescue the poor, dumb Irish from themselves?"

There was complete silence in the cave. Eyebrows shot up and elbows nudged sides as the other young men looked at Morgan with fresh appreciation. Morgan and the captain locked eyes and each considered the boldness they saw therein. The tension broke at last when Captain Evans laughed.

"Hah! A true man of action." He crossed his arms and regarded Morgan. "Well, Mister McDonagh, you've certainly got a point. I am English, it's true. And there is much about my country that I love."

With those words, the men grew suspicious and began muttering.

"But there are also things I cannot abide," Evans said clearly, his voice riding above their suspicion. "And one of those things is the occupation of Ireland and the domination of her people."

Eyes narrowed, but slowly the men nodded their heads and whispered, "Aye, 'tis true enough."

"Then why are you not in England, protesting your government and lending support to the others in power who feel as you do?" Morgan asked.

The captain considered this. "Frankly, there are not many who feel as I do," he said. "And even fewer whose voices might carry any weight. England is full of people who toil day to day getting their liv-

ing, just as you do here. They don't have time to think about the poor,
struggling farmer in Ireland because their mind is occupied with their
own struggles at home. It's not that they don't care, but that they *can't*
care. Those who are poor struggle against their own poverty, most of
those who are rich struggle to keep it that way. There was nothing I
could do to change things in my own country, but in Spain, I met others who also felt that the British occupation of Ireland must be dealt
with. It is my countrymen who hold your country, therefore I feel a
responsibility to pry open their fingers and loosen their grasp. Does
that answer your question, Mister McDonagh?"

Morgan looked at the man, minding the fine clothes torn and
splattered with mud, the boots run down in the heel, and the thin face
lined with fatigue.

"It begins to, Captain Evans." He looked around at the other
young men, who nodded their agreement. "Let you speak now on what
you'd have us do, and we'll all know more."

Evans ran his fingers through his shaggy hair and unfolded the
map he'd brought in his saddlebag. He had two men hold it up, then
pointed out the patrol areas in their region, and told them how to organize themselves into groups with one leader per dozen men. They
should meet in secret and keep their thoughts to themselves, he said;
spies were everywhere.

"Next to the English," he warned, "your greatest enemies are
those among you who seek their favor. And as things get more desperate, that number will rise."

He urged them to organize as quickly as possible and to meet again
the next week on their own. Rifles and pistols would be supplied, he
assured, as well as caps and lessons in how to shoot. In the meantime,
they must stockpile any arms they could lay hands on and put them
under lock and key.

When he was finished, men gathered around Morgan to hear his
opinion, but he said firmly that they must make up their own minds.
They hesitated only a moment, then began to talk among themselves.
The crush was overwhelming. Morgan got Sean to his feet and led
him out into the fresh night air, where they both breathed deeply.

"They'll be gabbing in there till the sun rises," he said.

Sean grinned. "Captain Evans ignored our strongest asset—we
could easily talk the English to death!"

They laughed quietly, then began the steep descent down the slippery hill to the waiting wagon. They weren't a mile down the road when the bushes parted above them and out jumped three horses.

"McDonagh." Evans touched the brim of his hat. "I wondered if I might ride along with you and have a word." He glanced at Sean.

Morgan saw the glance and frowned. "This is my brother in every way but blood. 'Tis himself brought me here tonight."

"I'm glad of that." Evans nodded his thanks at Sean, then turned back to Morgan. "I asked about you back there, and they all say to a man that you're a born leader."

"I doubt that," Morgan said, keeping his eyes on the road ahead.

"No, you don't." Evans was matter-of-fact. "You've just never thought about it. You took charge and spoke for the group tonight. I admire that. You're the kind of kind of man whom others gladly follow."

"And where is it you'd have them follow me to, Captain? The bushes above the roads in order to shoot a man in the back as he rides along it?" He snapped the rein and the horse snorted in protest. "There's no fairness in a fight like that . . . it's only murder. And I'll not be a party to murder."

"Good God, man, what do you think the English are doing to you right now? Is that not murder? To be slowly starved to death? Men, women, and children? What do you call that, if not murder?"

Morgan's face was grim.

"And it'll only get worse, my friend." Evans lowered his voice. "There's not been a famine in many years now, thank God, but your people are living on the edge, and if even one year of crop failure happens, you'll be wiped out. The English will have succeeded in ridding Ireland of the pesky Irish, and they will use your land as a great big back garden for England."

"It's God's truth." Sean spoke up from the back of the wagon. "You know it is, Morgan. They've already cut down the forests, the best pastureland goes to feed their cattle and sheep, they take our grain in great ships back to England. We have only the potatoes year after year to keep us alive."

Morgan shot him a look.

"Some have more," he allowed. "But not much. We don't own our land and we never will. We're not forced into hedge schools any longer, but the state schools steal away our language, our customs and religion, they take our history and change it to suit themselves, to make themselves look like our saviors. In another generation or two, we'll all be English—there'll be nothing left of Ireland but the name."

Morgan pulled up on the reins and the group of riders halted beside him.

"I know all that," he said evenly. "I live at the very bottom of that. But when we start shooting back, when we kill a soldier here and there, burn out a landlord, cripple an agent—what will happen to us?" He looked around him. "Are you Christian men, any of you? Captain Evans?"

"I am," the captain said. "I became one here."

Morgan nodded. "Then you understand me when I say that it's not death I fear, but the course of my own soul. I won't just be killing English soldiers, but men like myself, men with families and lives and faith in God."

Evans sighed, then reached out and put his hand on the edge of the wagon.

"This is war, son. No one is going to say, 'We made a mistake, the Irish are fine people, we'll be off now and they can have their country back. Sorry for the inconvenience.' Slowly, and without mercy, they will beat you down and wipe you out. Your children will only know an English Ireland."

"You're not giving him any news, Captain," Sean said softly. "And great men do not make hasty decisions."

"Fair enough." Evans nodded. "When you come to your decision—and I pray to God it's the right one—Kelley will help you contact me. Until then, I wish you well, McDonagh. And you, too . . . ?"

"O'Malley. Sean O'Malley."

"O'Malley?" Evans frowned. "You aren't Grace O'Malley's relation?"

Sean nodded. "My sister."

Evans turned wide-eyed to Morgan. "Then you're the McDonagh she spoke of so highly!"

"I am?" Morgan was confused.

"I met her at a dinner party at O'Flaherty's one evening—got to keep up my cover, you understand." He winked. "Young Gerald was up to some teasing with a maid—your sister, I believe, McDonagh—

and Grace came to her defense. I chided her about championing the poor, and she climbed right down my throat in saying what a fine family the McDonaghs were, finer than any at the table that night!" He chuckled, remembering. "I liked her tremendously. Great fire, that girl. I was hoping for more of her company, but they never extended an invitation to call, and I have not seen her since."

Morgan and Sean exchanged glances.

"Grace was with child," Sean said cautiously. "She gave birth to twins, but one died. She wasn't well for some time."

"I'm sorry to hear that," Evans said, genuinely distressed. "How did it die?"

Again, Morgan and Sean looked at one another.

"Was it a girl child?"

"No," Sean said. "A boy. He was weak from the start."

"Why?" Morgan frowned.

Evans paused. "Donnelly's got a bit of a reputation," he said. "Of which I'm sure you're aware."

Sean pulled himself up in the back of the wagon. "We know nothing of a reputation for killing babies."

"You'd best explain yourself, Captain, before my friend here gets himself too worked up," Morgan warned.

Evans sat back in his saddle and stared at his hands for a moment. "Ride on ahead," he spoke to the two men who had been waiting patiently on their mounts behind him. "I'll catch you in a moment."

When they were out of earshot, he said softly, "Gentlemen, I carry a secret that I've shared with no one until now."

"If it has to do with my sister, or the man she married, you'd best give it up," Sean said.

Evans studied their faces in the moonlight. "I was engaged, many years ago, to a young woman called Abigail Dunstone. I loved her very much, but was very slow in showing it." If he noticed Morgan's hands tightening on the reins, he gave no sign. "She was persuaded to elope with Bram Donnelly, who, as you know, is a very handsome, commanding figure. Very charming when he wants to be." He cleared his throat. "Donnelly quarreled with everyone, with his father most of all. Eventually, because of the scandal, he was sent to live here in Ireland and work the family's holdings. He hated it, but Abigail loved everything about it: the customs, the festivals, the superstitions, and most of all, the Irish themselves. Her first pregnancy nearly ended her life and changed everything for her. Every day became precious—life had enormous meaning. She had begun writing secretly to me, you see, I think at first, out of loneliness, but then because her life had changed so dramatically, and she realized her love for me. I begged her to return to England, but she felt that God had brought her to Ireland to be a voice for the people, who were virtual slaves. In her last letter, she spoke of Donnelly's rage over her political involvement, and his insistence that she have another child—an heir—of which she was deathly afraid. And then there was nothing."

His horse snorted and stomped. An owl hooted in the tree above. Morgan and Sean sat as still as they could, waiting for him to continue.

"I went to her family and begged them to bring her back, but they would not. She had made her choice, you see, and had to live with it. My family, too, would not intervene. They had received a letter from the Donnellys saying she was in confinement and that my continually pressing correspondence had greatly distressed her. My family then sent me to Spain on a fool's errand, and when I realized it, I left immediately for Ireland. By the time I got to Donnelly House, she was locked in her room, having had some sort of breakdown. The servants would not let me see her. She came briefly to the window and stared down at me in the courtyard, but there was no recognition in her eyes and she did not answer my call. I went to Dublin, to find a doctor or a solicitor who might know how to help, but while I was there . . . she died." He stopped to collect himself. "It was a long time ago, but I've never forgiven him. And I never will."

"You want to ruin him, then," Sean said quietly.

"Yes." He paused. "But after I met your sister, I could not. Watch out for her," he added. "Donnelly is not to be trusted."

"I know," Sean told him, and Morgan stiffened in the seat beside him.

Captain Evans looked at the two of them. "I failed Abigail, but you will not fail your sister. Abigail wanted Ireland to be free, and I have pledged my life to that cause in her name." He paused. "You will fail Grace only if you do not make the same pledge."

A light went on in a cabin up the hill; wisps of smoke curled out the chimney. Dawn would soon draw back the curtain of night behind which they hid.

"I must go." Evans pulled himself upright in his saddle and put out his hand. "Think about what I've said, McDonagh. Your people need you."

"I will, sir."

"And you, O'Malley." He shook Sean's hand. "They need you, as well."

"Thank you, Captain."

They watched him trot the horse down the road, catch up with the other two, then disappear at a gallop around the bend.

The gray sky continued to lighten until they were no longer shadows on the road, but visible to anyone who cared to look out.

"Take us home now, Morgan boy," Sean said at last. "We've work to do."

# Twelve

THE summer was hot and dry; men put aside their shirts and shoes, women tied up their skirts and wore only their vests in order to catch what little air might stir in the afternoon. Babies slept or fussed in the building heat of the day, children played in whatever shade could be found; every movement was slow, made drowsy with the heat. The potato crops—leaves sleek green and lustrous—rose up from dark mounds of earth in promise of abundance. It would be a rich man's harvest this year and no one minded the final meals of old, rubbery potatoes; there were plenty of berries to pick, the occasional eel or trout from the master's lake, a rabbit the dog brought in from the wood. They were warm at night, their bellies content. They grew brown in the sun and their faces relaxed with the assurance of what was to come.

Grace kept the baby with her everywhere, nursing on demand, the ache of her loss receding with every healthy ounce this one put on. When she went out to walk, she tied the baby to her with a sling fashioned from old bedsheets. She would stop to nurse under one of the broad oaks and often dozed off there, waking with a start to feel the heavy, sweaty head of her daughter on her arm. She would carry a basket lined with flannel out into the garden, setting the baby in the shade while she weeded and watered, pruned and clipped. Bram insisted she let Brigid or her daughter Moira do that, but Grace had found she needed the garden, needed the growing things. She felt closest to God there, far closer than she did on her knees in her bedroom. And, of course, from this place she could see the stone cross that marked Michael Brian's tiny grave. In the garden, she had both God and her children near to her.

As June burned into July, the lushness of the land filled her heart, pushing out winter's ache. Bram, too, was in better spirits. The potato crop looked so well this year that he was sure he would have no problem collecting rents. He did not seem to mind so bitterly anymore that his heir was a daughter—his son forever asleep on the rise—or that his wife had abandoned any pretense of gentility and was now a vigorous gardener, as brown as the earth she turned. He did not complain about her being improperly dressed for dinner, or even whether dinner was on time. Often, he did not return to the house until late, and although his breath was woody with drink, he was peaceful, falling quickly asleep and waking clearheaded and with purpose. They did not talk, Bram and Grace, and he did not come to her at night, as the baby still slept in her room. But neither did they argue nor stand stubborn. They were polite with one another—even cordial—and slowly, slowly, slowly, they put their disappointment behind them.

And then the weather changed. A dreary, misting gloom settled in the sky and continued, day after day after never-ending day for three long weeks. The temperature dropped with a succession of chilling rains and damp fogs. Grace sat in for the first week, afraid to take the baby out in such weather, but soon the gloom began to creep into her heart and she knew she must get out of the house.

One morning, as she looked out the upstairs window, she saw a figure sitting in a wagon on the edge of the wood across the field. It could only be Sean, and she lifted her hand. He waved in return, then pulled up the horse and turned the wagon around. She bundled up Mary Kathleen, tied her close to her own body, and drew a heavy cloak about them both in order to keep in the warmth, then headed out across the field. He waited and the look of delight on his face when he peered in at the little baby was all the spark she needed to get her heart's fire going again. He chided her gently, reminding her that she was a country girl, her baby a country child, and that they must get out and be in the weather God gave them, good or bad. There is beauty to be found in a dark day, as well as in one flooded with light, he reminded her, and she took it to heart, along with the Bible verses he'd written out for her to study. It was but a short visit, snatched in secret, but she hugged the comfort of it to her breast and pushed anxiety away.

Bram was not so easily consoled. The chill was damaging his feed corn, and he was uneasy about the potatoes, a crop as unreliable as the weather. The verses he knew best were those citing the dismal history of the Irish potato: 1728, major crop failure; 1739, entirely destroyed; 1740, entire failure; 1770, failure due to curl; 1800 and 1807, general failure, and loss due to frost; 1821 and '22, horrible distress in Munster and Connaught; 1830 and '31, failure in Mayo, Donegal, and Galway; 1832, '33, '34, and '36, crops lost to dry rot and curl in many districts; 1835, failure in Ulster; 1836 and '37, extensive failures throughout Ireland; 1839, universal failure throughout Ireland with famine conditions from Bantry Bay to Lough Swilly; and last year, 1844, the early crop had been widely lost. Bram hated the potato, hated his dependence on it for rents and tenants' livelihood, but he accepted that failure would come and go. There was, as yet, he told himself, no cause for alarm.

The sharp change in the weather was also affecting the animals; his horse, already high-spirited, had become nearly unmanagable, and the cows were fitful, producing poor-quality milk.

"Damn Irish weather," he muttered time and again, and only scowled when Grace pointed out that it could just as easily turn for the better come morning.

Which it did. The gloom lifted, the clouds turned from black to gray to white wisps that strayed across the blue, the sun returned to dry out the land, and the potatoes appeared undamaged. Bram's *Freeman's Journal* reported that "the poor man's property, the potato crop, was never before so large and at the same time so abundant"; the *Times* printed favorable reports from all four provinces of Ireland, and announced that "an early and productive harvest was everywhere expected." He was relieved. Grace was relieved. Relief breezed across the fields on a tumbling wind as people stayed out of doors, smiled and sang, dug a few early potatoes, and waited. In the evenings, children walked barefoot in the warm soil, hip-deep through bushy plants, knocking against the delicate white blossoms that released an invisible sweetness into the air. The days grew shorter, the nights a bit longer, and so the last weeks of summer passed.

Long before dawn crept over the mountains, before the birds began to sing or the animals gave thought to stirring, long before happy
dreams gave way to wakefulness, it came upon them: It had drifted
across the ocean, and now—tired of the journey—began to settle
on the ground, invisible, odorless, undetectable. As Ireland slept, it
coated thick, healthy leaves, seeping down roots to the warm nests of
potatoes, poisoning them with a foul rot that spread more quickly than
the blink of an eye. Plant after plant after plant, field by field, one district after another, across the entire island. Unaware, Ireland slept.

Granna was not the first one up. Her night had been disturbed by
dreams, and only at dawn had she finally slept. Now, she dressed
slowly, tying her apron as she came into the kitchen. She stood for a
moment, troubled, then pushed back the shutter, and there it was, in
her first breath. It could be no other thing, and she closed her eyes
against it, even as she became aware of the shouts from the fields
echoing down the valley, felt agitation in the very stillness of the air.
She knew, she knew. There could be no doubt. The blight had come
again.

"Dear Lord have mercy on us," she whispered, eyes still closed
against the early morning light that hung heavy about the landscape.

When she opened them, Sean was hobbling back toward the
cabin, eyes wide, face gone white.

"No need to say it, boy." She put a hand out the window. "I felt it
even in my dreams, though it wasn't till this very minute that I knew."

"What are we to do, Gran?" His voice was hoarse. "Da's just sitting down in the middle of the field, staring out. Ryan as well."

"Ever one is rotted?"

"Da says they're all gone for it." He shook his head in bewilderment. "But how can that be? They were fine! The leaves were green
and glossy, the flowers as white as can be!"

"Come in now." She eyed the shivering young man. "I'll make you
some tea for the shock."

"I don't understand."

Gran poured boiling water from the kettle over the tea leaves in
the pot, and when he'd come through the door, she spoke.

"Some say it comes in the night." Steam rose from the pot. "Some
say it's borne on the wind, an invisible thing we cannot see. It settles

on the leaves like dust, leaving little brown spots." She poured out his cup. "Many will tell you 'tis the demon fairies having their fun, or the heavy hand of God in punishment. Whatever 'tis, when you go to bed at night, they are a beautiful sight—when you wake in the morning, they are rot."

"'Tis a curse." Sean took the cup and blew on it. "Black, slippery muck like nothing I've ever smelled before."

"Aye. Sure and it's the vapors of Hell come to earth, the stink of bad death."

They heard a shout in the lane, then the door burst open and Aghna stumbled in. She'd been to her parents' overnight to tell them of the baby she'd started; she'd left rosy and proud, but now stood out of breath and deathly pale, freckles standing out on her face like the pox.

"Oh, Lord, has it fallen here, as well?" she gasped.

Granna took her hand and helped her to the bench. "Sit down child, before you hurt yourself. Aye, 'tis here. Sometimes the Aran Islanders escape it, but not always." She paused. "More as like, where it's not, it soon will be."

"Oh, Gran, what will happen to us?" The girl dropped her face into her hands and began to weep.

Sean looked hopelessly over her head at his grandmother. The back door opened and Patrick entered, followed by Ryan. Aghna jumped up and ran into the arms of her husband, who held her tightly but said nothing.

"Is there nothing to save, then?" Granna asked, bringing out more cups.

Patrick sat down heavily at the table and shook his head. "Here and there a good one, but most have turned to rot." He wiped a dirty hand over his face.

Granna went to the door and looked across the road, up the gentle slope where the cabins of their neighbors sat on small plots of land. There was Campbell Hawes in the field high up, digging with his bare hands like a frantic puppy looking for a misplaced bone. He stopped, turned, and dug in another spot, then another, then finally sat back in the dirt and raged at the sky, shaking his fist and cursing God. Down the lane, the young Ryans came out of their cabins, stunned as moles in the sun, cowering now back against the door as their mother threw her apron over her face and began to wail.

The calamity of the earth was betrayed by a nearly perfect summer sky: Thin wisps of cloud, blown lightly by a warm breeze, stretched across the endless blue. Granna turned away and came back into the dark cabin, knees shaking.

"Come now, girl," she murmured to Aghna, who sobbed in the corner. "'Tis not the end of the world."

Aghna lifted her tearstained face from Ryan's knee. "What will we eat? How will we make it through the winter?" Her hand gripped her belly.

"Nay," Granna soothed. "You'll not lose it. We're better off than most here. We've got other foods in the larder, and animals to slaughter. Arrah, we must be frugal, but we'll not starve."

Patrick stood and put a hand on Aghna's head. "You listen to Granna, girl," he said. "She's been through it enough times to know."

"Where are you going, Da?" Sean spoke up.

"I've got to clear away the weeds and stalks, then dig up what's left and burn. Any that haven't gone bad, we'll clean and store against the winter."

Sean got up awkwardly from the bench. "I'll help."

"No, boy," Patrick said, not unkindly. "I need a strong back to work quickly. Ryan'll do the digging." He saw the look on Sean's face. "There's other work you can do." He nodded toward the store shed. "See what's left, and take count of the pigs and chickens. How many to eat, how many to breed, what for eggs and to butcher when the time comes."

"We'd best harvest the garden." Granna looked at Aghna. "Come on, girl, and we'll see what we can spare for your folk."

Aghna's face went white. "They have nothing," she whispered. "Four children left to home, and ten shillings rent come due after harvest day. They'll not make it. They'll be turned out." She turned her wide eyes to Ryan's face.

He lifted her to her feet and held her tightly in his arms, looking at Granna over her shoulder.

"They'll not be turned out, not in times such as these," he said firmly. "We'll share what we have."

Granna nodded, even as she thought of the five mouths here, Aghna's six, the neighbors who never planted more than they had to and barely kept chickens enough for eggs. The winter would be long.

"Sean," she said quietly, nodding toward the back door.

He followed her to the store shed, where they kept apples and onions, and hung the ham in autumn.

"You're worried." Sean took her hand.

Granna sighed, and shrugged her small shoulders. "I've seen it before."

They looked around the room, taking into account the few crocks on the shelves, the store of last year's potatoes, two barrels of apples, sacks of flour and oats, herbs drying from the roof beam. What, by any neighbor's account would be plenty, now seemed meager.

Granna pulled him further into the room, lowering her voice. "We must be selfish now, boy, and make out we have less than we do, or it'll be everyone coming to our door and ourselves starving before the next crop."

Sean nodded. "I can dig a false floor to hide the crocks and spread out the apples. Should we slaughter the pig?"

"Too warm yet—it'll spoil. But soon enough the chickens and pigs will start to disappear, so keep a close eye. At first frost, we'll butcher what we can."

"All right, then." Sean's face was grim. "I'll start now."

"And you mustn't let Ryan or Aghna see you do it. It's only right that she'll want to help her family, and Ryan will want her to, as well, but we must get by on as little as possible. If they carry a load of supplies over the hill, it'll be eaten up, shared with other neighbors and gone in a month. If we send smaller amounts, they'll keep it for themselves and make it last. Do you see?"

"Aye, Gran."

"It sounds uncharitable, un-Christian . . ." She shook her head.

"No." Sean put his arm around her. "It's called 'rationing.' Giving out only what is needed, as it's needed. 'Tis the best way, Gran. You mustn't feel guilty."

"Easy to say now." She looked at the food. "But when they come crying to the door with their starving babies at empty breasts . . ."

"We'll feed them a bowl of porridge, put bread in their pockets, and send them on," he said firmly.

"Easy to say now," she repeated, leaning against him for a moment.

They stepped back out into the warm sunlight, aware of the stillness—no more wailing and cursing, all was quiet. A blanket of despair had settled over the hills.

"Arrah, we'll not have to worry about Grace and little Mary Kate," she said. "That's a blessing in itself."

"Aye." Sean nodded. "And perhaps she can put a word in with the Squire about Aghna's folk and the rent."

Granna turned to him in alarm. "No!" she said. "You mustn't ask her to do that! Nor for any help a'tall!"

Sean frowned. "But why? She'd be glad to do it!"

"'Tis not right with themselves, sure and you know this." Her eyes implored him. "He's not a contented man for all our Grace married him. She must step carefully in her own house, without us tripping her up."

Sean nodded, but said nothing.

"Sure and you know she's not as she was. She keeps something from us, some shame or worry." Granna looked up at the vast sky. "When the baby died, she went away from us, himself included. But she came back for wee Mary Kate, and is stronger now because of it. And yet . . ." She paused, searching. "Yet, I cannot help but think her strength has left her blind in some way, so she sees all's well, when all's naught." She shook her head. "I don't know what I'm trying to say to you."

"It's all right." Sean took her hand. "I understand. I'll tell her that we're fine here, that we've enough to see us through."

"You see her, then?" Granna's eyes brightened. "Sure and you do, being of one heart as you are."

"I drive over now and then to the wood behind her house, just to have a look at things," he admitted.

"That's a comfort to me, boy. 'Tis well on you."

"Sometimes she sees me and comes out with the baby. Other times she just waves . . . or shoos me away, I don't know which," he laughed.

"Morgan goes, as well, does he?" she guessed.

"He doesn't say, but I think he must. He's riding out from home two, three days a week now, carrying messages to . . ." He stopped suddenly, then glanced at her, appalled.

"I know all about the Young Irelanders, boy, if that's what's making your face go all red." She smiled grimly. "Better keep a closer watch on your tongue, though. There's as many spies as patriots in our land."

Sean gulped. "But how . . . how . . ."

"Women know to keep an ear to the ground, an eye on the land, and a finger in the wind." She patted his shoulder. "Don't look so caught. Your grandfather was an Oak Boy, and Ribbon Men have stood up for both sides of your family."

"You don't mind, then?"

"I mind if you get yourself killed," she warned. "So don't. Use the brains God gave you and get us out of this mess before the famine kills us all. You and Morgan are leading the rise in these parts, I expect." She paused, and looked out over the field. "The McDonaghs will be in a bad way now. That rascal Nally's not been back all of a year."

"Morgan planted other things beside potatoes," Sean told her. "Not much—some onions, peas, corn . . ."

"No good soil up there for corn," Granna said.

Sean shrugged. "It's come up. They'll be able to eat it, or feed it to the pigs."

"We'll not forsake them." Granna caught his eye. "You remember that's my wish. He's a son to me."

Aghna came out of the cabin then, drying her face on her apron, Ryan kissing her cheek before striding up the hill to join his father. Looking at her young body and straight back, Granna felt a great weariness unlike any she'd ever known. She was too old to face this again: too old to watch their faces grow thin and pale, their hair become lank, their bodies fragile and weak; too old to watch as Aghna suffered through an undernourished pregnancy only to lose the baby or give birth to a sickly child; too old to witness the loss of compassion as they hardened themselves to the misery of face after face appearing at the door begging for food when there *was* no more food; too old to guide them through the pain of watching good people and innocent children die in the road for want of a potato on their plates. She was too old to do this again, even as she knew no other choice; and, in her heart, she asked her Lord why it must be so.

\* \* \*

By October, the island was in a panic. Rumors flew with such speed that information gathered in the morning was easily refuted by afternoon. Good, healthy-looking potatoes could still be dug, but within days of storing them in the customary pits, rot set in. Farmers flooded the market with potatoes, unloading them before they turned worthless.

In an effort to combat growing fear, the Scientific Commissioners published seventy thousand copies of "Advice Concerning the Potato Crop to the Farmers and Peasantry of Ireland." Potatoes still in good condition were to be put in the sun, surrounded by a shallow trench dug on all sides and filled with mold, turf sods, and "packing stuff" made by mixing lime, sand, burned turf, and dry sawdust. Diseased potatoes were to be grated into a tub, where the pulp could be washed, strained, then dried on a griddle. Starch left in the tub could be mixed with dried potato pulp and meal, then made into a nourishing loaf. But the instructions were complicated, and even those who managed them lacked the proper equipment to see the process through. Everyone had a theory, and the papers printed them all; common sense was soon forgotten.

November came with a chill that cut to the bone; the reality of winter was now at hand. Those farmers with a good supply of corn and additional food stores might make it through, but not the thousands who had no food for the year nor a penny to their names. Late August, with its new potato crop, was ten months away.

"Damn it all to hell." Bram crumpled his newspaper, then threw it into the fire.

Grace looked up from the writing desk where she sat going over the household records; they could not count on any rents coming in for the year, but they were far from starving.

"Bad news?" she asked quietly, laying aside her pen.

"It's that bastard O'Connell." He spat the name into the flames.

Grace stilled her hands in her lap; she had become a private champion of the great man.

"What's he done then?" She spoke as if it were of little consequence.

"He's called for the end of corn exportation to England, and wants the ports thrown open for free import of food and rice and Indian corn from the colonies. He demands help, and to meet the cost, he proposes a ten percent tax to resident landlords, fifty percent for absentees!" He kicked at the pile of logs on the hearth. "We can't pay ten percent of rents we don't receive! The fool. It's all political. He doesn't care if the peasants live or die. He just wants the Corn Laws repealed. England will never stand for it." He walked over to the window and looked out at the black, frosty night. "Sir Robert Peel is going to back the demand—he's wanted this for years. Ireland will be divided. They'll forget all about the famine and any kind of real help. Damn Irish imbeciles."

Grace bit her lip, thinking. "But wouldn't that mean that the grain we grow would stay in Ireland, instead of being shipped to England?"

"A portion of it always remains in the country."

"Yes." Grace shifted in her chair. "But it's divided among England's soldiers and their horses."

"Nonsense." Bram spoke sharply. "Look here, we get a fair price for our corn in England, and that means money comes back into Ireland."

"But the tenant farmers don't see any of that money."

"They're paid for their labor during harvest, and for any extra crops grown."

"It goes for rent, as well you know. Most trade straight across, never to see a penny in their own hand."

Bram frowned in irritation. "Whose fault is that? Not mine!" He stalked to the fire and leaned against the mantel. "They're lazy, these damned Irish. Content with a plot of potatoes and a turf fire. They breed children like cats, just to pack warm bodies around themselves at night. If they really cared about all the grain leaving the country, they'd stop making liquor!" He pounded the hearth once with his fist. "But they'll not give up a drop of their precious whiskey to put food in their children's bellies, will they? They work only enough to get by, they plant only what is easy to grow, they save not a penny toward the lean years, which they know from experience are going to come . . . and yet, the minute disaster strikes, they expect to be rescued by the British government with little sacrifice of their own."

"That's not true," Grace said firmly. "There's always some give a bad name to the rest, but most of us are honest, hardworking people."

"Your family, perhaps," he conceded. "But you are not typical Irish. Most do not work, most do not save, most do not plan for the future."

"I'm not saying you're right, but could it be that those you speak of see no future worth planning for? They work, and yet they can never own their land. They're like slaves to the landowners."

Bram's face stilled and his eyes grew hard.

"They were denied education," she continued, unaware of his expression. "A place to worship, a chance to vote in their own country. The most a young man in Ireland can hope for is a bit of land to farm and a managable rent. And even those are becoming scarce."

"To whom have you talked of these things?"

Grace's eyes widened in surprise. "No one but myself."

"Does your brother come to see you when I'm away?"

"I only wish that he would," she lied.

Bram's eyes narrowed with suspicion. "Certainly you don't read the papers?"

"Once in a while," she confessed. "It fills the evenings when you're away. I didn't think you'd mind," she added.

"Well, I do," he said sharply. "I am head of this house, and my opinion is the only one that matters—is that clear?"

Grace nodded and looked down.

"I will not have you debating me on issues about which you know nothing. Political opinion is most unattractive in a woman, and I will not stand for it in my wife. It leads to feverishness and self-absorption. I have witnessed this firsthand," he added bitterly. "If you require reading material, take up that blasted Bible of yours, or any of those." He waved his hand at the wall of books behind her. "Romances and travelogues are all a woman needs. Anything more simply addles the brain."

"Yes, Bram," she said quietly. "I'll not read your papers again."

"Good. Lest you become restless and uncouth like that Martin woman—not fit for marriage, nor any kind of gentile society."

He turned away and began poking at the fire. Grace glanced at his rigid back, then resumed work on the household records, though her thoughts were miles away. An awkward silence grew between them, until Bram made a great show of pouring himself a large whiskey—something he'd not done in front of her since the night of O'Flaherty's party—and drank down half in a single swallow.

"It's been some time since we've had a letter from England," he said, his tone once again smooth and conversational, oiled by the alcohol.

"Nothing from your father, then?" she made herself ask, eyes still on her work as though absorbed.

He watched her, then took another drink, holding it in his mouth, savoring it a moment before swallowing.

"Nothing. But then, he's got problems of his own. The blight's just as bad in England. They've most likely gone abroad until the situation betters." He paused and looked into his glass. "I can always sell the mills. Those belong to me. We'll be fine, if we're careful. I'll check those numbers when you've finished entering them," he added.

"There's a great deal we can do without." Grace tapped her pen on the ledger. "We'll be able to set up a soup kitchen come winter when it's worst."

"We will not." Bram's voice hardened again.

Grace held still, then said carefully, "Your tenants will have nothing, Bram. They'll come looking for work . . . the least we can do is give them a bit of bread and soup for the hunger."

"No," he said firmly. "There will be no beggars littering the grounds of this estate. And you're not to ride out to them, either, is that understood?"

"But why?"

"Once they hear we're handing out food, they'll come from all over the district. Even the Catholics, who think they're risking their bloody souls by taking a bowl of soup from Protestants. They'll hang about, not even trying to survive on their own. I know this from experience." He finished his drink, set down the glass, and stretched, then came and placed his hands on her shoulders. "You may, of course, give some assistance to your own family, but not to anyone else. You may take them supplies as needed—but *only* as needed and *only* in small quantities, or they'll be robbed by their neighbors."

Grace sat speechless, the weight of his hands on her shoulders heavy and unpleasant. She was relieved when the baby began to cry and Bram let her rise. She hurried from the warmth of the drawing room, racing up the stairs two at a time, skirts held high in balled fists, teeth clenched in anger.

Mary Kathleen slept at the end of the hall; the fire was low, but there was no chill in the room when Grace entered and went to the crying child, who had pulled herself up and was standing in the crib, shaking the rail. The crying ceased immediately at the sight of her mother, and she smiled through wet eyes, gurgling and bouncing, unhappiness forgotten. Grace picked her up and felt an offending wet diaper under the heavy nightdress. She cooed over the baby, changing her quickly, then settled into the rocking chair to nurse her.

It calmed Grace, this weight of a sturdy child in her arms and the eagerness with which the baby suckled, breaking off now and then to smile up at her, small fingers reaching to explore her chin and mouth. The anger subsided, cooled by the peace that abided deep within her soul and arose only when she was alone with her daughter. Her anxiety over losing Michael Brian had eased and no longer compromised the joy she felt when holding Mary Kate. Indeed, when she thought of her Michael now, waiting in Heaven, she was thankful to God for keeping him there and grateful in the same moment for the child He'd left in her care. She had become keenly aware that He was in control of her life, and she saw His presence everywhere. She remembered her brother's words—that everyone was where they should be in the world, placed there by God so that they might do His will when the time came. She was as Joseph in Pharoh's Egypt, in charge of plenty against the time of famine. And now that it had come, she would not fail her Lord. He would give her the courage to act.

# *Thirteen*

CHRISTMAS showed itself in the holly berries that decorated windows and fire mantels, the pictures of Mother and Child that went up on the walls of even the darkest, most forlorn cabins. There would be no Christmas dinner for many this year, but Christmas would come nevertheless. Families made plans to gather for worship and song, and hid away humble gifts for the children. They looked forward to a day-long fire in the hearth, a warm loaf of brack, maybe oat cakes with butter, or an egg if they were lucky. Everyone would take a drink, then sing the songs they all knew and listen to the long stories they all loved, the children at their father's knee, babies in their mothers' arms. They were not ashamed of their poverty, and on this day, they would also put aside their fear, for God was very much with them. Hadn't He sent His own child to be born on a cold night in a lowly stable? And, even though kings came from afar to welcome Him, had He not called the poor His own?

Grace thought of this as she stood in the kitchen and looked out the window at the early morning. It was cold and gray, but there was no rain, for which she was thankful. Bram had said she might ride over to her family for a day and a night, to wish them a blessed Christmas and show them the baby. He had given her permission to pack a basket for them, and now she put into it everything she could think of. She had not spent money on gifts, gathering instead small trinkets from the house that would not be missed. A linen sheet for Granna's bed, a pile of newspapers and journals for Sean to read, baby clothes for Aghna, and for Ryan, a pair of old work boots Bram had thrown out as too tight. She had a good bottle of whiskey from the cellar for her father, and gloves for his hands, which had become stiff with age. She had been baking and storing food the past few weeks, so there were breads, small cakes, and rolls. The preserves were plentiful; she had put in three jars, along with a side of bacon, a piece of stew beef, and a sack of oats.

She covered the baskets securely with cloths and had Nolan carry them out to the carriage. He would drive, then stay the night in order to bring her home the next day. While he stroked and steadied the horses, she fetched Mary Kate, bundled against the cold in layers of flannel and wool, a cap tied snugly over her head. She was not surprised at the elation she felt when the manor house disappeared and they were alone in the day on the road. There was no talking to Nolan as he drove from the outside and she was tucked in with the baby, so she contented herself with the familiar view, growing more eager as hours passed, bringing her closer to her glen and the cabin she still thought of as home.

"There it is!" she called out at last to Nolan, though he'd had no problem knowing, as a small crowd of people came rushing into the lane to wave him down.

When the carriage stopped, the door was opened and her father appeared.

"There and isn't that the best present an old da could have, his own lovely girl and wee grandgirl!"

He reached in and helped her out, taking the baby in his arms and holding her up for the neighbors to see. They asserted loudly that she was of a fine size and had the bright manner about her face, a quickness in the eyes, and such rosy cheeks. But they fell silent when Grace emerged, shy suddenly of the girl who was now lady enough to come visiting in a carriage. Grace glanced around, then spoke quietly to her father. His eyes widened and he nodded vigorously.

"Neighbors! Hasn't our own Grace brought with her a fine bottle of the best whiskey to share with her family and friends? Come in now and God bless you all—let us drink a toast as is befitting a Christmas Day!"

A cheer rose and they all crowded into the cabin. Sean met her at the door and embraced her, then led her over to Granna, who sat near the fire. Aghna shyly greeted her sister-in-law and Ryan blustered,

"Merry Christmas," patting her vigorously on the back. They all exclaimed over Mary Kathleen, who had now been peeled to her true size and was sitting on Granna's lap, wide-eyed at all the beaming faces and excitement.

Nolan came in quietly and set the baskets under the table in the kitchen, then went back out to feed the horses. Although they did not want to stare, Grace could see the neighbors looking surreptitiously and with longing at what they knew must be food.

She leaned over and whispered, "Gran, have you enough to feed yourselves here at home?"

"Aye," Granna said quietly, holding her gaze, and Grace knew things had been put away against the worst of it.

"Then how about a bit of Christmas stew to go with the whiskey?" she said. "I've brought some cooked beef and carrots, and perhaps you've got the odd onion or parsnip, a bit of cabbage?"

Granna's eyes twinkled. "I'll bounce the baby, if you'll do the honors," she said. "Oh, and haven't we missed your cooking around here!"

Grace got Aghna to help in the kitchen, and before the first round of whiskey was poured, a stew bubbled over the fire, its aroma drawing neighbors who'd been too proud to come at first: Declan and Paddy Neeson came in with their da—their mother dead the summer past and himself too sad to make much of a Christmas; the Ryans were already there, Julia saying that Mary Kate was the spitting image of Grace as a baby; Missus O'Daly brought her shy boy, Shane, who spluttered and blushed when young Niamh Sheehan, sister of Big Quinn, came over to wish him well; Old Campbell Hawes was further along in his celebrating than any of them, and his wife shushed him with a slap to the shoulder each time he called for more drink; Irial Kelley had come with his family and his fiddle, and it didn't take much persuading to get him to play. Sean had found Nolan in the barn with the horses and dragged him in with the promise of a little fun; now the boy wore the first smile Grace had ever seen on him. Even Mary Kathleen, hesistant at first, now toddled around the room on the fingers of each loving hand that reached out for her.

After bowls of stew and soda bread went around the room, along with another splash of whiskey each, the neighbors came one at a time to bid Grace a blessed Christmas, to take up her hand for a moment or run a finger across her cheek, this girl of their own. And then, their stomachs eased of ache and their minds of worry, they wrapped their cloaks or blankets tight around themselves and walked home.

When the cabin was empty of all its visitors, Sean threw another piece of turf on the fire and set the kettle to boiling. Nolan was asleep on a pallet they'd made for him in the corner, and Mary Kate was drowsing in her grandfather's arms as he smoothed the hair out of her little face.

"Aye, Julia's right, sure enough. She's just like you as a babe," he said softly to Grace. "So busy, into everything you were, but happy as a lark in spring."

"She's a fine daughter," Grace agreed proudly. "I'm blessed to have her."

Aghna rose and brought the steaming kettle to the table to make tea.

"Let me help, Aghna." Grace took the heavy kettle and poured boiling water into the pot. "Do you feel anything yet?" she whispered.

Aghna nodded shyly. "Aye." Her hand covered her belly protectively. "It's mostly awake at night when I'm trying to sleep."

When the tea had steeped, Grace poured out the cups, then retrieved her Christmas bundle from under the table.

"I've brought you a little something," she said, handing the package of baby clothes to Aghna.

"And for you, as well, Mister Farmer."

Ryan took the boots, eyeing them with appreciation and gratitude.

Sean took his bundle of papers and magazines with delight, smoothing them out with a careful hand, barely pausing to kiss her in thanks before diving into the bold headlines.

"'Tis far too fine to sleep upon!" Granna fingered the hem on the linen sheets.

"I'm still enjoying my gift," her father whispered over Mary Kate's sleeping head, indicating the inch of whiskey that remained in his glass. "It made me feel lordly to have enough to share with my neighbors. Thank you, child."

"That was my gift to the family. These are for you." She put the gloves next to his glass. "I think of your hardworking hands on these cold mornings."

Her father shook his head, unable to say anything. He looked

down so that Grace might not see the mist in his eyes, but she knew
he was touched. She kissed his cheek and whispered, "You're a fine
man, Da," then went to sit near Sean, taking up the cup of tea to warm
her hands.

"I brought some flannel for the McDonagh girls," she told him.
"To cut up for winter petticoats and to make nappies for the baby."
She paused and lowered her voice. "And I've got a book for Morgan,
if you'll pass it on to him."

"A book!" Sean looked up from the newspapers. "What would he
be needing with a book—fine present though it is," he added quickly.

"Father Brown stopped in at the Sullivans' while I was there and
said Morgan was reading all the farming pamphlets he could get his
hands on. I found this . . . all about farming in the East."

Sean grinned. "Sure and won't he be happy to have it from you."
But then his smile faded.

"What is it?" Grace was surprised at the anxiousness she suddenly
felt.

Sean glanced at Aghna and Ryan, whose heads were bent over
the pile of tiny garments, lifting each one and holding it in wonder;
then he looked over at his father, who was humming a lullaby and sipping the whiskey.

"Nothing ails him," he said quietly. "He's just . . . he's distracted.
He's got much on his mind what with the troubles and all, and with
Aislinn gone missing."

"Aislinn!" Grace's tone caused Mary Kate to stir across the room,
so she lowered her voice. "She's not in service at O'Flaherty's?"

Sean shook his head. "She run off to London after young Gerald
months ago. He's come back to visit now, but no sign of her."

"Have they eloped, then?" Grace thought of that night nearly two
years ago, the look of fear and excitement on Aislinn's face, the fasci-
nation on Gerald's.

"I think he must've led her to believe that was the plan. He's been
living in London himself, you know—studying with a big solicitor. You
must know all this, traveling in the circle you do."

Grace shook her head, beginning to realize how isolated she'd become. "We don't go out much. Not since . . . the babies."

"Oh." Sean paused. "Well. They heard nothing from her all summer, just an envelope with a bank draft once in a while, no note. They

wondered, was she married, but then they were told that Old Man O'Flaherty referred to her as his son's tallywoman."

"And Morgan thinks she's still in London?"

"Aye." Sean smiled wryly. "He caught young Gerald coming out of a pub late one night, grabbed him up by the collar, and dragged him round the corner to the sidewall. The young master's a coward at heart. He didn't hold back a'tall."

"You talk as if you were there."

"And wasn't I, though? Sitting in the cart with a pistol in my hand in case further persuasion was needed."

Grace shook her head. "A pistol! Where would you get such a thing as that? The two of you could've been killed!"

Sean's smile slipped away. "We're all going to die, one way or another. We're at war, now, sister, or is that something else you're unaware of up in that fine house of yours?"

Grace looked down at her warm boots and felt the sting of his words.

Sean slapped his forehead with the palm of his hand. "Haven't I gone daft since you went away? I didn't mean that. Forgive me."

She nodded, determined to let it pass. "What about Aislinn, then?"

"The short of it is, he set her up in a room, then got engaged somewhere else—she made a fine mistress, he told Morgan, but was too common to be the wife of a gentleman." He paused, glancing again around the room. "I thought our Morgan would choke the life out of him right there, but he showed great restraint, he did." He took a swallow of his tea. "When Aislinn found Gerald had betrayed her, she flew into a rage and set fire to his house, then disappeared. Morgan fears she may be with child and afraid to show her face at home with the shame of it all."

Grace's heart fell. "Sure and her mother's not hard against her?"

"Not at all," Sean said. "She blames herself for letting Aislinn go in the first place, and took to her bed with sickness over it. All they want is to find her and bring her back to them. There's no money for passage, so he's been trying to find a boat that will let him work across and back."

Grace sat very still, her eyes on the tender flames of the fire. She set aside her cup, rose, and went into her old room, the room she would again share with Granna tonight. It was dark. She'd brought no candle with her, but she knew the feel of her coin pouch in her travel bag. She found it and went to the door, where enough light came down the wall to enable her to count out what she needed.

"Here," she said quietly, returning to her seat. She slipped the pouch into Sean's hand. "Give this to him. For his passage over, and two tickets back."

Sean shook his head. "He'll never take it from you, fool that he is."

"Then you shame him into it, Sean O'Malley. I know you've got the power to do it. It means less here for all of you," she added. "But—"

"We're fine," he interrupted. "Don't worry for us. You mustn't be asking the Squire for money, you know."

"I don't. This is what's left of the householding money. I'm a little better with the account books than he thinks." Her eyes twinkled.

Sean laughed. "You're treasure enough, Gracie." He slipped the pouch into his pocket. "I'll see that he takes it, and I'll thank you for him now."

"Don't thank me," she said soberly. "Has he not always been like a brother to us, helping with the work and cheering you up when you lay sick?"

"All right, then," he said. "I'll use that in my persuading speech."

They smiled at one another, their knees touching, close to the fire, and Grace felt as if they were children again, talking and mending through the long winter evenings.

Patrick rose slowly, and brought the sleeping bundle of Mary Kathleen to her mother's waiting arms.

"Time for us all to be in bed," he said, retrieving the whiskey bottle and pouring a last swallow into everyone's cup.

Granna eased herself out of the rocking chair and came to the fire; Aghna and Ryan stood close, hands touching. Sean helped Grace shift the baby to her shoulder and stand. The firelight played over their tired, open faces, flickering in their eyes as they all drew together.

Patrick raised his cup and said softly, "Here's to the warmth of our fire, and the peace in our hearts. May the good Lord bless and protect us, and keep us as one, for we stand together now a family, and there's naught matters more than that." He paused against the emotion in his voice. "To our family."

"To our family," they echoed, and drank.

"And let us not forget the others," he added, hand raising the cup even higher. "To young and old alike!"

"To Ireland!" they answered.

"God help us," Aghna added quietly, and Ryan took her hand.

# *Fourteen*

THERE was no freeze, but the winter passed raw and cold. Even when it didn't rain, clouds hung heavy in the dark sky and dampness clung to every surface. Chest colds were common, and with little food to nourish them, many of the very young and very old were carried away. Grace was vigilant in her prayers for Granna, who had taken to her bed with sickness, and for Aghna, whose baby would be born in June, God willing. Mary Kathleen had begun to cough and her little nose ran thick with it, so that Grace could not make another journey to her family. Instead, she sent Nolan twice with baskets of food and medicinal herbs, and a letter that Sean could read to them for comfort.

Then it was the end of February and the sun began gathering strength even as the wind blew strong across the sodden land. Grace and Brigid baked a cake for Mary Kathleen's first birthday, a cake Grace then sent home with Brigid, as the child was tired and fussy with her cold, and her father had not shown up for the celebration. Bram had been surly and anxious all winter, but Grace hoped that his mood would lighten now that they'd come through the worst of it and planting time would soon be here, bringing with it the outside activity he loved.

The subject of having another child was raised frequently; he wanted a son, but Grace was still nursing Mary Kate and afraid to give that up, even though the child could well survive on cow's milk and real food, both of which she'd been enjoying for some time now. This fear was equally weighted with that of Bram's anger should she deliver him not a son, but another daughter. She knew his past. She knew the depth of his rage. Would the disappointment of another daughter push him over the edge on which he balanced so precariously? Still, she could not continue to deny him. She had a duty. And she had not completely given up hope that a love might still be rekindled between them.

The decision was made the day she went out to the barn herself with the buckets. Moira had missed the morning milking and Grace could hear the cows calling insistently. As she neared the barn, she heard another sound beneath that of the cows; it was Moira's laughter, bold and teasing, and Grace suspected a suitor had found his way into her shapely arms. But it was not a suitor, nor some country boy come sneaking into the barn for an hour's entertainment. She stood quietly just inside the doorway, not wanting to watch, but unable to stop. They were lying in the hay, Bram on top of Moira, holding her arms above her head, and although they were still dressed, it was clear to Grace that soon they would not be. He was fondling her breast and kissing her neck; she called him something in a low voice and bit his ear, so that he became more rough with her and she shrieked, then laughed and arched against him. When his hand began to snake up beneath her skirts, Grace dropped the milk bucket. Bram turned his head, but instead of jumping to his feet, he simply smiled lazily. Moira was far more alarmed, pushing him off and scrambling to straighten her clothing as she got clumsily to her feet.

Bram watched her with amusement, then stood himself, casually brushing the straw off his pants.

"Why, Grace," he said with no trace of emotion. "What are you doing here?"

Grace looked for signs of remorse in his face, any hint of embarrassment, but finding none, turned and walked back to the house, untying her apron and throwing it on the kitchen floor before going upstairs to her room. She stood for a moment, the door closed behind her, then crossed to the mirror and looked at her reflection.

"Oh, dear God," she whispered, touching her face. "What has happened?"

The sound of his horse pounding down the driveway pulled her to the window, but he was already on the avenue and nearly out of sight. He would be gone all night. She knew that. She composed herself, then went to check on Mary Kate, who had awakened from her morning nap. The little arms around her neck were comforting and she pushed her face into the sweet-smelling hair.

When she went down into the yard, Moira was nowhere to be seen. The cows were now madly bellowing, so Grace took Mary Kate to the barn to relieve them. She relaxed with the rhythm of the milking and the warm smell of the cows; Mary Kate sat contentedly behind her, throwing handfuls of straw up into the air and letting them fall down into her hair. Grace had nearly finished when Moira came rushing at her out of the shadows.

"I'm sorry, Missus," the girl sobbed, sinking to her knees and clutching the hem of Grace's skirt. "'Tis ashamed of myself, I am." Her head shook as she wept. Mary Kathleen looked on in amazement.

Grace felt suddenly old, though Moira was but a year younger. She put her hand on the bowed head and sighed.

"He's a handsome man, the Squire," she said softly. "A hard man to deny."

"Aye." Moira looked up, her face wet, her eyes frightened. "And I'm too bold. I know I am. A right sinner, Mam says. He never paid me no mind afore, and there seemed little harm in teasing." She looked down again. "But then he took notice of me, started standing close and touching my hair, my . . ." She broke off and took a breath. "He wants me to have a baby, he says."

Grace closed her eyes and held so still, so very still. But when she opened them again, the breath was tight within her chest.

"Why?"

"Because you cannot, and doesn't he want a son, though? Sure, and it's not a matter of love," she added quickly. "He doesn't love me, and I know that. But he give me a new dress, and a promise of money."

Grace did not speak.

"You know me, Missus," Moira said desperately. "I've had my fun with the local boys and no good one is ever going to marry the likes of me. There's nothing for me here. I've got to go away if I'm to have a decent life."

"What about your baby?" Grace asked then.

Moira's eyes filled with tears, but she did not look away. "I'd be leaving him here for you to raise as your own," she said firmly. "That's the bargain."

"And if it's a girl?"

Moira swallowed hard. "You have a good heart, Missus. I know you'll raise her as a sister to yours."

Grace shook her head. "It won't be up to me," she said. "He won't keep your girl, Moira. He barely sees the one he has. He needs a son or his father won't sign over title to the land. He can't mortgage or borrow against what isn't his. He must have a son. Legitimately."

"I'd not say a word. I'd stay away till it was born," Moira pleaded. "Then you can keep your land, and I'll get out of this place once and for all!"

Grace grabbed the girl and shook her. "Wake yourself now! You're not thinking straight. Nor are you doing me any favors—I can have my own baby, you know."

Moira held still. "But he said you could not."

"He meant I *would* not. And that has been my mistake."

Moira stared at her, then let her head fall into Grace's lap. "Oh God, Missus," she moaned. "I'm going to Hell as sure as I'm sitting here."

"Sit up," Grace said firmly. "Wipe your eyes." She waited. "You've not gone through with it yet, have you?"

Moira shook her head meekly.

"But you've come plenty close, and that's danger enough." Grace thought for a moment. "I'll help you go away," she said. "Your mam's sister is over in Killarney. Can they take you in?"

"I don't know," Moira answered. "They wintered hard with no food and most of the children sick. Another mouth is how they'll see me."

"I'll give you food to take, and money. I want you to stay there and be of help to them. I'll send more when I can, and you can go to England if that's what you want. Do you understand me now, Moira?"

"Aye," she nodded. "But what shall I tell poor Mam? Not the truth, for Da'll beat the life out of me."

Grace bit her lip. "Tell her the Squire's been in the bottle too much and you're afraid of him. She'll understand, and she'll be glad you're well out of it."

Moira rose and brushed off her dirty, tattered skirt. Grace stood, too, and they regarded one another.

"You've always been good to me, Missus," Moira said. "I thought I was helping you, as well as myself. Can you not forgive me, then?"

Grace put her arms around the girl and held her tightly. "It's strange times we're living in," she said quietly. "Put your faith in God and look to Him for your forgiveness."

"I will," Moira promised. "I will."

Bram never questioned Moira's sudden disappearance, or Grace's acceptance of him again in her bed, and by the time planting was done and summer begun, Grace was pregnant for the second time. She was eighteen years old.

The usual gaiety of the summer months was quieter and more subdued, as thin country people contented themselves with standing in their doorways, watching haggard travelers make their way slowly down the lanes. The rot had wiped out nearly all the potatoes, and there were not many left for seed; most families put in only a quarter of what they would need to survive, but it was all they had. There was speculation as to whether the diseased potatoes would produce healthy crops or not, but not one person refused to put them in the ground, and as the summer passed, the plants grew green and hearty.

Grace was terribly tired and sick to her stomach most of the time. She could no longer pick up Mary Kathleen, and the child trailed after her, whining and fussy. Her impatience was great, but so was her lethargy, and the two left her dazed most of the time. So focused was she on the changes in her body and getting herself through each day, she was dissociated from the world around her. She got the occasional letter from Sean and sent her own news to her family through Nolan. They had all survived the winter and Aghna had given birth to a baby boy in June, called Thomas after her own father.

August was hot and the potato plants teemed with small blooms, each one a hint of the gold that lay beneath, each a promise to those who stood quietly in their cabin doorways, waiting to ease their gnawing hunger. Again, they went to bed with hope in their hearts, for now they were down to nothing. Many had pawned their bedding and the clothes on their backs for food, and now slept in rags on the dirt floor, no straw bed beneath, no food left in the cupboard. They were at the end of their resources; this crop, small though it was, was their last hope. But when they awakened one beautiful morning in August, even hope had fled their land, leaving behind the scorched, blackened rot of decaying fields, and a horrible stench that hung over roads and seeped into cabins. This time they had not the strength to weep and wail; they simply sank to their knees, stunned. And—as if the complete loss of their food was not enough—violent thunderstorms filled the air, lightning streaked across a dark sky, flashing eerily over demolished fields, torrential rains fell across the land causing floods, and finally a dense fog, cold and damp, closed in around them. It was, they all knew, the end of everything.

# Fifteen

THE letter from Lord Donnelly arrived in mid-October. Despite its brevity, Bram sat with it for more than an hour.

"Is it not the news you'd hoped for, then?" Grace entered the room quietly, surprised to find him sitting as he had been before she'd gone to put Mary Kate to bed.

"'As it is, we are stretched to meet our obligations,'" Bram read with little emotion. "'Your brother's colonial import venture has suffered a severe setback, and his debt is considerable. My own ventures have proved less lucrative than in the past, and I have no partner with whom to share the burden, now that Lord Helmsley has died. In addition, this year brings with it Caroline's marriage to Sir Bevin of Knightsbridge—you remember your mother's enthusiasm for societal display—it will be the wedding of the season.'" Bram cleared his throat. "'After these many years building the estate and speculating in the linen trade, one would think you had ready resources. But if, as you say, an increase in the annual remission cannot be met, nor even the usual amount paid promptly, then we must seriously consider the sale of Donnelly House, there being, as yet, no heir to claim it. We have done all we can here to ease the financial burden of the family and to repair our good name—we now look to you to redeem yourself once and for all.'" The hand holding the letter fell upon his knee.

"Is he saying they've gone broke?" Grace asked.

"He's saying that ready cash is not available to maintain their lifestyle, and he will not allow the family to be embarrassed. He won't hesitate to sell Donnelly House out from underneath us if I don't send them something immediately." His hand rubbed over the stubble on his cheeks and chin. "He's dangling the bait of redemption, as well. I know him. He wants me home but is too proud to ask. If I succeed, he gets his money; if I fail, he gets me."

"Does he not know about the baby?"

"He knows," Bram said. "He has to honor our agreement. But if it's not a boy, he'll put the house up at auction, and we'll have to go back. He'd like that. He'd like to have me under his thumb again."

Grace bit her lip, hands folding protectively over her large belly. One of the beautiful setters left the fire to nuzzle its master's hand. Bram took the dog gently by the ears and looked into its face.

"It's a bluff," he said finally. "He knows he'll get nothing for it, not with the troubles here, and the new estate tax." He paused, thinking, then came to a decision. "I'll sell the mill in Kildaire. It's done well— Hastings can easily buy me out. Then I'll have something to send to England, with enough left to keep things running here until . . ." He glanced at her.

"Until your son is born," Grace finished resolutely.

He nodded.

"God willing," she added.

"God owes me." He stood up, the dogs rising to follow.

"When will you go?" she asked.

He considered the possibilities, then decided. "Tomorrow. Don't know when I'll return, however. If Hastings thinks I'm desperate, he'll come in well below the price I need."

"I'll see to your clothes." Grace stood carefully, mindful of her aching back.

"Put in my evening suit," he said, checking the time on his pocket watch. "And two dress shirts. The black boots, gold cuff links."

She nodded as he strode out of the room, dogs at his heel. The front door slammed shut, and she knew he was going to the stable to speak to Nolan about readying Warrior for the ride across country. It would be a relief to have him out of the house for a time, though she knew he'd spend his evenings with women far more sophisticated than she. She shook her head, freeing it from those images, and went to see to his wardrobe. She knew that, especially in the city, Bram liked to cut a fine figure.

* * *

He'd only been gone two days when they began to come slowly down the avenue, turning up the driveway to the house. Grace had grown up amidst poverty, but rarely had she met with the desperate wretchedness that now stared her in the face with each opening of the back door.

"God bless you, Missus," they'd say, some sinking to their knees or holding out their starving babies for her to see. "God bless everyone in this house, for sure it is as good as Heaven."

She could not turn them away. So many were clearly dying, slowly starving to death, walking skeletons with skeletal children too tired to do more than turn their dark, sunken eyes to her face, not with hope, but with surrender. Sometimes with nothing at all. Those were the ones she fed first.

She listened to their talk and knew that most had been living on blackberries and cabbage leaves, but the berries had gone now and the remaining cabbages molded in the fields. In Skibbereen, they said, there was not a single loaf of bread nor sack of corn meal to be had by the common man. The Relief Committee had applied to Mr. Hughes, the Commissariat officer, and he had given up several tons of meal, but finally was forced to refuse, his superiors insisting that the locals should combine and import, or use home produce, instead of relying on government issue. Riots had broken out at Youghal when a crowd had attempted to hold up a boat laden with export oats, unable to bear the sight of food streaming out of the country. There had been loss of life in County Waterford when starving men entered Dungarvan and threatened to plunder the shops unless grain exporting was stopped. Two thousand troops had been ordered into the country with the intention of keeping the peace, as well as with private provisions of beef, pork, eggs, and biscuits. All ships loaded with grain or meal traveling up the River Fergus were given naval escorts, and warships were rumored to have been posted off Bantry and Berehaven.

As word spread that Donnelly House was feeding its tenants, a steady stream of ragged peasants found its way to the back door. Brigid had looked at Grace in fear when she first ordered the big pots set boiling for soup, the oven fired up for all the bread they could bake, but now the housekeeper came to the kitchen before first light so that those sleeping in the fields might have something warm as soon as possible. They worked together, and set those with enough strength to the task of helping them in order that everyone might get a cup of soup and a piece of bread that day. Most moved on after a day or two, lured by rumors of food ships landing at the docks in Galway or Cork City, or hoping to get passage to England. The Works Committees were still operating, although the number of people showing up for jobs outnumbered the tickets by the thousands. Anyone who could hold a shovel or a spade—young children, pregnant women, old men—stood in line in order to get their name on the list that would guarantee them two or three shillings a week. It was enough to feed their families one small meal a day if food could be found to buy.

The roads were a mess, made impassable by disorganized crews. Pay stations worked out of temporary shebeens, where workers were encouraged to drink up their small wage. The jobs officers were, by and large, unscrupulous men who paid the workers with a large bill, forcing them to walk to the nearest town in order to break it—and thereby losing a day's wage—or to spend part of it in the shebeen in order to get change.

Some stayed on at Donnelly House in hopes of living through this—mothers with small children, old people, cripples—and some stayed on to die in a place where they knew they'd get Supreme Unction and a Christian burial. Father Brown came nearly every day to comfort the dying, hear their confessions, and provide the last rites. Things were not much better for members of the clergy; Grace saw how he gulped down his soup, and put bread in his pocket against the gnaw that would strike late in the day. Despite his hunger, he would often forgo a meal until those around him had eaten something. He told her many times that God would bless her for her good deeds, to which she replied that God already had. She was thinking of the new man who'd come to help and who was now invaluable to her.

"Morning, Missus," he hailed her quietly from the doorway. "Two are dead—mother and babe, God bless their weary souls—but most still live to see another day."

"Morning, Abban." A mother and child, she thought, the woman who came in late last night, barely walking, the child so still in her arms, sores covering their mouths. "Will you cover them until Father Brown arrives?"

"Aye." He put his hand on her shoulder. "There aren't enough tears for all of them, Missus. The mother and her wee one are safe in the arms of the Lord now. Warm and fed. Aren't they the lucky ones, though, their misery ended at last?" He walked to the stove and lifted the heavy gruel pot to carry outside.

"Wait," she said. "Eat something first or you'll not get a bite all day."

He glanced toward the door. "Some are waiting already."

"Eat." She handed him a bowl. "I'll take out the tea to warm them. You'll be no good to me if you fall ill."

Abban nodded and ate quickly, standing near the stove. He was wiping out his bowl when Brigid came back in.

"Morning, ma'am," he said. "What needs doing?"

Brigid's eyes widened in surprise. "Abban Alroy, every day I think I've seen the last of you and every day I'm proved wrong. What's the matter with you, man, that you don't take what's left of your healthy self to the docks and get out of here?"

He handed her a bowl, then spooned in the gruel. "I'll not leave Ireland, ma'am. Not now I've buried my own, my son and his bride. I said to God, if You're leaving me alive, then give me a job of work, won't You? And He led me here, so here I'll stay. I'll be buried in Ireland with those I love."

Brigid nodded. "That's the grim truth of it." She ate the last of her breakfast. "Well." She looked out the window. "We're not sorry to have you. Take out the heavy pot and fill their cups. Those without will have to share. We've given out nearly all the crockery, including the good china, which won't fare the Missus any good with the Master."

"Is he not a Christian man, then?" Abban hoisted the pot.

Brigid laughed shortly. "No. I couldn't call him that, not in all the years I've been in this house, though I've cared for him well enough in my time."

Abban took the pot into the yard and filled the containers of each person who filed past, each one murmuring, "God bless you, sir," and, "Thank you, sir." He closed his ears to that and instead concentrated on making sure the children had a bit more and got what milk the cow gave. When the first pot was emptied, he scrubbed it out in the yard while Brigid and Grace brought out the second. A third sat on the stove, but that was all they had, and the pots had to be rotated. After the gruel was gone, they'd begin cooking up the soup, putting in whatever they could find for that day, slaughtering another chicken, although Grace was trying to keep enough for eggs. They had been at this nearly one month and their stores were running low. Twice, Grace had sent Abban with the wagon into town for more flour, and he'd bought up all he could, trading her silver spoons, but now there was no more flour or oats to be bought, although rumor had it the English would ship in corn meal from the colonies. The garden had been raided for everything edible, the jars of preserves nearly used up, and Abban wondered how she would feed herself and her young daughter, let alone the throng that grew larger every day. He'd thought at first that the Squire would bring back food, but now he understood that this was unlikely. Grace had said only that he was away on business and she expected him any day. She'd been saying that for the two weeks Abban had been here, and he wondered if she might not have been left behind. The Squire was an Englishman, after all, and liable to run home to his own people. He shook his head and sighed, scrubbing the pot a little harder.

"Abban!" Grace called from the side yard, where she'd set up a covered porch to house those most ill. She was very pregnant now and he could not abide to see her lifting or dragging anything heavy. "Two more going here. Send Father Brown as soon as you see him."

"Yes, Missus," he called back and went to the shed for the shovel. The hill back behind her garden was slowly being covered with mounds of dirt and stick crosses. She insisted on a cross for each grave, and the name of the person painted on a stone to sit beneath it, if they were able to find out who the person had been. Mothers and children were buried together. There was not time or material to fashion coffins, but the bodies were sewed into sheets or large pieces of burlap. Father Brown prayed over each one. Grace gave them words of comfort from the Bible if he was not there.

After he'd dug the graves, Abban went to the barn to see about the animals. They were a trouble to Grace; she did not want them to starve and suffer, but she could not put food in their mouths without taking it from people. They were making due with the hay, but the horses missed their oats and had become lethargic. The cow was still giving milk and the pigs were coping with bits and pieces, although Grace had said that soon they should be slaughtered and cured. When the animals were fed and cleaned, Abban went back to the house to carry out soup. Bread was sliced and placed on a long board. There was water to drink, some milk for the children, most of whom could no longer keep it down.

"You must go up and rest now, Missus." He took Grace by the hand and led her indoors. "The wee one needs a nap, and that one on the way needs your dreams."

Grace looked into his weathered face. "He'll be a worried child, then, if he's shaped by my dreams." She held out a hand for Mary Kathleen, who toddled quickly to her. "I have silver left to trade and some money, but where will we get the food?"

Abban pulled himself up to his full height of an inch taller than Grace, and attempted to frown down at her. "It will come from God," he admonished. "Just as it always has. Are you not like the wee boy who gave his lunch to our Lord Jesus? Two small fish and five loaves was all he had, but his offer to share it fed five thousand that day."

Grace smiled wearily. "Were that Jesus stood speaking in the yard today, eh, Abban?"

"He is, Missus. Now go on up and sleep awhile. Brigid and I can handle things for now, and I saw Father Brown coming down the road."

"All right," Grace agreed, climbing the stairs. "But wake me in an hour."

"Agreed." Abban watched with satisfaction as she and the little girl went up to bed. The Missus was much too pale, he felt, and an early baby would not bode her well in this time. The little girl, too, was feeling the worry and clung to her mother's skirts in an anxious manner. He had taken her down to see the animals, but after only a short time away, she'd begun to fuss. The Missus never seemed to mind—indeed, she kept her daughter close as if the absence were too much to bear.

He went back to the kitchen and helped Brigid start another pot of soup; there wasn't much to it: watery stock, strings of meat, some cut-up root vegetables, and a handful of barley. Still, it was warm and nourishing, if not enough to fill the belly, and no one was complaining. He saw many hands moving over their rosaries and heard the Missus' name mentioned in every prayer.

"Has there been no word yet from the Squire?" Father Brown asked, warming his hands around a cup of soup.

"None." Brigid shook her head. "Just as well, Father, or Missus Donnelly would have to shut this kitchen down."

Father Brown swallowed his mouthful of soup. "Surely the Squire is aware of and has approved his wife's actions? Will he not commend her for standing strong and doing her Christian duty in this time of great trial?"

Brigid let out a harsh laugh, startling Abban, who was chopping parsnips. "I don't think 'commend' is the right word there, Father." She turned to him, wiping her hands on her apron. "The day Squire Donnelly rides back up that road is the day someone pays for all of this." She motioned to the shambles of the yard, the lean-tos, the calls from the sick in the drawing room, the disarray in the kitchen. "And there'll be no kind words about Christian duty. No." She turned away so that only Abban saw the fear in her face.

Father Brown set down his empty cup. "I was not aware that Squire Donnelly knew nothing of this." His face was grim. "Certainly I know him by reputation—the farmers tell stories of his . . . firmness. I had thought—or perhaps *hoped* is a better word—that he'd experienced a conversion of sorts."

"No, Father," Brigid said quietly. "He most certainly has not."

"Well, you must send word to me the minute he arrives and I will speak on behalf of Missus Donnelly and what she has done." He turned and glanced down the driveway to the road. "In the meantime, there's work to be done."

"Two to be buried, Father," Abban put in. "And three in the drawing room looks like they won't see evening."

Father Brown nodded and reached into the folds of his robe for his prayer book and crucifix. "I'll hear confessions first, then see to the dead."

The afternoon closed in, bitterly cold and gray. Snow—rarely seen during the mild winters of the South—began to fall, as if Nature, too, had now turned against Ireland. Ragged peasants in dark, soiled clothing huddled around small fires throughout the yard, their talk not much more than occasional murmurs and low croons without melody sung in an effort to soothe their sick and starving children. They did not move about, as they had no extra energy to spend. Those still strong and hopeful had moved on after breakfast, warily eyeing the sky, sure that the next town would be better off with food and jobs for those who could still work. New folk had drifted in, their faces anxious, some with the terrible cough and wheeze that meant death was near. Abban tried to give everyone new a cup of warm broth and a piece of bread. He sorted out the terribly ill and dying, bringing them into the house, where they lay on blankets and rugs in the drawing room. It was more splendor than most had ever seen, and some called out in their delirium, sure they'd entered Heaven. He put women with young children in the barn or out on the back porch, which had been made into a kind of shelter by nailing up boards on the rails. The men made due as best they could, stacking boards into temporary shelters, or sitting near the fire through the frosty night. There wasn't one who didn't look ten years older than his true age. Those who could help did, but if they had the strength to walk on, they did that, too.

Abban and Father Brown had just finished burying the mother and her baby in the frozen ground when they spied a lone man on horseback coming down the road. The rider did not stop to speak to any of the travelers who shared the road, but nudged them aside with his great black horse. Father Brown and Abban looked at one another.

"I do believe the Squire is back," Father Brown said calmly, crossing himself and starting down the hill.

Abban stood another minute, looking up at Grace's bedroom window. It was still dark. He decided not to awaken her until Father Brown had spoken to the Squire, but his heart was pounding and he said a quick prayer to calm himself.

# Sixteen

"WHAT the hell is going on here?" an angry voice demanded from the yard. "Who are all these people? Brigid!"

The housekeeper came to the door, her face pale, her eyes searching out Father Brown, who was making his way through the garden.

"Good to see you home, sir," she said meekly. "Shall I get Nolan to tend your horse?"

Bram jumped down and snapped the reins around the porch post. Anger rolled off him in a sour wave; his bloodshot eyes told Brigid he'd found an open shebeen on the way home.

"Nolan!" He came running. "Take the Squire's horse to the barn, now, there's a good boy."

Nolan reached out hesitantly to loose the rein, then led Warrior quickly away.

All the men in the yard had risen to their feet and stood silently watching, as the snow fell on their shoulders and covered their way-worn hats. Father Brown slipped on ice near the well, regained his balance, and hurried cautiously toward the porch.

"Squire Donnelly." He made a slight bow. "May I be the first to welcome you home, and may I say what a fine thing it is you're doing here."

Bram squinted at the priest, then looked around the yard in disgust. "Who the hell are you?" He shoved Father Brown aside and walked up to his housekeeper. "What the hell is this, Brigid?" He peered into the kitchen behind her. "Where is Missus Donnelly?" He stormed into the house. "Grace! Grace!"

Brigid followed him. "She's resting, sir. Her time is near, as you know, and she's been so tired, she has."

He ignored her. "Grace!" Then he stormed into the drawing room, eyes widening when he saw the furniture pushed out of the way and what seemed to be bundles of rags lying on the floor.

Grace appeared at the top of the stairs, pushing her hair into place, then coming down as quickly as she could.

"Bram," she said evenly, taking his arm and pulling him out of the drawing room. "I'm so glad you're home."

He looked at her in amazement. "What in God's name is going on here? Who are all of these people?"

Grace swallowed and smoothed down the apron over her skirt. "They're your tenants, Bram. They're dying." She held his eye, un-flinching. "Father Brown comes to hear their confession. Then we bury them."

Bram became unnaturally calm. "And those able-bodied men in the yard?"

"Tenants trying to get to the city to find work. There's nothing left for them here," she explained.

"And are you feeding them?"

She nodded, her mouth dry.

"With our food?"

"Yes."

"So, not only are my tenants running off without paying their rent, but they're taking my food as well, is that right?" His smile froze her heart. "Do I understand the situation correctly?"

"They cannot pay you, Bram," she said quietly. "They have no money. They have no food. They are starving to death. And now they're freezing to death, as well. I could not turn them away."

"Oh, you could not?" His eyes widened in mock surprise. "Well, all right, then. If you just . . . 'could not' . . ." He grabbed her arm and dragged her through the kitchen and out into the yard. "You could *not* turn them away, but you *will* make them pay—whatever they've got: rings, watches, earbobs . . ." He shook her. "Look at them! They're se-cretive and sly. They sew coins into their clothing, they bury what they have in the fields or stuff it into tree trunks! I know they've got money hidden away, and it belongs to me! Tell them to turn it over!" he de-manded.

"I won't!" She struggled against him. "They have nothing to give you!"

"Then tell them to get off my property right now or I'll shoot every last one." He gripped her arm more tightly, then pushed her to the ground.

The men in the yard dropped their cups and moved forward as one body. Abban came around the side of the house, a shovel raised in warning. Bram backed into the kitchen, then burst out again, a six-shooter in each hand. His dogs came to his side and stood, quivering with anticipation.

"Get off my land, you lazy Irish bastards."

The men stood where they were, joined now by the women and children. Father Brown stood at their front.

"Start running," Bram shouted, his voice echoing in the muffled silence of raining snow. "Or I swear I'll shoot you where you stand. Bloody thieves! Bloody trespassers!"

Father Brown came forward, holding up his hands. "Please, Squire Donnelly. You're tired . . . you've had a long journey . . . this is all a surprise to you. But are we not reasonable men?"

Bram leveled the gun at the priest, who stopped in his tracks. "These are not reasonable times, priest."

Father Brown swallowed and took another step. "But certainly . . ."

Bram shot him in the foot. "Next time I aim higher. Now get out."

The men surged forward to catch the stumbling priest, who looked up at the Squire in shock. One man suddenly burst from the back of the crowd, charging with a battle cry. Bram shot him dead.

"Next," he said calmly, and when they still did not recede, shot again, felling a second man. Blood sprayed across the white snow.

"Run and live, or stay and die," he explained patiently, giving them another moment. When they still did not move, he sighed, shook his head as if they were errant children, and took careful aim at a young woman. Instantly, the crowd fell back, then began to run for the road, clumsily dragging the fallen and wounded with them, slipping and falling on the ice. Bram fired in the air to keep them moving, then set the dogs upon them. He turned, then, to survey the litter of the yard, and saw Abban, who had not run but stood near the barn.

"You!" he ordered. "Take that refuse out of the drawing room and dump it in the bog."

"Sir?"

"Clear them out of there or spend the afternoon burying them, with a space for yourself beside. Understood?" He waved the gun.

"Yes, Squire." Abban went quickly to the barn for the cart, which he drove around to the kitchen. Inside the house, he could hear Bram's rage increasing as Grace answered questions. He cursed under his breath as he carried out the dying men, one by one, and laid them in the cart. The last was his cousin Dick, who'd stumbled into the yard only yesterday and certainly wouldn't live to see tomorrow, so sick was he with the fever. He couldn't dump them in the bog.

"Go to the parish house." Brigid appeared in the doorway, pale and teary. "They'll give those poor souls a Christian burial." She glanced at the sky. "It's coming down hard. You won't be able to see soon. Leave the cart there, I'll send Nolan down for it tomorrow. You'd best not come back here."

"What will happen?" he whispered. "Will you be all right?"

She sighed, then set her jaw. "I'll not leave unless I have to. My Jack is sick, and there's Nolan. I've never seen such a cold winter as this. The roads would kill us all for sure."

"And the Missus?"

Fresh tears welled up. "I don't know," she whispered, shaking her head. "I don't think he'll touch her. Not with the baby so close." She paused and listened to a door slam upstairs. "But when he's had the drink, he's not himself. I've seen him terrible cruel, though never to this one."

Abban's face was grim. "I'll be back," he said. "Give him all the whiskey you can find and maybe he'll go out with it."

He climbed into the cart, but could not make himself go. Light spilled down from the upstairs window, blurred through falling snow, and he cocked his head, listening hard to the sound of raised voices; only when he heard Grace's, only when he had locked it firmly in his heart for safekeeping, did he pull his jacket more tightly around himself and urge the horses to move now.

"Surely you've taken leave of your senses!" Bram shouted.

They were in his study, Grace sitting in the chair by the window, Bram pacing the room, hands clenched.

"There's nothing left in the storehouse!" he said. "Do you realize what you've done to us? Do you?"

Grace faced him, but not defiantly. "I did what I thought was right. They work your land and pay your way. I cannot turn my back on them while they starve to death on our doorstep."

"And so you have decided to let your own family starve instead, is that it?"

Grace tried to quiet the fluttering within her. "Did you not sell the mill, then, and bring back supplies?"

"I am not running a poorhouse. I made that clear when I left. You knew what was expected of you and still you disobeyed me."

He was more angry than Grace had ever seen him, but not until she realized that Brigid had gone home and they were alone in the house did she feel the first trickle of fear.

"I was wrong to go about it the way I did, without your permission," she said humbly. "You have every right to be angry."

"Don't try to placate me," he spat. "You've dug yourself an early grave, Missus Donnelly." He pulled some papers out of his breast pocket and threw them on the desk. "Not only could Hastings ill afford to buy me out—he was himself in need of a buyer. We must have wined and dined every Englishman off the boat in an attempt to sell, but it's taken all this time to persuade someone of the bargain. All they see when they come are hordes of squatters begging in the streets. Fear hangs about the place like a stink. Who wants to invest in a country where death is all anyone talks about?"

"But you did sell it?" she asked hopefully.

"Yes," he hissed. "We sold it. But for very little. I wired most of it back to London, thinking I was safe. This is all that's left." He pulled a sack of coins out of his coat pocket and dropped it on top of the papers. "Little good it'll do us, though, with the country rapidly running out of food to buy."

"There are the animals," she offered. "And I've not touched the cellar."

"Someone did." He glanced out the window, his reflection stark in the glass. "Your precious Irish peasants broke in and stole what you didn't give them."

Grace bit her lip. There was no malice in her heart toward those who had taken the food, but she knew this would weigh against her in a trial where she was already most certainly judged guilty.

"God, I hate this bloody country!" He slammed his fist down on the desk. "Nothing but beggars and whores."

Grace said nothing, afraid to move.

"But I'll be damned if I'll go back to England defeated, and live with that smirk the rest of my days. He will not win." Sweat glistened in the creases of his forehead. "I may be stuck here, goddamn it, but I'm not going down with this tide of waste. I'll ride out this famine, and this bloody awful winter, and then I'll buy up all the land when they get desperate enough to sell—which they will! At the end, I'll be the richest man in the country, and when my father insists upon 're-muneration,' I'll have the extreme pleasure of telling him to fuck off." He smiled wickedly, then his eyes fell on Grace and the smile evaporated. "Get out," he ordered. "Tell Brigid to bring me something to drink. Then leave me alone to figure a way out of this mess."

Night came early. The gentle snow fall had become a fierce wind of icy sleet and hail that battered the house. It was not the west wind that Ireland knows so well, but a frozen gale from the northeast, and it ended the life of many on the road that night.

Upstairs in the battened house, Bram swigged straight from the bottle and looked over his accounts, oblivious to the wind howling around corners, whistling through tiny slits. Remembering Abban's advice, Brigid had gone out to the cellar and come back with a full bottle of whiskey, which she delivered to the Squire's study. Steeling herself against the tension in the house, but jumping at every sound of the storm, she tried to concentrate on roasting the last chicken for his dinner, along with a turnip, hoping a good meal and the drink would help him to nod off.

Grace cleared away the blankets and sheets from the drawing room and directed Nolan to put the furniture back exactly as it was. When this was done and all looked as before, she sent Nolan away—despite his protests and his anxious face—then lit the fire and sat staring into it, wondering at the chaos she'd created and wishing she were a child again on her straw mat next to Gran. Mary Kate, afraid of the storm, slept on the divan, firelight shimmering in her curly golden

baby's hair, a fist balled up, nestled against her mouth. She made sucking motions in her sleep and Grace worried for the future, as the un-
born child within her kicked and kicked. Occasionally there was a
thump from overhead, and once the sound of breaking glass followed
by a stream of curses. The chicken had gone untouched; she thought
of Abban and his dying cousin out in the night somewhere, unpro-
tected from cold and wind, but she held her tears, knowing she must
show no sign of weakness. She looked, instead, for answers in the face
of the warm fire until, at last, she fell asleep.

"You stupid, stupid bitch!" Bram screamed in her ear, hauling her
up by her hair.

She came awake quickly, her heart racing; one look told her that
he was out of his mind with drink. She began to fight him with both
hands, but was no match for his rage.

"All the household money is gone! Every penny!" He slammed
her up against the door, the hinge biting into her backbone. "And the
silver! That was Abigail's! You had no right to touch it! Where is it?"
His hands were around her throat, choking her.

Mary Kate was awake now, screaming in terror. Grace's hands
flailed against the wall until one fell on a porcelain statue, which she
grabbed and smashed over his head. Momentarily stunned, he let go
and she ran to the child, scooping her up protectively.

Bram recovered quickly, cornering them. "Bad enough you give
away our supplies," he snarled. "But to use the money, and to steal
Abigail's silver . . . for that trash . . . I ought to kill you for that alone."
He picked up the fireplace poker.

Grace set Mary Kathleen down, pushing the child behind her,
eyes flying over the room. There was no way out except the door. She'd
have to get past him.

"Bram, the baby," she begged, then stopped, remembering the
last time she'd said those words.

He darted in and struck her with the poker, knocking her to her
knees.

"The baby," he muttered, throwing the weapon into the fire with
disgust. "The damn baby . . ." He grabbed a thick hank of her hair and
dragged her out of the room, yanking her up, twisting her around and

shoving her against the stairs. She stumbled and he kicked at her, his boot smashing into her abdomen. She couldn't see for the pain, but struggled not to lose consciousness.

"Run," she called weakly to the child still screaming in the other room.

He snorted and gripped her hair again, close to the scalp, pulling her up the stairs and down the hall to the room off the nursery that had been Abigail's.

"Get in there, bitch." He shoved her into the room, then up against the wall.

No light, she thought, then realized the windows were boarded. Fear surged through her and she fought with fresh energy, bringing her knee up between his legs. When he doubled over, she shoved him and tried to run for the door, but he grabbed her ankle and felled her, then pulled her back along the floor. She struggled to her feet, only to feel his fist land against her face. Sinking back to the floor, she heard his voice as if from far away.

"You'll stay in here until you have the baby." He was breathing heavily in the doorway. "If it's a boy, I'll consider letting you out. If it's a girl, you can both rot."

The door closed on her and she slumped in the blackness, listening to the scrape of the key in the lock.

"Mary," she whispered, and then she passed out.

# *Seventeen*

THERE was no answer at the parish house and Abban realized the priests had gone up to the tiny convent of silent nuns on the hill. He could not bring himself to leave his cousin or the other men alone at the parish, although none of them was conscious. He urged the terrified horse on against the horrible wind, his hands and face numb, ice and snow coating the cart. He must have stood half an hour pounding on the convent door until they heard him above the shriek of the storm. Once inside, he drank some broth and took a cloak given by the nuns, who had little themselves but who gestured insistently and forced it upon him when they saw he would not stay and wait out the storm. He kissed his cousin Dick on both cheeks and looked long into the face of his last living relative, then asked the priest to bury him, say a special mass for his soul, and mark the grave with his proper name so that Abban might find it again one day.

The hour of midnight had come and gone, the wind had blown itself out, and the snow fell lightly again. He felt alone in the world, and was heartened to see, out in the bog, the flickering light of campfires shielded by the low, rough huts people had dug to make temporary shelter. So many had died, but there were others who were staying alive just as he was—day by day, night by night.

As, at last, he neared the avenue that would take him to Donnelly House, he was filled with dread and tried to hurry the exhausted horse. There was a low light in the drawing room window, but nowhere else. They're all asleep, he told himself, safely asleep in their beds. It was not until he neared the house that this illusion was shattered; a small figure burst out of the shadows and ran at him, his progress slowed by the deep snow.

"He's passed out now." Nolan was out of breath. "Mam's taken the baby. I don't know about the Missus—I'm afraid to go back in alone."

Abban hauled the boy into the cart and hurried the horse around the back of the house to the kitchen door. He stopped and listened, but heard nothing above the occasional gust of wind.

"Where's the Squire now?" he asked as loudly as he dared.

"On the floor by the fire in the drawing room," the boy replied, eyes wide. "He comes alive now and again, cursing and ranting, then falls back."

"And the Missus?"

"Above, I think. There's blood on the wall by the stairs." Nolan grabbed his arm. "We've got to get her out of there."

Abban nodded. "Courage, boy. Here's what to do." He glanced toward the open kitchen door. "Quiet as a ghost, you must take the cart to the barn and get a fresh horse. Then bring it back here. Quiet now. And quick as you can."

"Where will you go?"

"Does she have people in these parts?"

"Aye." Nolan's eyes widened. "On the other side of the great wood."

"That's where, then. Now, hurry. And not a sound."

Abban jumped off the cart and slipped into the kitchen. As he crept into the entry, he could hear Bram's snores from the drawing room. He picked up a candle from the side table and moved to the staircase, one careful footstep at a time. Lifting the candle, he made his way slowly up, pausing to cross himself when he saw the splotch of blood on the wall. Grace was not in the first bedroom, her own, nor in the second or third, nor the nursery at the end of the hall. It was not until he heard a moan from above that he spied the small staircase to the side of the nursery. There was blood and hair on the first step and his heart pounded in his ears as he climbed the short flight. He tried the knob—locked.

"Missus?" he whispered through the door. "Are you in there?"

The only sound was that of the house creaking, but he felt sure she was in this room. The Squire probably had the key in his pocket, and Abban did not relish the thought of searching him for it. He could just shoot the bastard in the head and be done with it, he thought. Burn the house down. End the whole thing. He shook himself. She'd be blamed. And hung. The English were hanging Irish with pleasure these days, and they'd love to slip the noose on one that rose above her station. No. He'd have to get her out of here and leave her husband to die another day. It wasn't much of a lock, he thought, turning the candle to it. Then he saw the nail holes around the door frame and knew the Squire had a more permanent restraint in mind. Bracing himself against the far wall, he kicked the door as hard as he could. It loosened but did not open, and Abban held his breath, listening for any sound from down below. He stood back and kicked again; this time the door swung open.

"Missus?"

He held the candle in front of him and stepped into the room. The windows were boarded. He played the light over the walls until it fell upon her crumpled form in the corner.

"Dear God in Heaven," he gasped and went to her.

The light showed up a face badly swollen and bleeding from a deep cut above the eye, a split lip and snarled hair, ripped out in bloody patches. Her hands were cut and fingernails torn off. He set the candle on the floor and gathered her into his arms. She moaned and tried to push him away.

"Hush, now, Missus," he soothed. "It's Abban come to take you home. You must be very quiet now."

He lifted her awkwardly, careful of her large belly, trying to manage the candle as well. She opened her eyes only once and looked into his without seeing him, then closed them again. Suddenly he was afraid, and moved swiftly down the stairs, through the kitchen, and out into the freezing cold. He placed her gently in the back of the cart, where the dying men had lain not so long ago, then went back in for all the blankets he could carry. These he wrapped under and around her to cushion the ride and keep her warm.

"She's alive, then," Nolan said with relief.

"Not for long," Abban answered, tossing him a blanket. "Climb up, now, and show me the way."

The O'Malleys were not yet up when Abban stopped in front of their cottage. It had taken what was left of the night to bring her this far; twice he'd had to stop to clear away snowdrifts, and twice they'd turned down a wrong lane, the snow having altered the landscape. Exhausted though he was, he jumped down from the cart and pounded on the door until it was opened.

"We've not much to spare, brother," Patrick said, yawning. "But if you wait till the fire is going, we can give you a cup of tea and some porridge."

"I've brought your daughter," Abban said quickly. "She's bad hurt. Help me get her out of the cart."

"Ryan!" Patrick was instantly awake, calling over his shoulder. "Sean! It's Grace." He followed Abban to the cart and looked in. "Sweet Jesus above, what's happened?"

Ryan hurried out, fumbling with his pants, his shirt unbuttoned and flapping in the wind. Standing across from his father, they worked together to lift the blanketed bundle out of the cart. Grace moaned and the cut on her lip opened, sending a fresh trickle of blood down her crusted chin. They carried her in and laid her in front of the hearth, where Sean was blowing on embers to start the fire. Gran rushed to them, tying a shawl around her shoulders. Abban and Nolan followed as far as the doorway, then stood, anxious and watchful.

"Come." Patrick motioned them in. "Close that door. Who are you, then?"

"This is Mister Alroy, helped up at the big house," Nolan told them.

Abban nodded and stepped into the small cabin room, which reminded him so much of his own; his heart turned over with yearning for the family he'd had less than a month ago.

"Sean," Gran directed, "get my kit and set a kettle to boiling." She turned to Abban. "He beat her, did he?"

"Aye." Abban knelt down beside Grace, picking up her hand. "She angered him by feeding the starving what come by her door. I was one of them, and stayed on to help. He was gone, you see, on business. And when they come, the folk, in this bitter cold, she couldn't turn them away."

"No," Gran said softly, smoothing the hair back from Grace's pale face.

"He turned up out of the blue and she had soup kettles boiling, dying folk inside the house, and Father Brown there to bury them."

He paused and looked at Patrick. "He shot the Father in the foot, killed two men outright for trespassing."

Patrick's face went hard. "And then he beat her?"

Abban shook his head. "'Twas later, after he'd been drinking and brooding upon it. He sent me away, but I come back to find her like this, locked in a room upstairs, and him passed out on the floor below."

"Where's Mary Kate?" Sean handed Gran her kit of herbs and salves, then limped to the door, looking out at the wagon.

Abban and Nolan looked at one another, then slumped. How could they have forgotten the child?

"She's safe," Nolan offered wearily. "Mam took her to our cabin."

"I'll go back for her." Abban stood and moved toward the door, stumbling.

"Sit down," Patrick said firmly. "You're in no state to go back out in this weather. Besides, he'll be waking up now and sorting through it. Will your mam bring the child to us?" he asked Nolan.

"I don't know." The boy looked downcast. "She was terrible scared when she come back up to the house and found the baby screaming in the corner and blood all over the walls. She told me to wait in the kitchen door for Mister Alroy and tell him what happened."

Aghna was up now, too, holding Thomas tightly in her arms. "Will she lose the baby, Gran?" she asked softly.

Gran ran her hand over Grace's belly, stopping in one place, then another. She frowned. "I cannot tell," she said. "I think the child moves a bit, but it's hard to know. Both have suffered." She looked up at the worry on Abban's face and the fatigue on the boy's. "Fix them something to eat, Aghna," she said. "They've had a long night."

While the men sat down at the table, Gran threaded a needle and sewed up the cut above Grace's eye. She rubbed salve along the girl's lips and into the torn places on her scalp. With scissors, she trimmed the broken nails and bandaged the fingers where the nails had been torn off. Then she directed Ryan and Patrick to carry Grace to the stuffed mattress in her old room, where they settled her as gently as they could.

In privacy, Gran unbuttoned the torn dress, blinking away tears that rose with each revealed bruise. She called Aghna to help bathe and clean the cuts, and get the battered body into a nightgown. Twice

Grace opened her eyes, but did not appear to recognize where she was or with whom. Each time she seemed to close them gratefully and sink back into the deep sleep of the battle weary.

At the table, the men discussed their options. Patrick was insisting that it should be he who avenged his daughter and rescued his granddaughter, but Abban calmed him down and made him see the foolishness of this. Patrick didn't know the lay of the land around the house, and would be easily seen against the brilliance of the snow, nor was he familiar with the dogs that roamed the property when their master was home; and if the Squire was shooting off his pistols . . . well, they didn't need another body to bury and that was all there was to it. The same went for Ryan, and Abban noted the relief in Aghna's eyes. After much talk and argument, it was finally decided that Abban and Nolan—no threat to the dogs—would return together, but not until they'd eaten and slept, and had the promise of darkness by the time they got there.

The storm had abated, the wind was but a gentle gust now and again, and the sky was free of clouds. The sun on the snow was dazzling; water dripped from the ice on the windows. They all stared out at the sight, so rare, and so beautiful, too, despite the fury that had brought it.

"It's like Fairyland," Nolan whispered drowsily.

Ryan brought out pallets and Granna bedded them down in a corner near the fire. The hot porridge and warmth of the room lulled their weary bodies into immediate sleep.

It was late in the afternoon when they awoke. Granna fed them bowls of thin soup with bits of hard bread to dip in it, then tied hats over their heads and wrapped torn bedding around their hands. The whole family walked them to the cart and stood until Abban insisted they go back in. He didn't wish to carry the weight of their worry any further than he had to. When he looked up, only the brother remained.

"Why did you not kill him, then?" Sean asked quietly, when Nolan had climbed into the back and gotten under the blankets.

Abban measured the small man with the withered arm and gimpy leg who looked so much like his sister around the eyes.

"I should have," he said. "I had it in me. But I wasn't thinking clear, what with trying to get herself out of there. I was afraid the English would hang her for the murder and be glad of it."

"Aye." Sean narrowed his eyes. "It's not safe to be Irish in Ireland anymore. If we're not starving to death, or dying of the fever, they're throwing us in prison for conspiracy."

"As long as there are young ones like this, we'll survive." Abban looked back at Nolan, asleep again under the blankets.

"The young ones are dying faster than the old," Sean said harshly. "And those that survive wander the roads and haunt the towns."

"The nuns are caring for them at Sisters of the Rose in Cork City," Abban said. "I've heard tell they take in any orphan comes to their door."

Sean put his hand on Abban's shoulder. "We've never needed orphanages in Ireland before. Ever. We've always taken care of our own. But they've taken that from us, as well. We don't need more orphanages," he said directly. "We need fewer English."

"I've heard talk of that, as well."

"And?"

"'Tis true enough that the English soldiers have become bloodthirsty."

"And have the Irish not become so parched that they have a thirst now, as well?"

Abban weighed this exchange, pausing before he answered. "I am a simple man. A farmer all my life. My grandfather wore the ribbon, but in his old age he swore that more lives were lost than won, and Ireland suffered more greatly because of it. He told me to follow the law, and live straight, and so I have."

Sean examined his face carefully. "All right, then." He nodded, and turned to go back in.

Suddenly Abban grabbed his arm, halting him, and it was Sean's face that bore scrutiny.

"But that was before," Abban added. "In another life."

"I understand."

Abban let go of his arm. "I am not a young man anymore."

"Nor are you old."

"I've been turned out of the only home I've ever known by soldiers who knocked it to the ground and laughed while they did it."

"Happens every day," Sean said.

"I watched my family die of fever beside the road and buried them with my bare hands in the wood so that the animals would not eat them, or the soldiers desecrate their bodies. I have buried more people than I can count in the last few weeks and seen more children die for want of oats in their bellies."

"Aye." Sean held still.

"I've seen English horse soldiers trample bodies still alive, and throw healthy children into infested workhouses, where they die terrible deaths." He paused and looked in the open doorway, lowering his voice. "And I've seen a fine, Godly woman beaten to within an inch of her life by her husband, an English landlord, who will never be held accountable for his crime under the law."

"We must change laws that give us no power over our own destinies."

"How?" There was anguish in Abban's voice. "O'Connell is dead, a broken man. Peel himself has given up."

"Does that mean that *we* must give up?"

"I was a Repeal warden in my parish, but I left it with all the backbiting. They were doing nothing about the suffering—it was all politics over the pulling away of those Young Irelanders."

"You're against them, then?"

Abban shook his head. "Not if they face the famine. Not if they stand up as the men of action they claim to be. But that Smith O'Brien, the man in charge, he's not much older than you are and a Protestant, in the bargain. A bloody intellectual, and what does he know of the common man, sitting all those years in Parliament?"

"He sat there begging the cause of Ireland, day in and day out," Sean stated. "There's Duffy stands with him, as well, son of a grocer. And 'Meagher of the Sword,' whose father was Catholic Mayor of Waterford. And young John Mitchel raised by a Presbyterian minister. All of them ready to speak for us."

"And what if I want to speak for myself?" Abban folded his arms across his chest.

"A single voice is easily drowned out," Sean said. "Add it to ours and they'll be forced to listen."

The sun broke through the gathered clouds just then, and a beam of light shone down on the two men, warming them briefly. Abban's face changed in that moment; despair left his eyes and determination took its place.

"I can shoot better than most, though I don't have a gun," he said quietly. "I can ride and I know these mountains better than anyone else. I've read Duffy's speeches in the *Nation,* so I know where you stand."

"If you're caught, you'll be tried for treason. Hanged, drawn and quartered."

"Then I won't get caught." He smiled grimly. "Where will I go now?"

"Back to Donnelly House for Mary Kate," Sean said. "If you cannot get her, then make your way up the valley to the Black Hill. Ask on the road for one called McDonagh. Give my name. When you get there, speak only to him and only in private."

"Have I not heard tell of this McDonagh?"

"Aye." Sean held his eye. "And he could use someone like you in his current line of work. We're not all saints, you know, and he needs a man he can trust."

Abban glanced through the open door one more time. "I am that," he said. "If nothing else."

# Eighteen

JULIA Martin paced the long living room, pausing at the end of each trip to look out the windows. She worried the rings on her fingers, fussed with the flowers, took books from the shelf and rifled their pages, only to shove them back into place or drop them on a side table. Finally, she flung herself into a chair and let out a long-suffering sigh.

"Dear God in Heaven, Julia, what on earth is the matter with you tonight?" Her father sat in his customary chair near the fire, papers folded neatly in a pile beside him. "Can a man not read the news of the day without fear of a book being dropped on his head?"

Julia picked at her fingernail, frowning. "You'll get no accurate news of the day from that rag," she said disdainfully. "Anything worth reading is in the *Nation,* Father, as well you know."

"Bunch of radical scalawag writers over there, I hear," he said, tongue-in-cheek. "Nothing but overeducated baffoons with romantic ideals."

She laughed and threw a pillow at him.

"Speaking of which, tell me how you are currently rousing the common man." He tucked the pillow under his arm, pulled out his pipe, and filled it from a silver box on the table beside his chair. "What are you writing about in fiery prose this week?"

"Revolution, of course." She straightened herself up and leaned forward. "John wants us to throw all our support behind the Young Irelanders. They've got nothing but opposition from O'Connell's group, the priests are against them, and there's little money from the gentry to arm an uprising."

"Armed uprising?" Her father sucked in the flame until the pipe smoldered steadily on its own. "Have we come as far as that?"

"Your head's been buried in the pacifist press!" She jumped up and strode across the room to the fire, flopping down again in the chair opposite his. "What do you think's been going on out there these past months?"

"I think we're in the midst of the most terrible famine Ireland has ever known," he said quietly. "I think the streets here in Dublin are impassable with dying beggars, that the workhouses are full, and that the hospitals can offer no relief. I think that ships full of grain leave our harbors every day, and that London refuses to send aid because it costs too much and will hurt agricultural prices. I think that all of England has turned a deaf ear to the screams of torture rising up out of our streets, and that they're wiping their hands as frantically as Pontius Pilate. That's what I think is going on."

"'Wiping their hands like Pilate,'" she repeated. "That's good. I'll use that in my next piece."

"This is not about rhetoric, daughter," he reminded. "This is reality. Behind all that impassioned language you use in your papers is the very real suffering of very real people. Are you writing *about* them, or *for* them?"

Her cheeks burned. "That's not fair," she said angrily. "I love my country and I'll not stand by and watch it destroyed."

"No," her father allowed. "But you wouldn't be the first to get caught up in the politics of revolution, when starvation and survival are the real issues."

"Don't I work at the soup kitchens, and drive the hospital wagon?" she demanded. "Don't I travel for weeks on end, begging money and food from every great house in the east? Haven't I emptied my own pockets and sold my mother's jewelry in order to raise money for food and medicine?"

"All that and more, my dear."

"If I didn't care about my people and my country, I would've stayed in England and finished my degree," she continued, still angry. "I'd be filling my evenings with dancing and dining instead of scrounging food and writing political articles that could land me in jail, not to mention wasting my best years waiting up late for renegades and wanted men!"

"Ah." He puffed up a cloud of aromatic smoke. "That explains the pacing."

She scowled. "He's late."

"It wouldn't be Mister McDonagh we're talking about, would it now?" His eyes twinkled with mischief. "Not the wild man from the Black Hill, that hero of men and heartbreaker of women?"

"The very one," she admitted, her anger dissipating.

"What's he doing up here, then?"

"William sent for him. To meet with John, and Thomas Meagher. David supposedly brought him up yesterday." She glanced at the clock on the mantel. "I thought they'd be here hours ago."

"Will we entertain them all this evening?" he wondered. "I planned on retiring early, but I suppose . . ."

She waved her hand. "Go to bed whenever you like, Father. It's only Morgan needs a room for the night."

Mister Martin studied his daughter's intense face, its pale color and anxious dark eyes. "You've a pen stuck in your hair, my dear," he said gently, reaching across to remove it and patting the loosened wisps back into place. "And isn't that your heart there . . . on your sleeve?"

Her eyes flew to his face, then to the fire. She bit her lip. "I've never been much good at romance, Father, as you well know."

He chuckled. "Therein lies your charm, my dear girl. They all think you are unattainable, and so they flock to your door."

"Flock is certainly the right word for the sheep I attract."

"But I thought you were far more interested in an independent life than that of marriage," he said, concerned. "You whirled through your debut and left at least ten good suitors in your wake when you went off to college, but you've always known your own mind, so it did not occur to me to give you advice on the subject of men." He sighed. "If only your dear mother were still alive, perhaps your life would have some semblance of order and . . ."

She smiled. "Are we talking about the only woman ever removed from Ladies Aid for her 'progressive and unseemly' ideas on training the poor for meaningful work? The woman who studied law on her own, and wrote a pamphlet on family planning—banned, of course, and all of us nearly excommunicated?"

He laughed. "The very one. Although she was always very gracious, even when arguing with the bishop, and she did run an orderly house. But you're quite correct—if she were alive today, the two of you would be living in the hills with the rest of them, teaching the peasants to write with one hand and shoot with the other."

"You've been very patient with us," she said fondly. "You always supported Mother even when she mortified you, and you've let me plot my own course, as well. And what have you got for all the tutors and college, for the traveling and free thinking? A daughter who's useless at housekeeping, wears clothes gone out of fashion, smokes and drinks, writes inflammatory political articles, and fills your house with anarchists!"

"Ah, but how interesting my life is because of you, Julia," he said proudly. "So dedicated and passionate. I'd never want you to be anyone other than who you are." He tapped out his pipe. "I do worry about you becoming eccentric at such an early age, however—what will be left for your later years?" he teased.

"When my eyesight goes and my fingers are too rheumy to hold a pen, I can always collect cats and go about muttering to myself," she retorted.

"Perhaps you will marry, after all."

"I don't know," she said simply.

"He's not interested in marriage?"

She shrugged her shoulders. "I've not asked him yet."

Mister Martin shook his head in mock exasperation. "It's the other way around, my dear. He's a Catholic, is he not?"

"Yes," she said. "We have that in common. But he counts among his friends priests and ministers alike, and carries no prejudice one for the other. He's not had any formal education, but he retains an amazing amount of information and he's a sponge for learning. And he's brave—not fearless, he admits to fear—but brave and courageous. He feels he's on God's mission."

"And you've fallen in love with him," he prodded gently.

She nodded. Then shook her head. "I don't know. I'm distracted and unhappy when he's not around, but when he's here, I get no work done, either! I have no control over this, and I hate that!" She pushed herself out of the chair and went to the window again. "Perhaps if we were lovers, I'd get over him."

"Julia!" Mister Martin dropped his pipe.

She grinned at him over her shoulder. "Oh, Father, I'm only joking."

"One might have good reason to doubt that," he admonished.

She turned back to the window and froze. "He's here."

Mister Martin sighed and got up from his chair, following his daughter out into the cold entry. The door opened and in came the man himself, much admired by the intellectuals who could only fight with their minds. McDonagh and this O'Malley fellow—a brilliant boy by all accounts—were already something of a legend in the heady group of students who were following the winds of change.

"McDonagh." Mister Martin shook hands. "Good to see you."

"And you, sir," Morgan said politely, his dark hair damp with melting snow. "Thank you for putting me up tonight."

"Anytime, dear boy. Anytime. And now, if you'll excuse me, I have a rendezvous with a hot brick." He turned and kissed his daughter's cheek. "Good night, my dear." His eyes held hers and he tapped the arm of her dress. "Mind that sleeve now," he said pointedly.

She smiled. "Good night, Father."

They watched him climb the stairs; then Julia hung Morgan's damp coat over a drying rack and led him into the drawing room, closing the doors to keep in the heat. Morgan went immediately to the fire to warm himself.

"It's so late," he said, hands behind him at the flame. "I've kept you up."

She waved that away. "I'm always up late. Drink?" She unstopped the whiskey decanter.

"We emptied the bottle at Smith O'Brien's," he admitted. "I'm not so steady on my feet."

"Well, sit down, by all means." She indicated the chair her father had vacated. "And have one more to call it a night."

"A nightcap it is, then." He sat and stretched his legs out in front of him, sighing with the comfort of it.

"And what did you think of our own John Mitchel?" she asked, handing him a heavy glass half full of whiskey.

He eyed it warily. "Sure, and he's quite the flamethrower, is he not?"

She laughed, standing next to his chair, her arm resting on the mantel.

He shook his head. "I could not follow half of what he said. He's either a lunatic or a visionary."

"Bit of both." She sipped at her own drink.

"But he appears to be strong behind us, and certainly we need the influence of such a man in the press and all. Meagher, I've heard his talk before, and I'm ever admiring of the man. Smith O'Brien, of course, is the best of the best, and I can't say enough good about him."

"How's David?"

"Captain Evans? Well enough, though tired of plodding about the countryside in this snow. He may go back to Macroom in a week's time and fetch Sean. They worry about him taking sick and dying now they know what a talent he is. Smith O'Brien wants him safe and dry in Dublin so as to keep an eye on him."

"What's he doing?"

"Maps." Morgan took another swallow. "He knows the West better than anyone, though how is a mystery to me, for the boy's never gone much beyond the Lee or Derrynasaggart Mountains! And he's what Mitchel calls 'a natural strategist' for planning ambushes and the like. He gets his inspiration from the great battles of the Bible, he says, and isn't that just like him?"

"It is," she agreed. "Will you come to Dublin, as well?"

"No. I'm away from my mam enough as it is, and she's not well."

"But don't you have a thousand sisters at home?"

He laughed. "Not quite. Barbara, the eldest, has gone to Holy Sisters of the Rose and is working her way up to full sisterhood. The next one is . . ." Worry flickered across his face. "In London somewhere." He took one more swallow, then set the glass firmly away from himself. "There are three more at home, plus the baby, but all have suffered with cold and hunger this winter, though Sean's sister, Grace, has sent them enough food to keep them going."

"She's the one who married Bram Donnelly?"

"Aye." He looked into the fire.

"I met her once," she said. "At a dinner party. I liked her very much. She was without pretense and her conversation with David was very interesting—I admit to eavesdropping. But that was ages ago."

"I've not seen her in ages myself, though I know she opened her kitchen before Christmas, and many's the life she saved, to hear people talk." He paused. "I can't see her husband allowing such a thing, but perhaps she's changed him."

"Not if he's the Bram Donnelly I know."

Morgan looked at her, then away again. "Anyway, she looks after her own family and mine when she can, but they're my responsibility and I don't like to leave them, especially in such bad times as these."

"We must all make sacrifices," she said, finishing off her drink and setting aside the glass.

"'To whom much is given, much will be asked,'" he quoted.

Julia glanced around the fine room with its comfortable furnishings, tray of biscuits, extra wood for the fire. "Do you think I should be doing more?"

"Ah, no, Julia," he said quickly. "I wasn't thinking of you, but of myself. No. You work like a demon, day in and day out, devoted to fighting for your country, instead of marrying a fine man and settling down to the comfort of family life."

"You've made the same sacrifice yourself."

They were silent for a moment, listening to the spit and sizzle of the dying fire. The clock rang out the late hour and a carriage slushed through the snow in the street outside.

"Have you ever considered marriage?" she asked, her voice too loud in her own ears.

He looked at her, surprised. "Have you?"

She shrugged her shoulders. "I like my freedom, and I'd lose all that."

"Not if you married the right man," he said.

"How do you know who's right and who's not?" she demanded. "A right man in the beginning may not be so right in the end."

Morgan nodded. "'Tis not the same for a woman, as for a man. Women's lives go round that of their husbands, while men just go round as they please."

"Would you want your wife's life to revolve around yours?"

Morgan thought. "I suppose in a way I would," he admitted. "But, at the same time, I would not want her to lose herself in my life. Rather, we should build a life together like this . . ." He made a circle with each thumb and forefinger, then overlapped them so that a smaller circle appeared between the two larger. "It takes a strong woman to resist being swallowed up in her husband's life."

"And you've never met a woman like that?" She kicked at an ember that popped out of the hearth.

"I have," he said. "But it wasn't meant to be."

Julia's eyes widened in surprise.

"She married someone else."

"Then she wasn't the right one for you."

"Sure and she was," he said quietly. "But just because you find the right person doesn't mean you get to have them. God may open the door, but He's not going to stand there holding it open forever."

"And is there only one right person for each of us?" she asked. "Are there no second chances?"

"I don't know," he said, pushing the hair off his forehead.

"But do you not miss romance, a young man like yourself?" She kept her voice light. "Are you never lonely?"

He looked at her face and saw the need. "Terribly," he admitted. "And the more I'm with people, the worse it gets."

She knelt down beside him and rested her cheek against his knee so that he could not see her eyes. "I know."

His hand smoothed her hair, and gently he turned her face up to look upon it.

"Julia—"

"I don't want marriage," she interrupted. "We're neither of us right for that. But we could be something to one another."

"Ah, Julia . . ."

She rose up and kissed him. His indecision lasted only a moment, and then he returned her kiss wholeheartedly, pulling her up into his lap, hands holding her firmly, bunching the fabric of her skirt in his fists.

"We can go to my room," she whispered in his ear, her breath light and quick. "We can be together."

He closed his eyes and pulled her tightly to him.

"Say yes, Morgan," she urged.

"No," he said, at last. "Julia, I cannot."

She slipped her fingers into his thick hair and kissed him again until he groaned. He broke off the kiss, but clung to her, shaking his head.

She pushed him away, stood angrily, and kicked him in the shin.

"Julia!" He grabbed at her, but she stepped away.

"You deserve that and more, Mister McDonagh," she spat. "I'm not asking you to marry me, for God's sake. I'm asking you to be my lover! What kind of a man says no to that?"

"A true eejit, sure enough," he said remorsefully.

"Then change your mind!" she demanded.

He looked at her standing there, hands on her hips, hair flying around her face, temper in full bloom, and he wondered why it was in the world that a man could not simply love where he wanted.

"Another minute and I will." He stood up. "And so I'll say good night." He strode into the hall, picked up his overcoat, and opened the front door on the black, frosty night.

"Morgan!" She stood behind him, shivering in the hall. "Bloody coward! Are you afraid I'll ambush you if you stay the night, then?"

"Terrified." He grinned, and then his face sobered. "Julia, I look upon you as a true friend . . ."

"Oh, bloody hell." She stamped her foot.

"Arrah, I've never been good at words. A man of action, only."

"Not tonight," she muttered.

He had to laugh. "You're a grand girl, Julia, and I'll curse myself till the day I die if I've lost your friendship."

"Better start now with a bloody good oath."

He put out his arms and she stepped into them.

"Just give me one good reason why not," she said into his shoulder.

"Because I don't love you that way."

"I'm not asking for love."

"You should be," he said and kissed the top of her head. "Never settle for less."

She clung to him a moment longer and he held her tightly until she was ready to let go. They kissed quickly on the lips and smiled into one another's eyes and anyone glancing up would have thought they were lovers parting for the night.

"Where will you go?" she asked, moving away from him reluctantly.

"I'll rouse that Smith O'Brien out of his warm bed and make him shove over." He smiled. "Though I doubt I'll sleep a wink."

"Serves you right," she said.

"Good night, Julia." He turned and stepped cautiously down the icy stairs.

"Good night, coward," she called and closed the door on him.

She rested a moment, her forehead against the cold wood, until her father cleared his throat behind her.

"Is that your man you've turned out on such a night as this?" he asked, coming down the stairs, nightcap askew, face tired and stubbled with gray.

"He wanted to go, Father," she said wearily. "It seems I am not quite the enchantress of my youth."

"No?"

"He loves another," she told him. "But she has married."

"How sad." He came down the last few steps.

"He would not entertain the notion of being my lover, but had to take himself out of the house in order to avoid temptation." She smiled ruefully.

"I knew I had good reason to be alarmed."

"My reputation is ruined."

"Highly unlikely." He put an arm around her shoulders. "It's late. Come up to bed now, my dear, and plot a new course for the morning."

They took the steps slowly, arms about one another.

"Are you terribly unhappy?" he asked.

"No," she said. "Strangely, I'm not. But if I cannot get a lover in the prime of my youth, what hope is there for my future?" They reached the landing and the door to her room. "I fear I am destined to become that eccentric old woman with pens stuck in her hair and ink on her nose."

He squeezed her arm sympathetically. "In that case, my dear, I shall be on the lookout for a suitable cat."

He kissed her good night and she entered her room, the low light of the lamp spilling over piles of loose papers, splotchy wooden pens, and well-marked books, clothes in a heap where they'd fallen, shoes scattered across the rug—it was so far from being a romantic den of seduction that she had to laugh. He was right, he had been right, she was not ready to share her life, and she thought of him walking through the snowy night, chilled to the bone. Served him right, she thought again, but with affection this time. She would tell him when they met again; she would forgive him and they would enjoy a long, long friendship that would encompass many evenings sitting together by the fire, drinking whiskey and throwing books at the damn cat.

# Nineteen

"SHUT that child up!" Bram burst into the kitchen, angry at having been distracted from his work.

"Yes, sir," Brigid said, quickly. "I'll try, sir." She lifted the little girl out of the chair and held her close, patting her back. Mary Kathleen arched away from her, crying harder now with frustration. "She wants her mother. Can't no one else feed her."

"If she's hungry, she'll eat," he snarled. "Keep an eye on her, Brigid, hear me?"

"Aye, sir." Brigid nodded meekly.

"I'll have no more kidnapping attempts or you'll find yourself out on the road with the other Irish trash," he warned. "And I want to know right away if that Alroy fellow shows his face around here so I can blow it off." He left the kitchen, muttering curses.

Brigid tried to soothe the little girl in her arms. "Arrah, now, musha. Don't anger your da so."

"Mam," Mary Kathleen whimpered pitifully. "Mama Mama."

Brigid carried her over to the kitchen door and opened it. "Your mam'll come for you soon as she's well," she whispered, looking out across the yard to the road and the wood behind. "'Tis just bad luck you're not in her arms now, God bless you both."

She had been sure that Abban would make another attempt to get the child and, fearful though she was of the Squire, had steeled herself to allow it. She had kept an eye out for him, but it was Nolan and not Abban who had finally appeared, slipping into the house after nightfall with the news that Grace had lost the baby, and Abban had gone for help. What kind of help, she had wanted to ask, but thought better of it. These were terribly uncertain times and her stomach was always in knots. Jack lay in his bed, dying of the drink, though he called it fever, and now Moira had come home from Killarney with a baby boy in her arms and no man to call it son; the shame of it so bad that Brigid was almost grateful for the famine and the attention it drew away from the fact of a bastard at the Sullivans. Nolan was as quiet and secret as the grave, slipping away at night and returning in the wee hours. She would turn and find him looking at her, searching her face as if he had a thousand questions, and she longed to gather him up—him the most noble of her children—and ask him what it was he needed from her, what it was he held in his heart. But she could not. If he'd taken up with the rebels, it would be best not to know. When the police came around asking questions, she could look them clear in the eye and say she'd heard nothing of wild boys shooting at soldiers on the hill, nothing a'tall. The only guns on the place belonged to the master; she could show them the locked cabinet where they hung, cleaned and ready. They need never know that Nolan could and *did* pick the lock, that he borrowed the rifle to scare up game, he told his mam, then cleaned and returned it so that the master had no idea of its absence. He never brought home a wild rabbit or grouse like he used to, but the woods were picked clean these days, everyone knew that. He was a different boy, sure of himself and determined. He'd begged her to let him take the child to the O'Malleys, but she'd said no, no.

"He'll shoot you dead as you stand. I could not bear that."

"Then I'll not come back to this place."

"He'll shoot me in your stead," she said to keep him from going alone into the dying world. Him just a boy.

He stayed on and did his work, and she noted that outwardly he was respectful of the Squire, though inside that head of his she knew he was taking note all the same. She saw the way he measured the Squire, marked his habits, and watched him warily from the barn, waiting for him to give the order to saddle up Warrior and load his rifle, an order that rarely came, as the Squire was reluctant to leave the house. Brigid saw the way her master kept out of doorways and away from windows, drawing the curtains at night and letting the dogs loose to roam the grounds. Two landlords had been shot—one on the road, one in his own yard—and another had lost his house to fire. Squire would never admit to fearing the lowlife he cursed, but Brigid knew and Nolan knew: There was good reason these days to slip the bolts.

"What!" Bram barked in answer to the timid knock on his study door.

"'Tis myself, sir. Moira."

"Ah, Moira. Do come in. Thank you for coming." The irritation was replaced by oily warmth. "Close the door behind you, my dear, will you?" He smiled and gestured to a small couch against the wall. "Sit down. Please. You must be tired. Your mother says you've gotten a ticket on the public works."

"Aye." Moira sighed. "Breaking rock on the road to Rosamare."

Bram's eyes widened and he regarded her again. "That's a long walk over and back. What's the pay?"

"Two shillings a week," she said. "Half that in this weather. We've still got to show our faces to collect it, even if there's no work."

Bram nodded. "Your brothers doing the same?"

"No, sir." Moira looked down. "They've gone to Galway, looking to get out."

"It's worse in the West." Bram picked up the hurricane lamp and set it on a low table next to the couch. "Empty warehouses, and soldiers shooting anyone who riots. Which is everyone." He paused, noting the horror on her face. "Old Jack go with them?"

"Too sick," she said quietly. "Road fever has him weak as a newborn. Can't keep nothing down, but the bit of broth Mam brings home."

"I don't mind her taking food," he said graciously. "Saves me paying her."

"You can't eat money, sir, and there's no food to buy."

"True enough." He eased himself into a chair near the couch and looked at her exhausted face. "Care for a drink?"

Moira glanced at him out of the corner of her eye, but didn't linger on his face. Her legs ached from walking eight miles that day, and she was so cold, she thought she'd never regain the feeling in her fingers or toes. In fewer than six hours, she'd have to get up and do it again.

"No, sir. I don't think I will, sir. Thank you very much for offering."

Bram shrugged and stood up. "Suit yourself." He poured out a tumbler of whiskey and took a long swallow. "Fire in the belly," he commented, his eyes on her apron. "Warms a body all through. Nothing like it after a hard day of work. Especially on a night like this one."

Rain beat steadily against the window and Moira shivered in her thin dress.

"I can't persuade you to join me?" He smiled invitingly.

Moira looked with sudden longing at the bottle. "Well"—she bit her fingertip—"'tis true enough a terrible cold night."

Bram poured out two fingers, glanced at her, added a little more. She took it more eagerly than she'd intended, and swallowed half in one gulp, wiping the back of her hand across her mouth.

"Drink up," Bram said, topping off her glass.

As the shivering stopped and drink eased the pain of her aching muscles, Moira began to relax, sinking back into the cushions, running her fingers across the plush velvet.

"Such lovely things," she murmured, her cheeks flushed.

"Yes," Bram agreed, moving a pillow out of the way in order to sit closer. "Nice things are a comfort in hard times." He paused, regarding her. "Tell me about your boy, Moira."

Her eyes narrowed. "There's nothing to tell, sir. He's but a wee thing, still."

"Looks like his father, does he?" he asked, casually.

"No, sir," she said. "A dead ringer for myself, he is."

"And who *is* his father?" He took a sip of his drink. "What does he do?"

"Nothing a'tall, sir, which is why he's not here." Moira worried her fingernail again, then forced the hand back into her lap. "Why would you want to be knowing about such a blaguard as himself?"

Bram shrugged his shoulders. "Just curious." He sipped his drink. "You haven't seen him at all since the baby was born?"

"Not that one," she laughed bitterly. "And never will, no doubt. He had his fun and now he's gone to Canada with a new bride."

This brought a smile to Bram's lips. "So you're left to raise the baby on your own?" he asked. "There's no one to claim him or you?"

Moira looked down. "No, sir," she said soberly. "We're lucky to have Mam's cabin to shelter us and a ticket on the works. That's all that keeps us from the workhouse."

Wind rattled the windows, the candles flickered, but the light in the lantern hissed a steady glow. Bram waited until the silence had grown and Moira had sunk into melancholy.

"You needn't settle for so little, Moira, when you deserve so much more." He paused, moving even closer. "Let me do something for you," he said quietly. "Let me help you . . . and your son."

Moira studied him. "I'm told the Missus took ill and went home, sir," she said carefully. "And that she lost the baby boy."

"Ah." Bram refilled her glass and his own. "Then you know I have a problem." He put a fresh drink into her hands. "I am in need of an heir."

"These things take the better part of a year, Squire," Moira smiled wryly.

Bram returned her smile quickly. "Not necessarily. You see, my dear, you have already given birth. The boy exists, and he is the right age."

"Are you saying you want to pass my baby off as your own son, sir?" Her eyes grew wide and she pulled herself out of the cushions, sitting on the edge of the couch.

"You are a clever girl, Moira," he said. "Clever and beautiful."

She looked down, smoothing her skirt. Bram leaned forward and gently tucked a piece of hair behind her ear.

"You and I shared something once," he said softly. "Something very special." He watched her, eyes half closed. "Do you remember that?"

She nodded, but kept her gaze averted. He lifted her chin so that she could not avoid looking into his face, and then his eyes.

"We have the same spirit," he whispered, his breath brushing against her cheek. "We are sensual, passionate people." His finger trailed down across her chest. He fanned his fingers over her heart. "I can help you." He kissed her ear. "And you can help me." He kissed her neck. "I need you, Moira."

Unable to resist any longer, she turned her mouth to meet his and they embraced. He lowered her onto the couch, knocking over her glass, warming her body with his own. Her heart began to surge with that strange excitement she'd known only with him, and she let go all doubt when he began to unbutton her vest, whispering that he needed her, loved her, would shower her with riches and be with her always.

By the time the pale sun fought its way through a heavy sky, she believed without a doubt that she had been the one to seduce him, and that his desire for her had driven him into making such a strange bargain. She would not have to get up this morning, or any other morning, to walk hours through freezing snow in order to break rocks with a small spade for a road that no one needed. She would not have to stand in line with all of the other shivering, starving, used-up women, hands out, waiting for a bit of money that would never pay the rent, let alone feed the crying children at their sides. She would not starve in the road or die of madness in a backstreet brothel, and her son would not grow up ragged and mean. Because of her, the Squire's fortune would be settled, and his gratitude for that along with his passion for her would secure her future as the mistress of a great man. And, in turn, their son would become a great man who would always take care of his mother. Her faith was complete in this vision of her future, but even more startling was the fact that he believed it, as well.

# Twenty

GRACE could now sit up for short periods of time and was in a chair near the fire when Brigid arrived in the middle of the day.

"He'll not give the child to you unless you come and do this," she said after she'd been given tea by Granna and set in the corner.

Grace's white face grew even more pale. "How is she?"

"Not well a'tall." Brigid shook her head. "Doesn't she cry for you day and night with no letting up? She won't hardly eat a bite, poor child. And her whining makes him so fierce with her."

"He's not hurt the child, has he?" Granna's eyes grew hard.

"Ah, no." Brigid put down her cup. "If I could've brought her to you, I would have. Abban tried, you know, right after you left. But Squire come riding down the avenue and scooped the little thing right out of Nolan's arms. Gave my boy a nasty bump on the head with his rifle butt."

"And if she doesn't go back?" Gran sat down.

"He says she'll never see Mary Kathleen again." Brigid sighed. "He says he'll send her away to England, to his sister who has no child and doesn't want one, from what I hear. And he says he'll throw you all out of this place, then tear it down."

Grace looked into the fire and the room was silent as the other two women watched her face.

"I can't let him send Mary Kate away. She needs me, and I her."

"No!" Sean stood in the doorway, his good arm cradling a basket of turf. "We'll get her back for you, Grace. I've promised you that."

Grace shook her head. "It's been nearly four weeks. Christmas has come and gone. She's all I've got left, and I can't bear it anymore. I've got to be with her. She'll take ill and die if I'm not there."

"Ah, no, child." Granna put her arm on Grace's shoulder. "She'll be all right. Brigid will watch over her."

Brigid bit her lip. "I do what I can," she said. "But now he keeps her near him, sleeping in the same room and tied on a rope all day. She's not well, Missus. She needs her mother's love."

"Damn it, Brigid!" Sean glared at the housekeeper. Then he dropped the turf basket and limped over to Grace's chair. "You're not going back to him and that's all!" He lowered his voice, the urgency in his eyes. "You've got to trust me, Gracie. Trust the Lord. We'll get her back for you."

Grace met his intensity with her own. "I do trust the Lord. And I know you're trying, Sean. But even if you get her back, we'll lose our land. We'll have nothing. We have nearly nothing as it is. I'd be condemning us all to death, and you know that."

"For the love of God, Grace, don't do this!" Sean pleaded. "Or the next time you come home to us, it'll be in a coffin. You and Mary Kate, both!"

Brigid stood. "He swears he'll never touch her again."

"He's a lying bastard, a bloody demon from hell!"

"Aye," Brigid said quietly. "He's both of those and more. But he needs her now. He can't afford to hurt her. It's only for a short time, while his father is here, to pass off Moira's baby as her own, to make a show of it until he's signed over the estate. And then she and Mary Kathleen are free to come back here. He says he'll sign over the lease to this property and you'll never see another Quarterday as long as you live."

Sean spit into the fire. "It's all lies," he said sharply. "Why does he need Grace if he's got Moira? Why not just pass Moira off as his wife?"

Brigid kept her chin up, but shame blazed in her cheeks. "Moira's too rough, she drinks too much. He's afraid she'll make a mess of it, and he's right. She'll come as nursemaid to the house to show the baby, then take him away."

"Why is she doing this?" Grace asked quietly.

"Money." Brigid sighed. "He's promised her a fistful and her own house in Dublin. He's leading her to think he might join her there in the future and they'll be a happy couple."

"Will the marriage be ended, then?" Granna asked.

"I don't know." Brigid looked away. "She's a fool, my one. I've tried to tell her so. He'll no more take up with her than with his horse."

Grace stood, pulling the shawl tightly around her shoulders. "Wait for me, Brigid," she said firmly. "I'm going back with you."

Sean put his arms out to block her. "Da will never allow it," he said.

"I'll be gone before he's home." She pushed him gently out of the way. "There's no other way, brother. You must let me go."

Sean stood bitterly beside the door, refusing to help carry out her bag, but in the end he came to her with tears in his eyes.

"Don't do this to me," she whispered as she kissed him. "Where's that trunkload of faith you're always carting about?"

He shook his head, but did not smile. "I'll be praying every minute of every day until you come back home."

"Aye," Granna said, embracing her one last time. "God be with you, child."

"Tell Da," Grace murmured, then stepped into the carriage Bram had sent and told Nolan to drive off.

Their hearts broke at the last sight of her, knowing that she was already in that other world where they could not protect her. For though they waved and called out their love, Grace did not once look back.


February passed, Mary Kathleen turned two on a day marked only by her mother, and still Lord Donnelly had not arrived. A letter had come saying that the island was too unstable for him to risk a visit at this time. The London papers were full of horrible news about land-lords being shot in their own yards or ambushed on the road; he'd read about the filth and disease that was everywhere now, and he dared not make himself vulnerable. He asked if it were true that a gentleman could not walk the city streets without stepping over the naked corpses of women and children.

"True enough," Bram mumbled and burned the letter.

His mood darkened daily, and he passed the time by shooting at stragglers who turned up the avenue from the road. He made Nolan sleep in the barn to protect the animals, but he'd allowed the dogs to roam at night and now only two were left. There was an eerie absence of living animals in the countryside; no dogs or cats should have meant an abundance of mice and rats, but these too were killed and eaten. The wood was empty of rabbit and fox, the lakes fished out, the shores picked clean of shellfish, seaweed, and kelp. The men he saw wore the wasted stamp of starvation, faces still and eyes gone blank. The children, whittled down to bone and little else, looked like old women with small bodies, their faces creased with anxiety and pain. And the women, the mothers, simply looked numb. He could not go out among them anymore, even as he despised them for their plight.

When Grace returned with Brigid, he stayed out of her way for a few days, spending hours in the barn with Nolan. Only Brigid and Nolan came to the house now, working for their daily food and the guarantee of their cabin. Grace had gone straight to Mary Kathleen, who had not cried, but climbed wearily into her mother's arms and fallen into a deep sleep. Grace had held her throughout the night and now did not go anywhere without her. Bram ordered them to stay indoors, away from the windows, and so they did.

She had seen Moira and the baby boy, who was called Phillip, after Bram's father. She did not acknowledge the deception in any way, except to hold the baby now and then so that he might be used to her touch. Moira was alternately aggressive and apologetic, depending on Bram's mood and Brigid's presence. Grace did not talk to her, spending much time in the nursery with Mary Kate, where she'd set up a cot for herself. She had gone into her bedroom only to remove her things, and after that had never so much as looked at it again.

When Bram decided she'd had enough time to settle herself in, he quit the barn, reentering the life of his house with bravado and good humor, determined to ignore the immediate horror of the countryside and his own devastating actions. He never mentioned the miscarriage of their second son, chattering on instead about the cattle he would buy and how rich he would be after Donnelly House became his. Grace did nothing to challenge his mood, wanting only Lord Donnelly's arrival so that the charade might be played out and she might at last take her daughter home.

But Lord Donnelly did not come, and the strain began to take its toll. Bram took up the bottle again, joined more and more frequently by Moira. Grace could hear them laughing behind the closed study door, but she did not put her hands over her ears. She did not care what they did.

And when yet another letter arrived, she expected Bram to sink even further into his true state, but was surprised instead to hear him laughing with glee.

"He's not coming ever!" He burst into the kitchen, where Grace sat at the big table giving Mary Kathleen her lunch. "But he's agreed to send the title anyway." He waved an official-looking piece of parchment in Grace's face. "Here it is, little wife," he laughed again. "The end of my troubles."

"And mine," Grace added quietly.

"Yes, yes," he said good-naturedly. "And yours, of course."

"Then I may leave?" she asked.

He frowned slightly. "I wouldn't be in such a hurry, if I were you," he clipped, his mood changed. "There's nothing out there but hard work and slow death."

"There is my home," she said. "The one you promised my family if I returned to you."

"Well, as it turns out, I didn't need you after all," he countered.

"Are you saying you won't keep your word?"

"I've always been a man of my word," he barked. He paused and looked into her face, moved suddenly by the lack of fear he saw there, the way she held his gaze unflinchingly. He'd beaten her nearly to death and stolen away her child, and yet, he knew, she wasn't afraid of him. He took her chin in his fingers.

"You have been a disappointment to me, Grace," he said softly. "We could have accomplished a great deal together had you obeyed me and become the wife I wanted you to be. We could have had a wonderful life together had it not been for your pride and stubbornness . . ."

"Or your cruelty," she added calmly.

His eyes narrowed briefly and Grace felt the pressure of his fingers on her jaw, but did not flinch.

"I have my weaknesses," he conceded. "Made worse by this damn country and the ignorant, lazy wretches who occupy it. A man can only take so much."

Grace said nothing and finally he released his grip.

"You may go after I've returned from the city. I'll be two days gone, and when I get back with the money borrowed against the deed . . ." He walked to the doorway, then stopped and looked at her with a yearning she couldn't understand. "I remember the first night I saw you standing in the light of the bonfire in the middle of town," he said. "Young and beautiful, and strong. And the first night I held you in my arms in Dublin, I was so sure that you were the answer to my loneliness, that you were the answer to my miserable life. I did love you, Grace," he said, and in the hard light of the morning, he looked suddenly old.

Grace watched him leave, heard his heavy tread going up the stairs. And, to her surprise, she felt a faint tug on the edge of her heart. She, too, had been so full of hope. But she did not allow herself to feel more than that; he might love her now, in this moment, but only because she was no longer fully his. If he thought there was a chance, he would try to steal her soul, and she could not allow that to happen ever again.

"Soon we will go away from here," Grace said softly to her daughter. "And then we'll have a new life."

But when Bram returned three days later, Grace knew there was little hope of leaving Donnelly House. He was not drunk. He had not touched a drop, and that was perhaps more frightening than if he'd come home reeling. His face was white with strain and anger, and the hope in his eyes replaced with flat, cold calculation.

He stormed into the house and went straight up to his study, dogs at his heel. Grace waited ten minutes, then followed.

"Is it bad news, then?" She closed the door behind her.

"We cannot borrow against the deed," he said flatly. "My father has already borrowed the full amount. We are mortgaged to the hilt!" He laughed bitterly. "He has not given me an estate! He has merely unloaded a debt!"

"Will you lose it?" She sat down across from him.

He nodded. Then shook his head. "I don't know," he said, staring at the wall. "The London banks will press for payment. They want more than my father ever did!" He reached for the whiskey decanter but didn't unstop it. "He's played the trump card, and now I am expected to fold and return to England with my tail firmly between my legs. And my son ready to begin training as the next Donnelly heir."

"The only Donnelly you have is Mary Kathleen," she said quietly. "There is no heir. Unless you take Moira and Phillip back with you."

"That's out of the question." Now he did pour himself a drink, downing it in one smooth motion.

"You could sell the other mills. Even at a loss, you'd have cash to put against the debt," she suggested.

"I thought of that myself. They're already on the market. But it will take time." He paused. "I carry insurance on two of them against fire."

Grace was still.

"If there were to be an accident . . ."

"What of the workers inside?"

Bram banged his fist on the table. "Damn it, Grace! Will you quit thinking about other people and think about your own family for once?"

"All right, then," she said. "Let me go back to my family and I'll trouble you no longer."

"No." He was firm. "I need you here. At least for now. Colonel Jones and Captain Wynne from the Board of Works are riding up next week to see how things are here. If I can get my tenants tickets for employment, they'll pay the wage to me and I can pay what I like, or apply it to their rent."

"They hardly make a shilling as it is." She looked out the window at the bleak, dripping landscape. "They'll be working for nothing."

"At least they'll have a roof over their heads," he barked. "And if they don't like it, they can get out. I'll call in the guards to knock down their cabins and that will be the end of their burden on me."

"No," Grace said quickly. "You're right. They'll be willing to work."

"I need you to set up the house for visitors and come up with some decent meals," he said. "I want them to think I'm doing well and am only interested in helping my laborers. Don't overdo it," he added.

The colonel arrived before the weekend, and over a dinner of scrawny chicken and a pie made from dried winter apples, he and Bram came to an agreement. The London banks would not foreclose on Donnelly House until after the crisis passed. The Board of Works would base another project on Donnelly land, digging ditches to drain water off the fields, which would then be cultivated, allowing the

Squire to plant to full capacity. Tickets for employment would be given to tenants who displayed need and who were able-bodied field hands. Bram would do the hiring. Spring was approaching and Ireland faced another disaster in that there were few farmers left to plant what seed could be found. Incentives were needed to get people back on the land, and to put seed in their hands. The suspension of Bram's debt would be arranged in accordance with his agreement to oversee the farming project. The two men shook hands and smoked cigars with a glass of the best whiskey in the house.

Again, Bram's mood was high and he left early in the morning on Warrior, two dogs following behind. He intended to cover the villages to the east of his land and hire workers for the rate of one penny a day plus suspended rent. He was not prepared for the sight that met him in the first village.

He had been to Skibbereen and ridden down the slop-filled, muddy alleys, where people lay in rat-infested cabins, dying of starvation even when the potato crops were good. These were the diseased, unemployed beggars and widows, the retarded, the orphans, the hard core of destitution that swamped Ireland every year; part of the two million, more or less, who starved to death no matter if there was famine or bounty. That was the hard fact of it. Most of them died in their cabins, undetected for days.

But what he was not prepared for was the sight of this miserable dying even in the more prosperous villages of Bantry, Crookhaven, and Skull. Everywhere he rode, he rarely saw a face in the window or a man sitting outside his cabin. And when he got off his horse to enter one, the smell nearly knocked him over. At the end of one lane he found a house with two children sitting, stunned, in the lap of their wide-eyed mother, who had clearly died a day or two before. They were naked and the body of their brother or sister lay not a dozen feet away, half buried under a pile of stones. They made no sound as he passed by, only their eyes followed him. They would be dead by nightfall. He got on his horse and rode to the next village. It was not much better there, but he did find two households surviving, on what he did not ask. The men and women were eager to come right away and asked if there would be food. He could not bring himself to say no, but answered instead that perhaps the Quakers would set up a soup kitchen nearby as they had in the West. He promised that for their work, they would not be evicted. Some clung to that promise, others turned away in disappointment.

When he returned home at the end of the day, he went straight into his study and closed the door. He did not come out for two days.

In less than a month, the Board of Works was declared a failure by the House of Commons. They cited the complete ruination of Her Majesty's highways by the building of roads that began and went nowhere, canals that never held water, and piers that washed out to sea with the first storm. The many accidents and delays, the corruption of officials, and the sheer amount of money paid out had all contributed to its doom. In their wisdom, the House of Commons put into effect The Temporary Relief Destitute Persons (Ireland) Act, known locally as the Soup Kitchen Act. As the distribution of soup became general, the Public Works, and their embarrassing mismanagement, would at last be closed. With drainage ditches partially dug and no more money coming in, Bram wrote the Board of Works and was told to apply for an immediate loan from the treasury. Fifty thousand pounds was to be lent to landlords, enabling them to buy seed for distribution to their tenants. Bram applied with little intention of distributing beyond what he needed to plant his own fields for surplus sale to the warehouses in Macroom and Cork City. Grace petitioned for, and received from him, enough seed to enable her own family to plant again; this in exchange for her continued presence at Donnelly House.

The winter snow melted, only to be replaced by sweeping spring showers. The earth, heavy with water, was hard to turn and work progressed slowly. She had seen the laborers hired by Bram slip seed potatoes in their pockets, or crouch low over the dirt to gnaw quickly, and she knew their hunger was great. She had heard that Father Brown was running a soup kitchen in Cork City, and that Reverend Birdwell was feeding them in Skibereen, but that the numbers were far greater than any had imagined, and not all could be fed in a single day. She was frustrated with her inability to do more for those around her, and roamed the house, going room to room, scrubbing and cleaning so that her fatigue at the end of the day might offer a dreamless sleep.

Even though Moira and Phillip rarely came up with Brigid, the house had become claustrophobic; when the rains eased, and the air began to soften with sunshine, she took Mary Kate to the edge of the wood to pick flowers and listen to birdsongs. She mourned the strange childhood of her daughter, but accepted it as better than no childhood at all.

It was on a day with the air swept clean and a breeze heavy with blossom scent that she left Mary Kathleen happily banging a pot on the kitchen floor near Brigid, and impulsively headed for the wood on her own. In her pockets were hard rolls of oatmeal and water; these she slipped to the workers as she walked past, pretending to chide them on their laziness in case Bram watched from the upstairs study window.

As she approached the trees, many in bloom, she heard a whistle unlike any birdsong she knew. She peered into the sun-dappled forest, scanning the shadows for Sean's face. Again, the whistle, now more purposeful; she followed it through a thicket of saplings and bushes toward an overgrown glen. Puzzled, she stopped and looked around, then gasped as a hand closed over her mouth and pulled her down behind a tree. She kicked and elbowed, then bit the hand so hard that her assailant let go, cursing. It was a voice she knew and she spun to face him.

"Morgan, you eejit! You scared the living right out of me!" She shoved him angrily against the tree, and he grunted in pain as his head smacked a low limb.

He rubbed his head, then shook the hand she'd bitten, looking at her in wonder. "Did you have a better plan, then?" he asked, laughter in his voice. "I've been coming here for days, but you always had Mary Kate along!"

Still glaring, but abashed, she took the hand she'd wounded and examined the bite mark.

"Always such a fighter," he teased. "The great pirate queen."

"Arrah," she scolded. "What would you be knowing about that, anyway, skulking about like a mountain man?" She peered more closely at him. "You're even growing a beard like an old bachelor!"

He leaned in and whispered conspiratorily, "It's my disguise, you see. I'm a wanted man in these parts, I am." He rolled his eyes as if looking for spies.

She put her hands on her hips. "I'll not laugh at that, Morgan Mc-

Donagh, as it's God's own truth," she chided. "You ought not to be out here."

"Ah, now, are you going to scold away the morning, or will we try to enjoy ourselves a bit?" His eyes danced with merriment.

Grace relented. "You caught me by surprise, is all. It's not every day I get hauled off into the woods by a bearded marauder, you know. I am happy to see you," she allowed. "But have you come alone?"

"Your old friend Alroy is covering my backside."

"Abban?" She looked over his shoulder into the woods.

"Aye. Good man that he is. Sean put him up to it. They got the seed you sent, by the way, and he took some to Mam and the girls. We all thank you."

Grace waved that aside. "How are they? How's Gran?"

"Well enough." He frowned. "Ryan had a ticket on the works, but that's all over and done with now. Aghna's been sick, and little Thomas. Not the fever," he added quickly, seeing her alarm. "She was working, as well, walking all that way in the cold. She passed it on to the babe, is all. Gran's taking good care of them. You know."

"I wish I were there to help."

"That's why I've come." He took her hand and pulled her down to sit beside him. "You know what I'm doing, then, don't you? What your brother and me have got up to?"

"Aye." She nodded. "I've heard about the ambushes on Her Majesty's guard and the riots at the shipyards. And I know that landlords are being murdered and their houses burned to the ground."

He put his hand on her knee and looked into her face. "Your husband's name is on that list," he said. "It's true he's put a few men to work in the field, but he's evicted hundreds and he's planning to evict the rest the next time the guards ride through."

Shame filled her heart. "I didn't think he'd actually do it."

"He's done many a thing he ought not," Morgan said grimly. "And to speak true, Grace, I could not believe you'd go back to him. It made no sense."

"I don't recall asking for your blessing."

Her curtness surprised him. "All right, then," he amended. "But still, I must say it—he's a hated man. They'll see him dead, and I cannot stop them."

"Why would you want to?"

"Because he's your husband," he said simply. "Because you've come back. But you must tell him to give it up and get out of here, now, or he's a dead man."

"He'd never listen to me. And he'll never give up. He thinks he's going to be the richest man in Ireland."

"Do you love him, then, Grace?" he asked softly.

She looked up into the trees, down into the ferns, anywhere but his eyes. "I can't leave him, and there's nothing more to say."

He watched her, unblinking.

"He promised to give Da title to the land so they'll never be evicted, and he lets me send them food. If I don't stay with him, we're all lost for it."

"You can't stay," he insisted. "I'm controlling them best I can, but I can't be telling them not to shoot this one because his wife's a friend of mine! I'm more than ready to let them have at him after what he's done, but they're not reliable—the power's in their hands, not their heads—and if they shoot at the carriage with you inside, or burn down the house with you and Mary Kate—"

"I know the risk," she interrupted.

"Then you must find a way to get out of there."

Grace pulled at the long grasses, tearing out one and another and then another, until Morgan stilled her hands, turning them over in his and rubbing his thumb over her dirt-creased palm.

"The last time I saw you, we sat under a shade tree talking in whispers just like this. And weren't you wearing white gloves and the prettiest blue bonnet, looking every inch a lady of the manor?"

She didn't smile, but stared soberly at his face, at the freckles still there, though hidden in part by his beard.

"And the time we danced the boards off your cabin at Ryan's wedding," he added. "Now that, I remember as a pure and happy day."

"Aye," she said, the word choking in her throat.

He stared at her in alarm. "Ah, no. All I wanted was a smile, and now you're crying!" He pulled her head against his chest. "No wonder you put up such a fight when you saw it was myself behind the tree! Old Melancholy Morgan, such a winning way with the young ladies, they all weep when they see him coming."

She laughed despite herself, and he hugged her tightly, closing his eyes.

"Sure, and it's been terrible rough since those happy days, there's no lie in that. But we're still alive, the both of us. And those we love."

"We're lucky," she whispered.

"We're blessed," he replied, and kissed the top of her head. "Now, dry your eyes and go back to the house before he comes looking for you." He got to his feet, then gave her a hand up. "I'll do what I can to hold them off, but there isn't much time. Will he not let you visit your family?"

"Not with Mary Kathleen," she said. "And I'll not leave her again."

"No," he agreed.

They brushed themselves off, and Morgan walked her toward the edge of the wood; from there they could see the field.

"I'll do what I can," he repeated. "Don't travel with him. Abban and I will try to watch the house. We'll think of something." A shrill whistle came from far off behind them. "I've got to go now."

She nodded. "God bless you, Morgan. I . . . it was good to see your face. What there is of it." She smiled and touched his beard.

"Good to see yours, as well, Pirate," he whispered and kissed her cheek, lingering there until another whistle broke the silence. He looked in her eyes for a long minute, then turned and waded into the thicket.

As Grace started back across the field, stepping carefully over rows, she caught a sharp glint of light from Bram's study window, which was closing. Her heart began to pound, but she quieted it, telling herself that he couldn't see her from there and that she had nothing to be afraid of. She hurried across the field toward the house and was met at the kitchen door by her husband.

"What were you doing in the woods?" he demanded.

"Walking." She forced herself to look him in the eye.

"Try again." He yanked Mary Kathleen out from behind the door, her upper arm tight in his grip. The child began to whimper.

Grace reached for her, but Bram jerked the girl out of her mother's grasp.

"Not so fast," he said. "I'll even help you out—who was that man you were talking to?"

"A friend of my brother's," she answered quickly, thinking. "He came to ask for food and seed."

"Why didn't he come to the house?"

"He's afraid. You have a reputation, you know."

Bram smiled drunkenly. "Yes," he said. "I like that." He shoved Mary Kate away from him and she bumped her head on the wall.

"Mam!" She began to cry.

Grace started toward her but Bram held her back. "No," he said. "Brigid!"

Brigid came rushing into the kitchen, then stopped, taking in the scene.

"Take Mary Kathleen down to your cabin and tell Moira to keep an eye on her," he ordered.

"Aye, sir." Brigid did not look at Grace as she lifted the child gently and carried her out of the room.

"So." Bram attempted a winning smile. "Now we're alone. Care to join me for a drink?"

"No, thank you," Grace said calmly, then turned and tried to bolt out the door. Bram grabbed her arm and pulled her to him.

"Stop now," he murmured as she beat at him with her fist. "Stop this. I'm not going to hurt you. Stop!" he demanded, losing patience and shaking her.

"What do you want?" she asked.

"I have been aroused," he said. "Seeing you out there in the woods with another man stirred my imagination. I have visions of you rolling around in the damp leaves, and sure enough . . ." He picked a small twig out of her hair. "Here is the evidence of your tryst."

Grace's heart began to pound. "Bram, I did not . . . I would never . . ."

"Of course not," he soothed. "But you are a young woman, and I have not been properly attentive to your needs."

"My only need is to be left alone," she said firmly.

He shook his head. "Now, now. I know best. You cannot respect me as your master unless I take control of the situation in a masterly way."

Grace turned her head from the smell of him, the closeness.

He nuzzled her hair, whispering. "I want to come back into your bed. That is where I belong as your husband."

"No."

"There is no yes or no, Grace," he said. "The past is over. Let it go. Let it go and you will not be sorry."

She felt herself go numb with this expectation: Forget the dead babies and the rape and the beatings, forget the misery, the famine, the heartache, forget starvation and betrayal, forget loss, the terrible loss . . . forget it all and resume her duties as wife as if nothing had ever happened.

Bile rose in her throat and disgust sent a chill through her body. He took it as a sign of desire, picked her up, and carried her swiftly to bed. She did not stop him. The only alternative to forgetting the past was to forget the future—for herself, her child, her family—and so, she took herself away and let her body respond automatically, doing the things she knew would give him pleasure and allowing him to feel as if he'd conquered her. Only once, while he rested on top of her, did she glance over his shoulder toward the open door. There, in the shadow of the hall, was Moira's shocked and crumpled face, but this only added to the suffering of her own tortured soul.

"All right, then!" Bram leaped out of bed the next morning and went to the window, pulling on his trousers. "They're watching me, you know," he said, looking toward the hills. "I've seen men running along the ridges when I ride out. They shot O'Flaherty in the leg." He laughed. "Then burned down the house when he packed up his family and retreated to Dublin. Hah! They don't scare me." He came back to the edge of the bed, and let his eyes roam over her body. "It's early," he said, pausing mid-hitch of his belt. "Plenty of time yet."

She did not encourage him, unable to fathom his thinking. He acted like a satisfied newlywed, despite the fact that he'd been unable to accomplish his goal. After several frustrating attempts, he'd simply passed out. Perhaps he didn't remember, and she certainly wasn't going to mention it.

"Do you not think they'll come after you, then?" That changed his course.

"Hah! The local boys are too simple, too cowardly." His eyes narrowed. "But they may have brought in a few outsiders to stir things up. Like your brother's friend—the one who said he only wanted seed—what's his name?"

"Dick," she said quickly, thinking of Abban's dead cousin. "Dick . . . O'Brien."

"I'll run that by the colonel and have him checked out." He tucked a shirt into his pants. "I'm famished. Get up and make me something to eat."

Grace got out of bed gladly, and hurried to the nursery to dress. Mary Kate's empty crib hit her like a kick in the stomach and she prayed she would not become pregnant. There were herbs she could use to prevent this, but she had to see Granna before his aim became true.

Down in the kitchen, she set before him a bowl of gruel and a piece of bacon fat from the storehouse. Brigid came in with Mary Kathleen and stopped at the sight of them, sitting at the table like husband and wife.

"Brigid!" he boomed. "Fine morning, isn't it? Take the child up-stairs and dress her for a day outdoors."

"Aye, sir." She glanced at Grace on her way out of the room.

Grace froze when she heard his order, but she managed to keep her voice casual. "Are you taking Mary Kathleen out today?"

He smiled at her and she saw that beneath the cheerful veneer lay his old character, more twisted than ever and dangerously close to becoming unhinged.

"Those bandits won't shoot at me if I've got a child tied to my back." His face was triumphant. "And an Irish child at that." He was proud of his plan—he had to go out, but he didn't have to go unpro-tected.

"But she's barely two years old!" Grace tried to laugh. "You can't carry a baby around with you all day, can you?"

"I can and I will," he announced. "Tell that to your brother's friend." He stood up, grabbed her face, and kissed her hard. "See you tonight, my dear."

Grace barely had time to murmur love and encouragement to the bewildered child before she was put up behind Bram on his horse, and the two of them roped firmly together. When they were out of sight, she went into the house and threw up her breakfast.

"Are you sick, Missus?" Brigid asked anxiously.

"Aye." She rinsed her mouth. "He thinks the rebels won't shoot at him if he's got an Irish child tied to his back."

"Jesus, Mary, and Saint Joseph." The housekeeper crossed herself, looking every one of her fifty hard years, and then some. "What's happened between the two of you, then?"

Grace shook her head. "He thinks he loves me again, and that he can make me forget all that's happened. It's madness. He must be losing his mind."

Brigid glanced at her sharply. "Moira has said the same thing to me." She lowered her voice. "You've got to be careful, Missus," she warned. "He's got the lover's sickness. And my Moira, as well."

Grace's eyes widened in shock.

"I don't know which one gave it to the other," Brigid whispered. "But Moira's swallowing arsenic on the sly. I found the bottle under her things. Where she got hold of such a thing, I'll never know."

"Oh, dear God, Brigid," Grace moaned. "I've got to get out of here."

"You can't leave us," Brigid pleaded. "If you go, he'll lose his mind for sure and kill us all or turn us out, which is the same thing. If the rebels don't burn us out before."

"Don't say a word to anyone, Brigid, you hear me now?" Grace demanded. "Not a word about Moira or sickness or murderers loose . . . or any of it."

"Aye, Missus," Brigid said humbly.

Grace wandered the house for the rest of the day, sitting in one room after another, looking at the paintings on the wall, the fine furniture, the books, the view out each window. She could not leave and she could not stay, she could not love and she dared not give in to hate; she was paralyzed with fear.

The sky darkened, showered the land, then brightened again and still they did not come home. The lamps were lit in the kitchen and a small supper of root vegetables and fried fat lay on the table. Grace sat, listening for the sound of Bram's horse, and praying to God for an answer, a sign, direction, anything: It came in the form of her exhausted daughter, wet, cold, and shaking—too tired to do more than whimper in her arms. Her little head was hot, her face bruised. One arm hung awkwardly from her side.

"What's happened?" Grace forced herself to remain calm.

Bram shrugged drunkenly. "She is whiney and horribly unpleasant. You have spoiled her." He brushed off his pants and handed Brigid his jacket.

"She's a baby!" Grace picked up the child gently and felt her shoulder. Mary Kate screamed, then began to cry in earnest. "It's out," she said to Brigid. "Help me with her. Bring the whiskey."

"You'll not waste good drink on that brat," Bram slurred.

Grace ignored him and carried her daughter up to the nursery. She could hear Bram cursing them, but she didn't think he'd follow and make more trouble. Brigid came in behind her, closing the door and speaking in a whisper.

"Here 'tis, Missus." She set down the bottle of whiskey, then watched as Grace cut away the blouse, exposing Mary Kathleen's arm. Both women winced at the sight of that small shoulder and the arm hanging loosely from it.

"Pour some of that into her cup," Grace said, supporting the child in a sitting position. "Bring it."

Tears rolled down Mary Kathleen's cheeks, but she was silent, numb from the pain and the long, difficult day. Her eyes never left her mother's face, and Grace had to steel herself to keep from crying out in rage.

"Here now, musha," she soothed. "Drink this down. 'Tis bitter, I know, but 'twill ease the hurt in your poor wee arm."

The two women exchanged a glance over the child's head, coaxing three small sips down before Mary Kate's eyes grew heavy and closed at last.

"I have binding rags." Brigid looked Grace in the eye. "Can you bring yourself to do it, or will I?"

Grace's face was grim. "I'll do it."

Brigid held the girl firmly, while Grace placed her hands on either side of the small shoulder.

"Ready?"

Brigid nodded.

With a swift motion, Grace snapped the shoulder back into place. Mary Kate opened her eyes and screamed, then fell back into numbing sleep.

"There now, Missus, there now." Brigid patted Grace's arm in distress. "You done it just fine, it'll heal well."

Grace had not realized that tears coursed down her own face until she put her hand to her cheek and felt the dampness there. They bound Mary Kate's shoulder and upper arm to her body, wrapping it securely so that it would not shift while she slept. Grace bathed her dear little face with warm water and brushed back her hair, noting the bruise on her cheek and the cut under her chin.

"I never dreamed he'd hurt her," Brigid murmured, shaking her head. She took up the child's cup, swallowing the last bit of whiskey in it.

Grace lowered the flame in the lamp, then sat down in the rocker near her daughter's bed.

"Is there anything else I can do, Missus?" Brigid stood near the door, her face strained and pale.

Grace thought of a thousand possibilities. "No," she answered. "Thank you, Brigid. You go on to bed now."

"I'll be on my knees for the both of you tonight," Brigid whispered, closing the door behind her.

Grace waited until the house was quiet, and then she, too, got down on her knees, clasped her hands together, and bowed her head against her child's bed, sick with the turmoil of what had happened. She had much to say to God, many questions to ask of Him, and so the battle between spirit and soul commenced.

When the long night had passed and its shadows had lifted, she rose stiffly from the cold floor and went to the looking glass. She knew herself there: the boots on her feet, the muddied skirt and crumpled sleeves of her dress, the cross at her neck and the chin that rose above it, the new tightness about the mouth, and the pale cheeks, the lines that drew down the corners of her eyes. She looked past the terrible sadness that had robbed them of color, traveling in and down, down to the place of her soul. And there, she looked with acceptance upon a blackened and empty house.

# Twenty-one

IRIAL Kelley's cave had long since been discovered and no one met there anymore. The men had broken into smaller bands, although too many of them consisted of independent marauders operating on anger instead of calculation. Still, they were enough of a threat to be discussed in the papers and bountied by the British army.

Barely sheltered from the wind and rain in an old bog hut, Morgan's men huddled around a small turf fire and waited for Captain Evans. Irial blew in with his men, Abban Alroy and Morgan right behind. Evans had sent a message to Morgan that Sean O'Malley was not to know of tonight's meeting; he was too close to the family and bound to be questioned should there be an investigation.

"Twelve more families thrown out this week." Irial warmed his hands in front of the fire. "Their belongings smashed and their roofs tore off. Hanlon and Donohue come back after dark thinking to shelter their families from the storm and the soldiers were there waiting on them. Killed Hanlon and his son, shot Donohue's arm off. And for what?" He looked around at his comrades. "For the few pennies those Brits throw his way. They say clear the land and plant for us—and he does it without any regard for the people been living there all their lives."

"He's an Englishman," Abban said.

"He's a dead man." Lord Evans came around the corner and stepped up to the fire. "He's gotten away with this too long. What say you?"

"Please, Captain." A young boy pushed his way into the circle. "I'm standing up for the job. I can do it, sir."

"Of course you can, Sullivan." Evans regarded the boy. "No one doubts that. And you'd have just cause, as well."

Nolan shook his head. "Not for Moira." He grimaced. "For the Hanlons—Dirk Hanlon's my mate—and for the others, as well." He paused and looked down. "For the Missus and what he's done to her. And to Mary Kate. If he'd hurt them, he'll kill us all soon enough."

"He hurt the child?" Morgan's face went white with anger.

"Aye." Nolan nodded. "He takes her out with him on evictions and oversees. She's roped to him, you see, so no one'll shoot him in the back."

"Christ have mercy," Abban said.

"Squire put her shoulder out yanking her off the ground, and even after the Missus set it, he forced her to go. Two days of that and she come down with fever." Nolan smiled grimly. "He's afraid of fever, he is. She's left in her bed, though he ties a bundle of rags in a cloak to his back so folk'll think he's still got her with him."

"Bastard." Morgan put his hand on the butt of the gun stuck into his belt. "I'll take care of this," he said to Evans.

"And me," Abban put in.

"Looks as if we all want a piece of this one," Evans said grimly. "But it won't be easy. He's an Englishman—they'll come after anyone they think is even remotely connected to us."

"It must be an accident, then." Morgan turned to Abban.

"Right," Evans agreed. "An accident is the only way." He took out a small flask, drank, and passed it around. "What are Squire Donnelly's weaknesses? What do we know of his habits?"

"He's a sure rider and a clean shot," Abban said.

Morgan nodded. "He knows the trails and cutaways, and he uses a different route every time."

"He's known to beat up whores," Irial put in. "As well as his own wife and daughter."

Nolan's eyes flashed. "And he's a drunk."

"Which makes him unpredictable," Evans added. He paused, thinking. The men were silent, watching his face, controlling their own urgency. "All right, then," he said at last. "Here's what we'll do . . ."

❋ ❋ ❋

Grace spread two pieces of bread with bacon fat from the pan, then sprinkled each piece liberally with arsenic before folding them together. She did not reflect on her action as she did this, did not let the word "murder" come to mind.

Mary Kathleen lay upstairs in bed, her fever broken. She would be well soon and Bram would take her again out on the road. It would kill the child. Grace could not take her and run; there was nowhere to go and she would only be condemning them to a more agonizing death than this. There was money in the house; she'd seen Bram moving his coin sacks late one night, but when she checked his room, she couldn't find it. After his death, she would take apart the house and leave this place. She wrapped the sandwich in a damp cloth, added a last piece of hard cheese, and put it in his saddlebag. Then she went upstairs so that he would not see her face before he left.

She watched out the window as Nolan tied the dummy to Bram's back, then stepped aside as Bram swung up on Warrior. Her face remained calm as Nolan handed her husband the saddlebag, but she did not breathe until he called the dogs and galloped down the avenue out of sight.

"Good-bye," she whispered, her open hand on the glass.

It was a beautiful day. Spectacular. Full of warm sunshine slanting through the trees, and the sounds of the birds and splashing water from the stream Bram followed through the east wood. He was going to make money today, but first he had to get rid of those squatters. No sense in giving them seed to plant, they'd only eat it. And anything he planted there would be dug up for the same reason. This particular group had always irritated him with their lack of initiative and their lazy, slovenly ways. No one ever wanted to work; how they scraped up their rent was a mystery to him. But now they were in arrears and he had other plans for the space they took up. The colonel had spoken to him of the English factory managers, many of them experienced farmers. If Bram provided land for them, the government would pay their rent and arrange for seed as part of a plan to put more food into circulation. They wouldn't pay for Irish hands unless the labor was needed, but they would aid experienced British farmers. He was on his way now to meet the soldiers and he looked forward to a full day of evictions. It was an hour before the scheduled rendezvous, and a good time to eat something. He pulled up Warrior, dismounted, and settled himself with his saddlebag against a tree; so absorbed was he with his own thoughts, and so confident in his ability to outwit those stupid Irish militants, he didn't notice the shadows flitting from tree to tree high up the rise on either side of him.

Morgan watched as Bram pulled out his bread and took a bite, then got up to fill his cup with water from the stream. Across the stream and up the other bank, Abban hid behind a pile of stones. Evans was further ahead where the stream crossed under the road, his carriage hidden just before the bridge. They had been waiting for Donnelly to dismount, worried that it would be another day when he did not. Once he had eaten, they were hoping he would close his eyes and sleep, but they were prepared to take him either way. He and Abban would come slowly down the bank and overpower him, knock him unconscious, and lead him on his own horse to Evans, who would then drive him up north to his favorite house of prostitution, where one of the Irish girls he'd beaten so badly was waiting to exact her revenge. He'd be given all the drink he wanted, then poisoned and left for the constabulary to find and report. Too much drink and heart failure in a whorehouse—it wouldn't be the first time this kind of thing had happened.

Morgan cupped his hands around his mouth and sent out a cuckoo's call, the signal to Abban that it was time to move in. There was no answer, but a moment later Abban sent back a different call. This wasn't the plan. What was he doing? Morgan moved out for a better look, and then he saw what Abban must have seen. Donnelly was standing, swaying, his head in his hands, shaking as if trying to clear his vision. He watched, stunned, as the squire called the dogs, then tossed to them the bread he'd been eating. The first dog wolfed it down, then went to the water and began drinking frantically. It vomited and went into convulsions. Donnelly watched, too, then pulled out his gun and shot the dog. He stumbled to his horse and got on, urging it downstream. Morgan and Abban ran through the woods on either side of him, racing to keep up and out of sight at the same time.

Suddenly, a figure jumped out from behind a boulder in the path of Donnelly's horse, shouting, "Hyah! Hyah!" The horse reared, startled, and threw the Squire from the saddle. His head hit a rock and he lay still.

Morgan started down the bank. "No!" he yelled as the boy cautiously crept toward the fallen figure.

Nolan looked up into the woods at the sound of Morgan's call just as Bram lifted the gun at his side and shot the boy in the chest.

Abban hollered from the other side, both men now sliding down the hills.

Bram stood slowly, swaying, blood soaking his collar, aiming the gun at one side and then the other. Morgan dove behind a boulder, Abban behind a tree. They waited, watching his frustration build.

"Come out, cowards!" He roared, firing off a shot. He grabbed Warrior's saddle and hauled himself up. "It'll take more than a boy to finish me!"

"How about a woman, then?" Moira stepped out into the stream and pointed the gun Nolan had stolen at Bram. She was dressed in her father's ragged pants and shirt, her hair stuffed up under a cap.

He was confused for a moment, then laughed. "Why, it's Moira! And is your mother behind you there in the wood? And old Jack?" He raised his gun. "Shall I shoot you like I shot your brother, Moira, or is it to be the revenge of the Sullivans this day?"

"Aye," she said, deadly calm, and pulled the trigger.

Bram fell from his horse and landed facedown in the stream. Moira walked to where he lay and shot him in the back of the head. The wood was silent.

And then came the sound of soldiers making their way downstream, shouting to one another. Moira did not hesitate, but mounted Warrior and rode off fast toward the bridge.

Morgan and Abban locked eyes across the river, and started down the steep bank. Abban splashed across, picked up the limp body of the boy, and carried him to Morgan. Together, they climbed again to the top of the rise and set off on a trail unknown to the soldiers, Nolan's blood soaking first one man's shirt and then the shirt of the other. He moaned and cried out for his mother, but when they finally arrived at the camp in the bog, young Nolan was dead.

# Twenty-two

"THEY'VE arrested him!" Ryan stood at the back door, his cap twisted in his hands. "They come for him right away this morning. Da says he'll never survive the questioning."

Grace pulled him into the kitchen. "Sean, you mean?"

Ryan nodded. "Conspiracy to murder."

"No!" Grace sank down on a stool. "He didn't do it," she said, then looked up at Ryan.

Ryan sat down, too. "No, he says, but that he'd gladly die for the man that did." He took her hand, something he'd never done. "What did they say, the guards, when they brought the Squire's body home?"

Grace's eyes filled with tears of guilt and confusion. "He'd been ambushed upstream near the old bridge, shot in the chest and head. He was facedown in the water and Warrior gone. They gave chase to two men in the woods, and a third on horseback, but lost them all on the trails." She paused. "That could not have been our Sean running through the woods?"

"He says he was downstream fishing when the soldiers came through. They asked him a few questions, then rode on. Not long after, he heard gunfire and decided to get out of there."

"They think he was a lookout."

"And maybe he was."

"You're not saying that to anyone else, are you, Ryan O'Malley?" She looked intently at his face, then sighed. "We've got to be careful, is all I'm saying."

Ryan glanced toward the door and his eye fell on Bram's boots. "You're not sorry he's gone, are you?"

A thousand emotions collided in Grace's heart, bringing fresh tears to her eyes. "He was my husband," she said softly. "For better or worse." She wiped her face with the hem of her apron. "But God could not have made a man so cruel. 'Twas the Devil claimed him for his own."

"That's what they're saying up and down the valley." Ryan squeezed the hand still in his own. "The news come quick and there's many say God has released you from a bad bargain."

"But is Sean's life to be the price?" She shook her head.

"I've sent word up the Black Hill, but no one's seen Morgan for days," he said.

Grace stopped and stared at the wall. Suddenly, she knew. "It's him they want. They know he'll come after Sean."

Ryan's eyes widened. "We've got to warn him." He stood and went to the door. "Where's your Nolan? He'll know the whereabouts sure as anyone."

Grace shook her head. "Nolan has disappeared, and Moira. It's just about done old Jack in, and Brigid's gone sick with worry. Just sits near the fire and rocks the baby."

"Moira wouldn't go off without her son?"

"Thank God she did," Grace answered truthfully. "I've got to have a baby boy in my arms when Bram's brother arrives for the burial or things will be worse than they already are."

"It's his brother coming then, and not his father?"

"Aye. Lord Donnelly's unwell, the letter says, though I think he's afraid more than anything else." She paused. "I know nothing of the brother—Edward, he's called—though Bram despised him."

"Dear Lord, what a mess." He glanced again at the boots by the door.

Grace stood. "Don't worry. I can do it. I'll keep the baby as mine until he's buried Bram and left us alone again, then I'll return him to Brigid, sell what I can, and come home to all of you."

"What about our Sean?"

Grace bit her lip. "Morgan won't let him hang," she said firmly. "And he won't let himself get caught, either. We've got to have faith."

"All right, then," Ryan said, relieved. "I'll tell Da what you've said and we'll wait to hear. Are we to come to the burial?"

"Aye." She nodded grimly. "There's not to be a whisper of trouble, we're a happy family in his brother's eye. Starving," she added. "But happy."

She insisted Ryan take half the oats she had on hand, two fresh eggs from the chicken she kept locked up at night, and the pigs' feet for boiling.

"Not much," she apologized.

"You'll hear no complaint from me." He kissed her cheek and went out to the cart, leaving her alone in a house that was, for now, hers.

# Twenty-three

THEY buried him in secret on a misty morning high on the hill above his home, his small body wrapped in a clean linen sheet, a ribbon with the green, white, and orange of Ireland pinned over his heart.

It was only men come to remember the life and mourn the death of the quiet, courageous boy. Only men, and a single woman, his mother, roused silently from her bed and brought to this place so that she might always know where her son would be. Her husband, weak and trembling with sickness, stood next to her, wrapped in his blanket, supported on either side by strong men whose eyes gave lie to their stoic stance.

Father Brown had come with no questions asked; he'd been up against the British interrogators before and his silence in the face of torture had earned the trust of the rebels. The smell of incense from the cantor he swung over the grave fought for recognition with the scent of pine. The air was damp. There was no wind, no breeze, no sound other than that of the priest's soft voice.

"To the earth we return this body," he intoned. "Ashes to ashes, dust to dust. We pray that our Lord Jesus Christ might have mercy on his soul and greet him at the gates of Heaven with open arms. Amen."

Brigid moaned and rocked, her hands together in a knot against her chest. Morgan put his arm around her shoulders.

"Will anyone speak?" Father Brown asked.

Abban stepped forward, cap in hand. "I will, Father." He addressed the group. "I knew Nolan Jack Sullivan through the worst win-

ter we've ever seen in Ireland, through the great hunger and terrible
dying, through cruelty and disaster such as a child should never witness. And I have this to say about him: Never was there a boy so steady
in unsteady times, constant in his devotion to his Maker and to the
people he loved. Never was there a boy so very brave and true of heart."
He looked at Brigid. "He was a son to make a mother proud. And no
better son could a father have. We were proud to call him one of our
own." He paused, then said, "Stand tall, now, men, and let's send him
off the way he deserves . . . Nolan Jack Sullivan, a true son of Ireland."

And so they stood gallantly, these men, their clothes hanging
loosely on gaunt frames. Each one carried in his heart the face of a
child he'd loved and buried, and it was of these children, as well, that
they sang; these children, they also mourned. Their voices broke with
emotion, but as one man lost heart, another found new strength and
took up the song.

His mother listened, tears streaming down her face; his father
mouthed the words as best he could, his hand over his heart. And in
this way, they sent young Nolan off to a land that better deserved him.

Lights flickered in cabin windows down in the valley and women
coming out to see another day put their hands to their ears and listened for the echo of what was surely a song of going away. Their own
children lay dying, most of them, on the cabin floors, and some wondered if this might be the end, at last—if God in His mercy might be
sending a host of angels come down through the misty morning wood
to take them all home where food would be plentiful and they'd never
know want again.

When the singing stopped, they waited a while longer, straining
their eyes against the shrouded hills. Then they sighed and went back
indoors to lie down on the floor with their children and wait.

Abban and Morgan stayed behind to fill in the grave and mark it
with a cross bearing Nolan's name. They did not pick up their spades
until the Sullivans were out of sight and the last of the men had vanished into the trees.

"I'll never get used to laying a child in the cold earth," Abban said,
tossing in a handful of dirt.

"Then you're a lucky man." Morgan rubbed his hands together to warm them. "It's those become used to it I feel for most."

They dug in earnest, working up a sweat. It was dangerous for them to be so close to Donnelly House with the soldiers in and out and the Squire's brother due to arrive, but they hadn't the heart to take him so far away from his mother now that she'd lost him forever. Their work was quick, but the sun was breaking through the mist when they'd finished.

"Will we tell Brigid about Moira?"

"No." Morgan set down his spade. "'Twas an accident, her being shot like that. Wouldn't do her folks good to know she was dead, as well. Better to let them think she run off and found a better life."

"How's Evans?"

"Arm's shattered, but he's coming out of it. Father Brown has him hid in the parish attic."

"Does he remember any of it?" Abban wiped his dirty hands off on his pants.

"He recalls seeing the great black horse come flying upstream toward the bridge. He says he got out of the carriage to take him down, then realized it wasn't Donnelly. Moira must've been in a panic what with the killing and the soldiers right behind her, and she just fired away. He didn't even know 'twas a woman, just fired back in self-defense. Irial and old Tom come in the wagon and got them out of there just ahead of the soldiers, him unconcious and her dead. They took the body to the nuns and Evans to Father Brown."

"Did they give her a Christian burial?"

"Aye. She rests in the rose garden with the other Catholic girls who, for one reason or another, couldn't go home."

He leaned on his shovel and wiped the sweat from his forehead, then paused as a light came on in an upstairs room of the big house below and the shadow of a figure crossed the window.

Abban watched him for a moment, then said, "Hard to be so near, to see her, but unable to offer a bit of comfort."

Morgan nodded. "They say she fainted dead away when the soldiers rode up with his body."

"I don't think it was from a broken heart, though, Morgan boy."

The two men looked at one another.

"Someone poisoned his food, and it wasn't Brigid or the wee child."

Morgan looked again at the house. "Are you saying our Grace is capable of murder?"

Abban moved closer for a better view; Grace was now in the yard, crossing to the barn. "I'd not call it murder," he said softly. "Who else was there to defend the life of her child and herself? Must be a terrible thing for her to bear," he added, shaking his head. "A secret like that."

Morgan watched her leave the barn and carry something to the house.

"Best we finish up and get away." Abban pulled him gently back toward the grave. "Nothing we can do for her now."

Morgan studied Abban's face for a long moment. "There is something," he said. "If you're willing to risk that old neck of yours yet again."

Abban gave him a weary smile. "And wasn't I just waiting for yourself to bring it up?"

The two men finished filling in the grave, smoothing the mound of dirt and covering it with a blanket of pine needles. Anchored in the ground at its head was a wooden cross that bore the inscription NOLAN JACK SULLIVAN, 1836–1847, IRELAND'S BRAVE BOY.

They took off their hats and bowed their heads in a moment of silent prayer, looking up again when a raven's cry broke the stillness.

"Where's he being held, then?" Abban asked.

"Cork City Jail." Morgan pulled his cap down low over his brow and turned up his coat collar against the chill.

Abban did the same. "Better pick up your feet then, boy," he said, starting off down the hill. "'Tis a long, long walk to Cork City."

*Twenty-four*

E DWARD Donnelly was disgusted with Ireland and everyone in it. How his brother could have taken an Irish wife and made a home here was beyond his comprehension, although the girl was certainly good-looking. By Irish standards, at any rate. Too thin to provide a man much warmth on a cold winter night, but that was merely his own taste in women, and Bram had always had an odd eye.

His first night in the house, damp even for late April, had been troubling at best. There were no servants to attend to his comfort and no head cook, other than this Brigid woman, a mere shadow of a person who was painful to look at and difficult to understand for all her mumbling in that strange tongue, and yet she alone inspired in him some sympathy as she knew to take his coat and put a whiskey in his hand. There appeared to be no other man about the place and it was the Irish wife who saw to the horse and carriage he'd hired. The house itself was in ill-repair. Several windows were broken and the roof was in need of attention, as one chimney had collapsed and shutters hung askew. He could see no animals other than a bony cow in the barn with his own horse, but chickens lived in a back room on the first floor. The Irish wife had apologized for this, explaining the necessity of hiding them from thieves, but he found this hard to believe, as he was familiar with the Irish penchant for keeping livestock in one's living quarters. He had witnessed the piles of hardened manure in front of cabin doorways throughout his ride to Donnelly House, and had observed the pale, listless children sitting on top. Horrible-looking children, most of them, sticks for arms but enormous bellies and swollen legs. And in the city—foul, disgusting place with lanes reeking of stink—he had even seen children with hair on their faces! A physician whom he'd befriended on the boat had said he might see such things as a result of poor diet and hygiene, and had advised him to avoid crowds, as the disease in this godforsaken place was on everyone. He'd expected the same kind of low-living degradation one sees in London slums, but he never imagined it to be so inescapable, and the sight of wizened children's faces covered with hair was something he sorely wished to put out of his mind.

His brother's daughter was no monkey, thank God. A weak, frail little thing, confined to her bed, a mess of reddish hair like that of her mother, but clearly the high forehead and strong chin that marked every Donnelly. The baby boy, too, appeared to have escaped the poverty of character predominant in his Irish countrymen. Though he showed no real sign of resemblance to the mother and lacked the strong features of the father, he was still an infant. In an embarrassed mumble, the mother explained that her milk had dried up and she was feeding it cow's milk instead. Apparently, it had not quite taken to this change, and was thin and spotty. It fussed a great deal and was only comforted in the arms of the Brigid woman, who sang an unfamiliar melody to it with great repetition.

He'd asked to see the body of his brother, and was surprised to find him laid out in humble field clothes on the drawing room table. There was no light and the draperies had to be drawn back in order for him to look upon the face he barely remembered. It had aged, and the trauma done to it had not enhanced any part of its appearance. The room was cold, as befit the keeping of a corpse, but Edward felt more than a chill of damp. There was no stir to the air, as if no one had looked in on the body since its laying out. The only mourners who stood in attendance in the outer room were the wife, the housekeeper, and an old man they called Jack, who looked as if he could crawl into a grave himself and be right at home there. Condolences had arrived from two former business associates, as well as from Captain Wynne and the O'Flahertys of Dublin. But that was all. He'd imagined the many tenants, caps in hand, women weeping, paying their respects to their dead squire, but not a one had come to the door. Ungrateful lot. Mean-spirited, he was sure of it. The books were a mess, but it looked as though none of them had paid any rent in over a year! No wonder his brother was unable to send money home if he could not run an estate any better than this!

All this trouble and annoyance, and he'd not had anything substantial to eat since he arrived—nothing more than a bowl of thin soup and some hard bread. Apparently, there really was a shortage of food in this godforsaken country. He had assumed that those of better class could buy what they needed, but the wife said this took special permission from the captain of the guard and entailed a trip to Cork City. Then the food had to be smuggled back home against the threat of looters and bandits. It was simply mind-boggling.

The funeral was to be held this afternoon, after which he hoped to look over his brother's affairs and come to some agreement with the Irish wife. She, of course, was not entitled to anything from the estate, but would act as guardian for her son's best interests. If, of course, she appeared competent, which he doubted. In the meantime, he would take a nap and dream of dinner in London.

It was a small funeral. Bram's landowner friends, those who were still in the country, refused to come out for fear of ambush. Grace's family was there: her father, looking tired and confused; Granna, who kissed Grace immediately, cooed at the baby in her arms, then somberly greeted Mister Donnelly, telling him quietly what a fine brother he'd had in the Squire and how they'd all loved him like a son; Ryan and Aghna stood wide-eyed and fearful, each with a hand on young Thomas, who stood between them. They'd brought a few of the neighbors to make a show—the O'Dugans and Julia Ryan—and Grace was grateful for that, as Brigid had stayed behind to watch over Mary Kathleen and Old Jack, in his bed and looking to die before the day was out.

The Reverend Birdwell, from her mother's old church, had come at Grace's request and had given a very tactful, Protestant service beside the grave. Grace did not realize she'd been holding her breath until it came time to throw in the fistful of dirt. This she did with a steady hand, much to her surprise. Relief bloomed within her with each shovelful of dirt that hit the coffin. The group then returned to Donnelly House.

Refreshments were meager, but no one said a word, until finally Reverend Birdwell broke the silence.

"And is Sean not well?" he asked Grace with concern.

Grace glanced at Granna, who moved closer and took the whimpering baby into her own arms.

"Sean's not well, no, Reverend," Granna said quietly. "He lies abed."

"Who is this Sean person?" Edward looked down his long nose at the old woman.

"He's Grace's brother, sir," she answered. "A fine boy. Crippled, though, and often sickly."

Edward wrinkled his nose in distaste. "This is not a family ailment, I hope?" He glanced at the baby in Granna's arms.

"Oh, no, sir," she said quickly. "He was in an accident years ago, trying to save his mother—my daughter, bless her heart—who drowned."

Edward's eyes widened in alarm. "Oh, my." He downed his glass of sherry and looked about for something stronger.

Grace brought out the whiskey and filled everyone's glasses. She was just about to excuse herself to look in on Mary Kathleen when the front door rattled, and in stormed Captain Wynne, followed by his guard.

His eyes found Edward's face in the group at once. "Forgive the intrusion, Mister Donnelly, sir, but we've come to search for a fugitive." He motioned for one of the soldiers to go upstairs, the other to search the rooms downstairs.

Out the window, Grace could see soldiers heading for the barn and storage sheds. "Who is it you're looking for?" she asked.

"Your brother, of course, Missus Donnelly." He eyed her carefully, caught between ready suspicion and necessary respect in the presence of her brother-in-law. "He has made an escape."

"This is outrageous!" Edward puffed out his chest and strode across the room. "As you may be aware, Captain, we have buried my brother today and are in a time of mourning."

"Yes, sir, again my apologies." Captain Wynne held his ground. "But Missus Donnelly's brother, who was being held in connection with the Squire's murder, has escaped, aided by two other wanted men, and we think they will attempt to see their families before trying to leave the country."

"Is this true?" Edward turned toward Grace.

"Absolutely not," she insisted. "My brother's a cripple!"

"You are not aware, madam, that he is accused of murdering your husband?" Red spots appeared on his cheeks as his voice rose in doubt.

Patrick cleared his throat and stepped forward. "The boy was taken in for questioning two days ago. We told Grace he was sick in bed as she's got enough grief on her shoulders." He stood next to his daughter, his hand on her arm. "We stand by his innocence, and we've heard nothing of an escape."

"But he's been charged with murdering my brother?" Edward looked incredulously from Patrick to the captain.

"Yes." Captain Wynne reached into his breast pocket and pulled out an official-looking document. "This is his confession."

"Confession!" Patrick spat. "The boy's no more guilty of murdering Squire Donnelly than I am!"

"Let me see that." Edward snatched the papers and looked through them. "This appears to be in order," he said. "Your brother has confessed to the shooting. He says he acted alone and not as part of a conspiracy, that he was motivated by your ill treatment." He glanced again at the last paper, then passed it to Grace. "This is your brother's signature?"

"I'm not sure," she said evenly, though with its confident hand and obvious flourish, it could be no other.

Edward's eyes narrowed. "What is this so-called 'ill treatment' to which your brother refers?"

"The Squire beat her near to death," Patrick said quietly but clearly. He did not lower his eyes.

"She lost—" Ryan began.

"*Nearly* lost the baby," Granna interrupted, kissing the cheek of the little boy in her arms.

An uncomfortable silence filled the room.

"It appears he is not here," the captain announced after a soldier entered and shook his head. He turned to Grace. "But if he should turn up and you do not report it, then I will arrest you, as well."

Anger flushed Grace's cheeks and she pulled herself up to her full height. "I'll not give up my own brother to British soldiers," she answered defiantly.

"He's a murderer." The captain stared her down.

"He's not capable of murder, and you know it, having seen his poor twisted body. And he's weak in the mind, as well. Swayed by the desire to be a hero."

"Ah, but I have his confession." He smiled.

"No, *I* have his confession." Grace held it up, tore it in half, and dropped both pieces into the fire.

One of the soldiers scrambled to the hearth, pushed her out of the way, and retrieved the singed and smoking documents, which he handed to the captain.

"I ought to arrest you right now for that," he said between gritted teeth.

"Here, here now." Edward put his hand on the captain's arm. "She's a grieving widow, not herself, as unpleasant as it all seems. I shall have finished my business here in a day or two, can you not wait until then to pursue this matter?"

The captain looked from Grace to Edward and back again. "You've not heard the last of me, Missus Donnelly," he said, then turned on his heel and left.

Edward waited until the soldiers had ridden to the road before he turned on Grace. "Now, my dear sister-in-law, perhaps you'd better explain yourself. It appears your family has been putting on a front for my benefit and I would like to know why."

Grace thought fast. "They have found it hard to forgive him the beating he gave me on one occasion," she said, moving to the fire and standing with her back to the heat. "They have come today only out of respect for me." She smiled at them, but her eyes warned them to agree with everything she was about to say. "I forgave my husband and came back to bear him the son he had so longed for. You cannot know how troubled he was this past year with the letters from your father about money and there being none to give. You've seen the books. He had to sell the mills and other things to keep us in what little food we have. Surely you can understand the frustration that builds in a man when he cannot provide for his family," she implored. "And indeed must sit by and watch all he has built come to naught." She lowered her voice and looked away toward the window. "I am ashamed for him to say it, but he fell into the habit of drink for a short time. I provoked his anger by giving away what little food we had to strangers on the road and he just went round the bend." She forced earnestness into her voice. "Never was a man more contrite and loving than my husband when he'd realized what he'd done. He swore off the drink, cleared his head, and turned his hand to the easing of our plight."

"And your brother did not realize you had reconciled?" Edward found himself wanting to believe her—she was beguiling in an Irish sort of way.

Grace shook her head. "Sean is no murderer. My husband was ambushed by a renegade band of evicted tenants—of this I am sure."

Patrick nodded. "Our Sean has always been too close to his sister, as she was his company all through their growing up. He's claimed the deed as his own to appear a hero in her eyes, but it's no more than that."

"That captain seems quite convinced of his guilt," Edward said dubiously.

"He must bring someone to justice," Patrick answered. "Squire Donnelly was a man to be reckoned with in these parts, and of course, he's English."

"Of course," Edward murmured. He turned away and looked out again at the dismal darkening sky.

"You must be exhausted," Grace said at once. "All the travel and turmoil."

"Aye," the others agreed, nodding and moving toward the door.

"We must be riding for home now, Grace." Patrick embraced his daughter, then stepped aside. "We'll stop at the Sullivans and take little Mary Kate with us. I'll bring her back in a day or two."

Grace nodded gratefully. They'd worked this out in private, knowing that Mary Kathleen might well let it slip that Phillip was not her brother.

"Good night then, Mister Donnelly. Sorry for your troubles. May your brother rest in peace and may you have safe travel home."

Edward accepted the outstretched hands offered him by the men, as well as the women's shy farewells. When Grace had ushered them out into the night, he ran a hand over his face and felt how deep the weariness ran. This was an odd house full of sly doings. The whole country was sly and unsettled; he would be glad to leave it. He poured himself another whiskey—the one good thing about this place—and was about to go upstairs when he heard a mewling from the cradle by the fire. He went to it and peered in at the face of the boy who lay wrapped within. A Donnelly boy. His own blood. He could see some resemblance now that he looked closely; it was there in the set of the eyes and the jut of the chin. Yes, clearly a Donnelly. He felt a kinship to the child and pictured himself the guiding mentor of a strong, intelligent young man. But that would never be. He didn't intend to ever see Ireland again. Perhaps when the boy was old enough for education, he would send for him, he mused, still enjoying the image of himself as benefactor. But no, he shook his head. Too Irish by then. The accent would keep him out of good society; his mind would be undisciplined, his will unruly. He laid a finger against the child's cheek and was rewarded with a smile and a coo. Phillip Edward, they called him. The old man would like that. For all his brashness and headstrong ways, Bram had been the favored brother in the Donnelly home, and his father had hoped until the end that the Irish estate would fail and he'd have his youngest son back again, contrite and grateful for reacceptance. Now Bram was dead and Lord Donnelly was being eaten away by guilt and grief. He'd lost interest in financial affairs and Edward was not yet ready to assume such responsibility— he still enjoyed a life of relative ease with little demand made upon him. But a grandson might rekindle the old man's interest in life; Bram's son, a namesake, might well convince the old man that he'd been given a second chance. And if Edward were to rescue this poor child from his ignorant Irish relations and bring him back to England under his guardianship . . . well, he might just rise at last in his father's estimations. Edward smiled warmly at the baby in its cradle. It might just work. He eyed the whiskey in his glass, then raised it.

"Here's to you, young Donnelly," he toasted, and they both gazed happily at the firelight that danced in the nooks of the heavy crystal.

# Twenty-five

OLD Jack breathed his last as the sun came up on the next day. Brigid patted his cheek and crossed his arms over his chest, then went outside to hang a bit of yellow cloth from the doorway. Her eyes were dry. Jack's death was a relief, and there were no mourners to call upon the deep well of grief she carried.

She had just finished wrapping him in a threadbare sheet when there came a soft knock on the door and three men slipped in, doffing their caps and lowering their eyes. They'd said they'd come, and they had. And now she need only wish them Godspeed and safe away, and they'd take her Jack to lie next to their Nolan on the hill above the house. She thanked them for that and tried to press her last coin into their palms, but they shook their heads. "No, Mother," they said and kissed her cheek, each one of them weary in the eye and needing a shave. She did not watch them slip away into the wood, nor mark the time she'd last set eyes on her husband's face. There was no need.

Grace was in the kitchen, rocking Phillip, when Brigid appeared in the doorway; the look on the older woman's face was so grave that Grace stood immediately and held out the baby. Brigid took him in her arms, sat down carefully in the chair, and began to rock, her eyes never leaving his sweet little face. Jack had died, true enough, but she could take comfort in this child, the last bit of her family.

Edward was not yet up. He'd been busy the last two days, sending messages and making inquiries with the help of a private the captain had put at his disposal. Grace suspected the private's true purpose was to keep an eye on herself and the doings of the house, but her brother-in-law had unwittingly thwarted that plan. For this she was glad, but she did not harbor any thoughts of charity, and only hoped he would not throw her out immediately. She had listened to him toasting some private grand thought and chuckling to himself through-out much of the previous evening, finally falling asleep on the divan before the fire. At some point he must have roused himself to go to the bedroom, as that was where he lay this morning when she got up with the baby.

Grace did not ask about burying old Jack; Brigid had said it would be taken care of and there'd been a man come quietly out of the barn at first light.

She made a cup of tea and set it down next to the woman who'd been with her through so much, and to whom she had so little to of-fer. "God bless you, Brigid," she said quietly.

"And you, Missus."

Edward's breakfast lay upon a tray. He'd said he must rise early in order to meet with her before leaving. She met him on the stairs, dressed and fresh-faced, rubbing his hands together briskly.

"Ah, lovely," he said with great cheer. "Bring that along to the drawing room and I'll breakfast there while we talk."

He sat and tucked the napkin into his collar, motioned her to set the tray down on the desk before him. "Sit, sit!" He indicated the seat across from him. "My, these are lovely eggs! And what's this? A bit of bacon?" He smiled. "Can't be too much of a famine if one can get a breakfast as fine as this each day, hmmm?"

Grace smiled wanly. "You're having the last of it, sir."

He tucked it all away in a matter of minutes, then sat back and regarded her.

"My dear sister-in-law," he began ceremoniously. "I've given the matter of my brother's affairs much consideration, and I've come to a resolve that I feel will give you much peace of mind."

"Thank you, Edward," she said demurely.

"As you know, the estate as it stands is quite worthless. It's not bringing in a penny against the cost to run it, let alone making any kind of profit. There's no sense in leaving you here in destitution when you have a family home to which you might return. As for the oversee of this house and its leases, I have made arrangements with a Mister Ceallachan . . ."

Grace shook her head quickly. "Oh, no, sir," she insisted. "You would not want to be doing business with the likes of him."

"What's wrong with him?"

"He's a ruthless man, and a cruel cheat."

Edward smiled. "You've just confirmed my faith in him, my dear. I need a ruthless man to collect the debts that are owed this estate, and for a generous percentage promised to him and the allowance of this house as residence, I am assured he will not cheat me. After all, it is your son's inheritance with which I concern myself."

"My son," Grace paused. "Phillip? Phillip's inheritance?"

"Estates traditionally pass from father to son," he said, then added, "I'm sorry for your daughter, of course, but she'll have a husband someday to take care of her needs."

"Aye," Grace said doubtfully.

"But about your son." He made a triangle with the tips of his forefingers and thumbs, proceeding gingerly. "I have a proposal to make and I would like you to hear me out before you give me an answer."

"I can do that." She kept all emotion out of her face.

"Phillip is a Donnelly," he began carefully. "And there is a long tradition of Donnelly men in our family, although my wife and I have not been blessed with children. Phillip is the only heir so far." He paused to see if this was registering. It appeared to be, as she'd sat up straighter in her chair. "As heir of the Donnelly lands and of this estate in Ireland, Phillip will have many responsibilities, responsibilities that he will be unable to fulfill without the proper education and training."

"Are you saying, sir, that Phillip should come to England when it is time for his schooling?"

Edward held up his hand. "Please, madam, allow me to finish."

Grace nodded, reluctantly.

"As I was saying, Phillip will need a thorough education in order to rise to his proper station in life. Yes, I would like him to come to England for proper tutoring, but these early years of his life are critical, as well." He paused and wet his lips. "What I am proposing is that you allow me to bring Phillip back to London with me now . . ."

Grace shook her head firmly in protest.

"Please, please," Edward insisted. "Hear me in full! As you yourself have said, there is much starvation in this country and pestilence, as well. His life is at risk here. In London, he will have the best physician and a private nurse; he will be raised with a nanny just as his father and I were, and a governess will begin his early education, followed by tutors, boarding school, and university. It is a fine life for a young man—he will want for nothing."

"What about love, Edward?" she said. "A mother's love?"

"My wife has longed for a child," he said quietly. "She will love him with all her heart. We will raise him as our own beloved son."

"I cannot give him up," she said simply, thinking of Brigid downstairs rocking her grandson.

"Madam." He was firm. "I had hoped you would see the reason in my proposal and be grateful for such a chance for your son, but I see this is not to be. So I must tell you that I am quite within my rights to take the child with or without your permission, as he is the only heir to a great fortune." He paused and, seeing no change in her face, added, "And as his mother is suspect in the death of his father."

Grace stood in fury. "Are you calling me a murderer, then?"

"No," Edward shook his head, trying to calm her. "I know you had nothing to do with Bram's death, nor your brother, but on paper it is suspicious and any judge in England or Ireland would hand the child over to me. I don't want to go through that. It would only tarnish your name and his."

Grace sat again, thinking. "Would I ever see him again?"

"Certainly. Though I would discourage too much contact in hopes that I might adopt him as my own son. He's young still—you'll forget him in time. It's not as though you've had him years and years. Not like your daughter."

"And what about Mary Kathleen?" she asked. "Is she to go, as well?"

"No," he said quickly. "A girl belongs with her mother."

"But she is as much Donnelly as her brother."

"Yes," he said, beginning to understand. "Yes, that is certainly true. She has Donnelly blood." He paused, regarding this woman anew. "What would you want . . . for your daughter's future, I mean?"

Grace thought. "For Mary Kathleen Donnelly, I would want a sum of money for schooling and a dowry. And when she is eighteen, I would want title of this land handed over to her. The title to be free of debt and the estate able to make a modest income for her and her family, if she has one."

Edward considered this. There was every possibility that the girl and her mother would not even be alive in a year or so, and the title could be reverted. "All right," he said. "That is a reasonable request. It will give the girl a chance at some decent society."

Grace ignored the slight. "For my son," she continued, "I would see his adoption papers notarized and know for my own peace of mind that he was your legal heir, never to be turned away from you no matter the circumstance."

"Gladly," he said with relief.

"And one last thing," she added. "I would have you take Brigid Sullivan along as the baby's nurse to watch over him till he's grown, and then to be taken care of herself until her natural death."

Edward frowned. "An Irish nurse? And she's a bit old, is she not?"

"She is not old and she loves him as her own. I could not send him off unless I knew she were there to care for him."

"I would not push too hard, if I were you, or have you forgotten that the advantage here is mine?"

"I'm not asking for more than is fair," she said. "And I believe, sir, the advantage is *mine*. Phillip is half Irish and this is Ireland; without my permission, you will never see him again until he is grown and ready to fight you for what is rightfully his."

He regarded her with a new measure of respect. "You make your point well, madam. I must say I admire that. I suppose you want all of this documented?"

She nodded. "I'll have the papers in my hand before you leave."

"All right, then." He stood and made a little bow. "You have my word. I'll send the private on ahead to Cork to have the necessary work drawn up and ready for our signatures when we arrive. Done?"

"Done."

In the end, it was easier than Grace imagined. Brigid confessed that Nolan was dead and buried, though she'd not say how and when, just that she had proof of it. There was no proof of Moira except what she knew in her heart. "I never dream of my children when they're alive," she said, "and Moira's come every night for weeks." All the others were in America and there was no one now but her grandson. She was grateful for the bargain Grace had struck. It meant she might live out her final days in ease watching Phillip grow into a fine and healthy young man. And she'd be there to whisper Irish tales in his ear as he fell asleep at night and sing him Irish songs in the morning. She even laughed at the great irony of it all—Moira's Irish bastard going to live in London as heir to the great Donnelly fortune! Ah, the Lord had a sense of humor in doling out justice!

It was a fast trip to the solicitor's in Cork City, where Grace secured a fine future for young Phillip. This gave her great satisfaction, as did the twenty pounds of gold in her pocket and the promise of title to Donnelly House upon the eighteenth birthday of her daughter, the true Donnelly heir.

# Twenty-six

GRACE drove the horse and carriage hard until she reached the lane that took her home. There, in front of the O'Malley cabin, stood her own daughter playing with a stick in the dirt. She greeted the little girl with a long embrace, and then explained that she would only stay the night, for she had to return to Donnelly House to gather up their things.

They waited for cover of darkness to unload the cache she'd brought back from the warehouse at Cork. All that food to be sent to England when so many were starving right here; it had maddened her and she'd used more than two pounds of gold and a great deal of flirtation to get what she wanted before it disappeared into the ship's hold. Hidden beneath her driving rug was a sack each of oats, wheat, and barley—she would not buy the coarse Indian meal that was given to the Irish—as well as one of sugar and a small keg of molasses. She'd gotten a box of tea, one of salted fish, and a basket of dried apples. It had taken all her charm and another flash of gold to talk the mess cook into parting with two dressed chickens and a bit of side pork. And then she'd driven with fierce determination, stopping for no one in case she was found out and robbed.

She begged her family to keep it well hidden, as there was enough to keep them all going but not enough to share with the neighbors. While Ryan, Aghna, and Thomas looked with wonder at their sudden good fortune, Grace took Patrick aside and pressed ten pounds into his hand.

"Keep five hidden away," she said quietly. "And try to get the other five to Sean so that he might escape the island and go to America."

Patrick shook his head. "I know not where he is, nor how to help him."

"He'll contact you," she said confidently. "He won't try to leave without getting word to you, and you tell the messenger that you must see him, that you can pay his passage out."

"Aye, that's what I'll do, then." His smile was weary, but his eyes grateful. "Do you not want Ryan or myself to come back to the house with you?"

"No." Grace was adamant. "I've got five days to take what is mine and pack the rest into trunks to be picked up by our devoted friend Captain Wynne and sent to London." She paused. "I need to be there by myself."

Her father regarded her. "Aye, that you do."

She slept fitfully that night, then set out early next morning. It was strange to come up the drive to Donnelly House and see not a single light nor any activity in the yard. The Sullivans' house had been equally empty when she drove by, but the thought of Brigid and Phillip on their way to England was comforting.

She lost no time in stabling the horse, then went into the house and lit the lamps. She also loaded Bram's shotgun and put it by the front door, then carried the pistol upstairs to put by her bed.

In the kitchen, she ate a bit of the chicken and some bread, and drank water from the well, while surveying the room. It was early May and the steady sun was welcome. Grace's father would use this day to plant the basket of seed potatoes he'd managed to hang on to in hopes that August would bring them a decent harvest. He'd have to plant and guard them, for the starving along the road might dig them up, so desperate were they still for food. She would be home to help him in a week's time.

She was still hungry after the bits of chicken and hard bread, but it was a feeling to which she'd become accustomed and she ignored it, licking the crumbs from her hands, then wiping them on her skirt.

There were trunks in the attic and these she lowered down to the upper floor with a rope and most of her strength. After dragging them to the main floor, she sat down on top of one and contemplated her next move. She could not bring home trunks of books and antiques, as there was no place to put them and no way to defend their presence if the captain should come calling. And yet, she felt in her heart that most of this was the rightful property of her daughter and she resented sending it back to England or leaving it in Ceallachan's thieving hands. She looked out the window and up the hill to the little cemetery where she and Abban had buried those who could go no further, and then she knew what to do. She would bury the trunks. They were watertight and she could also cover them with tarps. There might be some damage after years in the damp earth, but it was worth the attempt. She began to pack—one set to be sent to England, one to be buried for Mary Kathleen's future.

The days passed quickly in an exhausting routine of packing, loading the heavy trunks onto a sledge that the horse pulled up the small hill, digging the "grave," and lowering the trunks into them. In all, she buried three trunks for her daughter—each one filled with linens, small family portraits and landscapes, books, antiques, a miniature musical clock, silver, china, and crystal. Into the last, she dropped the earrings Bram had given her early in their marriage, the teardrop diamond, and her engagement and wedding rings. Each trunk was marked by a wooden cross with a different name: Mary Kathleen, Michael Brian, and Baby Boy; a trunk for each child she'd had with Bram, although only one lived to claim the inheritance.

This task done, Grace found her mind much more at ease and her pace more leisurely. She filled the remaining trunks with incidental books and pieces of art, family photographs and paintings, some silver and second-best linen. Bram's clothes would all go home to England, along with his boots, guns, and fishing tackle. She left in the house just enough to make it habitable: the odds and ends of crockery, flatware, the kitchen pots and pans, and linen for the beds. Some of the furniture would be shipped back to England, but the rest, she knew, would stay in the house where, hopefully, it would remain. She was not fool enough to leave Ceallachan nothing to sell for personal gain—here and there was the odd candlestick and vase, books to bring him a few pounds, the wine in the cellar and a half case of whiskey, and the rugs. To bring back to her old home, Grace packed up her quilts and samplers, the family Bible, extra blankets and pillows, and the bed frame in the guest room so that Granna might have a comfortable place to lie at night. She also took an extra pot from the kitchen and anything else she thought might add a bit of comfort to her family, including bottles of port and whiskey. She'd keep the horse and take back shovels and hoes for her father, as well as buckets, spades, hammers, and nails.

It was Thursday night. On Saturday morning she'd hand over the trunks to Captain Wynne and the keys to Ceallachan. This determined, Grace went into the bare library, lit the fire she'd laid that morning, and sat down on the divan to watch it burn. She was deep in thought, drowsy with the heat, when there was a rap at the back garden window. She squinted into the darkness, sure it was only a branch knocking against the glass. It came again, more insistent this time. She rose and slipped quickly into the kitchen, picking up the shotgun before stepping out into the dark and easing silently around the corner of the house. It took a moment to adjust her eyes, but she could see faintly outlined from the light of the window, the figures of two men, one supporting the other, leaning against the house. She shouldered the gun and cocked it.

"Who are you and what do you want?" she demanded, stepping away from the house and aiming at them.

The biggest of the men nearly dropped the other as he tried to raise his hands and hold on at the same time.

"For the love of God, Grace, don't shoot!" he whispered as loudly as he could.

Grace's heart stopped. "Name yourself, then!" she called, not daring to believe.

"It's me, of course!" He stepped closer, holding up the other man.

"Oh, dear Heavenly Father," Grace murmured, lowering the gun and moving quickly to him.

She slipped her shoulder under the other arm of the hurt man, helping to carry him into the kitchen.

"Morgan McDonagh, I near blew your fool head off! What are you doing here, for pity's sake, and who've you got under this great hood?"

They stepped into the kitchen and eased the man into a chair. Morgan pushed away the hood.

"It's Father Brown!" she exclaimed. "What's happened to his head?"

Morgan, too, sank into a chair and wiped a hand over his tired face. "Just grazed, but it bled a lot. They come for him again, you see." He looked at the older man. "And he'd not survive another round of 'questioning,' so we got him out of there, but he was hit and we got separated from the rest in the skirmish. I lost his horse, but it's just as well, we'd've been seen and . . ." He shook his head.

Father Brown roused himself at that moment. He opened his eyes and managed a weak smile. "Grace, my dear girl, forgive us coming like this."

"I'll have none of it, Father," she scolded him gently. "You know me better than that. Haven't we been through times before?"

"That we have," he said softly and put a hand over hers. "Can you clean me up a bit while we figure what to do next?"

"Aye." She nodded. "Come in here near the fire and warm your-selves."

They stood while she barred the back door, then followed her into the living room.

"Sit," she ordered, putting a glass of whiskey in each willing hand.

They sat on the floor in front of the fire, Bram's heavy glasses in hand, and looked at one another.

"Here's to a sight for sore eyes." Morgan raised his glass to Grace.

"Hear hear." Father Brown drank deeply.

Grace bathed the wound on his forehead and applied a bandage. The whiskey had restored the color to his face, and he was able to eat the weak soup she had left, a crust of oat bread, and a dry, withered apple.

"A feast, my dear," he said and sighed deeply. "Simply a feast."

Morgan nodded, having finished his food, as well. "We're grateful to you, Grace. I don't know what we would've done, but I saw the smoke rising from your chimney and hoped you'd be alone."

"Another day and it would've been Ceallachan who answered your knock." She smiled grimly.

"We heard." Father Brown looked at Morgan. "It's a bad bargain, being turned out after all you've been through."

Grace shrugged. "Not so bad as you think." She thought of Moira's son and mother in England. "And how could I go on living here, a poor widow, alone?" She smiled mischievously. "What with all the renegades and riffraff slinking about the countryside on dark nights."

They laughed. Then Father Brown put his hand to his head and grunted.

"Is there a corner for me to lay myself down, dear Grace?" he asked. "I'm feeling the day now and can't keep my own eyes from closing."

"Take my room at the top of the stairs, Father, and welcome to it."

He shook his head. "I'm sure to sleep like the dead . . . and if someone should come knocking in the middle of the night, I'd best be hidden away." He thought. "How about the pantry closet off the kitchen?"

Grace nodded. "If that's what you want, but the floor's hard and cold." She set down her glass. "Morgan, help me fetch the featherbed from the nursery. And blankets."

He followed her upstairs, stood patiently while she piled the featherbed and two wool blankets in his arms, then carried it all down to the kitchen and waited while she arranged it into a comfortable-looking nest beneath the shelves.

"And what about you now?" she asked. "You look as though you've not slept in a hundred years."

He shook his head. "I'll be fine. Someone must stay awake, stand guard."

She saw how terribly pale he was, how dark the circles beneath his eyes. His beard was gone, and his hair badly cut, hanging across his forehead despite the bit of leather that tied back most of its length. She'd become accustomed to the sharp, bony look of other people's faces, hers included, but it shocked her to see Morgan so gaunt, he who had always seemed as tall and strong as the Irish oak, whose handsome face had carried a smile no matter the day. Now it appeared that a smile might stretch the skin too tight, and that his collarbones might snap if he stumbled and fell.

"'Twill be me stays awake," she said firmly, taking him by the hand and leading him to the drawing room. "You'll have a night's rest and there's to be no other talk about it, do you hear me, now?"

He was too tired to protest, and sank down gratefully on the rug in front of the fire, laid his head back against the divan, and closed his eyes. Grace roused a sleepy Father Brown, took him to the pantry, tucked him in, and saw with relief that he was fast asleep.

She checked all the doors and drew every curtain against the night. She knew the house so well, there was no reason to carry a candle, and the firelight seemed bright when she came back into the drawing room. Morgan lay still, his hands folded across his chest. His jacket, which he'd never taken off, was thin and tattered. She put more turf on the fire and a bit of kindling, then quietly eased herself down next to him. He was asleep, his head tipped back at an awkward angle, and she gently drew it onto her shoulder, brushing the hair off his forehead and pressing her lips to it.

"Ah, lovely." His eyes stayed closed, but he smiled.

Grace drew back, embarrassed. "Here I thought you were fast away, but instead you're lying in wait, counting on the pity of an old friend," she scolded, shrugging his head off her shoulder.

Opening his eyes to her face, he grinned waggishly. "'Pity' was not the word I had in mind." He sat up and resettled himself, drawing her near again. "But 'tis true you are my old friend. I've missed you, pirate."

"And I you," she answered truthfully, glad to be close. "Have you not been to home in all this time?" she asked. "Your mam must worry after you."

"I've not been, nor will I ever go again."

Grace sat up and searched his face. "Has she died, then?"

"Aye." He nodded slowly.

"And what of your sisters?"

"Gone."

"All of them?" Grace whispered.

"Not all." He stared into the fire. "But Mam was never strong after the last baby, you know, and Erin at two was still a wee bit of a thing. They died within days of getting the fever, and then Fee. Maureen got word to me through Father Brown and I snuck back to bury them, but someone talked and the guard was laying for me." He shook his head, staring into the fire. "I got close enough to see the cabin and the girls walking to the road and back, looking out for me, but the soldiers were spread through the bush and I'd have been an easy target. The next day, Maureen come out and dug the grave herself, burying the bodies together and marking the place. It wasn't a week after, Ceallachan and his henchmen—every one Irish—threw them out. Sure and it was a just another plot to lure me in—no one could grow a crop on that scrappy land—but I was far gone and knew nothing of

it. She had no way of finding me, of course, so she took Katie and
Ellen up the mountain, believing those crazy rumors of food hidden
away in the caves. By the time I found them, Maureen and Katie were
dead—of fever or starving, I don't know. The animals had got to them,
you see . . ." His voice broke and he put his fingers across his mouth.
"Though Ellen tried to beat them off with a stick."

"Where's Ellen now?" Grace asked quietly.

"Buried at the Holy Sisters." His voice was steady now. "Barbara's
there, you know. Took her vows years ago, it seems. Sister John Paul,
they call her. Wears a great robe and barks orders at everyone, just
like at home." He smiled wearily. "Ellen died two days before I got
her there." He paused. "Wasn't she always my favorite, though, and
how could I leave her by the side of the road?"

"Oh, Morgan, I didn't know."

"Dying's not news anymore."

"But Aislinn's alive? And your da?"

"Da came back afore Christmastime to find the cabin razed and
the grave out back. They say he went on a roaring drunk, stole a man's
horse, rode it right into the fort and started shooting. They killed him,
sure enough, but I think he took one or two down with him."

"And you've got these." Grace touched the small gold rings in his
ear.

"Mam left them for me. I wear one for her, one for him." He
shrugged. "It's about all that's left. Along with this." He pulled out
from beneath his shirt a leather cord, on the end of which hung his
mother's wedding band. "Ellen had it round her neck, and Barbara
can keep no worldly goods, as you know."

Grace's heart went out to him. "Will you give it to Aislinn?"

"If I find her. Last I heard, she was still in Liverpool. Making her
way best she can, if I know that girl. And there may be a child, as
well." He looked at Grace. "Mam cared nothing for the shame, just
wanted to see her again. But now I'm glad she never come."

"Ah, Morgan."

He shrugged. "Barbara is alive, and Aislinn, maybe. I'm still here."
He turned from the fire and laid a hand upon her cheek. "And thank
God you're here, Grace."

She covered his hand with her own, then leaned forward and
kissed him, gently for his lips were split and sore. His eyes opened

wide with the shock, but he quickly recovered and pulled her tightly to him, kissing her in return, desperately and with fierce longing.

"I'm sorry," he whispered in her hair, breaking the embrace. "I forgot myself. Too many nights I've kept warm on a stranger's cold floor by thinking of you and a kiss such as that. You must forgive a foolish man."

She pulled away and narrowed her eyes. "You're taking a lot of credit for one that started nothing, Mister McDonagh."

He smiled despite himself. "It's all right, then?" he asked shyly.

She nodded and held his gaze until they kissed again, gently now, for there was time.

"Where will you go when you leave this place?" he whispered as she leaned back in his arms.

"Home," she answered. "And lucky I am to still have it." She squeezed his arm, then looked at him. "I've not thanked you for saving the life of our Sean! He'd be a dead man now, if not for you."

"I don't know about that." He laughed shortly, shaking his head. "Our Sean has never been short on guts. We could hear him yelling at the guards long before we knew which cell he was in! The whole day and through the night, even when they beat him, he cursed them all, cursed their families, cursed their mothers!" He laughed again. "He wasn't denying that he did it . . . didn't he say he'd do the same to them, as well? Abban and I thought sure they'd cut his throat before we could get him out of there."

Grace laughed with him, then sobered at the thought of how close her brother had come to the end of his life. "How did you?"

Morgan frowned. "I'll say only this—not all the English are against us. Some come from families poor and desperate as our own, and they help when they can. Plenty cannot bear the suffering, especially of the children."

"'Twas a great risk," she said. "I saw notices in Macroom and Cork City. 'The Outlaw McDonagh,' they call you."

"Well, I'm keeping respectable company then, am I not?" He smiled, then rubbed a hand over his weary face. "At least I'm wanted alive, or it'd be harder than it already is. Before they put a rope around my neck or ship me off to Van Diemmen's Land, they want to hear my lovely voice singing out names. One of them belonging to your own dear brother, of course."

"Do you know where he is, then?"

"I have an idea," he admitted. "But I cannot say."

"You must both get out of Ireland. Right away."

"It's not that easy." He sighed. "Even if I were to go, there's just not enough money—not for passage, nor food and clothes, bribes and papers."

Grace thought a moment. "How much?"

"More than you've got squirreled away, pirate." He smiled and kissed her cheek. "You who've been feeding every mouth in the county."

"How much?" she asked, ignorning him.

"A lot," he laughed. "I can't parade onto any old boat looking like my own wanted poster. There's a reward, as you well know, and many's the man wants that money—English and Irish alike."

"I have money," she said. "Plenty."

"No." He took her hand. "The Squire's got nothing in the banks and there's no one to buy what's left of his property."

She regarded him for a moment. "If you'll keep your manly opinions to yourself for a moment, I'll tell you a wee story."

He sat quietly as she related Bram's scheme to gain title to Donnelly House and all its lands, and Moira's return with an illegitimate son. His mouth fell open, however, when she went on to tell him of Edward's eager acceptance of the child and Brigid's position as nurse for life in exchange for money and eventual title to the Donnelly estate for Mary Kathleen.

"Sure and you are a pirate!" he exclaimed when she'd finished. And then he broke into hearty laughter, looking at her with fresh admiration. "Sweet Jesus, I didn't know you had it in you, Grace! And why are you not leading raids with the best of them? We could use a mind like yours, 'tis true. What other secrets are you keeping in that head of yours?"

Her face sobered immediately and he grabbed up her hand, reading her mind.

"You're no murderer," he said quickly. "I know you wanted to kill him, and that you tried—but it wasn't you did it in the end."

Grace's eyes filled with tears. "You shot him to cover up. He was already dead of arsenic."

Morgan shook his head.

"Sean, then."

"Not Sean, nor I, nor Abban, though we were all laying for him that very day."

"Then who?"

"Nolan had plans, as well. He was downstream from us, and when the Squire come riding through, he jumped out to startle the black, hoping the Squire'd be thrown and his neck broke. The horse reared and threw him, but he only played dead until the boy come close enough, then he shot him."

"Nolan." Grace's hand went to her heart.

"Moira was laying downstream, as well, and when she saw what happened to her brother, she didn't waver, but shot him cold in the chest and again in the back of the head after he fell into the stream."

"Brigid thought Moira was dead, or I'd've never given up her son!"

"She is. The soldiers were fast on her heels. Abban and I managed to grab Nolan and carry him out of there, but she jumped on that great wicked horse of his and bolted. Dressed like a man, she was, and when Captain . . ." He paused. "When another man saw her coming at him, and with her gun out and firing, he shot back."

"Moira killed Bram." Grace could barely take it in.

"Aye."

"I put arsenic on his bread that morning. I meant to kill him. If he'd come back alive, I'd've found another way."

Morgan put his hands on her shoulders and shook her gently. "Look at me," he said firmly. "God forgives you, Grace, if you ask Him. He knows the fear you carried for yourself and Mary Kate, and He took it out of your hands."

"Poor Moira," she said, and then, much to her horror, began to cry. Not just silent weeping, but loud racking sobs that rose out of a chest strained too tight with grief and fear. He folded his arms around her, pressing her face against his shirt, holding her tightly.

"It's over now," he whispered. "He can't hurt you anymore."

She struggled against him, unable to breathe, frightened by the noise that poured out of her.

"Shhhh," he soothed, stroking her. "Don't fight. Let the angels take it, now, for they've come."

She heard him, and stopped struggling, the slow rub of his hand on her back calming her and opening her lungs. Her tears fell freely, soaking the front of his shirt, but no sound accompanied them, save the deep sighs that expelled each painful memory: the babies who were dead, never to know life; the beatings that had ended her innocence; the torment of her marriage and the guilt she'd felt over not being able to repair it; the fear of losing her daughter and of damnation for taking her husband's life; the horror of mothers and children dying alongside the road and not enough food to feed all those who begged at her door; the gnawing, weakening pain of hunger; the fatigue of fighting for survival day after day. She breathed it all out, pushed it away, and let it rise in vapors to be taken by the angels and rinsed clean. Her heart emptied, the blackness of her soul began to lighten, and her mind cleared itself of torment until she knew at last the one truth left in the world.

"I love you," she said aloud.

"And I, you." He kissed the top of her head.

"Is it too late?" she asked.

He smiled against her hair. "Never too late."

They sat quite still, listening to the hiss of the fire.

"How much time do we have?" The cloth was rough under her cheek and she could feel the warmth of his body, hear the sound of his heart. She pressed close, knowing the answer.

"Not long," he whispered. "Tonight."

"'Tis nothing."

He paused. "'Tis everything to me."

She lifted her head and looked long into his eyes. He made no move until she began to take off his damp shirt, and then he took her hands and kissed them, pulling her down gently to lie beside him on the rug in front of the fire.

"I have this reputation . . ." he began and stopped. "It's not earned. I mean to say, I've never . . ."

Grace put a finger across his lips. "I've never been with a man who loved me," she said in Irish. "Nor have I ever loved a man as much as I love you."

He looked long into her face, then bent to kiss her, whispering now in the language of their childhood. He did not try to hide the deep emotion that swept over him by wiping away his tears or stilling the tremble of his mouth, nor did either of them close their eyes, but instead drank in the sight of one another. Even when they kissed, they spoke uninterrupted, and their bodies took comfort from the nearness of their hearts. They whispered and laughed softly, touched and marveled, then clung to one another until, exhausted, sleep carried them to a world in which they were never apart.

She awoke with a start. The fire had died down and Morgan had covered them with a blanket. He lay, deeply asleep, in the crook of her arm. The lines of his face were eased and there was peace about him. Grace allowed her eyes to close again and that was when she heard the soft crunch of gravel outside the window. Someone was walking around the house. Quickly, her heart pounding, she touched Morgan's shoulder, putting a finger to her lips for silence when he opened his eyes. He understood immediately and pulled on his clothes, motioning her to do the same. Dressed, they crossed the big room, Grace pausing to pick up the pistol, handing him the shotgun. In the entry, they heard a knock, so light as to be barely audible. They looked at one another. Morgan stepped back into the shadows behind the door and Grace moved closer, calling out, "Who's there?"

"Missus Donnelly?" a voice came softly from the other side.

She gave no answer.

"Are you alone, Missus Donnelly?"

"No," she answered firmly. "My gun is with me."

Suddenly, Morgan stepped out of the shadows, opened the door a crack, grabbed the man outside, and pulled him in.

"What are you doing sneaking around out there?"

"Good Lord, McDonagh, I've had the devil of a time tracking you down." A heavily bearded man wrapped in a dark, worn cloak took off his hat and bowed to Grace. "Good evening, Missus Donnelly, or rather 'Good morning,' as soon the cock will crow." He turned to Morgan. "Father Brown with you?"

Morgan nodded. "Aye, asleep. Took a shot across the head, but Grace looked after it and he'll recover."

"Get him up," the man said briskly. "I passed a soldiers' camp not an hour down the road, and they'll be here at first light."

"Lord Evans!" Grace could scarely believe it; but for the glint of humor in his eyes and the laughter in his elegant voice, this man was but a shadow of the gentleman she'd dined with so many years ago.

"At your service, dear woman." He made another small bow. "And I trust you'll keep that information to yourself?"

"I'm no telltale," Grace said indignantly.

Lord Evans laughed. "No, no, never that." He gazed at her for a moment. "From all accounts you are a fine, upstanding Christian woman who has braved the wrath of Satan himself in order to help her neighbors."

Grace looked down, embarrassed. "I'm not that, either," she said.

He took her hand and kissed it. "Ah, Missus Donnelly," he said, and his voice was full of mirth. "You are the stuff of Irish legend now. There are many who swear they caught a glimpse of your wings as you filled their bowls with soup, others who say your halo shone so brightly, they were warmed by its light. Yes," he said, looking at Morgan. "I have listened to more than one Irishman wax poetic on your bravery and compassion, your beauty and steadfast endurance."

Grace stood silently, cheeks burning.

"Right." He clapped his hands together. "I've got horses in the woods and a contact to take Father Brown to the Franciscans. Hurry up, man! You look as if you've actually gotten some sleep."

Morgan went to the kitchen to get Father Brown. Lord Evans smiled at Grace. "Thank you for taking them in," he said graciously. "That fool Mitchel printed every word of Lalor's call to arms and now the British are watching every move. They'd have had a field day with these two."

"Do you have food for the road?" she asked.

He shook his head. "If you have some to spare, madam, I would again find myself in your debt." He glanced at the doorway through which Morgan and Father Brown were now coming.

"Ah, Evans," Father Brown said sleepily, his bandage askew. "Bless you for coming."

Grace hurried into the kitchen and threw the last end of bread and a bit of hard cheese into a satchel; that and two withered apples barely covered the bottom of it. And then she remembered the gold.

"Don't go!" She threw the satchel to Morgan and ran upstairs. She ripped up the bottom of the wardrobe and took out the bag, stopping to remove five gold coins, which she pocketed before running back down.

"Here." She handed the bag to Morgan. "You know what to do with it."

"I can't take this, Grace." He tried to hand it back.

"You can and you will." She turned to Lord Evans. "There's enough gold in that bag to buy Morgan and my brother Sean a safe passage out of Ireland."

His eyes widened in surprise.

"Will you make sure that happens, Lord Evans?"

"Indeed I will, Missus Donnelly. It would be my greatest pleasure to see them safely away."

Grace nodded, then looked at Morgan, who pulled her into his arms and held her tightly.

"We must go," Evans said gently.

"Marry me." Morgan looked into Grace's face, and then at Father Brown.

Father Brown blinked several times. "Marry? Here? Now?"

"There isn't time." Lord Evans peeked out the door at the lightening sky. "I'm sorry. We'll find another way."

"No," Morgan said firmly. "It must be now. We're married in our hearts." His look told Father Brown everything. "Marry us now before God."

Lord Evans sighed with resignation. "Do it quickly," he warned.

"Very good." Father Brown neatened his jacket and stood before them, warming to the task. "Have you a Bible, my dear?"

Grace dashed up the stairs once more, then back down, tossing her Bible to Father Brown. "Hurry, Father," she pleaded.

He flipped through the pages, found what he wanted, and began to read. Grace and Morgan moved closer together.

"Rings?" he asked solemnly, when he'd come to the end.

Grace shook her head, but Morgan pulled the leather thong off from around his neck, cut it with his knife, and laid his mother's wedding band on the open Bible in Father Brown's hands.

Lord Evans sighed again, then pulled off his gloves, revealing an intricate gold band on the ring finger of his right hand. "My wedding gift to you both," he said, pulling it off and placing it on the Bible with Morgan's.

"Lord, bless these two lives that are now joined together as one without end. Amen. Take the rings." He held out the Bible. "Morgan McDonagh, do you promise to always love and be faithful to your wife through all the trials of life till death do you part?"

"Aye." Morgan took his mother's ring and placed it on Grace's finger.

"I do," whispered Lord Evans, nudging him.

"I do," Morgan repeated tenderly, smiling at Grace.

"Gracelin Donnelly, do you promise to always love and be faithful to your husband through all the trials of life till death do you part?"

"I do." Grace slipped Lord Evans's ring on Morgan's finger.

"Then let you live your life as man and wife with the blessings of our dear Lord Jesus Christ." Father Brown snapped closed the Bible. "Let's go."

Evans was first out the door, followed by Father Brown and Morgan.

"Lord Evans!" Grace called. She held out a slim, leather-bound book. "This was Abigail's. She has written in it. To you."

He came back and took it carefully from her.

"I read only the names," she said softly. "'Twas hidden 'neath a carpet in an upstairs room. I had hoped for the chance to give it to you."

He held it in his hands as if it were the most wondrous treasure.

"Thank you," he said finally, then took her hand and kissed it again. "I believe I see those wings, myself . . . Missus McDonagh."

He moved off the steps, tucking the little book inside his shirt.

Father Brown made the sign of the cross. "God bless you, dear girl," he said and turned to follow Lord Evans into the field.

Grace held tightly to her husband one last time.

"I love you," Morgan whispered. "I've loved you all my life."

"And I, you," she answered.

"If something should go wrong . . ."

"No." She shook her head, but he held her firmly so that she could not turn her face away.

"If I can't be with you in this life"—he paused, but held steady—"know that I'll be waiting for you in the next. Have faith in that."

She nodded, unable to speak, and they kissed farewell.

"Leave Ireland," she begged as he went down the steps.

"Not without you."

"Hurry!" Evans called, already crossing the field.

Morgan turned and began running to catch the other men.

"Go to America," she called. "I'll follow."

He lifted his hand and vanished in the rising mist.

# Twenty-seven

CAPTAIN Wynne and his guard had arrived early Saturday morning to oversee the transfer of Donnelly House from the widow to the agent Ceallachan. The captain, though still harboring suspicion of Grace's involvement in the death of her husband, was clearly disgusted by the fawning manner of the gross man who was to replace her in this fine house. He dismissed the atmosphere of conspiracy Ceallachan tried to induce, moving away from the man's side-of-mouth comments and raised eyebrows. Grace, on the other side, conducted herself respectfully, leading them through the workings of the house and explaining the keys. She neither rose to the bait when Ceallachan slighted her ("Won't you be happy to leave such a big house and return to the small cabin to which you are better suited?"), nor answered him when he sought information under the guise of aiding the captain ("Will you be joining your poor crippled brother in Canada, then?"), but did her duty with dignity, adding a final admonishment that this was her daughter's rightful home and they'd both return in fifteen years to claim it. She intimated with great tact that if it did not stand in good stead, his suffering and that of his family's would be never-ending. Captain Wynne had to chuckle over that, although he quickly composed himself and ordered one of his men, Private Henry Adams, to drive the widow home to Macroom. She had insisted she needed no guard, but he reminded her that the horse was to go on to the cavalry in Macroom and Private Adams would deliver it. He had other reasons for wanting the young, ingenious soldier to accompany Missus Donnelly, and he suspected she knew this as she locked eyes with him and seemed to peer into his soul. He had to admit he was not un-moved by this strong, suffering woman—he knew well the man to whom she had been married.

This was not the sort of assignment he relished, but his orders had been clear and he had felt not a little relief at getting out of Cork City and all its chaos for a day or two. The countryside held its own dangers with all the potential for ambush, but at least there was not the din and stench of the city. He breathed deeply the fresh, sweet air of spring as they walked out to the loaded cart.

"Good-bye, Missus Donnelly," he said, putting out his hand. "I wish you well."

"Good-bye, Captain." She gave his hand one hard shake, then climbed up onto the seat next to Private Adams. "Don't let them burn down my daughter's house."

"That would be more in your hands than in mine," he replied, stepping back.

She smiled, and he caught sight of that wonderful beauty that lay beneath her fatigue and hunger. Not for the first time did he wish it were another world and he might have a chance to know this woman.

"May God have mercy on your soul," she said quietly.

"And on yours, Missus Donnelly."

He raised his voice to speak to the young man who stood at atten-tion. "See her home, leave the cart, and take the horse on to the fort at Macroom."

"Yes, sir, Captain Wynne." Adams saluted, then climbed into the wagon and took up the reins, calling to the horse. The cart jerked, then began to creak down the driveway.

Ceallachan had gone back into the house to survey all that was his for now, but Captain Wynne stood and watched the cart until it turned onto the main road and traveled out of sight. Grace had not once looked back and he admired her for that. He had not expected weeping and wailing from this woman, but one never knew with the Irish—they were all so emotional.

Grace and Private Adams rode along in silence for most of the morning. The private, a friendly, outgoing boy, commented occasion-ally on the countryside or the beautiful day, but met only with stub-born resistance from the pale young woman who sat next to him. He did not consider that she might be exhausted from the events of the past few days and the lack of food, for it had been nearly two days since she'd eaten, having given the last of it to Lord Evans, and it had taken all her strength to keep up the appearance of vitality in front of the captain. Only when the private suggested, two hours later, that they stop and stretch themselves, did she rouse herself, walking a ways into the woods to squat, and then a bit further to drink water from a small, muddy stream.

When she rejoined him, he was sitting on a rock under the shade of a tree, eating bread and cheese and chewing dried meat. Saliva flooded her mouth immediately, but she sat down a ways from him, lay back, and closed her eyes as if to nap.

Private Adams was not unmoved by the hunger he had witnessed during his two years in Ireland, but he still assumed that those of some position had access to food. It did not occur to him that Grace might be hungry, though had she been a peasant, he would have looked for and seen this clearly.

The worst of it for him had been the sight of the Irish children, thousands of them, it seemed, lying along the roads and in the gutters, slumped up against the door of the workhouse that could not admit them or in the hospital yard, too weak to put a voice to eyes that begged for relief. Their parents he could blame for ignorance and laziness, the lack of foresight that put them in such a terrible situation, but the children . . . He shook his head. To see them suffer so greatly had troubled his heart, no matter how he tried to harden it. Many of his fellow soldiers passed out their rations and tried to ease the hunger, but it was as a drop of rain in the desert—there could never be enough to save the thousands who needed it.

He had thought this a beautiful country at first, and its people joyful and carefree, but he had come to hate Ireland for all her misery, and could not wait to be rid of the place. Not even in the London slums had he witnessed such a total collapse of humanity. The prevalence of death in Ireland was unrelenting and he could not say which was worst: the slow, painful death of a body eating into itself for lack of nourishment, crumbled with endless bouts of dysentery, hairless, toothless, covered with sores, bloated and caved; or the violent, dayslong death of black fever, where blood swelled the body, turning it purple, bringing severe vomiting and gangrene, and the most horrible stench; or yellow fever, with its burning temperatures and vomiting, drenching sweats and deep exhaustion that lasted but a few days only to strike again when the crisis seemed over—the pattern to be repeated three or four times if the patient lived that long. And of course, there was madness, brought about by one or all of these, its victims equally devastated, degraded, and hopeless.

This past March, he had been part of a detail that traveled the West erecting fever sheds, but his assistance had been required in every area, as there were too few doctors and nurses. He had learned a great deal about how typhus worked, and knew that the sight and smell of it would never leave him, not even in his sleep. He counted the days until he could return to the sweet pastures of Cornwall; he had thought to make a career in the cavalry, but that had changed. When his duty was done, he'd go home and never leave it again. He would marry the rector's daughter and bring her to live with his father, where they would raise fat babies and hardy horses, go to the seashore in the summer, and walk the heather moors in winter. How could anyone in their right mind choose to stay amidst this horror? This was a country that God had clearly forsaken.

"Will you emigrate, Missus Donnelly?" he asked with an urgency born of his thoughts. "Will you come to England or go on to Canada?"

Grace opened her eyes and sat up. She had been drifting, on the verge of sleep, walking in a garden somewhere with Mary Kate's hand in her own and Granna looking on, calling something to them and laughing. She shook off the yearning that swept up her heart, and looked at him. "No," she said, squinting against the sun. "I'll not leave Ireland."

"Plenty are." He ripped a piece of dried jerky with his teeth and worked it into his cheek. "Any man with a coin in his hand has gone off for a better life. More than a million gone to Canada and America. Half again as many to England, some to Australia."

Grace looked at him, shocked. She had not realized so many were gone. It was the rare Irishman who left Ireland and then only to the mournful keening of his friends and family. But this was the end of the world, as Morgan had said, and now, it seemed, they were running to get away.

"It only makes good sense," he went on, tearing off a piece of bread. "If you don't starve to death or go mad, then there's the typhus, or renegades shooting at anything that moves. In another year, there'll be nothing left here but graves and rotting fields." He swallowed his bread, wiping his mouth with the back of his hand. "Certainly, you should not stay," he advised. "Being a woman of means, surely you could make a better life for yourself in Canada."

"Woman of means?"

"You were married to Squire Donnelly, weren't you?" He brushed the crumbs off his lap onto the grass and Grace resisted the urge to pick them out and eat them. "The Donnellys are an old and well-respected family in London, always in the papers about this charity or that one."

"I am not one of their charities," she said shortly.

He blushed. "Begging your pardon, Missus Donnelly. I didn't mean that. I meant that the Donnellys have money, and with the annuity your husband left you, surely you could live anywhere you wanted."

Grace frowned. "I want to live in Ireland. In an old cabin on a lovely little lane outside Macroom." She studied the private, not much older than herself. "As for my husband leaving me anything . . . he suffered his own misfortunes years ago, and what I have in this cart is all I have left. I am Irish. That makes me nothing to the Donnellys of London."

Private Adams stopped chewing and stared in disbelief. "Bloody hell," he exclaimed. "That's terrible!"

Grace nodded, then covered her stomach quickly as it started to rumble.

He heard it and squinted at her. "Aren't you having anything to eat, Missus Donnelly?"

"I had a large breakfast," Grace said, unwilling to admit her position.

The private tipped his head and saw for the first time past her social position to the shabby dress that hung on her bony frame, the lank hair, gaunt face, and bruised eyes.

"You must have a bite to eat," he insisted tactfully. "I know it's rough food, but a little bread and cheese will see you well. We've a long trip still ahead."

Grace had no resistance left. "Thank you," she said quietly, taking from him the generous piece of bread and hunk of pale cheese he offered. "You are very kind to share your meal."

She held it in her hand, bowing her head to pray before taking the first bite. The relief of food in her mouth brought tears to her eyes and she was forced to chew slowly until her throat opened enough to swallow.

Seeing this, Private Adams stopped eating and wrapped up the remainder of his meal in a cloth, which he quietly slipped into her basket when she wasn't looking.

When she had finished the food, Grace turned away from him and licked her fingers, then closed her eyes again and gave thanks to God. She took his pail and brought water from the spring to drink, then feeling much refreshed, they started off again in the warm May sunshine, a fresh breeze blowing across the land bringing with it the scent of lavender and wild thyme.

"Excuse me for asking, Missus Donnelly," he said as they bumped along the road. "But if he's left you nothing to live on . . . well, isn't that all the more reason to leave this place? If not for yourself, then for the future of your children. Surely, you could sell what you've got here and buy passage for all of you?"

Grace wanted to repay his kindness with trust, but knew she could not afford this; Captain Wynne was a man of calculation and Private Adams, however unwittingly, had been sent on this errand for a reason. She weighed her answer.

"My son is already in England, adopted by my husband's brother, and I'll not see him again," she said evenly. "My daughter has been left to me, and I have done the best I could to secure a future for her, but it is here, in Ireland." She paused. "I've other family, as well, to look out for. There's my father, who will never come away from Ireland, and my granny, who's too old. My older brother, Ryan, is married now with a wife and young son, and he's just as stubborn a man as my father."

Private Adams shifted in his seat. "And what of your brother Sean? The crippled one?"

Grace bit her lip, then straightened her back and shoulders. "Sean's on his own right now. I expect you know that already."

"Yes," he said. "I was one of the guards on his cell. Listened to a steady stream of cursing for three bloody nights!" He shook his head, then laughed good-naturedly. "Tried to argue his way out of jail, cheeky bastard, then damned our eyes to hell when we wouldn't come round to his point of view!"

"Doesn't sound like our Sean," she said, trying to swallow her smile. "He's a Christian man, you know, educated and well-read, he is."

"That's for sure," he agreed. "Bloody man never ran out of things to quote."

Grace laughed, despite herself.

"I shouldn't say it, but I was half glad when he got away. Not just to give my ears a rest." He smiled at her. "He never shot your husband, not with his shoulder so crippled like it is. I'm sure he's guilty of other things, but murder's not one of them."

"Then why was he arrested?"

The private shrugged. "He knows plenty, Missus Donnelly. And a mind like his remembers everything. There's no doubt he's part of John Mitchel's group, and Captain Wynne wants to shut down that bloody rag of a newspaper before full-scale war breaks out." He glanced at her out of the corner of his eye. "And, of course, they're after his friend McDonagh, for ambushing Her Majesty's special guard outside Cork last spring and inciting riot at the docks in October. He's been a slippery one. The man that brings him in will get a medal for it and a ticket home."

Grace looked down at the wedding band on her finger, then covered it with her right hand.

"It's generally known that McDonagh and your brother work together—brawn and brain, so to speak. We think it was your brother planned the October riot, and McDonagh that carried it out." He paused. "But you wouldn't know anything about that, would you?"

Grace met his gaze and shook her head.

"Didn't think so." He turned back to the horse and slapped the reins along its backside. "Anyway, we're sure it's McDonagh that broke him out. Along with one other."

A silence settled between them until finally he asked, with an effort at appearing casual, "Been a long time since you've seen your brother?"

Grace chose her words carefully. "Aye," she said. "Not since the end of last summer."

"And McDonagh?"

She pretended to consider. "Longer still."

"Know him well, do you?" he asked lightly.

She nodded, Morgan's face suddenly rising before her, head thrown back in laughter, the morning sun on his face. "Didn't we grow up together, the three of us? Our mothers, best friends. When ours died and Sean was left a cripple, it was Morgan come down the mountain to cheer us. They're like brothers, the two of them." She bit her lip. "Sean could not survive without Morgan, so I pray they are together and not lying in a ditch somewhere, dead."

Private Adams hooted. "Not bloody likely! The one talks too much to ever give up his last breath, and the other has the lives of a cat. Besides, we'd know if McDonagh was dead—with a reward like that on his head, someone is bound to bring in his body."

Grace's heart stopped. "Is the reward not for bringing him in alive?"

He shook his head. "Dead or alive, now that Mitchel published Fintan Lalor's idiot call for peasant revolution. That's just the fuel the Young Irelanders have been waiting for. And, you know, of course, this new Irish Confederation—bunch of bloody militants—is led by McDonagh and some Englishman turned bleeding traitor. Certainly, your brother is mixed in with that lot now, as well."

"Maybe they've gone off Ireland," she said, then bit her tongue.

"That's what the captain thinks," he said casually. "He'd be glad to see them gone and ready to drop the manhunt . . . especially if he had the name of that Englishman in return."

Grace looked out over the farmland, most of it unplanted and wild, cabins seemingly abandoned, animals dead. The countryside was strangely quiet, absent of noise but for the few birds still scavenging for seed. She thought of Lord Evans and the song he'd played for her on his guitar the night they'd met. The guitar was long sold, she knew, and the hands too battered to play anymore; the fine clothes had worn to rags and the handsome face was weary and lined. He could have gone away years ago to live an easy life in Spain, but he had not; he remained in Ireland, devoted to winning freedom for men like her husband and brothers.

"I don't know who it is you're talking about," she said at last, turning to face the young man beside her. "But even if I did, do you really think I'd give you his name?"

He shook his head, accepting the truth of this, and they rode along in silence until suddenly the horse became nervous and threw its head.

"Whoa, steady on," Private Adams soothed, reining in the horse until the cart stood still. He put his face into the wind, then recoiled, gasping.

"What is it?" Grace asked.

"The smell," he said, tying his bandana over his nose and mouth. "Black fever. Cabin over there must have people dead or dying of it." He pointed to the first of several cabins built on a rise above the road. "Can't you smell it?"

And now she could, the stench so overpowering, she wondered how she'd missed it. She held her skirt up over the lower part of her face.

"It's a mile or more of cabins along the road here," she said, her voice muffled by the cloth. "But there's a lane goes up behind the hill with no cabins upon it. We'll have to go that way."

He backed the cart up and took the lane she pointed out, its entrance half hidden by overgrown bushes.

"Who tends to them up here, takes them to the fever sheds?" he asked when they'd gone behind the hill and the smell had faded behind them.

"No one," Grace said, lowering her skirt. "Even if the parish priest is still alive, all he can offer is water and last rites. They'll not go to the sheds."

"Then they'll die!"

"They know that those who go to hospital never come home again," Grace said. "So best to die in your own bed if die you must."

"What about the healthy ones?" he asked.

"Most likely none of those," she said quietly. "But if so, they'll bury the dead under the floorboards, collapse the roof over them, and set off for somewhere else, hoping to send a priest back later to pray over the bones."

He shook his head, not understanding.

"The Irish fear fever like nothing else," she explained. "'Tis the only thing that will send parents away from their children and children away from their parents. It's an awful death and they cannot bear it. But, of course, they almost always fall one after the other and die together anyway."

"So, no one will come to help?"

Grace looked at him. "There is no food to bring, and no medicine that will keep them alive. To go near them is to give up your own life."

He was silent, his young face troubled. "Why do these Irish rebels keep fighting for a country that is nearly dead?" he asked.

"You might ask your countrymen the same question," she replied. "And you might ask yourself why the people of Ireland have been allowed to starve while boatloads of Irish grain were sent to England. Why British landlords who have never set foot in this country are allowed to demand rent from families who have lived here for thousands of years. Why we have not been allowed to educate ourselves, own our own land, or make laws that better an Irishman. Why have our forests been stripped to build your cities, and our people turned off the land so that you might have more beef and wheat? Can you give me any answer at all, Private Adams?"

He shook his head.

"You have robbed us of our land and our right to live here with dignity. You have worked us as slaves, starved us to death, and left us to cope with terrible sickness. This is what we have come to under British rule." Her eyes flashed. "Ireland has provided you with an endless cradle of our best young men to be fodder for your enemy's cannons. We fight against you now, because we have little left to lose."

"Except your lives," he said.

"And soon we will not even have those. The Irish will have disappeared from Ireland and your country will finally have what it wants."

"That's not true," he insisted. "We don't bloody well want the Irish to die out! We're here to help you survive!"

"And do you think it's enough to just survive?" she asked. "Well, it's not. We want more than that. We want to live. What is your Christian name, Private?"

"Henry," he answered. "Henry James Adams."

"Henry," she repeated. "And where is your home?"

He thought of the clean, orderly farm high on the cliffs above the sea. "Cornwall," he said. "My father is a horse breeder."

"Will you go there when your time is up?"

"Yes," he said definitely. "My father is old and my mother has died, so I will take over the stable."

"Will you marry?"

"The rector's daughter," he said shyly. "Isabel Benton."

Grace nodded, then thought a moment.

"And what if I said to you, Private Adams, that when you return home, I shall come and live in your house and run your farm, although you will do all the work and pay me rent, as well? I will take the best of your harvest, the best livestock, and all your money. You may marry, but you must ask my permission and pay me a tax. You may not have any say in the running of the farm your father has worked all his life, and he may not deed you any title to it. If, in another year or so, I decide to grow wheat over all the land and turn you out, it is my right and the law stands with me."

His eyes opened wide.

"That is *my* father's life," she said quietly. "He has worked every day on that land and pays the rent four times a year, but will never own it, can never own a bit of it, or pass it on to his sons. They can work it with him if he divides it, but their future is not secure." She paused. "Can that be right?"

"No." He shook his head. "No, it's not right."

"We are a happy people, never minding what we don't have. We look to God for our fortune and are thankful for our daily bread. But now God is telling us to stop throwing our pearls to swine. It is not just the Irish people who are dying, but the Irish way of life. Only there will be no Oisin come back from Tir na nog."

He squinted into the sun, puzzled.

"Land of the Young," she explained. "Oisin was a poet who disappeared into Tir na nog, but returned hundreds of years later to argue the old ways and beliefs with Patrick the Crooked Crozier. Only this time we'll all be dead or gone away, and there will be no old ways to pass on." She looked earnestly upon him. "In another life, you and I might have been friends, but you are my enemy as long as you try to rip the heart from my body."

"I understand," he said quietly.

"Good. Then there is hope for us all."

The afternoon light had begun to soften and great bands of pink and purple filled the sky around the mountains. The effort of her argument, along with the food in her belly and the rocking of the cart, lulled Grace into a light sleep and she drooped against the private's shoulder. Driving with one hand, he carefully eased her into a more comfortable position, holding her against him with the other hand. His mother had been a woman of opinion like this Missus Donnelly, and he realized with a start that they would have liked one another very much.

When at last she came awake, the sun was lower in the sky and her neck terribly stiff. She lifted her head immediately, and he removed his arm so that she might move away from him and not feel embarrassed.

"I'm sorry," she said. "I fell asleep."

He smiled. "Quite all right. You left me with a great deal to think over."

Grace smoothed her hair and drew her shawl up over her shoulders. "You must be tired, Private," she said. "Will you let me drive the rest of the way?"

"No," he said. "For then I'd be completely at your mercy, and I see now that you are a woman to be reckoned with. Much like your brother in speech, all that passion for what you believe. Your family must be very interesting people."

"Aye, and you must meet them," Grace answered. "We're nearly to my lane." She sat up, suddenly excited to be home and in the warmth of her family's love, with her dear daughter sitting on her knee.

"I don't dare!" he laughed. "If they're at all like you and your brother, I'll be recruited to the Young Irelanders by morning!" He turned up the lane and started down, his smile fading as he silently noted the lack of light in any cabin windows. "My orders are to take the horse on to Macroom and billet there."

"You'll reach it by midnight. Stay on this lane to the road and follow the signs to Macroom. Be careful, Private," she added.

"I will," he nodded. "Thanks."

Half a mile down the lane and there stood the cabin, a bit of smoke drifting out the chimney, lantern light in the front window. The windows of the cabins both right and left were dark. She sat on the edge of her seat eagerly, hands clapped together in her lap. And then her smile slipped away and she felt the private's hand grip her own.

"Smell it?" he whispered in alarm.

She nodded, unable to speak.

"I can't leave you here," he said, but the horses had already drawn up in front of her cabin and she had jumped down.

Patrick flung open the door and embraced her, then looked into her face and said, "It's the children."

Grace went white. "Mary Kathleen?"

"Thomsy's worst, yellow and high fever for two days," he said quickly. "Hit Mary Kate this morning. And I think Aghna is ill, as well."

She looked back over her shoulder at the private. "Don't come in." Her face was tense and worried. "You know what we've got."

He stared helplessly as she turned to go in. "Wait," he called.

"Go on, now," she warned. "Ride out of here, quick as light."

He hesitated only a moment. "I can help. I watched the doctors at Cork."

"No," Patrick said firmly.

Grace paused, undecided, then nodded. He climbed down immediately and followed her into the dim cabin, where the smell nearly knocked him off his feet.

"Open the windows," he said at once to the shadows that sat near the hearth. "I'll need sheets and long poles or sticks."

Grace put a hand on his shoulder. "I was wrong about you, Private. Forgive me."

"It's Henry," he said and knelt down to look at her daughter.

# Twenty-eight

JULIA had warned him, had written to him in excruciating detail while he traveled the south counties rallying support, but now that he was back, Smith O'Brien could see for himself—Dublin was a cesspool of filth and disease. Previously tolerable, despite lack of drainage and sanitation, it now stank of death and decay. The people were filthy; any extra clothing had been sold, and now they wore the same dirty rags day after day. He knew their furniture and bedding had long since gone the way of their extra clothes, and they slept on muddy floors covered, at most, by empty grain sacks or scraps of rag. Any money went for food instead of fuel, so washing clothes and bodies was out of the question. Julia reported that food was eaten half-cooked or raw, which did nothing to ease the constant dysentery; their weakened condition made going to the outhouses nearly impossible, and slippery, bloody filth lay in puddles all through the lanes. They huddled together for warmth at night, further spreading the louse that carried typhus. He had seen them during the day—those who could, even with fever upon them—troop to the soup kitchens where they stood shoulder to shoulder, sometimes two hundred or more sick and infested people.

It was no secret that typhus had spread like wildfire, killing off entire districts in a matter of weeks. In the papers, Julia praised the courage of the doctors, nurses, priests, and nuns who continued moving among the people trying to stave off further infection, and offering comfort as best they could to those who were dying. It was a labor of love, Smith O'Brien agreed, since not only had they to deal with typhus, but with hunger edema, the disease of starvation that now afflicted most of the population—walking skeletons whose limbs swelled to three times their normal size before bursting and causing a painful death. Scurvy, too, was widespread now that the Irishman's diet of potatoes had been replaced by Indian corn, which provided no vitamin C; gums grew mushy, teeth fell out, joints became swollen, and legs turned black up to the thigh—"Black Leg," the locals called it. There was so little in the way of medicine to ease the advancement of these diseases, and because of the highly infectious nature of typhus, doctors and caregivers were dying at alarming rates.

Writing under the name of Patrick Freeman for the *Nation,* Julia had blasted the British government for being slow in admitting that Ireland now faced a fever epidemic of immense size in the midst of the third year of famine, and for not immediately reinstating a Central Board of Health to oversee funds for additional hospitals or dispenseries, despite the fact that only twenty-eight hospitals existed in all of Ireland, not nearly enough to serve the hundreds of thousands now desperately in needed of such services. Smith O'Brien had visited some of these hospitals, quickly realizing that they were completely overwhelmed—as caregivers died, fever patients lay naked on the dirty straw, suffering without medicine, water, or heat. It was the same in the workhouses; already overcrowded and understaffed, they had became morgues where the dying and dead lay side by side. As rumors spread that food and water were to be had in jail, people committed random crimes in the hope of getting arrested.

There were fever sheds, but too often their assemblage was sloppy, amounting to little more than a lean-to on the side of the hospital, where typhus continued to spread. The *Times* answered editorials condemning the British government by pointing out the success of the new Irish Fever Act, which was leading to the erection of wooden-floored tents in fields and the removal of piles of filth from the streets, cabins cleaned and disinfected, corpses properly buried, and provision made for additional hospitals, dispenseries, doctors, and nurses. John Mitchel's reply in the *Nation* was that it was too little too late and that half the population had already been lost. He adamantly opposed any posture of gratitude to the British government, and instead began foreshadowing the resistance, calling for every able body to prepare themselves. While Julia continued to argue in the papers as an intellectual, there was no denying that Mitchel had taken up Fintan Lalor's impassioned plea, "Will Ireland perish like a lamb, or will she turn as turns the baited lion?"

Smith O'Brien, well aware of the exhausted state of the people, had been horrified at Mitchel's inflammatory rhetoric and clung to the hope that the revolution would be bloodless. He cringed these days whenever he opened the pages of the newspaper, and tried as best he could to instill some business sense into the revolution, urging groups to form and report to one another, to organize whatever strength was left in Ireland. Unorganized, and with Britain growing less tolerant and more angry every day, the revolution would be a disaster, and so many more lives needlessly lost. Smith O'Brien could not control Mitchel, but he could organize greater cohesiveness with the help of a few good men. And he had them: Sean O'Malley had been brilliant in planning the October raid, Morgan McDonagh was a hero in the eyes of the men he commanded for his courage and stealth, and Lord Evans had supplied endless cash and years on end to live like a criminal in order that Irish soil might at last be owned completely by Irishmen.

O'Malley was, even now, poring over maps in the cellar of Smith O'Brien's Limerick house. With his twisted frame and ill health, he would not survive another winter in Ireland. Evans had arrived with gold in his pockets and instructions that O'Malley and McDonagh be smuggled out of the country immediately. O'Malley was easy enough—he'd nearly finished his work and had been convinced that more could be done from America in the way of raising cash and arms. He was to recruit some of the lads who'd left Ireland years ago with the promise of a homeland once again theirs.

The United States had already rallied strong in support for the Irish, sending in the past months vessels loaded with grain, corn meal, and clothing. Most of this had been organized by the Society of Friends, and Tammany, the central organization of the Democratic Party of the United States. Catholic parishes and Irish communities across the country had also raised money to be sent for the relief of the destitute in Ireland. Most of this found its way to the right places, thanks to the Quakers, and certainly the suffering had been eased somewhat. But the relief would end in the autumn, as channels began to freeze and ships could no longer make the journey across with food. Now was the time for O'Malley to go and passage had been booked for him on the *Lydia Ann* returning to Manhattan out of Limerick. There were enough ships in and out of Ireland, enough emigrants filling the hold, that Sean could travel safely. He would board at night and stay below until well out to sea. He had readily agreed to this mission; he was a dreamer.

However, McDonagh, the realist, could not be convinced to leave before the revolution had taken place. Rumor held that he'd a wife hidden away in the country, and would not leave without her; Smith O'Brien had offered to get her safe passage as well, but Evans had dismissed it as fancy, saying McDonagh would rather die in Ireland than live in America. And that was what Smith O'Brien was afraid of. A dead hero might rally the passion of his men and inspire their attack, as Mitchel had so bluntly pointed out, but Smith O'Brien knew it would more likely lead to disenchantment and doom. McDonagh had proven himself a brilliant leader and readily deserving of the praise heaped upon him by the people of Ireland. They thought him invincible, and as long as he traversed the countryside speaking of victory and showing them the way, they continued to hope that the battle would indeed be won. They hid him and fed him, loved him and called him their own son; despite those among them who turned on their own and tried to collect the reward for his capture, McDonagh had remained free—and freed others. Surely God marched with such a man as this, they said, and had McDonagh asked them to swim across the sea and fight England on her own land, they would have done it!

No, Smith O'Brien shook his head, he could not afford to lose McDonagh to death. Nor could the English, for that matter, but they had become desperate, and were willing to lose the information he had in order to avoid a battle. Smith O'Brien had even heard it whispered that they had offered freedom for O'Malley and McDonagh in exchange for their emigration to America and the traitor Englishman's identity. It had become a deadly game of cat and mouse, with Mitchel all the while openly baiting the British government and Smith O'Brien trying desperately to buy more time before things came to a head.

❖　❖　❖

"Smuggle him quietly out of the country," Sean suggested, when Smith O'Brien sought him out in the cellar. "Not far, maybe to one of the little islands in the North. Or off to sympathizers in Scotland."

"But won't the people think he's abandoned them?" Smith O'Brien asked, warming his hands on the candle flame by which Sean worked.

"Can you not do it in secret? Sure and there's plenty of other clandestine activity about the place," he replied, that eternal gleam in his eye. "Let him simply disappear, and a few well-planted rumors will keep him alive and well here in Ireland."

Smith O'Brien thought seriously about this. It was true enough that rumors flew like sparrows across the land and no one really knew what was true or not anymore.

"With me rousing the men in America—raising arms and ready cash—and Morgan close enough to advise by letter, can we not have everyone in place come spring?"

"Have we that much time, do you think?" March seemed a thousand years away.

"Aye." Sean nodded. "England won't be committing more soldiers to Ireland with France tickling their underbelly, and can you not feel the change all over Europe?" He had spent his long days underground with newspapers from all over the continent, and now he warmed to the subject. "Vienna will rise and get rid of Metternich, and Sicily's putting all kinds of pressure on its king for a new constitution. The Brits are getting nervous with all that rumbling, and don't we have our own Fergus O'Connor leading the Chartists right there in England herself? Millions he's got standing behind his demands now and all threatening revolution!" He rubbed his hands together in glee. "Ah, Willy, it's a fine time to be alive!"

Smith O'Brien frowned at him.

"Well, you know what I mean," Sean amended. "Great change cannot occur without great sacrifice, and the price has been paid in Ireland."

"Do you not think that all this discontent might make the British clamp down even harder on us? Revolution in Ireland would be an enormous embarrassment, and surely it would stir up trouble even at their own doorstep." He shook his head. "There's no doubt the pot is boiling—the question is, how long can we keep the lid on?"

"Long enough," Sean answered firmly. "Keep Mitchel to a dull roar in that paper of his, and we'll be ready to rise up before summer." He reached behind to his lower back, kneading out the stiffness, a grimace of pain passing briefly across his face. "Bring Morgan back to Dublin at the end of April, and his appearance after so many months of rumor will make them wild."

"Can he be persuaded to lie low until then?"

"He's not completely unreasonable, you know," he said and smiled. "Though hardheaded, without doubt. But hasn't the man gone without a decent meal and steady sleep in a soft bed for years now? And hasn't he missed the company of a good woman?"

"They say he's taken a wife." Smith O'Brien watched Sean's face carefully. "Would you know anything about that?"

Sean was clearly surprised. "He's not said a word, and I know of only one woman he's ever loved." He paused, thinking hard. "It would be some kind of miracle, if it's true, but . . . but I don't know for sure."

"If it were true," Smith O'Brien said cautiously, "would she be a strong enough person to influence him?"

Sean dug his long fingers into the hunched shoulder and rubbed. "Aye," he laughed. "She's strong enough to pick up a gun and lead the battle herself."

"How do I find her?"

Sean was reluctant. "Have you asked Evans about it?"

"He says only that McDonagh's married to the fight, and that's all."

"Could be I'm wrong," Sean said. "Stranger things have happened, you know."

Smith O'Brien ignored the joke. "They say he wears a ring."

Sean thought again. "If he's keeping it a secret, he's got good reason." He bit his lip. "What is it exactly you want from her?"

"Only a letter," Smith O'Brien said convincingly. "For his eyes alone. Just a letter persuading him to stay safely hidden for now. Would she do that?"

"Aye." Sean nodded. "But she'll be looking for a trap. You'll have to send Evans. He's the only one she'll trust."

"He knows her?" Smith O'Brien's eyes opened wide in exasperation.

"Well enough, and where to find her."

"Could've bloody well saved me a lot of bloody time," he grumbled. "Now, I've got to find him all over again."

Sean looked at him in amusement. "Everything in the Lord's time," he said. "Will you ask Evans to send her a message from me, as well?"

Smith O'Brien scratched at the heavy muttonchop sideburns that framed his face, eyes puzzled. "From you?"

"Just that her brother sends his undying love!" He laughed gleefully at the look of astonishment on the other man's face.

"Oh, bloody hell," Smith O'Brien said and threw a book at him.

And so, with that strange combination of irritation and relief that seemed to reside in him at all times, Smith O'Brien sent Evans on one last assignment: to get a letter from an unknown wife in an unknown place and carry it to McDonagh—wherever he might be—in order to convince him to go somewhere else that no one else knew of.

He smiled wanly, and in his heart he hoped O'Malley was as right about this as he had been about everything else. His greatest fear was that McDonagh would be captured and imprisoned before they got him to a safehouse. All communication would be cut off; there'd be no way to get him out. And, Heaven knew, Lord Evans was not good for much more, though he'd cut the throat of any man who suggested it. One had only to look at the sallowness of his face, the yellow eyes and bloodless lips, the shaking hands and terrible fatigue, to know that he was not long for the world unless he took to his bed and had the constant care of a good doctor.

"Bloody burning hell," Smith O'Brien muttered, running his hands through his hair. "The best men in Ireland and look at them! One'll be dead any day from sheer exhaustion, the other's crippled and coughing like an old woman, and the third can't show his face for more than a minute without someone taking a shot at it!"

He poured himself a large drink. When it had settled to a slow burn in his gut, he knew what to do. He hoped the letter from a beloved wife would be enough, but just in case, he'd send Meagher out to see McDonagh, as well. If ever a man could sway another man with fancy rhetoric, it was Meagher. They'd take him up to the Aran Islands and hide him away like Robert the Bruce until the time was right. Sean was set to go to America on the next boat, passage paid and the captain bribed to keep him in food and water until they landed, money in his pocket and a list of sympathizers who would take him in when he reached New York. He, too, had been blessed with a fiery way of talking, and a month or two of evenings in the pubs would rally enough young men to return and claim their land. Evans would be sent to the south of France on the pretext of meeting with men who were in the midst of brewing their own kind of trouble. O'Malley's vision was clear, and word from abroad was that Louis Philippe was preparing for flight, while Lamartine, the poet, was being positioned for Minister of Foreign Affairs. If France indeed revolted and sent their king back to England, Ireland would be greatly encouraged to make her own stand and England, they hoped, too divided to hold her down. In addition, Evans would get the very best medical attention in France and return in the spring with renewed health to witness the fruit of his long labor.

"That's it, then," Smith O'Brien mumbled to himself and stood to stretch, going to the window and looking down into the filthy streets. The sun was coming up on another wretched day and already those who had survived the night were stirring. He watched them, these soldiers-to-be, Fintan Lalor's words echoing in his head:

". . . unmuzzle the wolf dog," Lalor had written. "There is one at this moment in every cabin throughout the land, nearly fit to be tied— and he will be savager by and by."

"Cabins are empty now," Smith O'Brien murmured into the chill morning air. "And the wolves have come to town."

# Twenty-nine

THE O'Malleys survived the feverish spring, though not without cost. Thomsy was dead and buried in the glen beside the grave of Grace's mother, and Aghna sat there every day, murmuring and rocking, unable to recover from her grief.

"Our Aghna's away," Granna told travelers who stopped to beg food or a night's rest.

"Aye, away," they'd repeat and nod knowingly, having seen others who'd gone away often enough in these troubled times.

Unable to bring his son back to life or his wife back to the world, Ryan poured his hopelessness into daily foraging. He was not alone in the wood or on the hills, and too often met with berry bushes picked clean, and tree limbs stripped of fruit. Angrily, he would thrust himself into the sharp, thorny thickets until, scratched and bloody, he reached those that no one else had found; fiercely, he scrambled to the tops of old trees for small, tart apples and green plums; furiously, he waded out past the rushing currents into the deep pools, standing still for hours in the freezing water until he bagged an eel. He hit birds with rocks, caught squirrels with his bare hands, tore apart rotting tree trunks for grubs and snails. All day he stalked, until at last he brought home food enough for another meal, and fatigue enough to sleep next to his wakeful and disturbed young wife.

Granna had been ill with fever, as well, but hers, like Mary Kathleen's, left her exhausted, not dead. They lay together, the two of them, on Granna's pallet pulled into the big room, and the old woman spent long hours whispering old stories in Irish to the little girl who'd never heard them before. She made Mary Kate a soft doll, which the child called Blossom, and she fed her the bits of food that Ryan brought home, putting into the child's mouth most of what was meant to keep her old self alive. It gave her satisfaction to watch the color come back into her great-granddaughter's cheeks, and to see the little tummy fill out over bony ribs. Though keen and watchful, Mary Kate was a somber child without the sparkle of life in her eyes; she spoke her few words seriously and listened to everything her elders said, nodding as though she understood what no two-and-a-half-year-old child should.

It was Mary Kathleen's time to live, and Granna's time to die; every morning the old woman awoke with a start when she realized she was still here, still in the cabin on her straw bed. Although she longed for Heaven, she was not unhappy, and counted each precious hour with her beloved family as a gift from her Lord. There was no need to speak of it to the others; they knew, and in their eyes, she could see the beginnings of their mourning. She was most content to lie in her bed, surrounded by the younger ones, watching Mary Kathleen gain a sure foot again, clutching her mother's skirts for balance. She rarely stirred herself anymore, except to sit on the bucket near her bed or lift her head for a glimpse of the sky out the window, but in her mind she wandered all the hills and glens of her youth, and visited all the people she had ever loved, and she was so very happy in those places.

It hurt Patrick to see his old mother-in-law wasting away to naught, and in his dreams he saw the reproach in his dear Kathleen's eye for not making her passing less painful. But he could not force Gran to eat when, in his heart, he knew she was right; it was the young who must be kept strong. He had hoarded a small number of seed potatoes against the gnawing hunger and fear of death that haunted them all, and these he had planted in the spring. Now the tiny fields were lush and green, with blooms that promised an abundant harvest. All day long he sat, like other men, watching the waxy-leaved shoots with a sharp eye. Each day he watched the sky, measured the rain, examined the earth for strange bugs, checked the leaves for blight. Any odd insect, any imperfection, was immediate cause for alarm, and Grace watched her father age a year each time a discovery was made. He kept his panic in check, however, and left the potatoes where they lay, resisting the urge to dig them up too soon. In other fields, tall stands of corn grew strong, but the farmers dared not eat the grain themselves for fear of having nothing left to sell to England, and no money then to pay their rent. Patrick had an occasional newspaper from government people passing through the lane, and all accounts were optimistic; but he knew, as did anyone who followed farming in Ireland, that the crops were small, and that too few seed potatoes meant there would not be enough food to feed the people again this year.

Patrick would have to dig what he had and hide it from thieves and beggars; even then, it might not be enough to see his family through the winter. He did not let his mind wander that far. He only wanted to dig what there was and fill their bellies. Granna would not live the summer, and he feared that Aghna would become violent as he'd seen so many others who'd become lost in grief. She had lucid moments, but then she would beg and plead for Ryan to take her away from here, from this place that had swallowed her son. He could see the heartbreak in Ryan's face and worried that the boy would give in before harvest, so much guilt over the son's death and his wife's pain. His darling Mary Kate had survived, thank the good Lord, and was getting stronger every day, her sweet face in the morning the one thing that gave him strength to keep on. But of them all, it was Grace he worried after most; Grace and the secret he knew she carried. He'd waited for her to come to him, but she had not, and so he watched her eat and tried to make sure she got a bit more than her share, and he saw to it that she rested herself and did not work too hard. If she could just hold on to it for another week, there'd be food enough to nourish them both.

Grace, unaware of her father's watchful eye, kept herself busy on the long days caring for Granna and Mary Kathleen, and for Aghna, who was like a child again, mute and helpless, unless she was in the midst of a childlike rage. Grace stretched the food that Ryan brought back so that they might all have a small meal in the evenings, and ate the extra her father slipped her without protest. On hot afternoons, with Granna, Mary Kate, and Aghna all sleeping in the cabin, Patrick sitting on his bench in the shade, and Ryan long gone up the hill, Grace would walk up and down the lane, twisting the wedding band on her finger and watching the sky as if news might fall from it. There were no neighbors to ease the worry in her mind, no women to help her in her time: Katty O'Dugan's cabin was empty, the family having given up and emigrated the year before; Bully Ryan had died on the works, walking through the cold day after day with his bad chest, and Julia had taken the children to the workhouse in Cork City where, by all accounts, they'd perished. The Kelleys were gone, and Old Campbell Hawes had drunk himself to death, leaving his widow to be cast out by Ceallachan for lack of rent; she'd turned down the offer of shelter with the O'Malleys and set out on foot for her brother in County Kerry. There were two families still living in cabins at the end of the lane near the avenue—Mister Neeson and his two sons, and Shane O'Daly, who, at fifteen, was the young husband of Niamh, herself but a girl and soon to bear her first child. Shane and Niamh were the only survivors of their respective families, and it was a blessing they'd found one another. They had joined together for work with the Neesons, planting potatoes on a plot behind the O'Dalys' cabin, which Paddy and Shane guarded now the time for digging was at hand. But these were all the people left on a lane that had once been crowded with folk. Grace often caught out of the corner of her eye the flit and shiver of spirits drifting behind trees or rising up from hills, and to her ear, from out of the blackness of abandoned cabins, came echoes of songs sung long ago. She felt as though she walked more among the dead than the living, but she was not afraid. It was only the sadness of her people that drifted among the trees, left behind now that their souls had entered Heaven.

At night, weary of their own thoughts, the family would gather near Granna's pallet to drink a little water and eat whatever had been found that day. They'd talk a bit or just draw comfort from the nearness of one another until, at last, it was time to lie down and escape into sleep where fields were full of gold and tables heavily laden.

On a morning late in August, Patrick left his post by the field to follow a movement in the grass, returning an hour later with skinned meat that he said was rabbit. Grace knew well enough it was but a skinny field cat, though she roasted it anyway and ate her share, thankful for the feel of meat in her mouth. There was still corn meal to be had in Macroom, but the trip was risky and, having survived the fevers in the spring, none of them were wont to go. Only Aghna spoke of leaving—when she spoke at all—but the place she yearned for was Galway.

"Does she know what she's saying at all, then?" Patrick was irritated now that she'd been rambling for thirty minutes.

Grace rose and led the girl outside to sit on the bench, Aghna still insisting that their only hope was to be fishers of men, to go to the sea of Galway.

"Thank God for that," Patrick sighed when they'd left the room.

"I'll not be having you speak poorly of her, Da," Ryan warned. "Isn't she still my wife, for all I love her?"

"Musha, boy, she breaks my heart," Patrick said. "Would we could bring the child back and ease her suffering, but we cannot."

Ryan stood and paced in front of the open door. "I don't know what was worse, that terrible silence for months or the talk that's come upon her now!"

"Maybe she'll start another baby and that will stop her thinking of going off." Patrick fingered the stem of his pipe.

Ryan said nothing, but the look on his face did not escape Granna. "What is it?" she asked him, her voice weak.

"I don't think she can have another," he said, and looked out the door to where she sat. "Her body's not right, somehow . . ."

"Does she have the monthly blood?"

Ryan shook his head, turning red. "A little. Sometimes. Grace takes care of her that way."

"And does she have pain?"

"All the time," he told her, glad to speak of it. "Deep inside, she says, where the babies are meant to start."

Granna's lips drew tight and she looked at him with sorrow. "It happens in the terrible times," she said. "The body knows it has not enough nourishment to keep two hearts beating, so it sends away the weaker one before it ever takes."

He shook his head. "That's not it," he said. "She keeps to herself and won't let me near, not even to comfort her! Oh, Gran"—he looked at her—"what am I to do, for the love of God?"

She gestured for him to come sit on the edge of her pallet and then she took up his hand in her own. "A woman goes away like your Aghna, because she cannot bear to be in the world anymore. Her pain is so great that her mind travels with the spirit world while her body stays on earth. She is with us, but not with us. All we can do is wait. And pray."

"I'm afraid for her, Gran," he said softly. "Sometimes I see in her face that she knows where she is, but she's not making any sense. All this talk about going west." He paused. "What if she just walks off by herself one day, and me not knowing anything about it?"

"What's in the West? Does she tell you?"

"I know it sounds daft, but she says that the Jesuits in Galway have prepared a safe place for faithful Catholics among the Claddagh."

Granna's eyes grew wide.

"Aye," Ryan said. "I know. She's got Jesus and the fishermen of Galilee all mixed around with the Jesuits in Galway."

"There are no Jesuits in Galway, boy, only the ring fishermen— and they'd not let Jesus Himself in their huts without proof of His birth among them."

Ryan took a deep breath. "She thinks she belongs there, because an old relation of her mam's was Claddagh."

"Did her mother pass on the gold ring to her and does she wear it?"

"Nay." Ryan shook his head.

"Does she speak the Claddagh tongue?"

He said nothing.

"Then they'll have naught to do with her, and you know that. She'll be just another transplanter."

"She's sure that miracles happen there every day—water turning into wine, manna falling from Heaven, fish and bread from a basket that never empties . . . she says we must go or there'll be no room left!"

Patrick cleared his throat. "Well there are other folk beside the Claddagh, but even if you did find family to take you in, they say it's no good in the West now the shore's been scraped of dillisk and all the shell life picked clean. They're not fishing the waters for want of boats and nets gone to buy food. Folks are eating the very sand just for the weight of it in their bellies."

"I know, I know." Ryan's head fell into his hands. "It's madness to think of it."

"Five days and we'll dig," Patrick said reassuringly. "With solid food in her, her mind'll come right again, and her body, as well. You mustn't lose heart, son," he added gently.

"If I did, I'd have nothing left." Ryan got up from the bed and walked to the door. "I'll go sit with her now, give Grace a break. She's been looking too tired with caring for all of us of late."

Patrick and Granna exchanged a look after he went out, Patrick raising his eyebrows in question.

Granna shook her head. "Not a word," she whispered.

Patrick took the pipe stem out of his mouth and set his jaw firmly. "'Tis time we spoke of it," he said. "She cannot carry this alone any longer."

Grace came in, shaking the dust off her apron.

"I don't know, but Aghna's living in Galway already!" She smiled, but spoke softly so Ryan would not hear. Slowly, she lowered herself into the rocking chair and looked at Gran's pallet.

"Mary Kate's asleep already, is she?"

Gran nodded, stroking the little girl's light hair.

"I'll be glad when Lug Day comes," Grace said, closing her eyes and resting her head against the back of the chair.

Granna and Patrick exchanged another look.

"Aye," Patrick said. "It'll mean a good birth for the wee one you've started."

Grace's eyes flew open and she sat up straight in surprise. She looked from one face to the other, unable to speak.

Patrick chuckled around the pipe stem in his mouth, and even Gran gave up the ghost of a smile for the look of amazement on Grace's face.

"Do you think we're daft, girl?" Patrick asked his daughter. "Haven't we seen enough babies started to know the look of a woman carrying one?"

"I said nothing for fear it would come to naught," she said softly. "I've lost others better fed than this."

"Aye, but 'tis a full Irish child you carry now," he paused. "A fighting child."

"And how would you be knowing that, pray tell me?" Grace was stunned.

"Faith, your Gran is a wise woman and knows the way of everything. Always watching over you, she is. 'Tis her pointed out your wedding band." He looked at Granna and his eyes twinkled. "And doesn't it look just like the one Mary McDonagh wore all those years, but her dead and buried now?"

Grace had to laugh at their conspiracy, but then she became serious.

"You mustn't speak of it," she said quickly. "Not even to Ryan."

Patrick frowned at her. "Have we not proven we can keep a secret, girl? We all know the trouble your one is in."

Grace's heart fell and she nodded weakly.

"And can you tell us anything about that brother of yours?" he asked.

"No," she answered. "Morgan would not say, but I think they are together. They've got a good man looking out for them, and sure, he'll get them out of Ireland before too long."

"Your one'll never go." Patrick took the pipe out of his mouth and tapped it by habit before putting it into his shirt pocket.

"He must, Da." Grace sat on the edge of her chair.

"And Sean?" Granna spoke softly.

"He's meant to sail for America if he's not already gone. Morgan is to follow when he can."

Patrick rose and crossed the room, laying a hand on the damp head of his granddaughter. "So I'll not see this one grow up, then."

Grace looked across at his grizzled face, the white hair shaggy over his forehead. "We'll not be leaving you, Da, nor Granna. When Morgan has got himself clear, he'll send for us and we'll all go. Ryan and Aghna, as well."

Patrick shook his head. "Your gran and I are too much gone to make a home in another world," he said. "And your brother and his wife must make their own way, the two of them."

"Well, I'll not be going without my family, and there's no more to say on it," she said firmly, fighting back tears.

Patrick walked over to the rocking chair, and in a rare show of affection, pulled his daughter up and into his arms. "You're a fine girl, Gracelin O'Malley, and every bit the fighter your husband is and your ancestor was."

She closed her eyes against his shoulder.

"We're your family that *was*," he said gently. "Your family *now* is that beautiful child lying over there, the wee babe growing inside you, and your husband, fine man that he is." He leaned back and smiled at her. "This cabin is not your home—Ireland is your home. And always will be as long as she's got the likes of you and McDonagh to fight for her. And, of course, your brother, the revolutionary," he added with a laugh.

"And you, Da," she said softly.

"They're coming in now." He nodded toward the door, where Aghna leaned on Ryan's arm. "But I want you to know that I curse the very day you married that Donnelly—may his soul rot in hell—and I'll die a happy man if you'd only say you'd forgive me."

"You're never to say that, Da," she admonished. "For I thank God he was my husband."

Patrick glowered.

"Otherwise, I'd not have Mary Kathleen, and isn't she the very light?"

"Bless you, child," Patrick whispered, his face softening. "And may God bless your marriage to McDonagh, for he's the man you should have had all along."

Grace kissed his cheek, then stepped away as Ryan and Aghna came through the door, Aghna tired now, and silent, and Ryan's face etched with worry and fatigue. Still, Grace thought with envy, they have each other at this moment, the feel of a hand on one's arm, a beloved face to look upon. She put her hands across her belly and, at that moment, felt the quickening of life within. She put away all thoughts of anxiousness and worry. She must not lose this child.

August blazed into September. The potatoes had come up with nary a spot or blemish, and they had been stored in the bothan after all had eaten their fill. Grace had paid the rent and, with the last of her money, had bartered for three chickens and a rooster, which Shane O'Daly brought back from Macroom on the promise of eggs for himself and his wife, whose time was coming near. The city was fair starving, he reported back, even with warehouses full of grain and the stores stuffed with food again. Food prices were lower than ever anyone could remember, and Grace was happy for the oats and molasses they now had. But for the others it was not so easy; there had been no employment in Ireland and no wages—all the food in the world mattered not, if a man had no coin with which to buy it. The soup kitchens closed and no more meal was given out; England was glad to get the Irish off relief and off its hands. But still the Irish starved, and it was all the more bitter for what they'd survived the past three years.

Ryan and Aghna had gone to Galway, despite Patrick's protests. They'd eaten for a week, and Aghna began to fill out, so she grew more determined to get out of County Cork. Ryan saw no reason to wait any longer, so hopeful was he that, with food, and in the company of the priests she loved so much and her own family, she would at last grow well.

On the day of their leaving, Patrick followed them out into the lane, insisting they take a sack of bread and potatoes, and then, to their astonishment, he embraced them both, clinging to his eldest son and looking long into his face. Ryan was moved by his father's farewell and promised fervently that he would see them again, that they'd send word from Galway when they were settled.

Grace kissed her brother and sister-in-law good-bye, then stood in the middle of the lane with Patrick until the two figures had faded to nothing.

"They'll be back, well and strong," she reassured.

"No," Patrick said, staring down the lane. "We'll not see them again."

The days crept by and Grace waited, walking to the door every time she heard someone in the lane, hoping for word from Sean or Morgan. They had enough food to last the fall if they ate carefully, rationing each meal. They did not talk about what would happen when the potatoes were gone. There was no money left now, and rent was due.

Granna had stopped eating altogether, and would only sip water. She was so weak now that she could barely lift her head from the pillow, and her arms and fingers were mere bones. Mary Kathleen seemed to understand she was going, so she sat for hours beside her bed singing Irish songs in a high, thin voice. At night, she insisted on sleeping with her gran, and it was she who woke Grace one early dawn to tell her the angels had come now and were waiting beside the bed.

Grace came quickly, and mother and daughter lay down beside the old woman they loved—one on each side—their arms across her thin body, listening as her breathing grew more faint. Grace pressed her mouth to Granna's ear, whispering her last words of love and devotion. Granna lay still, staring up at the ceiling, her lips trembling with the effort to speak. At last, a single tear fell from her eye and ran away down her cheek, where it pooled against Grace's lip. Grace kissed her, eyes squeezed shut against the pain, as Granna drew a final breath and slipped away at the moment of sunrise.

An hour later, Grace woke Patrick and together they dug a grave between Thomsy and Kathleen. Patrick tore down the lower sheep hut to make a rough box and into this they laid her before lowering her into the ground. Mary Kathleen, clutching Blossom, watched while they filled in the hole and read from the Bible. When Patrick closed the great book and put it under his arm, Mary Kate tore at a clump of strawflowers, flinging them at the mound of new earth, before burying her face in Grace's apron.

Patrick patted the little girl's shoulder. "There now," he soothed. "We'll miss her true enough, but she's with the Lord now and happy as a lamb in a spring meadow."

Mary Kathleen looked up at him through her tears.

"And you," he said softly to Grace. "Have you not buried two mothers, then?"

She nodded, her mouth trembling.

He lifted her chin and wiped the spilling tears with his finger, leaving a smudge of dirt that made him smile. "I see both their faces in yours. Are they not, the both of them, standing even now at Heaven's Gate, gazing down with pride at you—the mother they've raised?" He paused, then added, "Don't ever forget the strong women from whence you came, girl. You and Mary Kate, you're a part of them and that's a thing to remember."

She tried to answer, but could not, tried to smile, but could raise no more than a tremble. He put his arms around her, then took her hand firmly in one of his, Mary Kate's in the other, and led them both back down the hill.

## Thirty

THE cabin was terribly quiet now, without the voices of Ryan, Aghna, and Granna. Grace tried to fill the corners with song and chatter, but rarely got a rise out of her little daughter or her father. Patrick spent his days sitting by the empty potato field, or counting their stores in the bothan; Mary Kathleen played quietly on Granna's pallet, having claimed it for her own. She was too sad for a child, and rarely spoke, her heart heavy with the knowledge of death and despair. Grace could not even get her to sing the songs Granna had taught her, or say aloud her prayers at night; desperately, she sought for something to make the little child hopeful again. One evening, as they lay together in bed, Grace put Mary Kathleen's hand on her belly.

"Can you feel that?" Grace asked.

Mary Kate's eyes opened wide.

"'Tis a baby I'm growing." Grace looked into the pale face of her daughter. "A wee brother or sister for you."

"When will it come?" Mary Kathleen asked.

"Before Christmastime," Grace told her. "In December."

Mary Kathleen's large gray eyes clouded and grew sad again. "How long will it live with us?" she asked plainly.

Grace took the little hand and kissed it. "Forever," Grace said, and added silently, Please, God, let it be true.

Mary Kathleen gave the ghost of a smile and put her hand back on the small mound of Grace's belly, falling asleep without the lines of worry that had so crowded her brow.

\*   \*   \*

They went on that way, day to day, as the leaves changed from green to red, and the long grass to gold, until, at last, it was the final day of September, chilly enough to have brought the turf fire back to life. When the sun had gone down, there came the sound of a slow horse down the lane, and a knock fell upon their door. Grace's heart started as she opened it a crack and peered out. When she saw who it was, she stood back and glanced at her father, who remained by the fire.

"Ceallachan," he said curtly. "What brings you out on this night?"

The agent had not fared much better than the rest of his country-men; his once large frame was haggard and there were dark circles under his eyes. His hands were grimy, the nails ragged and black with dirt, his beard a sparse stubble over his chin.

"You see, O'Malley, I've had a letter from Lord Donnelly him-self," he announced importantly, swaggering past Grace into the room. "And he's given the order to throw everyone off the place. Through with supporting layabouts, he says. Time to turn a profit, he says. Wheat is the moneymaker now. Wheat and corn." He hooked his thumbs into the armholes of a greasy vest.

Mary Kathleen began to tremble and Grace went to her.

"It's nothing to do with us," she said confidently. "I've the word of Edward Donnelly that we'll be left alone long as we pay what we owe."

"Letter said nothing about no promise." Ceallachan cocked an eye at her, pleased with himself. "Nor nothing about O'Malleys a'tall."

"Have you forgotten that I am a Donnelly?" she asked coolly.

"No, ma'am." He smiled. "But I think they have."

"Well, you're mistaken, Ceallachan." She pulled herself up straight and eyed him sharply. "And it'll cost you your job."

Under her gaze, Ceallachan squirmed ever so slightly. "My orders is my orders," he said plainly. "Everyone is to go out. Starting with this lane here."

"I'll ride into Macroom and send a letter myself," she announced.

Ceallachan shrugged. "Won't do you no good. They've all gone abroad for winter, leaving Captain Wynne in charge of affairs."

"Then I'll go to see him first thing in the morning."

"Well, and isn't he off to Dublin to ready a transport of criminals?" Ceallachan was pleased with his game of cat and mouse. "And wouldn't one of them go by the name of O'Malley? A weak, cripple boy, guilty of conspiracy?"

Grace's heart fell to her stomach and she glanced at her father.

"What do you know of it, Ceallachan?" Patrick challenged.

"What would it be worth to you?" the agent asked coyly.

"It would be worth sparing your miserable life another night," Patrick said, stepping forward and grabbing the agent's shirtfront, lifting him off his feet.

"Bloody hell, O'Malley," the agent spluttered. "You always were a man of little humor."

"Talk." Patrick shook him.

"Set me right first," Ceallachan said, trying to break Patrick's grip on his shirt.

Patrick let him fall.

"I don't know anything about it a'tall." The agent made a weak attempt to restore himself to authority, brushing off his clothes.

"Is Sean in prison?"

Ceallachan squirmed. "Rumor has it he's arrested on conspiracy. Sent off to stand trial in England." He paused. "Then again, he might have gone off to America on some eejit errand for those rebels think they can run things."

Patrick's face grew red. "Which is it, man? And you'd better speak true or I'll rip the tongue from your mouth!"

Ceallachan backed against the wall and put up his hands. "God as my witness, O'Malley, I only know what I hear in the pubs! Captain Wynne's been called to Dublin to organize a transport for some secret prisoners they got. Tongues are wagging about your one being in that group." He gave them an innocent look, as if it was all beyond his comprehension. "Same men turn around and swear he's gone to America with money in his pocket and orders to bring back our boys for the fight."

Patrick looked at him in disgust, then glanced at Grace.

"What exactly do you want from us, Ceallachan?" Patrick asked.

"Money," he spat, then pulled back, his body tense for another assault.

"And why would we be giving money to a rat like you?"

"I'll buy off the captain for you," he said quickly. "You'll still have to clear out, but you can stay through winter."

"Haven't you just told us that Captain Wynne's in Dublin?" Grace took a step toward him, her arm protectively around Mary Kathleen.

"So I did, but I can buy off the guard what's coming in the morning even easier than the captain!" He spoke rapidly. "Aren't I doing you a favor by all this, and what's the harm in asking for a bit of gold for all my trouble?" he asked, wide-eyed as though he believed it.

"We've got no gold," Patrick said. "Nor any money a'tall."

Ceallachan cocked his head, and shifted his gaze from one to the other. "Sure, and the widow's got a little something put by . . . something against next Quarterday?"

Patrick shook his head.

Ceallachan's face grew stormy. "I could take something of worth, then, and sell it myself." He looked around at the cabin, long since stripped of anything valuable. "There must be treasure hid about— eating silver or costly plate. Left me nothing at the big house, she did, though by rights it's mine."

"By rights it's my granddaughter's," Patrick said calmly.

"I know you've got money hid away!" Ceallachan exploded, his face turning red in the firelight. "And you better come up with it, Mister High and Mighty O'Malley, or you'll find yourself tossed out on the road with the rest of them come morning!"

He glared at them once more, then stormed out of the cabin, jumped on his horse, and galloped down the lane. Patrick let out a long sigh and sank down on the stooleen near the fire.

"Have you anything left, then?" he asked.

"No." Grace shook her head. "I buried three trunks full of treasure among the graves at Donnelly House—for Mary Kate when she comes into it—but there was little money, and what I had has all gone now for food and rent."

Patrick nodded. "Well, I wouldn't let you give it to that filthy rascal anyway," he said. "He'll not turn us out. It's all bluff and blubber."

"Are you so sure?"

"Aye. There's been no rent paid but ours and he owes money to everyone, especially Donnelly."

"Is that not all the more reason to have us turned out?" she asked, pulling Mary Kathleen onto her lap and stroking her hair.

"What's the purpose? Donnelly growing wheat here?" He snorted. "And who's going to run the place? Not Ceallachan, who's never turned a spade of earth in his life, I'll wager." He paused. "No, 'twas just a bit of trickery to get out of you what money he thought you had."

"And what about Sean?"

He sighed and shook his head. "I don't know," he said. "If he's caught and living in a prison cell, it'll be the end of him."

"Morgan would never let that happen," Grace said firmly. "I know they've got him out of here. He's in America, sure enough."

"I'd say true enough for you, daughter."

They sat quietly, and Mary Kathleen fell asleep, as she always did when she could not bear the tension.

"Where would we go, Da?" Grace asked quietly. "If they turned us out."

He stirred himself and frowned. "We'll not leave this farm, nor this cabin where you and your brothers were born, and no man will take it from us."

Grace rocked and thought, and when Patrick stood and announced that he was going to bed, this day had held enough trouble for one man, she nodded and let him go without further conversation.

An ominous feeling of foreboding stole into Grace's heart and she looked around the cabin in the dim light of the turf fire. She stood and carried Mary Kathleen to Granna's pallet, tucking her in with her doll, Blossom. Then she went quietly into the back room and took down from the high shelf her carpetbag, the one she'd married away in and the one she'd used to come home. She opened it and looked inside at the emptiness. "Just in case," she told herself.

Back in the main room, she checked Mary Kathleen, then unstuck from the wall the postcards her mother had always loved: the Mourne Mountains, the cliffs at Kilkee, the grasslands of the Golden Vale that her mother kept near her worktable, the sunset over Bantry Bay. Granna's rag rug still lay on the floor near the hearth, but it was more rag than rug now, and terribly dirty beside. The bawneen curtains were gone from the window, having been used to make bedding for wee Thomsy's cradle; the luster jugs had been sold to passing tinkers, as had most of the cooking pots and tools. There was Granna's cashmere shawl, and her mother's Bible, a glass brooch her father had given Kathleen and put away for Mary Kate, and Patrick's old clay pipe. Last, she put in the funeral cloth she'd embroidered for Michael Brian. What else, what else, she thought and looked around the room. Only clothes and her sewing basket. Quickly, she gathered up what she needed: Granna's flannel sleeping shirt and her favorite flowered skirt; Sean's rough trousers and his muslin shirt; Patrick's old jacket, full of the smell of rich earth and tobacco; Ryan's wedding vest and Aghna's pretty apron; Thomsy's baby blanket; the quilt her mother had made. Building up the fire, she settled before it and began to cut a square from each garment, turning the edges neatly with needle and thread. When she had a pile of squares, she stitched them together quickly, no pattern in mind, just a simple square with a bit of each of those she loved. She worked all night, and the sun was coming up when she finished backing it with a piece cut from her mother's quilt. It wasn't large enough to be of any use, but when she held it close to her nose, she smelled her family and the farm, felt the life of them next to her cheek, and that was all she wanted. She rolled it up and put it in the carpetbag, along with the silver spoons and Mary Kathleen's baby cup. There was a drawing of her mother and father, done on their wedding day, but none of Gran or any of the others. Finally able to rest, she lay down beside her sleeping daughter, put her arms tightly around her, and drifted off.

It was Patrick's hand that shook her awake and told her to gather up the child and come quickly. She rose, rubbed her eyes, and picked up Mary Kathleen, awake and clutching her doll. There was shouting down the lane, and the sound of horses stomping.

"They're turning out the O'Dalys," Patrick said, now searching through the baskets above the kitchen shelf. He pulled one down and took out Bram's Colt revolver, which Grace had hidden there.

"Can you fire this blasted thing?" he asked, holding it up gingerly.

"Aye," she said. "It's not loaded, though."

She came and yanked down a second basket, tipping out a powder horn and six caps. Quickly, she poured gunpowder into each chamber, then popped in the caps with a practiced hand.

"Ready," she said, tucking the revolver into the waist of her skirt. "Let's go."

Patrick shook his head. "Take the child up to the high sheep hut and don't come down till you see me waving for you," he commanded.

"What good am I up the hill?" she asked angrily.

Patrick put his hands on her shoulders. "Do as I say, Grace," he said. "You've a child to protect. Keep the gun at the ready, and hide yourselves."

"What good are you to them now?" she begged.

"Not much, true enough," he said, shaking his head. "But I'll not forsake them. 'Tis my own fault they had no warning."

"Da," she pleaded.

"I've got to get that boy and his wife away from there," he said firmly. "When they start throwing his things about, he'll go wild and they'll shoot him down sure enough. But maybe Neeson and I together can talk sense to him. Maybe the soldiers will see the way things are and leave us a day or two to get ready."

"Don't count on it," she said.

"No." And then he grinned wickedly. "But am I not the father of a feared revolutionary? And might there not even now be rebels in the wood?"

Grace's face was grim. "God only knows where he is, Da."

"But God knows right where we are, Grace, and He'll not abandon us."

She hugged him quickly, nearly crushing him to her, then scooped up Mary Kathleen and the carpet bag in one arm, the other hand on the handle of the pistol, extra caps and powder in her pocket. Patrick kissed his granddaughter's head and tousled her golden hair.

"Off with you now, wee Mary Kate." He winked to ease her fear. "We'll play a bit of a game, if you like."

She nodded soberly.

He put his finger to his lips. "Now hide away with your mam, like a good girl, and I'll come find you when it's time."

The shouting was louder now and Grace slipped out of the cabin, crouching behind the low stone wall as she made her way up the hill past the bothan to the sheep hut. She looked back once and saw Patrick standing in the door, urging her on with his hand, and then he went around the side. From the hill, she could see him start down the lane at a trot.

It was only a matter of minutes before she smelled smoke and realized they were burning the roof off Neeson's cabin, and most likely

O'Daly's next. She could hear the screams of a girl and the angry
shouts of young men, but not the low voice of her father. Suddenly a
shot rang out and all fell still. Another shot followed.

Grace looked into the frightened face of her daughter.

"Come," she whispered. "We'll go higher up."

They crept out of the hut and up to the top of the hill where Grace
and Sean had played in the hollow tree as children. She'd not been
there in years, but was relieved to see the tree still stood.

"Pretend you are a wee elf," she told Mary Kathleen. "And this is
your home in the wood. Crawl away inside and I'll lay these branches
across the opening to make you invisible. Here's your elfin child." She
put Blossom into Mary Kate's arms. "Hold her close and sing a quiet
lullaby whilst I go and hunt our supper."

Mary Kathleen looked doubtful, but crawled into the hollow trunk
and sat down, her eyes wide with uncertainty.

"And now to make you invisible!" Grace said with desperate
cheerfulness, covering the hole until she could no longer see her
daughter's face.

"Mam!" came a frightened cry from within.

Grace closed her eyes, hand on the branches. "Be brave, wee elf!"
she whispered. "Sing your song, and I'll be back before it's done."

There was no answer and Grace's heart was torn. She tucked the
gun more firmly into her waistband and began to run along the top of
the ridge until she was above the O'Daly and Neeson cabins.

Lying in the road were Shane O'Daly and the younger Neeson
boy. A soldier sat nearby pressing a bloody cloth to his head. Patrick
was trying to calm Niamh, his arms around the hysterical girl, while
Mister Neeson attempted to pull his son Paddy off a soldier who had
drawn a knife. Ceallachan stood across the road, watching the out-
break with scornful amusement. At his command, soldiers were carrying out the meager possessions of the O'Dalys and dumping them in
the road. Furniture smashed and dishes shattered, curtains were torn
from the windows and the glass of a small picture frame was ground
under boot heels. Niamh stopped shrieking and sat on the ground,
dazed, cradling her husband's head in her lap.

Ceallachan yelled to one of the soldiers, but they pretended not
to hear and continued razing the cabin. He screamed again, and when
still they ignored him, he walked over to the dead boy himself,

grabbed his feet by the boots, and tried to drag him away from his widow. Patrick moved forward to stop him, and Neeson let go of his son long enough for the boy to escape and attack the agent. Ceallachan scrambled away, drew his pistol, and fired wildly. Patrick crumpled to the ground, and Neeson and his boy moved back in horror. Grace stuffed her fist into her mouth to keep from crying out, and froze, crouched against the wall, until Ceallachan drew back his pointed boot and kicked her father viciously in the head, shouting curses all the while.

With a stealth that belied her pounding heart, Grace crept down through the bushes and sparse trees, staying low behind Neeson's wall until she was close enough to take a shot. Her hand shook, but she steadied it with the other, supporting the barrel in a crevice of the wall as she drew a bead on Ceallachan. She held her aim for a split second, then fired, ducking down behind the wall, eyes squeezed shut in hurried prayer. Cautiously, she rose again to see what had happened, and there was Ceallachan fallen to his knees, a dark red stain spreading out on the cloth that covered his thigh. He clutched the leg with both hands, screaming in pain and fury, spittle flying from his mouth. The soldiers froze where they stood; no one came to his aid. She aimed and fired again, this time hitting him square in the forehead. His eyes went wide with surprise and he toppled over, facedown in the dirt. Then panic set in. The soldiers—afraid of being fired upon—grabbed Neeson and Paddy, and pounded them with small clubs, while another hauled Niamh to her feet and held her in front of him as a shield. She struggled to get away as Neeson and Paddy began to crumple beneath the relentless blows. Grace made herself wait for a clear shot, sweat running down her forehead and stinging her eyes. There it was—and the soldier holding Paddy collapsed, dead. Paddy rushed to help his father, but was immediately attacked by the knife-bearing soldier, who plunged the blade up to the hilt into the boy's arm. Grace inched forward, fearful of hitting Mister Neeson or Paddy; closer, closer, and then she aimed and fired another round. In the confusion that followed, Niamh twisted away and the last two soldiers ran for their horses, leaping upon them and galloping at full speed away from the wreckage. Grace fired her last round at the backs of them, then stood and shook out her hand, cramped from squeezing the trigger.

Niamh saw her first and called to the others, who stared at Grace as though she were a ghost. They watched the apparition pick her way through the rocks, and then their mouths fell open in amazement when they recognized Patrick O'Malley's daughter. She ran across the road and knelt by her father, her hand slipping under his shirt to his chest.

"He's still alive," she said grimly. "Help me get him up."

Neeson and Paddy came at once and together they carried him to the stone wall across the road, propping him up so that he sat. He gasped and hacked against the lack of air in his chest, spit up, then weakly opened his eyes.

"By God, if this is Heaven, I've been cheated," he wheezed.

"Hush, now." Grace felt along his shoulder for the place where the bullet had entered. "You're a long way from dying, Da, but you're hurt bad enough."

Neeson had gone to his youngest son, kneeling beside him in the dirt. He laid a hand upon the boy's chest and said his name, shaking him when his eyes did not open. Blood bubbled up between his lips and trickled down the side of his face. Neeson crossed himself and bowed his head. His shoulders shook as he wept. Paddy came quietly to his father and put an arm around him.

"There's not much time," Grace said quietly.

"I'll not leave him lying in the road." Neeson choked back his tears, reaching out to touch the boy's face and smooth back his dark hair.

Grace's heart raced with anxiety; any minute the soldiers might return with help to finish the job. "Put him in O'Daly's cabin," she directed. "Burn it down." Her eyes fell on Niamh. "Best to lay Shane there, as well," she added, gently.

Niamh let out a wail and clung to her husband, sobbing, "No, no, no," as Mister Neeson rose slowly to his feet and went to her. He put his great arms around her shoulders and eased the pregnant girl to her feet, murmuring in her ear all the while. She moaned and began to crumple against him, but he held her firmly, forcing her to take one step and then another, guiding her away from the boy who had been her husband.

Paddy lifted up the body of his young brother and carried it into the empty cabin, returning a moment later for Shane, eyes lowered as he picked up the boy and bore him inside, as well. Mister Neeson led

Niamh to the wall next to Patrick, then, with Grace helping, made small twists of long, dry grass with which to set the cabin on fire. They circled the small hut, lighting the edges of the roof, then throwing their torches in the door. The fire caught and spread, and they backed away from the heat to stand beside Niamh and Patrick, silently watching as the flames consumed it, sending into the air blackened bits of straw and thatch. There was a great *whoosh* as the roof collapsed and yellow flames shot out the windows. Mister Neeson helped Patrick to his feet and they backed even further down the road, still unable to take their eyes off the funeral pyre.

"We must go," Grace said at last. "It's too dangerous."

"Aye," Neeson said. "But where?"

"They say there's food to be had in the city, if you can make it that far."

"Is that where you're headed?" He watched the thick black smoke pile up overhead.

She put her arm around Patrick's waist, supporting him. "I've got to get the shot out of his shoulder and let him rest." She looked up at the hills. "And I've got my daughter, as well."

"We'll wait and go together."

Grace shook her head. "They'll be looking for us." She glanced at the dead soldier in the road. "We've killed one of their own, now, Ceallachan, as well, and they'll be back with a hanging rope, sure enough. You must go on ahead. We'll be but a day or two behind you."

"Will you go up into the woods, then, until he's fit to travel?"

"Aye." Grace bit her lip.

Neeson examined her face, then nodded reluctantly. He turned to his son. "We'll keep Niamh with us?" he asked, and the boy put his arm around her shoulders protectively in answer.

"God be with you, then," Grace said, tears welling in her eyes. "Go safely."

"And you." Neeson gave a little bow, dignified to the end. "We'll be looking out for you in the city."

She watched them start off down the road—the fraught, weeping, widowed girl supported on either side by a man gone suddenly old and his last living son—and then she tightened her grip about her father, turned him around, and guided him slowly back down the empty lane.

# Thirty-one

GRACE eased Patrick onto the pallet still lying on the floor of their cabin, then scrambled up the back path to retrieve Mary Kate, whose hands were covering her face, mouth opened in silent scream. She calmed the child as best she could, then carried her back to the cabin, setting her in the corner with Blossom while she tended to Patrick. When she looked up, Mary Kate had escaped yet again into the safety of sleep, clutching her doll and breathing heavily. Relieved that the child would not have to witness yet another grim scene, Grace quickly sterilized her sharp paring knife over the fire. Patrick grunted when she slit the ragged wound in his shoulder, and again when she dug out the blunted ball with her fingers. She cleaned and dressed the wound, and made a cold compress for the knot on the side of his head. After brewing up the last of the medicinal herbs for him to drink and filling her pockets with bits of raw potato, Grace again picked up Mary Kate and they all crept over the hill to sleep in the woods in an abandoned botha, though Grace sat wakeful that long first night. She roused them at first light and led them for two days through the woods until she felt it was safe enough to join the silent travelers on the road to Cork City, relieved at last to be anonymous in the throng. She had Mary Kate tied to her back, the carpetbag in one hand and a walking stick in the other. Patrick walked slowly beside her, a blanket over his shoulders, a hat pulled down over the mess of a bruise that shadowed half his face. She'd thrown the revolver and caps into the river in case they were stopped by soldiers.

She had not been in the city since the day she'd ridden to the docks with Brigid, Phillip, and Edward Donnelly, and it was worse than she'd remembered. The streets were packed with ragged beggars, and filthy crowds sat outside the workhouse and hospital. Loaves of bread were piled up in the bakery window, and sausages hung visible in a butcher shop, but now that there was food to be had at last, few had money to buy it. As mouths salivated and eyes narrowed furtively at meat and bread and cheese so close, yet unavailable, the smell of riot hung thick; the smell of sickness mingled with it, clinging to clothing and doorways, fetid and dank, as ripe as the smell of death that blew overhead from bodies piled up behind the hospital waiting to be burned. Patrick pulled the blanket tight across his nose and mouth, Grace tied a cloth around her own and adjusted Mary Kathleen's face so that it pressed into her shoulder. Now that they were here at last, she wondered what on earth to do. The days on the road had been spent trying to keep moving, keep fed, keep warm against the chill of early October nights. She had only thought to get to the city, get to the docks. Here, she had hoped to find word of Morgan or Sean, and some kind of a plan, but as she looked around at the hundreds of exhausted, starving faces, her hope turned to hopelessness. She dared not ask for anyone by name and she had seen no familiar faces. Irish could no more be trusted than English; reward money was too tempting in light of the food that could be had. She made her way along teeming streets to the docks, where several vessels were loading, masts and spars waving in the choppy sea; there, she sat down on a crate and untied Mary Kathleen, shifting the child to her lap.

"Musha, we're here now," she murmured, pulling the kerchief away from her mouth and breathing in the salty air.

Mary Kathleen roused herself and looked around, then faced her mother.

"Where's this?" she asked plaintively.

Grace mustered a smile. "Cork City," she announced. "A grand place once, and grand again, sure enough, though crowded now and smelly."

Mary Kathleen nodded, wrinkling her nose. She laid her head against her mother's chest and sighed.

"We need to eat." Patrick rose unsteadily to his feet. He had not weathered the trip well, and his wound was beginning to stink. He was pale, despite the purple and green of his bruise, and sometimes he frightened her by not knowing where he was upon waking. "I'll fish here."

She looked into the greasy water and spied an arm floating out from behind a piling. "No, Da," she said. "We'll eat nothing out of here. Sit and rest a bit while I think on what to do."

She bit her lip, remembering the Dublin docks where she'd stood as a bride, watching the emigration of sons and daughters, mourned by families weeping and wailing and praying over their beads for children they never expected to see again. Leaving Ireland was like leaving life, and no one wanted their children to go from it. But that had been before—now, the emigrants waited quietly, thin and haggard, holding the hands of gaunt children, no one mourning their leaving, as it was death they left behind and life they sought in the far away. These weary travelers would be weeks on the sea, but few carried much in the way of provisions, having nothing left to carry, and Grace wondered what would happen to them when they landed in the new land, empty-handed. Would clothes and food miraculously appear? Jobs and food and cabins be handed out like ale and tobacco? She prayed God it might be true, for sure she was that Sean had landed with little more than a coat to keep him warm and a cough rattling around his chest from the damp at sea. She stood stiffly and stretched, then put out a hand, which Mary Kathleen took at once.

"I'll walk a bit and see about food and shelter for tonight, Da," she said. "You stay here and don't move, for I'd hardly know how to find you in all this crowd."

Grace marked the street and the name of the boat that anchored closest to her father, then walked along the dock, turning into an alley when she smelled the tantalizing odor of roasting meat. It was strongest in front of a small, grubby pub for soldiers and Grace boldly took up a place outside the door, lifting her hand to each group that came reeling out.

"Please, Captain," she begged. "Have you not a penny or a bite of meat for my hungry child?"

Some turned a piteous glance in her direction, but most ignored her, having become numb to the sight of starving women and hollow-eyed children. Others, full of drink, offered lewd suggestions as to how she might earn the odd penny and more. Grace's face turned red with these propositions, and she pulled Mary Kathleen into her skirts, covering the child's ear with the palm of her hand.

"Missus Donnelly!"

She glanced up warily out of the corner of her eye, and then raised her head and smiled with relief.

"Henry!"

He was with a group of young men who hooted and nudged one another until he glared at them and barked a reprimand. When they'd staggered off, he took Grace by the arm and led her away from the pub.

"What in God's name are you doing here?" he asked anxiously. "This isn't a fit place for a person like you."

"Then what is it you're doing here, Henry Adams?" she scolded.

They stopped at the end of the alley and he smiled, despite his alarm at her condition. "It's good to see you," he allowed. "I've thought of you often. And how's the young patient?"

"Hallo, Henry," Mary Kate said shyly, peeking out from behind her mother's muddy skirt.

He bent down and patted her head.

"You've had a long trip, haven't you?" he said, then looked at Grace. "What on earth are you doing here?"

"We've come to find . . ." She stopped. "I don't know. Gran has died, you see, though not of fever. And Ryan and Aghna have gone to Galway . . ."

"Oh, no." His face went pale.

"Aghna never got well, you know, after Thomsy died, and Ryan thought that maybe being with her own people . . ."

He shook his head. "They'll be lucky to reach it alive," he said. "Let alone find any family. What about your father?"

"Shot by Ceallachan and the soldiers come to evict our lane and tear down the cabins."

He slumped. "Oh, Grace, no."

"But he's alive," she added quickly. "We've left him to rest on the docks. There was nothing left for us at home and word is there's food in the cities."

"There is," he agreed. "But only for those with money. Have you got any?"

"Well, it wasn't ale I was begging outside that pub, you know."

He laughed—a tired, short sound—then dug in his pockets and pulled out a handful of coins. "Take this," he insisted. "It won't go far, but it'll feed you for a day or so. Where will you sleep?"

"I've not thought. We've only just come in."

"Stay away from the workhouse," he warned. "It's full of disease. The whole place is still pretty bad off." He thought for a moment. "There's a convent takes in orphaned children, at the edge of town, up on the hill. Rose . . . something."

Grace brightened. "Holy Sisters of the Rose! I'd not thought of that. I've a friend there."

"Excellent," he said, relieved. "They don't take in men, as a rule, but if you know someone . . . Can you get there by tonight?"

"Aye." She nodded. "Haven't we come this far?"

They stood and looked at one another, reluctant to part.

"Will you go home soon, Henry?"

"Ten weeks," he sighed. "In time for Christmas goose."

"And a fine Christmas it'll be," she said lightly. "You in Cornwall, sitting round the fire having tea with the rector's daughter. And will you be giving her a ring, then, your Miss Isabel?"

He laughed. "Yes. Yes, I'll spend the rest of my Christmases with Isabel, if she'll have me."

"And why wouldn't she, now, a handsome young soldier like your-self?"

His smile faded. "I'm through with all that," he said soberly. "I won't be coming back to Ireland, Grace. Ever."

"That's all right, then." Grace's smile stayed firmly in place. She put out her hand. "I'll say good-bye to you, now, Henry, and good luck. Thank you for all your kindness to us."

He looked at her hand in his, then made a gallant bow and kissed it. "Good-bye. I won't forget you."

Mary Kathleen shyly put out her own hand and he kissed it, as well.

"Take care of your mother, now, Mary Kate, and promise me you'll bring her to Cornwall to see my pretty horses."

"I promise, Henry," she said seriously, then smiled, and Grace was happy, as it was the first one in days.

They turned and walked away down the alley until his shout stopped them, and he came running up behind.

"I don't know where my mind is, Grace, but I've news for you." He stopped and glanced around, pulling her close to the wall and lowering his voice. "I'm not meant to give out a word of it, but your friend has been arrested."

"My brother?" she whispered.

He shook his head, confused. "No, not O'Malley. We think he sailed on the *Champion* bound for America the end of August."

"Thank God," she said, and then the color left her face. "Is it Morgan you're speaking of, then? Morgan McDonagh who's been arrested?"

"He's being held in Dublin."

"Are you sure?" she asked. "Could it not be another rumor?"

"No," he said and took her arm, for suddenly she looked faint. "I know for a fact that he was arrested with Thomas Meagher and Lord David Evans. On charges of conspiracy. Meagher is out on bail, but they've been after Evans a long time and he's set to be transported back to London. McDonagh is under tight guard. I don't know when he's to be tried. Or where."

"Dear God!" Grace's eyes went wide. "I must see him!"

"Absolutely not." Henry was adamant. "You'd never get to within a mile of him, and you mustn't try."

"I will," Grace insisted. "I must!"

"You'll only get yourself locked up, as well," he told her. "Seeing as how you're the sister of the one that got away."

"And the wife of the one that didn't," she murmured.

His mouth fell open. "I didn't hear that," he said, shaking his head. "That's just something I don't want to know."

"Please, Henry," she begged. "Can you not help me to see him?"

He stared into her face—dirty, tired, eyes haggard and bloodshot. "You're McDonagh's wife."

"Aye."

"They say he wouldn't leave Ireland without you."

"Fool that he is." Her eyes filled with tears.

He sighed, his lips drawn tightly together. "There's no way I can get you to him, Grace, and you mustn't even consider going to Dublin. It's too risky."

"Is there any chance you might see him yourself, Henry?" she asked. "Any chance a'tall?"

He hesitated, unwilling to commit himself to this outrageous idea.

"Then I'll go myself," she said desperately.

In light of her determination, he relented. "It's a long shot," he said.

Her face lit up.

"Mind you, Grace, I can't promise anything."

"If you promise to try, Henry, that's good enough for me."

He shook his head, exasperated with himself. "I can't believe I'm telling you this, but as luck would have it, I'm meant to ride into Dublin at week's end. I'm part of an escort for prisoners to be transported to the boat for Liverpool."

"You're sure to see him, then," she said eagerly.

"He's not part of that group, Grace, and I've no idea where he's being held."

"I have faith in you, Henry."

He looked out at the water, then back at the hope in her eyes. He sighed. "All right, then. I'll do my best. What is this very important message?"

"Tell him . . ." She paused. "Tell him we're alive and well, and that . . ." She put her hands on her belly. "And that he's to be a father."

His eyes widened in surprise. "My God, Grace!"

"Can you do that, Henry?" she begged. "It will harm no one, and it might give him hope."

"Yes," Henry agreed thoughtfully. "It would certainly give him that."

"Tell him we'll come as soon as we can."

"No," he said firmly. "That will give him no peace of mind. Dublin's a madhouse right now."

She looked down at Mary Kathleen.

"Then we'll go to the sisters, and think what to do there."

"That's best, Grace," he reassured. "Rest there and build up your strength." He glanced at the slight bulge under her skirt. "I promise I'll do everything in my power to give him your message."

Relief flooded her eyes. "Thank you, Henry. You're a fine man. Your mother would be very proud."

"Yes, she certainly would," he agreed. "Now, go along before I realize how much trouble you're getting me into and change my mind like a sensible man."

"God bless you, Henry!" she called, towing her daughter back down along the dock toward the edge of town.

"Ah, Grace," he said wonderingly to himself, watching them go. "Who are you?"

It was evening by the time Grace reached the convent, Mary Kathleen again tied to her back, Patrick at her side. She rang the bell at the gate and told the nun who answered that she must see Sister John Paul immediately. The nun told her to wait and disappeared for half an hour. Just as Grace was about to ring the bell again, a tall figure in black robes came hurrying across the courtyard, a giant key ring jangling in her hand.

"Who's there?" She stopped short at the gate and peered through the bars at the old man, ragged woman, and limp child.

"'Tis Gracelin O'Malley, Barbara, come to beg shelter for myself, my father, and my daughter."

Barbara's eyes went wide and she immediately unlocked the gate, pulling them inside. "Lord have mercy," she exclaimed. "I'd have never recognized you, Grace! Nor your father!" She tried to see the face of the little girl hiding her eyes in Grace's shoulder. "But I'd know Mary Kathleen anywhere," she said softly, her eyes as warm and comforting as they'd always been. "Morgan has told me all about *you*." She stroked the little girl's cheek with her finger.

"Can we stay a night or two?" Grace asked. "We're going to Dublin, but we must rest first. I have money." She held out the coins in her hand.

Barbara pushed them away. "We'll talk about that later." She untied Mary Kate from Grace's back and held the child in her own arms. "Let's find you a bed first, and something to eat.

"We don't shelter men," she apologized to Patrick. "But our caretaker died not long ago and you're welcome to his room. It's small, but nearby."

"Any bed a'tall would be a welcome thing tonight, Barbara, and thank you."

She showed him the shed and left him sitting on the bed—a lamp burning low on the table—with the promise of turf for the fire and a bowl of soup before too long. Then she led Grace back into the main building, up the stairs, and down a long stone hall, past many narrow white doors with tiny windows in them, like cells. Grace suddenly realized that the nuns slept in these small rooms and that many of them were occupied. They turned down one corridor and then another, until they were in the west wing of the convent. Barbara led the way up a second short flight of steps and opened a heavy door that creaked from lack of use. She crossed the room and laid Mary Kathleen gently on the bed, then lit a lantern that sat on a small table nearby. There was a hook for clothes and a cracked washbasin with a tiny mirror above it.

"The guest room," Barbara joked. "Yours for now. I'll bring hot water so you can wash and whatever's left from tonight's meal. Won't be much, I'm afraid."

"We're grateful for anything."

"Grace." Barbara hesitated. "Your da, he doesn't have the fever, does he? Because I can't treat him nor risk keeping him among us if he does."

"There was a fight when the guards came to turn out our lane. He took a close shot to the shoulder," Grace said. "I cleaned it up best I could, but it might well have gone bad."

It wasn't contagious then, and Barbara was relieved. "I'll have a look at it right away. What about that awful bruise on his face?"

"They kicked him when he fell. Swelling's gone down some, but it still looks sore and he says he hears a ringing in his ear . . . sometimes he's not sure where he is."

Barbara nodded. "Could be the shock of it all. How many days on the road were you?"

"Five, I think. We slept by the side of the road and had little to eat."

"It's a wonder he's alive, at all, then," she said grimly. "How are you?"

"Tired and hungry," Grace admitted. "Like the rest of the world."

"And the child?"

She paused. "Sad. Very quiet and sad. She sleeps so much . . . as if she can't cope with being awake."

"She can't," Barbara said quietly. "We see that a lot here. But once they get regular food and rest, they begin to come back to life. It will be the same for her." She smiled reassuringly. "I'll leave you to settle in, then come back with a meal. I'm glad to see a face from home," she added before closing the door.

Grace sank down on the rough bed and nearly fell asleep right there, so exhausted was she from the past days of travel. She had been on the verge of telling Barbara about the coming baby and Morgan in prison, but her head was heavy with fatigue and she hadn't known where to begin. Tomorrow, she promised herself. I'll tell her everything tomorrow.

Mary Kate stirred and awoke, then settled against her mother wearily. They lay quietly together until Barbara reappeared with a steaming kettle of water and a large bowl of broth; she poured half the water into the washbasin, the other half into an old pot with a handful of herbs to steep for tea. The soup bowl was placed squarely on the nightstand with two spoons and a generous chunk of brown bread.

"We're so thankful to you, Barbara." Grace sat up, pulling Mary Kate close to disguise the evidence of her pregnancy, and feeling guilty in the process.

"Best to call me Sister John Paul around here," Barbara said, wiping her hands on a small cloth. "Some of the older ones get quite put out. 'Tis another world for them, you know—contact with the outside, family coming and going, all the wee children about, services at odd hours. A long way from those quiet, contemplative days of prayer and householding. Familiar names, now, that just might push them right over the edge."

Grace smiled sympathetically. "And has it been hard on you, as well, then? Do you miss the old life?"

Barbara paused, considering. "No," she said. "I mean yes, of course. The starving and illness, the orphans—that's been awful. Well, and wasn't I a part of the old way for such a short time, though I miss the beauty and stillness of the days, the quiet, the prayers, the inner life we led." Her hand went to the cruxifix that hung from her belt. "But I've come to feel such a sense of purpose that wasn't there be- fore." She glanced upward. "Forgive me, Father, but it's the truth. I know that this is what the Lord prepared me for. This is my true calling."

"I understand," Grace said, eyes unwavering.

Barbara nodded. "I know you do." She glanced around the room, seeing that they had everything they needed. "You wash and eat, then sleep. I'll come in the morning and we'll talk then, for sure and you've more to tell me."

Her face was so much like Morgan's, strong cheekbones and high brow, the large, dancing eyes and freckles down one cheek. Grace's eyes filled with tears and she stood quickly, wrapping her arms around her old friend.

"Ah, now, it'll be all right," Barbara soothed, patting her back. "You'll feel stronger and better able to cope after a good night's sleep. I'll go see to your father now. God bless you both."

She left them, and they listened to her heavy robe swishing around her as her footsteps faded down the hallway. Grace stood at the washstand, soaking a rough cloth, then came to the bed and began dabbing at Mary Kathleen's face. The cloth came away grimy black and, horrified, she scrubbed harder until finally the little cheeks glowed pink and not a speck of dirt remained. Hesitantly, she approached the mirror to have a look at her own face—a face she'd not seen in months. She touched her cheek, barely able to recognize herself for the cuts and streaks of mud, the dark circles under her eyes . . . and the hair—the hair shocked her most. Where before it had gleamed with rich glints of red and was thick and luxuriant, now it hung lank and matted, twigs and bits of leaf stuck in the snarled ends, the color dull and lifeless, shot through with gray. She looked like a woman going on forty, rather than a girl of nineteen. She scoured her own face and then her hands and arms, until the water in the bowl was muddy brown.

Famished, she and Mary Kate soaked the bread in the hot soup, wolfing down great bites, then spooning out the rest. Afterward, they drank two big cups of the twiggy tea. When they'd finished, they stripped off their dirty clothes and put on the stiff, homespun nightshirts that hung on pegs by the washstand—a large one that swallowed up Grace, a smaller one for Mary Kate. Grace sat on the bed behind her daughter and began working a wooden comb through the child's tangled curls. She took from her bag a pair of sewing scissors and, with tiny snips, cut away the fine hair until it was cropped close to her head in soft waves. It combed easily then, and framed the pretty little face and dark eyes. Grace closed her eyes and breathed in the scent of her, covering her silky cheek with kisses until Mary Kate gave up another smile.

"I love you," she said, hugging the child fiercely.

She rose and went to the mirror, scissors in hand, and began snipping away her own hair until it hung just above her shoulders. When she combed it, great handfuls came away from her scalp. She looked again in the mirror and, with relief, recognized more of herself than before.

Warm and clean, she and Mary Kate knelt on the cold stone floor next to the bed and bowed their heads over folded hands. They thanked the Lord for bringing them safely to this house, for the food in their stomachs, and a warm bed before them. They asked Him to look upon those who suffered on this night, and to bless the people they loved: the Neesons and Niamh O'Daly somewhere in the city, Uncle Sean in America, Ryan and Aghna on the road to Galway, Brigid and Phillip in London, their old friend Abban Alroy, Morgan and Lord Evans in Dublin, Henry Adams, and dear Barbara, whom God had placed in their path. And then they blew out the candle and crawled into bed, Grace's body curled around that of her little daughter until a deep warmth spread through them both and each fell into a safe and welcome sleep.

# Thirty-two

MORGAN sat in the dank, dripping cell, listening to the coughs and groans, the wretched spewing of other prisoners around him. The jail was crowded, but he shared his tiny space with no one, his influence considered too dangerous to allow access to others. Despite a well-paid and trusted lookout who was surely even now sitting in some pub with food in his belly and reward money in his pocket, Morgan and Evans had been captured at the house of Meagher's cousin, where they had been drafting a speech about the forming of an armed National Guard. Morgan had listened, engrossed, as Evans read aloud the passage that stated that an Irish Brigade was even now being recruited in the United States—the reminder to their countrymen that one third of the British Army was made up of Irishmen, and that there were now over ten thousand Irishmen serving in the constabulary. It was a speech intended to give courage and move all men to action, and certainly it was passionate. There was another letter to be written that night—a formal congratulation to the soon-to-be new French Republic—and Evans was meant to be part of a delegation that would carry a letter to Lamartine in France. Meagher would give the speech about the National Guard, and Morgan was meant to travel north, where he would organize what was left of the recruits there, then lie low until the spring. Smith O'Brien talked about revolution by Easter, but Morgan was more of a mind to wait for summer and the American recruits with their guns and good health.

As wary as they had all been, as careful as they always were, the ambush had been successful and there had been no time to organize a rendezvous. After the arrest, Morgan looked for the chance to catch Evans alone, but had seen him only once, outside the interrogation room door: Morgan shoved in, Evans dragged out. Bloody and beaten, his eyes swollen nearly closed, Evans still managed to raise his head and say weakly, "Long live Ireland," which earned him a vicious kick from the guards.

Morgan had not fared much better in the end, reconciling himself to the blows that came when he refused to answer their questions or give up names. He had, instead, unleashed a torrent of insults and accusations at the Irish constabulary, who were participating in the torture of their brothers and hindering the future of their own children. This had not served him well, and it was the last thing he remembered until he regained conciousness in his cell with one of the jail priests in attendance, dabbing at the dried blood on his chin.

"God be with you, my son," the priest said when Morgan opened his eyes.

He shook his head to clear his vision, then struggled to sit up, leaning against the cold stone wall. "God is always with me, Father," he mumbled around his split and swollen lip.

"You must keep in mind the trials of Paul, and not give in to despair." The priest, a black-haired Irishman, leaned closer to examine the gash in Morgan's forehead. "Even in prison, the Apostle Paul did not dwell on his plight, but set his mind to the future of the new faith." His hand paused midair from water bowl to wound, and he added pointedly, "You will remember his letters to the flock, and how they were able to carry on, made strong by his words."

Morgan narrowed his eyes, then winced with the effort. "Aye." He watched the priest's face carefully. "Paul was a devoted servant of the Lord."

"Unfailing."

They regarded one another, then glanced at the man posted outside the cell; he was turned away from them, but still the priest moved so that Morgan could not be seen from that angle. Stealthily, he pulled from beneath his soutane a small sheaf of papers and a quill. He slipped these under the straw on which Morgan lay, along with a bottle of ink. Morgan understood.

"I will think on Paul," he said as the priest stood up. "Thank you, Father."

"Shall I hear your confession, my son?" The priest winked. "Or do you need time to reflect on your sins and prepare yourself?"

"I do, Father," Morgan answered soberly.

"Tomorrow, then."

Morgan nodded.

The priest gathered up the bowl of bloody water and the rags, made the sign of the cross, and asked the guard to let him out.

Morgan did not touch the paper and pen. He would have to wait until the guard moved down the hall or was absorbed in eating his supper, and this gave him time to think. An Irish priest could just as easily be a pawn of the church as an English priest, and lately Rome had taken to disciplining those who acted for the people. Certainly, this priest was no one familiar to Morgan and there had been none of the secret words used to show he was a sympathizer. Tomorrow, he'd want a letter, but to whom was Morgan meant to write? He dared not call out names or write of specific events. Was this to be his salvation, or his damnation? At that moment, he longed for Sean's ability to reason, or the clear thinking of Evans.

Cursing his own thickheadedness, he prayed God to show him the way. His aching eyes were closed, and his head hung over tightly folded hands, bruised forehead resting on bony kees. He thought not of Paul, but of Christ in the garden of Gethsemane, facing certain death with faltering courage, pleading with God for strength: "Not my will be done, but Thine, O Father." The words came to him as they always did when he was deep in prayer, and now he spoke them aloud, although they were lost in the cursing and moaning of other men in other cells. Because of Christ, he need not fear the end . . . nor would he face it alone. Of that, he was certain. Peace flowed into his soul at last, and then he slept.

"McDonagh!"

The whisper, hissed through the bars, shattered his dreams. His eyes opened, rough and blurry in the dark, and he lifted his head, heart pounding.

"McDonagh, wake up, man!"

He squinted and saw, in the flickering light of the hall torch, a young soldier he'd not seen here before.

"What is it?" he asked, his voice scratchy with fatigue.

The soldier was turned slightly away from the bars and Morgan saw a profile that was decidedly English—slender and straight, shoulders back, neat blond hair and trimmed mustache rising above a familiar uniform.

"I have a message."

First a priest and now an English soldier. Did they think he was a fool? He remained silent.

"From your wife," the soldier whispered, urgently. "From Grace."

His heart thudded against his chest, but he forced his voice to remain dull. "I have no wife."

"Bloody hell," the soldier muttered. He glanced up and down the corridor, then turned and faced Morgan. "I've no time for games, McDonagh," he hissed. "You'll just have to trust me."

Morgan narrowed his eyes and leapt up, moving quickly toward the bars.

The soldier backed away.

"Then you'll have to trust me, as well," Morgan hissed back.

The soldier hesitated, then returned to within easy reach of the most dangerous assassin in Ireland.

"I've seen her myself," the soldier said, measuring the other carefully. "In Cork. She's well enough, though road weary. Mary Kate and Patrick are with her."

Morgan nodded, reluctant to give anything away, a thousand questions on his tongue.

"They were turned out. Family's dead or gone." He paused again, listening to the sounds overhead, squinting into the shadows at either end of the dark hall. "I gave her what money I had and sent her to the nuns."

Good, Morgan thought, Barbara will look after them.

"But she says she'll come to Dublin as soon as she's able."

Morgan's eyes widened in alarm.

"I couldn't put her off that," the soldier said, adding, "You know how strong-minded she is."

Morgan allowed himself a small smile, which the younger man saw and echoed ruefully.

"She's with child."

Morgan's hand flashed through the bars and grabbed the soldier's collar, yanking his face toward the cold iron.

"If you're lying to me, man, or if this is some kind of bloody trick, I'll break your neck, so help me God."

"Let go, damn it," the soldier spluttered. "Why would I lie?"

Morgan glared at him in frustration, then suddenly released his grip. "'Tis no safe place, the road . . . not for a woman alone, not in these times." His voice was full of anxiety.

"No." The soldier understood. "But that's not it. The child is yours. She was determined for you to know."

Morgan eyed him warily, hesitant and confused.

"She's a fighter, your Grace," the soldier said. "As much mettle and pluck as any man . . ."

"Unlock the cell."

The soldier stepped back, alarmed.

"Please," Morgan urged. "I'll wait till you're well away before I make any attempt to escape."

"I can't," the soldier said quietly, though not without regret. "I haven't the key."

Morgan held still, then shrugged, struggling to hide his disappointment. "'Twas worth the asking."

The two men regarded one another through the bars.

Grace loves this man, Henry thought.

She trusts this one, Morgan told himself. "What are you called?" he asked.

"Henry Adams. Private, Cavalry."

"Will you see her again, Adams?"

Henry shook his head. "Not unless she comes to Dublin."

"She says she will."

"She'll not be able to find me in the chaos."

"She might." Morgan thought. "Do you believe in God, Adams?"

"Yes."

"And do you believe He works in ways mysterious?"

Henry nodded hesitantly.

"Then might He not be working through you?"

"He must be," Henry answered. "Or why would I risk this?"

"Help her to see me," he urged. "If she comes. If she finds you."

Doubt welled up in the eyes of the young soldier.

"And if you cannot, then let you deliver a letter to John Mitchel, who'll see she gets it."

Henry was aghast. "I can't go waltzing into the office of John bloody Mitchel at the bloody *Nation!*"

"Aren't the English in there all the time?" Morgan argued. "They've not passed the Treason Act yet—he can't be charged with sedition—but there's nothing to stop them harassing the place day and night, and you know they do!"

Henry shook his head adamantly.

"The truth of it is, Adams—I'm a dead man, sure as you're not," Morgan said simply. "I can't bear to think of her hearing it off the street . . . what with rumors as foul as they are these days."

Henry's heart was conflicted, but he felt a sudden surge of emotion for this man—an enemy of the empire, true enough, but hero of the heartland, truer than even that.

"Don't give up hope, man," he urged. "You're not going to die."

Morgan pressed as close as he could. "Have a listen around us."

Henry did. And he heard coughing and moaning from almost every cell down the corridor, the restless tossing of feverish men, retching and gagging, weak calls for water. He knew those sounds only too well.

"It's fever, true enough," Morgan said in a low voice. "Some of the guards are sick with it, as well, though they know it not. No need to beat me to death or hang me by the neck, for sure I'll lay myself down before another week passes."

"You might survive," Henry insisted. "Other men have."

"I've no strength left for surviving," Morgan said matter-of-factly. "I'm starving and tired, cold and beaten. There's a pain in my chest from broken ribs and an ache all through my body. We've no doctor here—no blankets, nor fresh air; we breathe in our own filth. I'm not without hope, Adams, but these last years have made me a realistic man."

Henry had no answer.

"I knew my wife but a moment, and will never know our child. Let me say good-bye to them," Morgan begged. "Hasn't God already provided the means, and are you not the way?"

Henry's mouth went dry and his mind shouted warnings: *You cannot,* it said; *you've stayed too long already.* He heard the dull sound of boots on the floor above his head, the keen jangle of keys, the slow drip of water on stone—the risk was too great, he must go now or surely he would spend the rest of his life listening to these sounds. He turned in panic, ready to bolt, but then the full weight of God's hand fell upon his shoulder and held him fast, searing through his doubts, burning his fear to ash. He had not asked to be here, but here he was. It was part of a plan to bring him to this moment, to provide through him this comfort to an enemy. As this became true for him as no thing ever had, strength grew out of his weakness, his cowardice turned to courage. He lifted his head and looked around him in amazement, seeing for the first time his place in the world. With greater compassion than he'd ever felt for any man, he turned and met openly the weary, troubled eyes of his brother.

Morgan's hand gripped the bar; Henry wrapped his own around it. "Write your letter," he said quietly. "I'll do what I can."

# Thirty-three

SEAN sat at his desk in a small rented chamber above The Harp, a saloon for Irishmen owned by Mighty Dugan Ogue. It was late—Sean was in his nightshirt with a blanket around him—and the sounds of good-natured argument and challenge were punctuated by the occasional shattering of glass. None of it interrupted his thoughts, however, which were wholly concentrated on the paper in front of him and the urgency of his message.

*Dear Grace*—he began, alarmed at the shake in his hand. He paused to steady himself—*Come right away. If this be the only message you receive from me, let you take it to heart and not delay.*

He dipped his quill in the inkpot and frowned at the window glass, his pale reflection distorted by blowing rain. Should he tell her that his dreams had been filled with nothing but death and disaster since he'd arrived in America? Cabins filled with dying children, all of them with Mary Kate's little face; a second dream of them running down the road, trying to get away from soldiers who fired upon them and hit their shoulders, their arms, their feet; the dream of them stuffing their mouths with dirt to silence the screams of hunger. But it was the last dream that had been the worst, and he shuddered with the memory of it: Grace lying in a pool of blood by the road, weakly fighting off ravens who tried to pick at her eyes as the child beside her wept helplessly, herself under attack. Sweat had drenched his nightshirt and he'd awakened with a shout loud enough to bring Mighty Ogue himself bursting into the room, waving his pistol wildly at the shadows. That had been less than an hour ago, and he knew he must not waste another minute before urging her to get out of Ireland.

> *I know well your reasons for wanting to stay, but rest assured that I am only saying what he himself would say to you. If he is able to travel, he will; if he cannot, know that he will follow in the spring. Don't wait any longer! Come, and bring our Mary Kate with you, for I have prayed to God to keep her alive through all the suffering. I know our da will never leave, nor Gran if she lives, and my heart aches to know I'll not see them again. There is only enough to bring you and Mary Kathleen now, but in the spring we'll send for Ryan and his.*

Even as he wrote, he felt sure that Granna was dead and perhaps Patrick, as well, for they had visited his dreams in the way of Grace's visions. Patrick's face had been battered, but Granna bore no signs of a violent death; peace radiated from her hands when she laid them upon Sean's shoulders and said that he would never return to Ireland. God had plans for him in America, she said, but he must find his sister first, he must bring her away. In the same dream, Aghna wept over a small grave, and Ryan beside her, and then they drifted to sea in an open boat that sailed into the night until it was no more.

He checked the receipt that lay near his inkwell and wrote again.

> *I have booked and paid for your passage out of Cork the first day of November on the American brigate Christina, captained by John Applegate, a man of solid reputation. It is he who customarily pays the commutation fees, but I have advanced this to him in order to ensure your disembarkment. Still, nothing is certain in these uncertain times, so you must be prepared.*

He steadied his hand again, remembering his own horrific voyage on the overcrowded vessel, *Lydia Ann.* Several of the water kegs had leaked and another was contaminated from wine; the captain had had to ration the meager provisions daily so that a week's worth of food would not be consumed in a single day. There were lice and fever, and the hold stank with the sickness and filth of its passengers.

> *At all cost, you must keep yourself and Mary Kate well, for they will not allow any sickness to come off the boat in New York and will instead send you on to Nova Scotia, which is no good. Dress warmly, laying garment over garment, with a blanket wrapped round as a cloak. Gather what food you can and bring this instead of extra clothes in your satchel, as you cannot count on the kindness of the captain or the measure of shipboard provisions. It will be hard to fire a pot, so think on that, and bring dried fish or fruit, hard bread and cheese, if you can come by these things.*

Ogue's tiny wife had brought him a cup of hot water with a little whiskey and lemon spice, and he reached for this now, sipping it carefully and warming his hands. He had run out of food five days before sailing into port.

> *Get up into the air each day and avoid the rank fever that will spread among those in the hold. Do not tend the ill. Do not risk yourself. Again, I say that you will not be allowed to disembark if you show any signs of sickness!*

He underlined the last sentence, remembering the howls of those who were kept aboard and the riot that had nearly ensued. Out of food and water, having come so far and landed so close, the passengers were loath to put out to sea for the trip north to British America. They had all heard the horrors of landing at Grosse Pointe and were afraid of dying there. He himself—sure to be kept on with his crippled arm and leg, and his terrible cough—had jumped overboard on the last night the brig still harbored. He had snuck up to the deck, avoiding the watch, then waited until a log drifted past before jumping into the water and clinging to it, praying all the while he would not be taken back out to sea. Near dawn, he was picked up in a dory by angels disguised as drunken sailors, who merrily rowed him back to shore and tossed him on the rocky bank.

*When time comes to leave the boat*—his pen scratched furiously against the paper—*cling fast to Mary Kate and your satchel. Hand it over to no one, even if the man be Irish and convincing. These hooligans are runners, and they'll speak our tongue and snatch your bag, forcing you to follow them to a crowded, filthy room where they'll charge you sixpence for a meal and six more for a bed. They are liars and cheats, and will try to wrest the satchel from your hand or worse, Mary Kate's hand from yours so that you will be obliged to follow. Cling hard and stand fast. I and some of my boys will be on the lookout for you.*

He stopped, worried now that this might frighten her from coming at all. Then he shook his head. Not Grace.

*You'll not have it as rough as the others coming here with no one to look out for them, and you'll not have to stay in the cellars, which is where many go. I have a small room above a pub owned by a fine man who has agreed to let you stay next door down. He is a believer in the cause and a good Catholic, so we can pay what we have when we can, for now. It is not as rough a place as some, and Mary Kate will be safe off the street.*

That sounded better—she would be happy to know that. What else could he tell her? He pondered, then dipped his pen again.

*This is the Land of Plenty, true enough. Walk down any street and there lie crates of apples and tomatoes, squashes, corn, and onions. The butcher's shop is full of hanging meat—hams and great sides of beef—and there is a bakery on every street with breads, rolls, and cakes. Men with carts full of fresh fish come every few days, and you cannot imagine the abundance of cod and turbot, red snapper, crabs, clams, and mussels. And none of it so dear as to put it out of your head. On the pennies I earn, I have eaten well enough, and you would not recognize me for the flesh on my own face! Mary Kate will grow and thrive here, I promise you. There are plenty of jobs to be had, though the work is hard.*

He would not tell her that the Irish were known for taking hard work at little pay, and that they were resented for this by most of the other immigrants. He would not tell her about the shantytowns or the parish burnings, the prejudice and harassment. He would not say that lately newspaper editorials had been calling for the end of the tremendous flow of destitute Irish into their communities.

*Please come*—he urged—*It will do my heart good to look upon the bold eyes of an Irish pirate come flying in from the bog with mud on her feet. Your daughter will have a fine home here, as will your husband, when he comes. And he will come, Grace. Have faith in that. He has loved you with all his heart and God will grant you a life together in this new land until our own is safe again. For now, we must be like the Israelites wandering in the wilderness, but it is a fine wilderness the Lord has provided, and we can all grow strong here. Come right away. I am counting the days until the ship docks.*

He stopped and blotted the ink carefully, then read it over. It was too full of warnings and high emotion, but he would send it anyway. It would have to go out tomorrow to reach her by the end of October. If she did not delay, she could sail in November on the last ship out before the winter storms. She must sail then. She must.

The letter had come addressed to William Smith O'Brien at his residence, and when he opened it, there was a second envelope with the name "Gracelin O'Malley" scrawled across its front in Sean's unmistakable handwriting. He did not think twice, but slit it open and took it to the window to read in better light. He read it once, and then again, and when he'd finished, he set it down and stared out over the browning autumn garden. There was little he could do now, but certainly he could arrange for her to be on that boat. As the light faded from the garden, he resolved that, in this, he would not fail. He owed that much to McDonagh.

Thirty-four

IN the Autumn of 1847, Ireland continued to starve, much to the dismay of authorities who had overseen the influx of food from the United States and Great Britain. Most maddening of all was the decline of communities along the coast who were subsisting on old cabbage leaves, roadside weeds, rotten turnips, and dillisk, an edible seaweed. They ate raw limpets pulled from the rocks, but no one fished the teeming sea that could have saved their lives. Herring and mackerel, cod, turbot, and sole swarmed in the deep, cold waters off the coast, but no attempt was made to catch them. What fishing gear that once existed had long been sold to buy meal, and now the most a determined fisherman could hope for was one of the fragile curraghs to carry him into the ripping currents. Fishing off the rocky coasts was dangerous, but not impossible, and so it was hard to watch many coastal communities, including Galway, continue to starve.

The fisherman of Galway lived in the settlement of Claddagh, where they had their own dialect and their own mayor, a "king" whose word was law and who was strictly obeyed. Strangers were not allowed to live here, and harassed if they dared try. Mothers passed down to daughters the Claddagh Ring, a band of thick gold that signified their membership. They were a strange and clannish bunch—living in clustered, thatched black beehive huts—suspicious and hard to deal with. Even the Quakers had experienced frustration in providing relief to the obstinate Ring Fishermen.

The Claddagh claimed exclusive rights to some of the best fishing in Ireland and they guarded those rights fiercely. Sometimes they would go out and bring in a fine catch of herring, but then they would refuse to go out for days and neither would they allow anyone else to go out. This was their way. But now, they could not go out, because their boats and nets were sold or ruined, and so they lay like the rest of their countrymen, quietly starving in their huts. This was the community Ryan and Aghna came to at last, and this was where they died.

Road fever had hit them two days from Galway, but still they staggered on, Aghna much more ill than Ryan and raving like a madwoman by the time he half carried her into Claddagh. Though people clearly lived in the huts, no one would answer their call for help, or bring them food or drink.

"I belong here!" Aghna screamed, shaking her fist. "Ask the Jesuits!"

Dark faces appeared at the windows, but they were full of suspicion for the strangers who did not speak their dialect and who were yellow with fever.

The sun was high all through the day as Aghna and Ryan wandered among the huts, then finally down to the beach where they sat, exhausted and stunned, on the damp sand. Splintered curraghs were littered around them, and when the wind came up in the middle of the day, they got into one that seemed most whole and lay down together on the warm, salty wood. Fever washed through them; it hurt to move, and the talk that wove around them was only in their minds. No one brought them food or fresh water. No one came to see if they still lived.

Night fell and stars emerged in a perfect, cloudless sky. Ryan opened his eyes and looked up at them, felt the heavy weight of Aghna's head on his arm, tried to curl it around her more tightly but could not. The tide was coming in; it crept up the beach an inch at a time and finally began to lap against the stern of the small boat, swirling and pooling until the curragh rocked as gently as a newborn's cradle. They heard not a thousand farewells, but only the one voice calling them home, and when at last they drifted out to sea under the endless night sky, they had already answered it.

Under the same, watchful sky but across the island on the eastern shore, Henry Adams left a boat at Youghal Bay and hired a horse, the fastest horse he could find at this hour of the night and from such reluctant company as crouched over tables in the sailors' pub. He had been missing now nearly two days, and it would be another two days before he could get back. There'd be questions to answer, but he was not afraid. McDonagh was dead, and the letter to Grace burned a hole in the pocket over his heart.

The road was unfamiliar and he was thankful for a way lit by the bright moon and star-scattered sky. It came upon him that he should have worn something other than his uniform, but he had not thought to change; indeed he had not paused a single minute once word reached the post that the outlaw McDonagh had died of fever in his cell, having made his last confession to the prison priest, not a word of it any use to the British. The strength of conviction that had come upon Henry at the jail had not left him and had, in fact, grown so strong that he had not hesitated when word came, but had gone immediately to his bunk and reached up into the slit in the bottom of the mattress where the letter was hidden. He had written a quick message to his captain saying that one of the hospital doctors was in need of assistance down South, and as Henry had helped before and no current duties held him here, he'd set off immediately. He had added his assurance of the captain's understanding, and promised to be back in four days' time. This was not military protocol, but Henry had been called away in the past and the captain had always given his permission. Henry would say, upon his return, that the fictional doctor had died of fever and he, himself, was feeling unwell. He hoped for immediate quarantine, with no time for questions until he'd had time to review.

So caught up in his plan was he as he rode through the night, that he did not hear the muffled shout on the hill in front of him nor sense any danger. He did not notice the men moving through the trees on the uphill side of the road, nor did he find a warning in the growing skittishness of his unfamiliar horse. His soul was right with God, for he was on God's errand, and his heart was finally free from the misery that had muddied it since he'd come to Ireland. Henry was now the man he'd wanted to become, though only days old.

The end of life came not with pain and thunder, nor with torture and despair, but quickly, without realization or the chance to doubt himself. It came in a brief flash of light, barely caught from the corner of his eye, before all light dimmed within him and he toppled from his horse, a single bullet having found its mark.

The terrified horse reared and screamed, then bolted, dragging the body of the British soldier whose boot was caught in the stirrup. Three men and a boy appeared in the road, hands raised to quiet the horse. When they had calmed the frightened animal, they loosed the soldier, dragging him into the bush where they searched through his clothing.

"Take his gun and caps," a rough voice ordered. "And any silver."

"Here's a letter in his jacket pocket." The boy held up an envelope, white in the moonlight.

"Is he just a messenger then?" mumbled another man. "Throw it away."

"Nay," the rough voice spoke again. "Might be important. Can anyone read?"

No one spoke.

"Put it in the saddlebag, then, along with the rest of it."

When they were done searching the body, they moved him out into plain sight, as though sitting by the road, having a nap against the stone wall. They even crossed his legs in fun, and tipped his hat down over his eyes. Let the Brits find him that way and be warned off this road, they told themselves. Let them know fear as others knew it.

The moon had left the night sky and the last of the stars stood brave against the dawn when they reached the cabin of the old woman who doctored in secret. They rapped on the door and called out the password, then entered and went immediately to warm themselves by the hearth. Here, they squatted, too tired to talk, gratefully accepting the small bowls of runny porridge offered by the midwife's daughter. They ate silently, then stretched out on the floor to sleep, all except the boy, who picked up the saddlebag and carried it to their captain, abed with a leg blown to bits. The old midwife had skillfully removed his foot and now talked of taking more, as the leg had turned green to the knee and gave off a terrific smell. The boy took a deep breath before entering the small, windowless chamber where the captain lay.

"Morning, Captain Alroy," the boy said respectfully, peering into the dim room at the shape on the bed.

Abban pulled himself up to sitting and winced with the pain of it. "Has it come again, then, boy?" He turned up the whale oil lantern, casting shadows on the wall. "Well, I've lived to see another day. What have you got there?"

"Saddlebag." He held it up. "We laid for a soldier on the main road, and didn't we leave him to warn off the others from riding through there?"

"Did you now?" Abban spoke quietly.

"Aye," said the boy. "We brought back his horse and gun, and there's papers in here, as well. Might be important to yourself," he added proudly.

"Bring it here." Abban held out his hand. "Then go rest yourself."

"I'm not tired, Captain!"

"Have you not been out all night, and on a fearful errand?" Abban frowned. "'Tis bad enough that men must do such things . . . let alone mothers' sons." He remembered with sudden clarity young Nolan standing alone in the river. "Are we not fighting these battles so the likes of you won't have to?"

"I'm not afraid to fight," the boy answered defiantly. "And I'm as brave as any man, with no mother left to mourn me nor no father, as well."

Abban sighed. "We'd mourn you, boy. And I tell you true, my heart is sick with burying children."

"I'll not be left behind to cook and mend," the boy announced. "I joined up as a fighter, not a sweep!"

"When you joined up, you put your life in my hands, and that is where it now lies, do you understand me?" Abban put as much menace into his voice as he could muster.

The boy said nothing, but did not hide the hurt in his eyes.

"Get some rest, now," Abban ordered, then added less gruffly, "You're a fine boy and I want you to live to be a fine man, is all. But you must obey me, for the arm of death has a long reach and you're no good to us six feet under."

The boy nodded soberly, respectful again in light of this approach. Abban shook his head after the boy left the room, then reached for the saddlebag, his nose wrinkling in disgust at his own rotten smell. It wasn't mending, he knew that. Better to have it off and be done with it. If only the old woman didn't seem so gleeful about her surgeries.

He emptied out the papers, which did not appear to be military, but personal and belonging to a farmer: grain receipts, hog prices, an auction sheet—nothing of any real importance.

"Bloody hell," he mumbled to himself. "They've gone and shot a bloody Irish farmer instead of an English soldier."

He sifted through the papers again, picking up a crumpled envelope, sealed, with no name or location. Frowning, he tore off the end and pulled out a letter, folded into which was a gentleman's engraved wedding band and two gold earrings. He recognized the earrings immediately and his heart scudded into his throat. It was a hurried message—words had been crossed out and the ink was smeared from folding it up before it had dried. Steadying himself, he brought the lantern closer and began to read Morgan's letter.

> *Dear Grace*—it said—*If reading this you are, 'tis only because I could not come to you myself. I have asked your friend to carry it along, so that you might not hear false tales of it in the street. I know you are with Barbara and that she will comfort you. Weep for me, and then be done with weeping, for I am watching over you now as I never could before.*

Abban's vision blurred and he swiped angrily at his eyes with the rough sleeve of his shirt. He read the letter through to the end, then set it down and stared at the three gold rings in his hand.

Morgan must have died in jail, Abban thought, and his grief was so intense that if God had appeared and asked was he ready to leave this earth, his answer would have been a solemn "aye." Riding hard on the heels of his grief, though, was the terrible anguish of guilt. The soldier his men had killed had been a messenger between the two people Abban loved most in the world. This soldier had managed to see Morgan and was carrying out the man's last wishes. Grace and Morgan had somehow wed, and their child was coming into the world, a child that Morgan would never see but that he loved and took comfort in. Morgan had wanted her to know the truth of his sure death before it became distorted into something wildly heroic or agonizingly brutal, so that she might have some peace. And the messenger had been killed by Abban's own men. His hand clenched into a fist around the rings and he smashed it against the wall, roaring like a bull.

The old woman rushed down the hall. "Is it the pain again, Cap'n?" she asked from the doorway, barely stifling her hopefulness.

"Aye," Abban snapped.

"Shall we have it off today, then?"

"To ease this pain you'd have to cut out my heart," he growled.

Her eyes widened in astonishment, and her hand flew to her mouth. He got hold of himself as her look became one of growing anticipation.

"Never you mind," he said quickly. "I'm not myself. Today the leg comes off," he added. "But only below the knee!"

"Ah, 'tis a pity," she said unconvincingly. "I'll boil the saw."

"Fine." Abban grimaced. "Send me the boy."

She went away, rubbing her hands briskly, calling to the boy, who jumped down from the hay loft and came running.

"You need me, then, Captain?" he asked, breathlessly.

"Aye." Abban folded the letter carefully and returned it to its envelope. "Wait a moment." He wrote out a short note of his own, saying only that the soldier who carried the letter had been killed, and that he, Abban, was praying for her. This he added to the envelope. "I have an errand for you."

The boy's eyes flickered, but he did not allow disappointment to cloud his features. "Aye, sir," he said evenly.

"I want you to carry this letter to a convent in Cork City. Holy Sisters of the Rose. Give it into the hands of Sister John Paul and tell her to read it in private. Got that?"

The boy nodded. "Sister John Paul at Holy Sisters of the Rose in Cork City. Read it in private."

"This is terrible important, boy," Abban warned. He paused, then said in a low voice, "Do you know the name 'McDonagh'?"

The boy's eyes widened in awe. "Oh, aye, sir. Doesn't everyone know the name of the most fearless man in all of Ireland?"

Abban swallowed the lump in his throat. "Do this for him, then, boy. And do not fail him."

"No, sir, I won't, sir. You can count on me."

"Draw no attention to yourself in the city," Abban admonished. "Take Lewis with you for safety, but go alone to the convent gates."

The boy listened carefully. "Do I wait for an answer?"

Abban thought for a moment. "No," he said. "Come back straight away."

The boy took the letter reverently and put it inside his shirt. His eyes were shining as he stood tall and gave Abban a smart salute.

"Deliver that letter and come back alive, and you'll have proved your worth as a soldier to me," Abban said soberly.

"I'll not fail you, Captain. Nor him."

With that, the boy left, and a moment later Abban heard him calling to the new man from County Wicklow, heard them go out into the courtyard and ready one of the jennets. They knew the roads, and could make it to the city and back in good time. There had been no need to have him wait, Abban told himself, for how could she ever answer a letter such as this?

## Thirty-five

PATRICK, Grace, and Mary Kathleen had been at the convent for nearly ten days, sleeping much of the time and eating the meager meals Barbara brought to them each day. Grace had tried to give her the rest of Henry's money, but Barbara had refused, insisting she keep it for the trip to Dublin. Tomorrow, they would go.

After many walks around the convent courtyard, Barbara heard the entire story of Bram's death and Grace's secret marriage to Morgan. Her eyes had shone with joy when Grace revealed that she was carrying Morgan's child, as she still suffered greatly from the loss of her own family and daily tended Ellen's small grave. She had hoped that Grace might have had word of Aislinn, but she accepted that nothing further could be known, and she thanked the Lord for the comfort of a new sister and the coming birth of her brother's child. She and Grace spent hours in the tiny cell at night, trying to plan the future, sure that Morgan would soon be free. Barbara was adamant that Grace, Morgan, and the children join Sean in America and start a new life, though she knew it would take strong persuasion for her brother to leave Ireland on the eve of revolution. The best argument, she felt, was to urge him to take his family to America only temporarily—just until the British government had forgotten about him and the country was free from illness and famine; they could return in the summer. The Young Irelanders were strong now, it was believed, and nothing would be gained by risking his life. He could work with Sean in America, then accompany the recruits back to Ireland. In the meantime, they'd all be well out of it.

They were often joined in these discussions by many of the other nuns at Holy Rose, women young and old who would trickle into Grace's room one by one, speaking softly so as not to wake Mary Kate. They sat on the cold stone floor, their shadows long on the wall, hands tucked inside their great sleeves for warmth. They had become militant under their own authority—this order—first by taking in famine orphans and breaking vows of silence, then by offering sanctuary to renegades, and now by indulging in worldly views by reading the very newspapers their parish priests damned as seditious. Their talk over meals was often political, and not one among them was unaware that Morgan McDonagh was the brother of their very own Sister John Paul, as well as the husband of their latest fugitive. Early on, they presented themselves as a contingency to Grace, offering her the tiny bounty of coins they had raised in order that she might bribe her husband out of jail and get him safely to America. Grace had been deeply moved, thanking them profusely, but refusing the money, insisting that Morgan would want the children fed first and foremost, for didn't he always say that the hope of Ireland lay in her children?

It was agreed that Mary Kathleen would remain at the convent with Patrick, while Barbara would go to Dublin with Grace; as Sister John Paul, she stood the best chance of gaining an interview with her brother. Letters of introduction had been acquired from two sympathetic priests, stating that religious inspiration from the outlaw's own relation might very well encourage him to turn over his heart and stand within the law. The other sisters laughed heartily over that one and prayed that the British might be gullible enough to believe it.

On the morning of their departure, Grace sat quietly in the courtyard saying good-bye to Mary Kathleen, who clutched her doll, while Barbara went to the gate to look out for the cart that would transport them to Dublin. A boy, no more than twelve, came boldly up the road and waved to get her attention. Something in the way he glanced furtively about made her hurry.

"Yes?"

"Do you know Sister John Paul?" he asked.

"Aye." She looked him over, but could not place him as one of the orphans she'd cared for.

"I must see her," he said firmly.

"And why is that, then, young man?"

He glanced around again, his confidence slipping. "I've a letter for her that I must place in her own hands."

"I am Sister John Paul," she told him.

The boy hesitated. "How could I know that for sure?" he asked. "For haven't I been sworn to deliver it into her hands, and her hands alone?"

Barbara glanced around, and motioned to one of the younger nuns. "Tell this young man who I am," she said.

The young nun frowned. "Why, this is Sister John Paul, boy. Who else would she be?"

Barbara thanked her and asked her to check on Grace, then turned back to the boy and held out her hand.

"Go on and give it to me, now. And rest assured you've done your duty."

He pulled the crumpled envelope out of his shirt and placed it carefully into her hand through the bars of the gate. "There's something else," he added.

Barbara turned the blank envelope over, looking for a name.

"He says you're to read it in private. In private, do you hear, Sister?"

She looked up at him. "In private," she repeated. "Is there anything else?"

He shook his head.

"Do you need something to eat?" she asked gently, though he looked better off than most.

"Nay," he said, eyeing her boldly. "My orders are to report right back." And with that, he turned and ran down the hill to the road that led through the city.

Swallowing against her rising anxiety, Barbara carried the letter into the convent and looked for a place to read it. There was too much commotion from the children in the great room, so she stepped into the quiet of the chapel, sat down in a back pew, and took out the letter, hands suddenly shaking.

"Oh, dear God, no," she whispered as she read her brother's words. "No, no, no." Her voice was like a chant until she reached the end. Her hand fell into her lap and through eyes blurred with tears she saw the wavering image of Christ on the cross that hung in the front of the chapel.

"How could You take him from us?" she whispered, anger rising in her heart. And then she was filled with remorse. "Forgive me, Father. For sure and You've shown him mercy by sparing him a death far worse." Tears coursed down her cheeks. "But how, in Heaven's name, am I to tell his wife?"

She knelt down in prayer until the tears ceased and resolve made her strong, and then she rose and went into the courtyard, asking the young nun to take Mary Kathleen to the kitchen while she spoke to Grace. But in the end, no words came and she simply placed the letter and the gold rings in her sister-in-law's hand, waiting quietly while Grace read the words that ended all her dreams.

"Prayer is all," Barbara told the anxious faces outside Grace's bedroom door. "There's nothing more to do. The shock brought on the baby, but it's too early and Grace is not strong."

The sisters were tearful as they fingered the beads on their rosaries, eyes dark in pale faces. They had been all night in the chapel praying for the soul of the great Morgan McDonagh, and now they would return to ask that his child be spared, though all knew that God's will must be done.

Barbara turned back to Grace, who was white as the sheet upon which she lay. Her knees were up and she slipped in and out of consciousness, babbling about people and places far removed from this room. She called for her grandmother, shouted for her brother, but said Morgan's name only once, and then in a whisper. It was safer in the madness, Barbara knew, but she worried whether Grace would be able to stay with her long enough to deliver the baby. The baby was surely coming, but the pushing needed to bring it into the world could not be coaxed from the mother, and finally—in desperation—Barbara slid her long, thin hand in as far as she could and cradled its head, guiding the wee thing out at last. She had braced herself to accept a dead baby—so early it was and born of great shock to an undernourished mother—but within the tiny chest beat a weak heart. It was a boy. Morgan had had a son. She cut the cord and cleaned the white paste from his body, swaddling him tightly, the ministrations second nature after so many years of helping with her own mother's many deliveries. He was so tiny, this little boy, and his skin translucent; his limbs seemed short for his body, though he had all his fingers and toes. He opened his eyes for only a moment, and what she saw was pale and unfocused; she feared he might be blind. When she tickled his lips with her fingertip to encourage him to suck, he gagged instead. Indeed, he seemed barely able to draw a breath, and she knew not what to think. Grace had passed immediately into a heavy sleep without knowing he was here.

There was a soft rap on the door and Sister James peeked in.

"A gentlewoman's come," she said, quietly. "With a letter from America for Grace. We thought she'd best speak to you." She glanced at the still form in the bed, and the quiet bundle in Barbara's arms. "Is it born, then?"

Barbara nodded. "A wee boy. But sickly."

"Has she seen him?"

"No." Barbara thought for a moment. "Let her sleep. He doesn't look well and it might just be the end of her after everything else."

Sister James came into the room and sat down in the rocking chair, preparing to pray. "I'll stay with her now. You must be exhausted."

Barbara shook her head. "Keep her quiet if she wakes. I'll hurry."

She placed the boy in Sister James's waiting arms, then left the room, hastening down the corridor, down the long flight of steps, and through the great hall to the room where visitors were received. She paused and took a deep breath, collecting herself for a moment, before entering.

"I'm Sister John Paul," she said, closing the doors firmly behind her and turning to face the well-dressed woman waiting by the window. "Sister James says you have a letter for Grace?"

The woman's eyes, taking in Barbara's state of dress and the blood on her apron, widened in alarm.

"I've just delivered a baby," Barbara said matter-of-factly.

The woman bit her lip. "Did it live?"

"Aye."

"Good, good," she said, as though dazed, then handed Barbara a letter. "This has come from Grace's brother Sean, who is in America."

Barbara looked at the envelope, and thought of another letter received only the day before.

"Forgive me," the woman said. "I'm Julia Martin from Dublin. I knew both Sean O'Malley and your own brother, Morgan."

"I see." Barbara glanced through the letter, then looked up at Julia. "He wants her to come straightaway. This is very urgent."

"It is," Julia said. "We all think it's best. Especially now that Morgan is gone."

"And who is this 'we' you speak of?" Barbara asked directly, taking in the fine coat and gloves, out of style, but of good cloth.

Julia did not hesitate. "William Smith O'Brien, John Mitchel, Fintan Lalor, Thomas Meagher . . ."

"Ah, the men in charge."

"Yes."

"And why could these great men not save my brother?" Barbara asked.

"They were being held—"

"But released," she interrupted.

"Not in time to raise the money to hire the solicitors to get him moved," Julia admitted. "No one knew where he was at first."

"He should not have died in a cell," Barbara said angrily. "Not alone like a criminal."

"No," Julia said. "Not like that."

The two women stared at one another.

"Why have they sent you, then?" Barbara asked. "Why not come themselves?"

"They're all being watched. I have worked quietly and out of sight for some time now," Julia told her. "The English do not know me. I write under the name of Patrick Freeman."

Barbara's look turned to one of surprise. "I have read your writing in the *Nation*. You are very bold and free thinking."

"Not bold enough to write under my own name, however." She paused. "Not bold enough to lead a protest over his imprisonment or to try to see him in jail."

Weariness replaced some of the anger in Barbara's eyes. "Sit down please." She led Julia to the fire. "Do you know where they buried him?"

"His body was burned with all the others who died of fever," Julia said. "There was nothing left." She frowned hard, her face working to hold emotion at bay. "He wore those bloody earrings, you know, and I tried to find out what became of them, but . . ."

"They were my father's," Barbara said softly.

Julia nodded. "I know." She looked into the fire. "One for his father, one for his mother. Such a bleeding heart. Was there ever a man so noble, do you think?"

It took Barbara a moment to understand. "You loved him."

Julia held still, unable to speak.

"Did he know?"

Again, she nodded, this time managing a weak smile. "I've never done a subtle thing in my life . . . but his heart belonged to Grace, even though she was married to that great beast of a man, Donnelly."

"He was murdered." Barbara waited a moment—deciding—then added, "Grace and Morgan wed secretly soon after. 'Tis she who bore a son today."

"I knew that . . . somehow." Julia bit her lip, then composed herself. "When they said she wasn't well, and then you appeared looking like that . . . I'd not seen him in over a year, but word of his marriage spread like wildfire. A great romantic legend to add to all the others. He died a hero in the eyes of so many."

"Were he but a dull workaday farmer, still alive."

Julia nodded, eyes filling with tears.

"What will you do now?"

She wiped at her eyes with the back of a gloved hand. "I'll stay in Ireland and continue my work," she said firmly. "I believe we will be rid of the English by this time next year."

"Morgan would be proud of you for carrying on."

"Thank you," she whispered gratefully.

They sat for another moment, and then Julia rose and went to the window.

"We can help Grace. Clearly she cannot sail tomorrow, but there is a boat from Dublin in five days' time that will get her to Liverpool, and there she can make the passage to America."

"I don't know." Barbara thought of the lifeless woman lying upstairs, and the weak baby she'd just borne. "I don't think it's possible."

"Let me send a carriage for her in the morning, and I'll make arrangements for her to stay at a private hospital under the care of my personal physician," Julia offered. "I'll travel with her to Dublin, then on to Liverpool to see that she makes the connection to America."

Barbara tried to take it all in.

"She will be among friends," Julia reassured. "We will take good care of her. We owe her that, and we owe it to Morgan."

"But the baby," Barbara said. "And she has a three-year-old daughter. What of them?"

"They'll come, of course."

"The baby would die," she said absolutely. "He's so weak as it is, and Grace has no milk for him."

"How will you feed him?" Julia asked.

"We've a woman here lost her own baby and acts as wet nurse for those who come to us with no mother. She'll have enough."

"Grace would never leave him behind," Julia said.

"No." Barbara shook her head. "Though sure I am he'll not live the week."

"Too late then. The ship will have left Liverpool and there's no guarantee of another until spring."

"Must she go now?" Barbara asked. "Can she not wait until spring?"

"She's wanted in connection with killing a guard, and the land agent, Ceallachan, and she's wanted for questioning in connection with the murder of Squire Donnelly, not to mention she's Sean O'Malley's sister and Morgan McDonagh's wife."

"But no one knows she's his wife."

"It won't be long," Julia predicted. "There are few secrets kept safely on this island. I was able to find her—word came to us through an old friend of hers—and soon the guards will know where she is, as well. She can't go into hiding with a sick baby and a small child, and she'll do neither of them any good if she starves to death in prison."

Barbara drew a sharp breath, then let it out slowly. "What you say is true enough," she admitted, thinking. "Perhaps I could persuade her to go on to America, leaving the baby here. If he lives, he'll be stronger for it and well enough to travel come summer. Her father could bring him across."

"Her father is still alive?"

"Aye," she said. "He's here, as well."

"Word has it he was killed during the skirmish with the guards."

"Let you not say otherwise, then, and no one will be the wiser."

Julia nodded, considering. "It could work. We'll book the ship and pay his passage across when he and the baby are ready to travel."

"And if the baby dies?"

"He can still go, or stay, as he chooses."

"When would you come for Grace and Mary Kate?"

"In the morning," Julia said. "First light. We'll keep her well-hidden and with the best medical attention until it's time to leave Ireland."

Barbara laid her hands in her lap and looked at them. She tried to think of what Morgan would want. "All right," she said at last. "I'll have them ready to go in the morning." She looked hard at the woman before her. "I pray to God I'm doing the right thing in this. If anything happens—if Grace should die—I must have your word that you'll give her a Christian burial and that you'll return her daughter to me."

Julia put out her hand. "You have my word," she promised.

After Julia Martin had gone away into the foggy morning, Barbara closed herself up with the Reverend Mother and together they prayed for guidance. In an hour's time, they had come to a decision: With God's help, they would persuade Grace to see that her only hope for a future with her children was to get out of Ireland now and go to her brother in America. It was risky to undertake such a voyage after a difficult birth, but they would count on the attendance of a good physician. Mary Kathleen was young, but steadfast, and she would give her mother no trouble on the long journey. With the promise of her father and child well looked after, then sent on in the good weather, she might just agree to go.

When Grace awoke in the late afternoon, she learned she had given birth to a living son and that the only course open to her was to give him up. At first, she would not hear of it, would not even consider the possibility of leaving the boy behind. Only after being faced with the reality of his most certain death under the bleak conditions of hiding out and moving often, with her inability to nurse him properly in a land of little food and fatal illness; with the impact such a life would have on Mary Kate, whose childhood was already so terribly stunted; with losing her father, who could not survive such stress; and with the likelihood of her own imprisonment and long separation from her children, did she at last fall silent. Yet, despite all their pleas she still could not bring herself to agree to their plans; in the end, it was Patrick alone who convinced her.

"I'll not fail you in keeping the little one alive," he vowed fervently. "I'll watch over him night and day, and he'll never leave my arms when I bring him across the sea."

"I know you'll try," Grace said wearily from her bed.

Patrick pounded his fist into his thigh. "I will not *try,* girl! I will do it! As God as my witness, I will do it! Don't you see, Grace? It's why I'm still alive after all this. Haven't I asked the Lord why He's spared my life and taken so many others worth so much more? And now I have His answer." He reached across the bed and picked up her hand. "I understand that you can't be sure—all the wrong turns I've made—but please, Grace, please give me this chance to do right by you. Please, darling . . . for I see no other way."

Grace wept and Patrick wept, but at last they were calm and talked quietly through the afternoon about the future, even laughing a bit when Grace explained to him about changing nappies.

In the evening a priest came to baptize young John Paul Morgan McDonagh, and with the last of the Holy Sisters' medicinal whiskey, they all drank to his future—may it be strong and sure—before leaving him alone at last with his mother, who held him long and whispered the tale of his father's days and how she'd loved him all her life.

# Thirty-six

EXHAUSTED, but resolved, Grace rose early to spend the final hour with her son and her father; Patrick kissed her and urged her to be strong, then picked up Mary Kate and held her tightly, promising to see her in the summer sun.

When the carriage arrived, Grace and Mary Kate left them sitting in the small room. At the foot of the stairs, in the entry hall, Barbara and the sisters stood waiting for her. They came forward shyly, murmuring prayers for a safe voyage, pressing into her hand small cards with drawings of Mother Mary and the Sacred Heart, rosaries, a crucifix, Saint Christopher medals, dried flowers pressed flat in pocket prayer books. She accepted each gift gratefully, watching her own slow movements as if in a dream, hazy from the laudanum Doctor Branagh had left for her. He had arrived this morning with Miss Martin from all those years ago, and Grace could still not quite make out how events had turned. She kept looking around the crowded foyer for Mary Kate, though the child clung to her hand.

They helped her out to the carriage, and Doctor Branagh called to the driver to take it slowly down the road. Grace heard the iron gate clang shut behind them, and when she turned, the nuns were pressed against it, watching her go. She looked up to the top floor of the somber gray building and saw her father holding the baby, standing in the window, his hand raised in silent farewell.

The pain of leaving them behind, of having lost Morgan forever, of having lost so many, even Henry—not home and married and raising horses with his father, but dead—seared her heart and rose as such an anguished moan from her throat that Doctor Branagh gripped her shoulders and called to the driver to hurry up now, never mind what he'd said before, be quick about it.

She had thought to die when the letter came, when she read his last words and held in her hand his wedding ring. She had closed her eyes and willed herself away, but a small hand, anxiously wandering over her arm, had kept her from leaving the world, had made her open her eyes again and see the worried, pale face of her daughter, a face that pleaded to be seen, begged not to be left behind. And that had ended her wish to die, for how could she have even considered abandoning this child who had survived against all odds, this child who had lived through so much and still clung to life? She had taken that small, fluttering hand and stilled it against her own heart, had pulled her daughter close and felt the heat of her, the beat of her heart, and had drawn from this the courage to live. The terrible loss of the many was not greater than the love of the one, and so she would endure.

Dr. Branagh's interns carried her into the private hospital, which was light and airy, despite the lateness of the season. A nurse undressed her and put her to bed; she was soothed to see a cot made up next to it for Mary Kathleen. She watched Miss Martin sit in a chair in the corner of the room and take the child upon her lap. The sound of her voice as she told an old story and the rhythmic rocking of the chair assured Grace that it was only sleep she was falling into and that she would awake before too long.

Within days, Grace was remarkably improved. The nurse had awakened her regularly for sips of beef tea and bites of oatmeal, letting her sleep in between. The heavy bleeding had ceased, though she still wore rags against the spots, and yesterday, she'd gotten up twice to walk, gratified that her legs were steady and her mind clear and lucid. Miss Martin—Julia, Grace called her now—was to arrive after breakfast and make the journey to Dublin with her; from there they would travel to Liverpool, and then Grace and Mary Kate would board the ship for America.

"Well, and isn't that my favorite sight in all the world?" Doctor Branagh said gleefully, coming in. "Pink cheeks and sparkling eyes!"

Grace was dressed, sitting in a chair near the window, Mary Kate on her lap.

"I'm much better," she told him. "Thanks to your good care."

"Isn't that grand?" He rubbed his hands together briskly, then sat down on the edge of the bed. "And do you feel well enough to travel up to Dublin?"

Grace nodded.

"That's fine, then. I have complete confidence in you." He glanced at his pocket watch. "Julia will be here within the hour, and off you'll go!"

Grace nodded again, slowly this time, as her heart began to pound with great thuds against her chest.

Doctor Branagh noticed her anxiety and put away his watch, glancing at her surreptitiously until she regained her composure. He was suddenly flooded with the memory of the first time he had seen her—so gay in the first days of her marriage, so fresh and beautiful that one wanted to hold her up to the world and say, "This, this is Ireland!" And now she sat, robbed of her youth, robbed of her gaity and her innocence, the luster of her magnificent hair faded and her face marked by grief—yet still hauntingly beautiful beneath it all.

"You've suffered more than most, Grace," he said quietly. "God has dealt you a heavy hand, but you bear up well and we're all proud of you."

Tears filled her eyes and she bit her lip.

"McDonagh was a fine man," he pronounced. "The finest."

"Aye." She turned away as if to look out the window. "I can't speak of him just now, Doctor, if you don't mind."

"I know," he said. "When Missus Branagh died, I wanted to keep the whole of my life with her to myself, for fear it would fade if I shared it out." He paused. "But I learned that, after a while, talking about her made her more real to me, kept her alive, don't you know. Because other people had their memories of her to share, as well. I believe you've got one yourself."

"That night at O'Flaherty's dinner party," she said, turning back to him. "I was but sixteen then, and didn't she take me right under her wing like a mother hen?"

He chuckled. "Oh, she liked you tremendously, you a country girl like herself. And she always hoped things would go well for you. We were uneasy about the Squire, you know," he added. "I'd attended his first wife and the second, and I had reservations as to his . . . stability."

Grace said nothing.

"The Missus died of fever last year—so tireless she was looking after those in the lanes that couldn't make it to the hospital. I warned her, begged her to take heed . . ." He shook his head.

"She went where God led her," Grace comforted. "And she did what she felt she must."

A nurse came in then, bearing a covered tray. The doctor rose and pulled a small nightstand over by Grace's chair.

"There now, my dear. Your breakfast." He took the tray from the nurse, uncovered it, and set it beside Grace. "You must eat it all now, both of you."

Mary Kate's stomach rumbled and she folded her hands in prayer in order to eat right away.

Doctor Branagh laughed. "That's the right idea, wee girl," he said. "Tuck in and put it all away." He turned to Grace. "Julia will be here shortly. I'll see you then."

Grace fed Mary Kathleen and ate her own porridge. There was plenty and it came with milk and butter, the taste of which still sometimes brought tears of relief to her eyes. She thought again with gratitude of the kindness of the nuns in taking her in, of Doctor Branagh's attention, and Julia's concern. God had taken away, but truly He had given in return.

When they had finished, she wiped their mouths, brushed her own hair and braided it, and tied a hat around Mary Kate's short locks. They were dressed warmly in clothes provided by Julia, and their faces glowed with the heat of their nourishing breakfast.

"Soon, we'll go," Grace whispered.

"To America." Mary Kate tucked Blossom into her pocket. "To Uncle Sean."

"Aye. And won't he be the happy man?"

"Will it be like Heaven, then?"

Grace shook her head. "No, though they say the streets are paved with gold and every man has a whole chicken in his pot each night!"

Mary Kate's eyes widened. "Do I like chicken?" she asked.

"It was your favorite."

She nodded soberly. "I thought . . ." She hesitated. "If it was like Heaven . . ." Her voice trailed off.

"Aye?" Grace encouraged.

"I thought I might see my brothers there," she finished quickly. "If it truly is like Heaven."

Grace's heart turned over and she pulled the little girl close. "I'm sorry about your wee brothers. Don't I wish they were with us even now?" She felt the hot sting of tears, but willed them away. "But I thank God for you, Mary Kate," she whispered into her daughter's musky hair. "You are ever a blessing to me, and come the summer, we'll have little John Morgan with us, as well."

They sat quietly until a commotion in the corridor announced Julia's arrival. There was the clatter of dropped breakfast trays, a nurse's admonishment about running in the halls, and Julia's loud cursing. Mother and daughter looked at one another and giggled.

"I like her," Mary Kate whispered.

"And I," Grace agreed.

Julia burst into the room, bringing with her the fresh bite of autumn wind. To them, she was warm and funny—winking and making sly jokes about bedpans and disinfectant—but with the nurses she maintained a brisk and businesslike demeanor lest they think her a flighty eccentric making off with reluctant wards.

She organized them into the fast carriage that would carry them to Dublin, their satchels stashed away inside out of the weather, a basket of rolls tucked between them. They all received a warm embrace from Doctor Branagh, who begged Grace to write of their wonderful new life in America, and to remember those who loved her here. And then they were off.

Not an hour out of Cork City and Mary Kate was fast asleep, her head in her mother's lap. Julia was scribbling away on a pad of paper, cursing every rut and dive the carriage took, so Grace pulled back the window flap for the company of nature. They were in the countryside now, trees nearly stripped bare of their leaves, grass gone brown and withered, awash in mud. The sky was low and threatened rain, but it was a rare cabin that sent smoke up through the rough chimneys— there seemed to be no one about on this day, and she knew then that they still lay weak in their cabins, starving and dying of fever. Her world had changed, but theirs had not. She gazed out at the sweeping landscape, the low stone fences that marked out each holding, one next to the other away off across the valley to the hills, toppled cabins, thatched roofs, empty yards. Her eyes ached with straining to catch the glimpse of a farmer crossing the yard, his wife at the butter churn, children in the lane shouting out their game. There was no one. And then there was a child, solitary, batting at a colored ribbon that hung from a tree branch. She looked for faces in doorways and saw none, but recognized the color of another ribbon. And another.

"What are all the ribbons tied about?" she asked, puzzled.

Julia looked up from her writing, and pulled back her own curtain. "Those are the colors of Ireland," she said quietly. "To honor our fallen hero."

Grace stared at her.

"Your husband, Missus McDonagh!" she exclaimed, her smile wry. "The rightful King of Ireland, to hear them talk in the pubs."

Grace turned to look out the window again, her eyes filling with tears. The trees blurred, and the colored ribbons were smudges of bright and dark streaming past. She wiped her eyes. They were everywhere. Now that she looked, she saw them tied to trees and bushes, fenceposts, gates and shutters, over doors and windows, sailing from pubs and shops, houses, cabins, and hovels. In the bogs, they hung from lean-tos and the handles of spades stuck in the turf.

"It began when word spread of his death," Julia said. "His men went round and tied them where they'd be seen. The guards caught wind of it and ordered all ribbons to be removed or those responsible would be arrested." She paused. "The next day there were hundreds tied everywhere, and the day after that, thousands. They say the colors fly for him up and down the coast, and inland all the way to the West."

"And have men gone to jail for this?" Grace asked, her eyes still on the passing scenery.

Julia shook her head. "They can't arrest us all," she said simply. "So they've let it go. They think that now our hero is dead, the uprising will die, as well."

Grace looked at her. "Will it?"

"Never."

They smiled at one another.

"Did you know him well?" Grace asked after a moment.

"Not as well as I would've liked," Julia replied. "But that's a story for another day. He was a good friend to me," she added.

"Aye, he was always that." Grace leaned back in the carriage, her fingers brushing lightly over her wedding band. "And you've become one, as well. I don't understand it, Julia, but I thank you for all you've done."

"We owe him this," she said matter-of-factly. "We owe you, as well. You'd have been married to him all your life had the Young Irelanders not caught him up and carried him away."

Grace shook her head slowly. "'Twas not what God intended. I was married to another, and even if Morgan and I had wed, there's no saying we'd have lived through the famine or the fevers. No, this was how it was meant to be—God put me where I could be of service to Him, and He did the same with Morgan." She paused, then smiled. "Did you ever hear him sing?"

Julia laughed. "All the time. What a beautiful voice on that man. He and David—Lord Evans—would sing for hours if we kept their glasses filled and the logs burning. Your brother joined in once or twice, as well, if I'm not mistaken."

Grace looked doubtful. "Sean? Waste breath on song when he could be talking?" She shook her head. "That doesn't sound like my brother."

Julia laughed again. "No, but it's true. Are you glad to be going to him?" she asked gently.

Grace hesitated, worrying her lip. "Sure and I'll be glad to see his face again, though don't I wish it were here in Ireland and times the better for it."

"Are you afraid?"

Grace looked down at Mary Kathleen lying in her lap. "No," she answered truthfully. "I've lived through everything there is to be afraid of."

After two fast days of travel, they arrived in Dublin. Julia had booked them into the same hotel where Grace had spent her honeymoon, but in the face of the continued starving outside the door and the gaunt look of the doorman, it was a bitter reunion. She asked at the desk after Alice and was told the maid had lost her husband to fever, and had emigrated with her two children. Grace silently wished her well.

Worn out, Julia drank down a tall whiskey and water, had a bath,

and went to bed, leaving Grace and Mary Kate alone to bathe themselves in faded splendor, and to spend their last night in Ireland kneeling before the windowsill, looking out at the gaslights spread across
the grand city of Dublin.

"There's the River Liffey." Grace pointed across the city. "You can
see the lights on Halfpenny Bridge where your father and I walked
one night."

"What is that great dark forest?" Mary Kate asked.

Grace laughed quietly, mindful of Julia sleeping a bed away.
"Phoenix Park. There's a lovely teahouse in the very center. I'll take
you there one day."

"Will we come back to Ireland, then?" She looked up at her
mother.

Grace smoothed the hair out of her face. "Aye," she promised.
"We'll come back to Ireland. 'Tis our home, is it not?"

Mary Kate nodded. Grace pointed out the spire of Christchurch
Cathedral and told her daughter all about the wonderful dress shops
in Sackville Street, where she had once ordered a scarf of Limerick
lace and a velvet evening gown, French gloves, and the most beautiful
blue bonnet. She whispered about going to the theater and concert
halls, to fine restaurants, and to Dublin Castle and the University Library. Mary Kate listened in wonder, her chin resting firmly in the
crook of her little arm until she fell asleep and Grace carried her to
the grand bed they would share on this, their last night.

And then it was the last morning, the sun bright in the clear, crisp
autumn sky. Julia organized their bags and had them carried down
to a carriage, which transported them to the docks. There again, she
was all business, arranging their tickets and the small cabin that would
be theirs for the short crossing to Liverpool. Grace and Mary Kate
stood on the dock, hand in hand, looking at the tall masts that rocked
in the harbor, watching the bustle of seamen around them.

When, at last, it was time to board, Grace found she could not lift
her feet off the ground, could not step away from the land onto the
gangplank.

Julia, lone witness to the growing anxiety, pulled her quietly off to
one side and told her to wait. As Grace watched, she hurried down
the dock, up the low bank, and across the street to someone's fenced

garden. Glancing around, she opened the gate furtively, disappeared into the shrubs, then reappeared, hurrying back to Grace.

"Give me your handkerchief," she demanded upon her return.

Grace handed it over and watched in amazement as Julia put a handful of soil in its center, then knotted it thoroughly.

"It's dirt!" she exclaimed.

"It's Irish dirt," Julia said, wiping her hands on her own skirt. "The stuff that grows potatoes and pookahs, shamrocks and warrior kings. Take it to America. And for God's sake," she added, "don't throw it in the wash!"

They laughed and Grace was able to follow her up the gangplank to the main deck, where they found a place at the rail. Within minutes, the lines were untied and thrown back on the dock. The captain stood solemnly next to the first mate, who called out orders to the men who scrambled over the rigging and raised the sails. Slowly, slowly, the ship inched out of the harbor, past the other ships and fishing curraghs, past markers and buoys, then out into the sea and beyond. As Dublin faded, Grace fell silent.

"I'll take Mary Kate to the cabin for a story," Julia said gently, her hand on Grace's arm. "We'll leave you alone to say good-bye."

Grace nodded gratefully, reluctant to take her eyes away from the disappearing land. And then she was alone, Ireland but a speck in the distance. Panic suddenly overwhelmed her and she gripped the rail to steady herself. There were others beside her, sick to their stomachs on the choppy sea, but it was a sickness of heart that afflicted Grace. How could she have agreed to leave? What madness had overtaken her thinking? How could she have ever considered risking her life and Mary Kate's on a voyage halfway around the world with winter coming? She could have kept them hidden and alive until they were all strong enough to travel in better weather—somehow she could've done it. What if she never saw her father or son again? No matter that Sean waited on the other end. No matter that there was nothing left for her in Ireland—no food, no future. She bowed her head and prayed to God to still the fear that threatened to break her. In only a moment, He gave His answer, and she had a clear vision of Morgan's face before her—head thrown back in laughter, white teeth flashing, eyes sparkling with mischief, freckles dancing down a sunburned cheek. He was singing and she heard the echo of his voice over the splash of the sea against the ship. She strained her eyes to see him clearly and there he stood, waving her off with Ellen holding his other hand, and his mother and sisters behind him; Mary with her arm around Kathleen's waist, Gran beside with Ryan and Aghna, the little boys rolling at their feet. Moira stood beside her father, Jack, both of them with a hand on young Nolan's shoulders. Next to them were all the faces of her neighbors and friends—Ryans, O'Dugans, the Haweses, Shane O'Daly, young Neeson—people she'd known all her life. And there was Henry, standing off to one side; Morgan beckoned him to join them, to stand with them, with her family and those she loved. They all waved and she lifted her hand and waved back, waved until the vision had faded and they were gone, and still she waved.

"Land!" someone called from the far side of the ship and Grace was left alone at the rail, her hand in the air, as the others went to see their first glimpse of England.

There was nothing but whitecaps in her wake now—no land, no family, only fleeting glimpses of what had been her only life. She pushed the palm of her hand into the ache beneath her chest and felt the rigid paper of Morgan's letter buttoned inside her shirtwaist. Her hand flattened out upon it.

*Weep for me and then be done with weeping*—he'd written—*for I am watching over you as I never could before.*

She looked up into the clear sky.

*I cannot tell you whether to go or stay, to struggle with the past or fight for the future*—it said—*but you, Grace, you know what is best. Listen to your own heart, and pray always to God for guidance. Trust in Him.*

"I have," she whispered. "I do."

"Then look away now, love."

She turned toward the strong sound of his voice, toward the front of the ship, but he was not among the passengers gathered there. She let go of the rail and stumbled with the sway, moving unsteadily across the deck to the bow from where she could see the spot of looming land. There the future lay, she knew, though the past rode hard on its heels.

"Hard to leave them all behind, agra, is it not?" asked the old man who made room for her at the rail.

She nodded.

"Where is it you're off to, then?" He kept his eyes on the sea, squinting against the glare.

She studied his profile for a moment, the face of a thousand Irish men. She knew he had a clay pipe in his jacket pocket and the woody smell of whiskey in his beard, she knew there was soil under his fingernails and a hundred songs in his heart, she knew he'd lived a long life and lost too much hope, and that hope was the mantle of the young.

"To America," she said, but the wind whipped the words from her mouth and hurled them into the sea. She moved closer to his ear and put a hand on the mended sleeve of his best jacket, felt beneath her fingertips the nubby Irish cloth worn old.

"Tir na nog," she said, "Land of the Young," and this time the words were clear and strong.

Ann Moore was born in England and raised in the Pacific Northwest. She lives in Bellingham, Washington, with her husband and two children.

# Gracelin O'Malley

❖

## ANN MOORE

This Conversation Guide is intended to enrich the
individual reading experience, as well as encourage us
to explore these topics together—because books,
and life, are meant for sharing.

# A CONVERSATION
# WITH ANN MOORE

Q. *You have written a novel of remarkable passion and historic sweep. What drew you to set your characters in this turbulent period of Irish history?*

A.  When I began plotting this book, it actually took place in the Pacific Northwest region of the United States, years after the great famine of 1845.  Gracelin O'Malley was a secondary character, an Irish immigrant hoping to make a new life for herself and her young daughter.  In order to make her voice authentic, I began reading Irish history and journal excerpts and discovered all of the dramatic and complex elements that made the Irish famine such a profound tragedy.  Though the Irish were no strangers to hardship—blights and crop failures were regular occurrences in their lives—I was struck by their continued optimism in the face of extreme poverty, their spirit and simple joy in living each day, their love for their children and pride in their heritage as the descendants of kings.  It became almost immediately clear that what I was truly meant to write was the story of this young woman and the incredible people who were her countrymen.

Q. *There's such vivid historical detail and richly imagined dialogue in this novel. How did you prepare yourself to recreate the world of Gracelin O'Malley?*

A. I tried to steep myself in writings of that period. I read novels written during that time in history or written about that time, as well as journals, books of letters, and as much history as I could digest in order to render the world as clearly as possible for myself and the reader. Finding a rhythm for the beautifully lyrical Irish speech was my greatest challenge, so I paid close attention to sentence structure in diaries and letters until I heard those voices clearly in my own mind and could translate them to the page with confidence.

Q. *All writers are influenced to some degree by the authors they love. Are there Irish writers you particularly enjoy?*

A. I was greatly taken with the traditions of mythology and folklore that the Irish have kept alive in stories, ballads, and poems, despite centuries of oppression. Irish writers I especially appreciate are James Joyce, William Butler Yeats, and Edna O'Brien. Other authors who have influenced my writing are Elizabeth Gaskell, Eudora Welty, Anton Chekov, V.S. Pritchett, and Zora Neale Hurston. For the sheer beauty of language, I read poetry and the King James version of the Bible. There are also a number of first-time novelists I've read lately who impress me tremendously with their seemingly effortless prose and excellent storytelling.

Q. *The character of Henry Adams is drawn with great sympathy even though he's an English soldier. Was this a conscious decision?*

A. No matter which side incurs it, loss of life in war is a tragedy. Henry was a good man caught up in circumstances beyond his control, a man who came to understand his place in the world just before his life was taken. The truth is, there were many sympathetic English, many young soldiers who entered Ireland with one mind-set and left with another after confronting the reality of the Irish-English struggle. Their story is a deserving part of the whole and one that applies to war in many parts of the world.

Q. *Ireland was a predominantly Catholic country in 1845. Why did you choose to make Gracelin a Protestant?*

A. As a Catholic, Gracelin's options in 1845 would have been much more limited, so part of that decision was about providing a more complicated storyline for Grace. For instance, marrying Donnelly would have been out of the question. But I also wanted to show that this historical struggle, which is so often portrayed as religious, is really about centuries of poverty and oppression. And as in any moral struggle, there are representatives of good and evil on both sides; to be English or Protestant did not mean that one was devoid of all decency, nor did being Irish or Catholic ensure an honorable character. By allowing Gracelin O'Malley to be the Irish daughter of a disillusioned Catholic and a devout Protestant, with a child who is half English, and a lover who is Catholic, with friends and enemies in all camps, I hoped to represent the real participants in history as the complex individuals they were rather than simply "good" or "bad."

Q. *Self-sacrifice emerges as a major issue in this book. Why is that?*

A. Often, people who lead struggles against oppression and tyranny are those who believe that man's right to govern his own life with freedom and dignity is God-given and that the battle is really between good and evil in the world, a battle that then transcends the individual. In Ireland, steeped first in a tradition of fierce, noble warrior poets, and then in the stories of the saints, they were well-versed in the higher calling of self-sacrifice; and of course, by the time of the 1845 famine, they simply had nothing left but that higher calling to give them hope.

Q. *Now that you have written of Gracelin's life in Ireland, will you continue her story in the next book?*

A. Reading the history of the Irish immigrants who came to America was deeply moving, and I realized I wanted to bring Grace full circle to the place where we first met in the plotting of the original book. In the second novel, Grace and her daughter sail on a famine ship to New York, where they are reunited with Sean and begin a new life. Manhattan is an incredible place at this time in history, so many levels of society intersect and are impacted by the flood of immigrants who pour into the city each day. This was only 150 years ago—the blink of an eye in history—and an irresistible time about which to write since these are the great-great-grandparents of so many of us.

# QUESTIONS FOR DISCUSSION

❖

1. By the end of the novel, Grace has lost nearly everyone she ever loved, and yet she is not without hope nor has her spirit been crushed. What has prepared her to survive such terrible emotional blows? Why is it that the spirits of some are so resilient, while those of others are defeated?

2. What do you think about Grace's decision to leave the infant boy behind with her father and head for the New World? Do you think she did the right thing? Can you imagine making the same choice in similar circumstances?

3. How much of Gracelin's spirit and will to survive derive from love of her family, particularly her children? Do you think people often summon the strength to go on despite enormous loss because of their children?

4. Faith and redemption are major themes in this book. How does faith, or lack of it, shape the lives of these characters? Do you know people whose lives have been sustained by great faith? Do you know anyone who has redeemed herself, turned her life around with an act of generosity or heroism that compensated for a previously selfish existence?

5. Has reading this story changed your perception of the 1845 famine? Is there anything you know now that you did not know before? How does it affect your view of the current struggles in Northern Ireland?